SISTERLAND

SISTERLAND

Linda Newbery

LAUREL-LEAF
BOOKS

Published by Laurel-Leaf
an imprint of Random House Children's Books
a division of Random House, Inc.
New York

LAUREL-LEAF and colophon are registered trademarks of
Random House, Inc.
www.randomhouse.com/teens

Educators and librarians, for a variety of teaching tools, visit us at
www.randomhouse.com/teachers

Reprinted by arrangement with David Fickling Books,
an imprint of Random House Children's Books

RL: 7.4

ISBN-13: 978-0-553-49450-1
ISBN-10: 0-553-49450-3

Printed in the United States of America

July 2006

10 9 8 7 6 5 4 3 2 1

For David, Bella and Maggie, with love,
and thanks for letting me throw
another stone into the swamp

Copyright Acknowledgements

Contents

1	Going . . .	1
2	Only a Visitor	4
3	A	23
4	Leavings	44
5	Heidigran	50
6	Dangerous Corner	65
7	Hello, Goodbye	82
8	Doppelgänger	87
9	Gone Away	98
10	Games	109
11	Letters to Rachel	116
12	Preludes	126
13	Encounters	147
14	Hands Together	163
15	Shopped	175
16	Snakes and Ladders	191
17	Window Dressing	209
18	The Night of a Thousand Bombers	223
19	Looking for Rachel	231
20	Heidi Thornton	254
21	Secrets	263
22	Dumped	278
23	Sarah Reubens	289
24	Survivor	307
25	Out of the Blue	319

26	Long Shadows	336
27	Catch 22	353
28	Going . . .	362
29	Gone	367

Acknowledgements | 371

Chapter One

Going . . .

. . . this feels so weird, in mid-air somewhere over eastern Europe, heading for your country, your places, but so far from you. I miss you. I miss you so much that it hurts. I know that's a corny thing to say, but it's also true. That's the point of corny old sayings, isn't it? They say something so true that you don't take notice. Then you realize in time just <u>how</u> true.

When I was packing, Dad started telling me about a play he'd heard on the radio. <u>Dangerous Corner</u>, it was called. It was about a group of people, family and friends, having a meal together at someone's house. One of them makes a chance remark about a musical box that's in the room. Someone else says they've seen it before, but another person disagrees and says no, that couldn't be right, because it wasn't here last time they came. They start asking questions, and from then on,

1

everything that follows — the whole play — shows that they've all told each other lies, and covered things up, and kept secrets from each other. Now it all comes out — who was where they shouldn't have been, and why — and by the end nobody's quite who we thought they were at the start. There have been all these secret things going on — dodgy deals with money, a killing, an affair. Things that will pull the family apart, now that they're known. And what they know, they can't _unknow_.

But the clever and surprising thing about this play is that about five minutes from the end it all starts again — the same, but not exactly the same. The same person asks about the musical box, just like before, only this time, before the other person can answer, someone turns on the radio and there's dance music, and they all start dancing and laughing. The musical box gets forgotten and all the other questions never get asked. They're safely round the dangerous corner. So this time they stay happy, but the audience knows that all the secrets are still there, hidden. It makes me wonder: Are they really happy? Or do they only think they are? And therefore is it wrong for them to be happy?

That's just like us. I keep thinking that I might never have known the truth — that

2

is, as much as I know now, which can't be all — without the dangerous corners. But it could have been like the second version of the play. Now, if I had the choice — know, or not know? — I'd have to choose knowing. It must always be better to know, mustn't it?

It's funny, the name of that play, because it's something Heidigran always used to say. When we'd been to visit her, and we were in the car ready to go home, she used to say: 'Go carefully now. Mind the corners.'

Chapter Two

Only a Visitor

Thursday

Dear R,

Yes, I know this is a weird place to visit on holiday. We arrived by accident. Dad and I went in, Mum and Z wouldn't. It felt all wrong to be a tourist — like we should have worn black, or armbands or something. But everyone was silent. Next pc will be back in holiday mode, promise!

Lots of love, H.

They came across Natzwiller-Struthof by chance. Not at all sure that she wanted to go in, Hilly knew she would, as the road had brought her to the gates. It wasn't the sort of opportunity you could miss.

With their baguettes and Camembert and other picnic items stowed in the boot, they had been look-ing for a place to stop for lunch. It was another hot day, too relentlessly hot for walking round villages or for visiting Strasbourg. The forest offered coolness and shade, trickling streams and grassy clearings. Hilly, in the front passenger seat with the road atlas on her lap, had noticed the roadside signs with the three crosses indicating some sort of war memorial.

'Natzwiller-Struthof?' her father said, changing to a lower gear for a sharp uphill bend. 'It's a concentration camp. Was. Open to visitors now, I think.'

'In *France*?' said Zoë, in the back seat.

'Zoë, this part of France was taken over by Germany at the start of the war.' Her father glanced back. 'You know, the Occupation of the Rhineland! We were talking about that yesterday, remember?'

Zoë lifted her chin and stared out of the side window, haughty and withdrawn.

Hilly said, 'I know, though – it does feel a bit peculiar, doesn't it? Here in the hills – the signs pointing up and up. It's like we're not in any particular country – as if the mountains are a sort of barricade between the Rhine and the rest of France.'

'Barricade against British tourists, as well,' her father said. 'Anyone noticed how few Brit number plates there are? Dutch, German, but very few GBs – I've only seen one or two since we got here. Looks like Alsace is a well-kept secret.'

'No beaches, that's why,' said Rose, the girls' mother. 'Lots of people want beaches.'

'So why do we have to be different?' Zoë said, still huffy. She hadn't wanted to come on this holiday, and was making sure everyone knew. She complained about the room she was sharing with Hilly; she complained that self-catering meant they were forever shopping for food; she complained that it was too hot.

'*I* wish you'd stayed at home, too!' Hilly had told her earlier, in a fierce, muttered conversation in their bedroom, before their parents were awake. 'It's Dad's birthday today, so you might make a *slight* effort.'

How many more times would they go on holiday like this, all four of them? Hilly wondered. This was possibly the last time. For their parents, this Alsace trip was revisiting the past; they'd come here nineteen years ago, the summer they got married. Although she had seen photographs, Hilly was surprised by the wooded slopes of the Vosges mountains, the deep valleys, the almost ridiculously picturesque villages along the wine-growing route. It was as she imagined the Swiss Alps: high meadows rich in wild flowers, remote farmsteads with logs stacked under the house eaves.

As they followed the memorial signs the road narrowed between stands of spruce, the young trees clustering so thickly that the farther slopes looked furred in green. Through the open window Hilly smelled warm grass and the resinous tang of pine; she saw verges bright with the purply mauves of wild thyme and harebells. It seemed an unlikely journey to a concentration camp, she thought, remembering documentaries she'd seen at school: bleak industrial areas, windswept flatlands, and those terrible railway tracks that led one way.

A sign to the left took them to a levelled parking area. The Craigs' car nosed into line next to a Peugeot with a French number plate, facing trees and a grassy slope. The large car park was two-thirds full; there was a blockish building that looked like toilets, and a sign asking visitors not to picnic or play ball games. Looking towards the entrance, Hilly saw iron gates, a high wire fence.

'You must be joking,' said Zoë from the back seat. 'You're not seriously expecting us to go *in*?'

'You can wait here if you like,' their father told her. 'I'd like to see inside. Anyone coming?'

'Me,' said Hilly.

'You would.' Zoë was sliding out of the car, trailing the lead of her Walkman. 'Just up your street, isn't it? – holiday combined with doom and gloom. Why be happy when you can be miserable?'

'You'd know all about that!' Hilly stood up, stretching. 'Coming, Mum?'

Rose glanced towards the gates. 'You go with Dad. Don't think I will. I'll wait with Zoë.'

Zoë reached for her magazine, slammed the car door and moved into the shade of a silver birch, settling herself on the grass. 'I hope you're not going to take ages – I'm starving! Can't we start on the lunch, Rose?'

Zoë had recently taken to calling her mother by her first name; although Rose didn't mind, Hilly couldn't do it without feeling self-conscious. She noticed, too, that Zoë always called their father Dad, even Daddy: never Gavin.

'We can't picnic here.' Rose nodded in the direction of the sign that urged Silence and Respect.

'No one's going to tell us off, are they?'

'We'll wait for Dad and Hilly,' Rose said firmly. Zoë sighed, rolled over onto her front and flicked open her magazine with the martyred air she was so practised at conveying; Hilly gave her a disparaging glance, which went unnoticed.

'Get a shift on, then, if you're going,' Zoë said, while Hilly hesitated about whether or not to take her camera. 'Great choice for your birthday outing, Dad.'

'Take as long as you like.' Their mother was delving in the glove compartment for her paperback. 'There's no rush. We'll be fine here, reading in the shade.'

Walking towards the ticket office, Hilly had the sense of stepping out of the sunshine and into cold shadow. Her father nudged her and nodded towards a sign in French: Entry free to children under sixteen. 'That'd put Zoë in an even worse mood,' he remarked, sorting Euros, 'being classed as a child. *Deux adultes, s'il vous plaît.*' The woman in the booth glanced behind him to see where the other adult was, before realizing he meant Hilly; quickly she covered up her mistake. '*Voilà.*' She handed them their tickets. '*Bonne journée.*'

They passed through gates into a large wire enclosure, surrounded by a high double fence with watchtowers at intervals on the perimeter. It was incongruous, high on the hillside: rather like coming across a floodlit football pitch in the middle of a forest. The area inside, on a downhill slope, was terraced steeply; there was one barrack-style building

8

at the top, with a sign saying MUSÉE, and two others at the lower end. Hilly felt a constriction of fear at her throat, and her heart beating. But I can walk out again, she thought, whenever I want to. She felt all wrong, dressed for the heat in cut-off jeans, a purple T-shirt and wide-brimmed hat; but everyone else was similarly clad. She saw crop-tops, painted toenails, sun-dresses; men in shorts, with hairy legs. We might be on a beach, she thought, or visiting a theme park. But this was real. And in spite of their holiday clothes, people were subdued, speaking to each other only in whispers. Seeing a woman in front remove her straw hat as she entered the museum, Hilly did the same.

TU N'ES QUE VISITEUR DU PALAIS DE LA MORT, she read on a framed card inside: YOU ARE ONLY A VISITOR IN THE PALACE OF DEATH.

* * *

Several hours later, in the main street of Orschwiller, Hilly felt strangely dislocated – plucked out of Natzwiller and transplanted to this busy village, festive in the early evening. Tonight being her father's birthday, they were eating out; he wanted to find a restaurant he and Rose had visited on their honeymoon. They wandered along the narrow streets, past intriguing alleyways, wine cellars, and windowboxes of pink or scarlet geraniums. The street names, Hilly noticed, showed the region's confused past: most had both a French and a German name, on separate plaques. ALTE WEG. RUE DES MARTYRS. Orschwiller itself sounded more German than French.

'Perhaps it wasn't here at all, Rose,' her father was saying, standing in the middle of the road till Zoë yanked him out of the way of an approaching four-by-four. 'I don't recognize it, do you? These villages are all so alike.'

Eventually they settled for a small courtyard place with tables set under a canopy of vines. A waiter greeted them: '*Guten Abend!*' He showed them to a corner table and handed out menus. With an air of reproach, Dad ordered drinks in the very correct French he'd been practising with study tapes for the last month.

'Do we *look* German?' Hilly asked, after the waiter had returned with mineral water, Coke, two Pernods and a basket of bread; this wasn't the first time it had happened.

'He could tell.' Zoë looked up from a grudging scrutiny of the menu. 'One look at Mum, that's all he needed.'

'No,' her father said. 'Nine out of every ten tourists here are German, that's why.'

'It's her Aryan look that does it,' Zoë insisted. 'Blonde hair, blue eyes – you could be a perfect Rhine maiden, Mum.'

Her mother was looking at the wine list. 'I get my colouring from your grandad, not from Heidigran. As you well know.'

'Would Heidigran like it here?' Hilly wondered. 'She might feel at home. She could order for us all in German.'

'I think she's all but forgotten,' said her mother. 'She can't have spoken German for years and years.'

'But can you ever forget your first language?' Hilly persisted. 'Your mother tongue? Even if you don't use it, does your tongue remember?'

'Good job she wasn't with us at that place today.' Zoë was gazing round the courtyard with bored interest. 'Heidigran's a Nazi.'

'*Zoë!*'

'Zoë, that's a ridiculous thing to say,' said their mother. 'As well as offensive. You know perfectly well it's not true.'

Unabashed, Zoë tore at a piece of bread. 'And you know it *is* true. She's racist. Isn't she, Hill? The sort of things she comes out with!'

'I—'

'I think we'll change the subject, shall we?' said their mother, turning back to the menu. 'Has everyone decided what to have?'

* * *

Earlier, in the museum, Hilly had been struck by the associations of the word 'camp'. It brought to mind guide and scout camps, or fields of mud at the Glastonbury Festival; it suggested a willing denial of comfort, a wacky makeshift arrangement enjoyed by people who would go back to duvets and central heating after a few days. It was a kind of pretending. But Natzwiller-Struthof was not pretending.

The German word was *Lager*. She had seen it at the entrance: KONZENTRATIONSLAGER. I wonder if Germans have lagering holidays, she found herself thinking, ridiculously; or signs in lay-bys saying NO LAGERING . . .

11

The museum was a long, single-storey building; inside the entrance you could turn left or right. Her father had gone on while she stopped to read the 'Only a Visitor' poem; she followed him into the left-hand end and found herself confronted by rows of wooden bunk beds. This wasn't a purpose-built museum, she realized, but a – she wasn't sure what the word was. *Dormitory* sounded far too cosy, like something from an old-fashioned boarding-school story, with midnight feasts and prefects. Accommodation block, then. People had lived in here, imprisoned. There were photographs: skinny men, not very old by the look of them, with big eyes, huddled together, several to a bunk.

She looked away, out of the window. If you ignored the foreground – the hangman's gibbet positioned there starkly, the wire fences and the watchtowers – the view was glorious. The sky was hazy blue, above the undulating outline of hills opposite, thickly clad in trees; a bird of prey soared high.

Did that make it better or worse, she wondered – if you were shut in like a battery hen, no hope of escaping – to know that, beyond the fence, streams trickled over rocks, the earth smelled of pine needles, and buzzards roamed the sky?

But the stream would trickle and swell and join bigger streams flowing down to the Rhine, the broad slow river that had proved inadequate as a border. In the dusty, respectful hush, the marching boots of documentaries sounded loud in Hilly's ears.

* * *

'*Choucroute garnie?*' The waiter held a loaded oval plate at eye level; Hilly goggled at it.

'*Pour moi, s'il vous plaît,*' said her father. When everyone was served – a cheesy potato gratin for Hilly, sausage platters for Zoë and their mother, leafy green salad for all – Hilly stared across at the mound of sauerkraut, potatoes and various kinds of meat her father was regarding with some awe.

'Dad! How many people's that for?'

'He had that last time, didn't you, Gavin?' Mum poured Riesling from a slim green bottle. 'I remember then it looked like something a farmer might tuck into, after a hard day digging turnips.'

'Gross,' Zoë remarked, 'all that cabbage stuff.'

'I like to try the local delicacies,' her father said, attempting dignity.

'*Delicacies!* How many kinds of dead animal can you get on one plate?' Hilly said.

'It's his birthday – he can have what he likes,' said Rose. 'Even if it's not exactly healthy eating. Are you going to try the wine, Hilly?'

'Thanks.' Hilly pushed her glass across.

'Me, too.' Zoë clinked hers against it. 'How come you're encouraging under-age drinking?'

'We're in France,' their mother said, watching the cool trickle. 'French children learn to drink wine with meals from an early age. It's civilized, not like the British teenage idea – drinking isn't drinking unless you end up vomiting in a gutter.'

'Charming, Mum! Just what we want to talk about

with our meal. Anyway, happy birthday, Dad.' Hilly raised her glass.

'Happy birthday, love.' Mum leaned sideways to kiss him on the lips. He raised a hand to her shoulder, prolonging the moment; an older couple at the next table looked at them and smiled.

Zoë made a retching sound, rolling her eyes at Hilly. 'Do you *have* to do that in public? Honestly, adults! Don't they show you up? Anyway, Dad – if you've finished slobbering over each other – what's it feel like, being forty-eight? Nearly *fifty*. I hope I'm never forty-eight.'

Hilly took a cautious sip of wine. Interesting, the way it flowed into her mouth, cool, flowery and even bland at first, then the flavours developed and changed on her tongue and in her throat into something muskier and longer-lasting. She saw Zoë's wincing expression as she gulped hers; it was typical of Zoë to insist on having wine, even though she didn't like it.

'Forty-eight's not old!' their mother said. 'I promise you, when you're in your forties you won't even think of yourself as middle-aged, let alone old!'

Hilly looked at her. She had seen how the waiter – thirtyish and dark-eyed – had flicked a glance over Mum, Zoë, herself, then back to Mum again. No, no one would take Rose for middle-aged. She was tall, blonde, well-toned from exercise; she wore a green sleeveless top that showed off tanned shoulders and arms. Zoë – already taller than Hilly, though eighteen months younger – resembled her; Hilly did not.

Resigned to the fact that she was never going to be as sleekly attractive as her mother or sister, Hilly had decided there were other ways to look.

They started to eat. 'Have some salad, Zoë.'

'Don't want any.'

'Mmmm, delicious. How's yours?'

'Hot!' Hilly said, having burned her tongue. 'But scrummy.' Potato, soft and waxy, in a creamy sauce flavoured with mustard, and topped with melted cheese that put strength against mildness. Green salad with the clean tang of vinaigrette. Bread, in chunks, that wasn't quite the same as French bread in England.

'So,' Zoë said, lifting a slice of sausage with her fork, as if she expected to find something unpleasant underneath. 'This time next week, you'll have your results, Hill—'

'Thanks for reminding me. Here was I thinking I might forget all about it, on holiday.'

'You're not worried, are you, Hilly?' her father said, with a heaped forkful of sauerkraut halfway to his mouth. 'Not really? You'll have done fine, don't worry.'

'*That's* what worries me. You and Mum assuming that.'

'– and we'll have Heidigran with us,' Zoë continued. 'How long's it for, Rose?'

Hilly saw the quick glance that passed between her parents.

'You know the situation, Zoë. We can't make long-term plans, not yet.'

'So,' Zoë said. 'Let me get this straight. When you say she's coming to stay with us, what you mean is she's coming to *live* with us? For ever?'

* * *

In the museum Hilly had seen children's drawings in a display case, in crayon and coloured pencil. They might have been in an infant classroom – they showed mums and dads, houses, trees. Good children, she thought, or bored children, impatient with captivity: sit down quietly and do a nice drawing. While you wait. While you wait for someone to decide it's time for you to die.

Maps, photographs, posters, lists. Some of the exhibits were familiar to her: a yellow star marked JÜDE, even one photo, of Jewish children with a nurse, that she thought she'd seen before, in a book. Maps showed how many camps there had been: names she had never heard of alongside the ones everybody knew, the names like Belsen and Dachau and Auschwitz that had come to mean concentration camp and nothing else. Though even those must have been ordinary places once, towns or villages, oblivious of the weight their names would come to bear.

She found Natzwiller-Struthof on the map, then her eyes flicked higher up the Rhine, looking for Cologne. Köln. That was where Heidigran had lived until the end of the war, when she had come to England as an orphan, both parents having been killed by Allied bombs. They were Hilly's great-grandparents, yet they seemed so distant from her – no photos in the family album – that she had to remind herself that they weren't just Heidigran's relations, but her own. I am part-German, she thought. A quarter of me.

People were moving slowly from exhibit to exhibit, not talking. Only a fretful baby cried, soothed and shushed by its father. The silence was making Hilly very conscious of herself. Why are we here? she wondered. What are we looking for?

Much of what she saw was blunted by familiarity, as if its presence in the pages of history and on the exam syllabus meant that the Holocaust had to have happened, that it could not have been otherwise. But some items jumped at her with the shock of immediacy: a face, a typed instruction, a letter to parents from a young partisan due to be executed later that day, a line of children walking obediently towards a waiting train. This last looked so innocuous, as if they might be infants at school being led from their playground.

There was a visitors' book. Hilly caught up with her father, who was turning the pages. She saw comments in French and in German, one in English: '*Will we ever learn?*'

Her father wrote a single word, '*Heartbreaking*', and then his name, Gavin Craig. 'Want to write something?' he whispered.

Hilly considered, then shook her head. She could not think of anything adequate.

* * *

The waiter brought coffee, milk in a jug, sugar. 'What shall we do tomorrow?' Gavin asked, unwrapping lump sugar. 'What'd you like to do, Zoë?'

Zoë shrugged.

'How about the castle – the Haut Kœnigsbourg?' Hilly reminded her. 'You said you liked the look of it.'

'Liked the look of it from *here*, I meant. Doesn't mean I want to trudge round it for hours, staring at bits of rusty armour.'

Hilly looked at her father; a look that said, *Well, we tried.* Since the conversation about Heidigran, which her parents had been trying to avoid, Zoë had gone into full-scale strop. Nothing would please her now.

'The stork place?' Mum suggested. 'Or perhaps just a walk? We could do a good walk from Thannenkirch. Take a picnic, go up into the woods.'

Zoë shook her head. 'Too boring. Too hot.'

* * *

Now that Hilly had been inside, the place would not leave her. Conversation and laughter from the other diners, lights trailing over the pergola and through vine branches, the clink of glasses, could not drive it out of her head.

The sun had struck fiercely as she walked with her father down the slope towards the lower end of the camp. In the intervening space there were only marker stones, like headstones in a graveyard, each bearing the name of another concentration camp. Hilly heard crickets chirring in the long grass beyond the fence; a small aircraft droned overhead.

An area hollowed out in the ground between two buildings had once been a cesspit and was now a memorial to members of the Resistance. There were wreaths and a flagpole. A man and woman stood there, the man taking photographs; the woman wore a long floaty dress, a white hat, sunglasses. They turned to walk away without looking at Hilly or her father.

And the buildings. A prison block. Punishment cells. An execution room. Oven.

Rooms where medical experiments had been carried out: experiments on humans. Rooms where the victims had been kept handy, like laboratory mice.

'Dad. I think I'll go outside.'

'You OK?'

Hilly nodded, though suddenly she was finding it hard to breathe. It was different here from the main part of the museum. Out of the sunlight the air struck cold. It was hard to believe that there wasn't something left here, in the air, in the dust, getting into her lungs and clogging her ears in the echoey silence. She felt tainted by evil.

'I don't want to see any more. D'you mind if I go back to the car?'

'Too much, is it?' Her father put an arm round her and pulled her against his shoulder. 'Come on, love. I know. Let's go back to the others and get out of here.'

* * *

'Who you writing to? Not Rubes *again*?' Zoë leaned over Hilly's bed to look, hairbrush in hand.

'Every day. I promised. And don't say Rubes.' Sprawled on her front, Hilly moved a hand to cover the writing.

19

'You're mad!'

'If you say so.'

'Might as well write mine, as well. Can I have two of your stamps?'

'If you must. In my address book, inside cover, over there on that chest-of-drawers thing.'

'Thanks.'

Hilly raised her eyebrows; this, for Zoë, was extravagant good manners. She watched her sister move across to the open window, against a gauze curtain that moved with the breath of air. Zoë was ready for bed, in a long blue T-shirt that reached to her thighs, her hair brushed straight down her back. Hilly could never look at her without feeling admiration spiked with envy. Why couldn't she have had Zoë's willowy build, her effortless grace?

'Which cards did you get in the end?'

'These.' Zoë showed two cartoon drawings of storks.

'For Nadine, and . . . ?'

Zoë smiled. 'Secret.'

'Oh?' Hilly said, rolling over. 'Male secret, you mean?'

'Secret secret.' Zoë clasped the postcards to her chest. 'Got a spare pen?'

In the early hours of the morning, before the first grey light, Hilly woke to the sound of her own voice yelling. 'No! No!' She was forcing the words out against a constriction in her throat, a strangling tightness.

'For Christ's *sake*!' Zoë clicked the bedside light on. 'What's the matter?'

'Nightmare,' Hilly said, as the strange room came into focus. She put an arm across her face to shield her eyes from the brightness.

'What sort of nightmare? God, you nearly gave me a heart attack!'

'Can't remember. I'm OK now.'

'Go back to sleep, then.' Zoë turned away, burrowed her head into the pillow, and reached for the light switch.

Hilly lay still, aware of the rapid pounding of her heart. She did remember. She had been drawing a picture; she saw her hand clasping a black crayon, drawing with quick, confident strokes. What she drew was a high gate, strong and barred. Why hadn't she chosen something else – trees, rabbits, daisies, a sun with a smiling face? The gate was already much bigger than she had meant it to be: huge, solid, fencing her in. And she must have drawn herself on the wrong side of it, as everyone else had gone through. There were guards – uniforms, badges, shining boots. 'Sorry. You're here now,' said a voice. 'You're never leaving.' She was alone. The others, tourists in bright-coloured clothes and hats and trainers, were chatting, holding each other's hands, moving farther and farther away, and Dad was a small figure walking to the car, not even noticing he'd left her behind. Her hands were on the bars, reaching up; she saw spikes of barbed wire gouging them, and blood trickling over her palms and wrists. The guards stood and watched her, laughing. 'Let me out!' she begged them, knowing it would only add to their amusement. 'It's a mistake! I'm only a visitor—'

Chapter Three

A

TOLD U U R BRILL

'How's it going?' Hilly's mother's head appeared round the door of the bedroom.

'Nearly done, thanks,' Hilly said, from the floor.

Her mother came farther in, stepping between a heap of shoes and a stuffed bin bag. 'Oh, you're moving out completely, are you? Books and everything? I didn't mean you to go as far as that!'

'Good excuse for a clear-out.' Hilly nodded towards the bin bag. 'All that's for the shop. I did think of throwing out some old books, but it's hard.'

'Aha!' Rose's gaze fixed on a paperback, *A Bottled-Cherry Angel*, that Hilly had hastily put face-down on the carpet. 'I thought it was a bit quiet in here. You've got sidetracked! Fatal, to start reading.'

'Well, it's good. Must be years and years since I've read it.'

'Grade A in English Literature, and engrossed in a book for a ten-year-old!' Rose teased.

'Dad's still got *Winnie-the-Pooh*.' Hilly got to her feet. 'Anyway, it makes sense to put all my books with

Zoë's. She's got space on her shelves. The wardrobe's more of a problem – you know how many clothes she's got.'

'Put some of your stuff in mine if it helps. Thanks, love, for being so good about this.' Her mother sat down on the bed. 'I don't think I could stand it if *both* of you were being awkward.'

Hilly digested this with the usual prickle of resentment. Good old Hilly. Reliable Hilly. Sensible Hilly never makes a fuss. Not like Zoë, predictably unpredictable, who's allowed to indulge herself in sulks and tantrums.

'Zoë'll be OK,' Hilly said, sounding more assured than she felt. 'Mum?'

'Mm?'

'Heidigran – the – her illness.' She could not bring herself to say the word. 'There's no cure, is there?' Why was she asking? She knew. She was being a little kid, wanting her mother to say, *Don't worry. Mummy will make it better*. But this wasn't going to get better.

Her mother looked at her. 'No, love, there isn't. But what we don't know is how quickly it'll get worse, the Alzheimer's. We'll find ways of coping. We'll have to.'

Hilly thought of the times when her grandmother was clear-headed enough to realize what was happening to her; aware enough to be frightened by it. How awful, she thought, to lose your sense of who you are, the person you've always thought was you. If that goes, what are you? How lost you would be, how alone!

'What'll happen,' she asked, 'if – if it gets to the

stage that we can't cope? If she needs someone with her all the time, can't be left even for half an hour?'

'We'll cross that bridge when we get to it.' Her mother started pairing up the socks that Hilly, emptying a drawer, had tipped on the bed.

Bad sign, Hilly thought, talking in clichés. It means she doesn't know. Her parents had been reading all they could find – guidance leaflets from the health centre, books, information from websites – but they still didn't know, not really, how it was going to affect them all. Alzheimer's, the big A, was beginning to seem like a new member of the family. Heidigran was coming to live with them, bringing Alzheimer's with her. Sometimes it was referred to as dementia, which Hilly thought was possibly even worse. *My gran's going demented.* At least Alzheimer's made it sound like Alzheimer's fault.

'The thing is,' Rose said, looking in vain for the partner to a red-and-white striped ankle sock that Hilly was sure wasn't hers, 'not that we're at that stage yet, but Heidigran's always dreaded going into residential care. She made me promise I'd never put her in a home. And I wouldn't think of it, not yet, but what if – like you say, what if we just can't manage?'

By now, Hilly could hardly believe that as recently as Christmas Heidigran had been with Grandad, living as they had always lived: busy, independent, apparently contented. Then Grandad had died in February – quite suddenly, after a stroke – and now A had made its presence felt, and everything had changed. Hilly's parents were leaving for Heidigran's, in Banbury, as soon as Dad got home from work; they would spend the whole weekend there, helping her pack, doing all the things that needed doing to a house when it was being left for an indefinite period. They were bringing her back with them on Sunday, and from then on this would be Heidigran's room, not Hilly's.

'It'd be awful, putting her in a home,' Hilly agreed. 'But there's you to think of, too. What about your job?'

Her mother made a bleak face. 'I'll have to be flexible. She looked after me when I was little – now it's my turn to look after her. Anyway,' she said, in a brighter tone. 'What are your plans for the weekend? More celebrations?'

'Oh no, that was yesterday.' Hilly still felt a glow of surprise when she thought of her GCSE grades: three As – History, English and English Literature – and the rest all Bs and a C. Better than she'd expected, and certainly good enough to let her go on to her chosen AS levels. 'The shop tomorrow, and I'm meeting Reuben, maybe see a film with Tess.'

'You'll be OK, won't you? There's plenty of food in the fridge, and Valerie's next door if you need any help.'

'Thanks.' Hilly couldn't imagine any crisis that might be eased by Valerie's presence. Valerie was a fussy, childless woman in her fifties who termed herself a housewife, with no sense of post-feminist irony. Wife to a three-bedroomed semi, Hilly thought; spouse to a house?

'I've told Zoë she's to be in at a reasonable time,' said Rose, 'and not give you anything to worry about.'

'That'll be fine, then,' Hilly said, with only the faintest edge of sarcasm.

With two of them sorting and carting, the room was soon cleared. They stripped the bed, and Rose went downstairs for the vacuum cleaner. Hilly stood looking at the room that had been hers all her life, hers alone since the loft conversion had been made for Zoë four years ago, but was hers no longer. Denuded of her clutter it looked smaller, just a box with one window. It was oddly disturbing, seeing her territory stripped and emptied; as if she were being tidied up with it, plucked out of her habitat.

She lugged the computer, a piece at a time, up the open stairway that led to Zoë's room. It was lucky that the attic room was large – the whole upper floor of the house, with eave-space made into sloping cupboards you could crawl into. The spare bed, now to be Hilly's, had always been kept here, usually strewn with several layers of Zoë's clothes. Zoë had grudgingly cleared space for Hilly's things, and as it was the summer holidays she had no school stuff on the desk; Dad had put in a new modem point, for the internet connection. Hilly arranged the computer – monitor, keyboard and printer – and crawled underneath to plug everything in. Zoë would moan about the space it took up, but would be appeased by being able to use it for homework and e-mails.

To check that it all worked, Hilly switched on, clicked the on-line connection and then MAIL.

'Receiving mail', the message came up, and then, in her inbox, 'Reuben Jones. Hot News.'

She clicked, and read: 'Xciting developments with S after I saw u yesterday! This is it – I'm in lurve. Tell u all about it, only not here. R.'

'Where is Lurve,' Hilly typed in reply, 'and why haven't you sent a postcard? You never know, I might want to go there myself one day. But seriously, can't wait for a full update! See you 7, park? H.'

From Friday to Sunday, while her parents were away, Hilly was supposedly in charge. The first night was fine. The second was not.

They left after a quick pizza meal on Friday evening. Zoë was at her friend Nadine's; Hilly went to meet Reuben in the park, at their favourite rendez-vous by the round pond, halfway between their two homes. First to arrive, she sat on their usual bench, watching a family of moorhens bobbing among the lilies and walking over the leaves.

Reuben was Hilly's best friend, and had been since primary school. He was not her boyfriend, though at one time she had thought he might be, and still found it useful sometimes to pretend that he was, just as he sometimes used her as a smokescreen. Since leaving school and starting at sixth-form college, a year ahead of Hilly, Reuben had stopped pretending that it was girls who attracted him. S, Hilly assumed, was for Saeed – a shy, handsome Middle Eastern boy Reuben had met earlier in the summer. Certainly, before she left for France, Reuben had been in a most uncharacteristic mope, after Saeed – scared off, Reuben said – had ended the short-lived flirtation. Hence Hilly's promise of daily postcards to Reuben, a small effort to cheer him up.

Staring at the moorhens, she wondered how she felt about Reuben's news. Reuben always kept her fully informed of various fancyings, skirmishes, misunderstandings and embarrassments, but – even allowing for his typical extravagance – this was the first time he had used the L-word. She had seen him only yesterday, but it was results day, dominated by exam hysteria. Hilly had spent the day with Tessa and her other friends, collecting and comparing grades, talking over and over again about successes, disappointments and plans, and finishing up in a pub in town. Reuben had gone to school with her, seen the results, then drifted off on his own.

And now here he was, approaching from behind a bed of scarlet dahlias: mop of unruly hair, broad grin, quick bouncy walk. 'You look pleased with yourself!' she called.

'So do you, Miss A-Grade.'

'Only three. I'd better make the most of it. Next year it'll be Zoë's turn, and she'll get starred As without even trying. Sickening, the way she does it.'

'Never mind about her. And three's two more than I got,' said Reuben, who only really put himself out for music. He plonked himself on the bench next to her.

Hilly elbowed him. 'Come on then, tell me! About lurve. Is S for Saeed?'

'Course! Who else? How fickle do you think I am?'

'Come on, then. I'm all ears.'

'Right.' Reuben settled back. 'After you went off boozing with your mates yesterday—'

'I went boozing, you went cruising?'

'Hilly!' Reuben's expressive eyebrows moved independently of each other – one up, one down. 'What have you been watching? OK then. I cruise into the music shop and there he is. Like it's meant to be – eyes meeting across a crowded shop and all that. I'm thinking, s'pose he's still not talking to me, and stand there dithering. But my feet decide to walk over, and next minute we're having a conversation with subtitles.'

'Subtitles?'

'Yeah. I say Hi, and he says Hi, and I go How's things, and he goes Oh fine. You? And I go OK, thanks. Another minute or two and we'd have been on to the weather and the Test Match. But the subtitles are zapping like crazy, and luckily they're a lot more interesting. *God, I've missed you. Me too. It's been awful. Can we have another go? You bet.*'

Hilly giggled. 'Lucky you could both read them. Then what?'

'We went to McDonald's – lucky we didn't bump into your lot. Ditched the doublespeak and did some straight talking – well, you know what I mean. Spent all day together, and sorted out a load of stuff.'

'And?'

'We're fine. It was all a bit of a mistake, before. Family pressure, and all that.'

'What, his folks know about him and you?'

Reuben shook his head vigorously. 'No! No-o-o!

He got scared of what'd happen if they found out – they'd go ballistic, he says. So he tried to kid himself he didn't need to see me. Problem was, he couldn't stand it – well, you can't blame him, can you?' He pretended to preen himself. 'Which was lucky, 'cos it was doing my head in. The whole time you were away. Lucky I've had the concert rehearsals and hours of practice, or I'd have gone completely up the wall.'

'Sorry,' said Hilly. 'Bad timing. But they'll have to know some time, won't they?'

'He's not ready for the kamikaze dive, not yet. But he knows and I know. That's enough to be getting on with.'

'Well, I'm glad for you,' Hilly said, trying to inject a note of genuine enthusiasm into her voice. 'Saeed's lovely.'

Reuben gave her a stern look. 'You fancy him as well?'

'Wouldn't be a lot of point, would there?' Hilly said. 'What's it feel like, then – Lurve, the Big L? How do you *know*?'

Reuben looked up at the sky, down at his feet, made a vague gesture with both hands, smiled a smug, private smile. 'I just know. Can't explain it.'

'Go on, though,' said Hilly. 'Try.'

Hilly's Saturdays were spent in the Oxfam shop in the High Street, where she had worked for nearly a year. To Zoë, who had a part-time holiday job at their father's sports shop, this was derisory.

'Why do that when you could easily work at Dad's?'

a typical conversation would go. 'You're mad, you are. You really *like* sorting through heaps of grungy old tat? Careful you don't get fleas.'

'I like grungy old tat, thanks.'

'I wish you wouldn't,' Zoë would grumble. 'It's em*barr*assing. Suppose one of my friends saw you in there?'

'Why should it bother them?'

'It bothers me! 'Specially when you actually *wear* Oxfam stuff, like a bag lady. Anyone would think you *had* to.'

'Recycling,' Hilly said. 'All my favourite things come from Oxfam. And if you're talking about tat, how about all that High-Street Clone-Wear you love so much? Those shops rake in more than enough money, without me contributing.'

'Oh, you're weird. Why can't I have a normal sister?'

'Why can't I have a *nice* sister? You used to be nice.'

'You used to be sane.'

'As if you could tell!'

And so on. These verbal spats rarely meant much, and were instantly forgotten. But Saturday night and Sunday morning were more serious.

By the time the shop closed, Hilly knew from the tightening in the back of her neck that a headache was imminent. For as long as she could remember, she'd had mild headaches, but nothing a couple of aspirin couldn't shift. Recent ones had been more persistent, accompanied by groggy sickness and lasting two or three days; often they coincided with her period, as if that wasn't enough to put up with. Damn. She had to go to Sainsbury's on the way home; she and Zoë had agreed to cook lunch tomorrow for Mum and Dad and Heidigran, and she wanted to make a lemon cheesecake tonight, to avoid a panic in the morning. Later she was meeting Tess and some other friends at the cinema.

She took two paracetamol from the shop's First Aid box, swallowed them with water, said her good-byes, did the shopping, lugged it home, unpacked, made the cheesecake and put it to set in the fridge. The pills weren't helping much; the headache tightened its grip around her forehead, stabbing into her right eye. She thought about the cinema and knew she couldn't go; the intensity of sound and picture would send the pain into overdrive. She rang Tess to explain. That done, she had a slice of buttered toast and a glass of milk – all she could face – and sat down at her piano in the front room. Zoë had said she'd be out, refusing to specify where, who with, or what time she'd be in.

Hilly knew that she'd never be able to play the piano as well as she wanted – as well as Reuben did, the music seeming to flow from his fingers – but nevertheless here it was: sturdy, willing, hers. She had bought it for twenty pounds from someone who had come into the shop with a card for the notice board. A place had been cleared, it was carted in with much heaving and straining from Hilly's father and Geoff from next door, and a man had come round to tune it, which cost more than the piano itself. Hilly's progress was laborious and uninspired, working from a book Reuben had romped through before he was five, a book of jingly little tunes for child beginners. Reuben was her teacher. He had promised her a new book next week if she could play all the pieces and scales to his satisfaction.

She started with the exercises and arpeggios he had set her, flexing stiff fingers. When Reuben played he made it seem a different matter entirely, his hands roaming over the keys as if by instinct. Her wrists and fingers lacked the strength for a regular touch, aching whenever she practised. And practising wasn't easy, with the piano in the main room where everyone gathered for meals and TV. Tonight, with no one to be annoyed, she ought to practise and practise for hours, but the headache was affecting her vision; when she gazed at the staves, the notes danced and blurred. Instead of playing properly she doodled a tune, picking it out with her right hand only. One hand was manageable; using two was a feat of co-ordination she thought she'd never master, even when she was able to concentrate properly. The gap between notes on the page and the required finger-action was too much for her brain or her hands to process.

A hot bath, that was what she needed. She would soak and unwind, and think the pain out of her head, wafting it away with the steam. With no one at home, she could wallow for as long as she liked.

Ten minutes later she was lying in scented water. A candle, the radio playing soft music, the mirror steaming up. Eyes closed, she found herself thinking about something Reuben had said yesterday in the park: 'It'll happen to you one day.' After he'd explained about Lurve. Well, would it? Did she want it to? And did it happen by some inevitable process, or did you *make* it happen, by wanting?

She had only the vaguest idea of her imagined Someone. Older than her, he'd have to be. Someone she could respect. Someone she could talk to. Someone she could be herself with. But which of her selves did she mean? By now she could recognize several. The self that inhabited her at school wasn't the same self she was with Reuben, and the version Reuben got was different from the one Zoë knew; Tess got another one again. So which, Hilly thought, is the real me, the real Hilary Craig?

And would it be frightening, to find someone who could see through the layers of selves? At the moment all she wanted to do was retreat deep into some peaceful core of herself, if it were there to find, beyond sense, beyond feeling . . .

She was half-dozing, drifting into a pleasant steamy haze that soothed away the pressure in her head. Then, in a moment, jolted into alertness by the sound of the front door crashing open, and loud voices at the bottom of the stairs.

For a second her mind blurred with panic. Then, hearing Zoë's voice among the others – a whole crowd of them, it sounded like, mostly male – she pulled out the plug and climbed quickly out of the water to close and lock the bathroom door, which she had left wide open. So much for her peaceful evening! Fear was replaced by annoyance; it sounded as if Zoë had brought a football team home. Hilly heard them moving into the main room, voices raised; the front door slammed shut. While she was drying herself, someone started thumping the keys of the piano. *Her* piano! Really thumping, not playing: like a boisterous child ramping over the keyboard. Maybe it *was* a boisterous child. She dressed quickly, rubbed her glasses on the towel and put them back on. The front door was opened again, and she heard sounds as of removal men carting boxes of stuff through.

Reluctantly she went down. A strange boy was lounging on the sofa, feet up. The one at the piano continued to attack the keys. Someone else was unravelling the lead of an electric guitar; two others were positioning black boxes that could be amplifiers. They all looked older than Hilly – eighteen or nineteen. She recognized none of them. The one on the sofa stared as if she were the intruder; no one else took the slightest notice.

'Where's Zoë?' she asked the room in general.

The boy on the sofa jerked his head towards the kitchen. Hilly marched through, tripping over the guitar lead. Someone holding it – partially shaven head, both ears multi-pierced and studded – glared at her. 'Watch it, can't you!'

'Hello, nice to meet you too. I'm Hilly, I live here, in case you were wondering. And that's my piano,' she added to the boy who sat at the keyboard.

He changed to a plinky-plink little tune in the

upper octaves that somehow seemed patronizing. 'Is that a problem?'

'Since you ask, I'd prefer it if you didn't.'

The boy was big-faced, with hair unbecomingly parted in the middle, and a cigarette between his lips. He banged down the lid. 'It's crap anyway.'

'Thanks. And would you mind not smoking?'

'Christ – laugh a minute, aren't you?'

In the kitchen, Zoë and yet another boy were wrapped in an uncomfortable-looking clutch, like drowned and entangled swimmers: mouth to mouth, as if in a desperate attempt at resuscitation.

'Zoë!'

Zoë made a token effort to detach herself. The boy – tall, gelled fair hair – still held her, giving her ear a last lick; she looked at Hilly, mildly discomfited. 'You said you were going out!'

'What's going on?'

'What d'you think?'

'I don't mean in *here*.' Hilly turned her head. 'I mean in there. The guitar. The equipment.'

'Oh.' Zoë giggled. 'Didn't I say? We're having a band practice.'

'We? Since when have you been in a band?'

'Since now,' said the boy, holding Zoë by both shoulders. 'She's our female vocalist.'

'Vocalist! Since when have you been able to sing?'

'I've got hidden talent,' Zoë said. 'We're called Doppelgänger.'

'Doppelgänger? Meaning?'

'Fuck knows,' said the boy. 'Clyde got it from somewhere.'

'Zoë, you can't play here,' Hilly said. 'What about the noise? The neighbours?'

'Oh, don't be so stuffy! Grant, this is Hilly. My sister.'

'Not much alike, are you?' Grant gave Hilly a quick up-and-down – not impressed, he made that clear.

'No, we're not,' Hilly said, aware of how she must look: barefooted, in jeans and a striped grandad shirt, one of her Oxfam bargains; hair lank and bedraggled from bathroom steam; wire-rimmed glasses. 'Zoë, make them cart all that stuff out. You'll have to find somewhere else.'

'You tell them, then. Spoilsport. We only want to go through a few songs. It's all right for you and Rubes, isn't it? Same thing.'

'Oh, come on.' Grant flashed a smile. 'Don't make such a big deal about it. We'll keep the noise down, promise. I'll make sure you don't get in trouble with Mummy and Daddy.'

'Big of you.'

'It'll be OK, Hilly, honest,' said Zoë, trying a different tactic. 'You can go upstairs and leave us to it if you want.'

'I'm not going anywhere.'

'Yeah, have a listen, I would,' Grant said. 'We're red-hot, I'm telling you.'

Was this, Hilly wondered, the recipient of the jokey stork postcard from Alsace? He was tall, bland-featured, but with flawless tanned skin and eyes of strident blue, and a cocky, confident smile. Acknowledging his attractiveness, Hilly disliked him on sight. He was too old and surely too experienced for Zoë.

'Well . . .' She felt too weary to continue arguing. Her headache was returning, throbbing and insistent. In the next room, the boy with the electric guitar played a series of chords that filled the house with a loud and – she had to admit – thrilling sound. Zoë, obviously thinking she'd given in, said, 'I'll make sure we clear up after, honest,' and moved past her to join the others. Grant, as he went, put a hand on Hilly's arm – obviously thinking he had her mesmerized with the sexual glow that radiated from him. 'You can audition for backing vocals if you want.'

'Thanks, no.' Irritably, Hilly moved away, went to the sink and ran herself a glass of water.

Now what? She was handling this badly: showing herself as a bad-tempered prude, but failing to do anything definite about the situation. She urgently wanted to go upstairs, take more paracetamol and lie down, soothed by quiet music. Instead, she was going to have to listen to whatever came out of the amplifiers, and she felt a duty to loiter downstairs. Typical Zoë, she huffed to herself: ruining my evening (more than it was ruined already) . . . making me feel responsible . . . doing just as she likes . . . all precisely as per usual!

Hilly hung around. Fortunately, no one took the slightest notice, giving her the chance to observe. Nothing she saw or heard encouraged her to like

Zoë's new friends any better. Although the music –
produced by a guitar, an electronic drum kit and a
synthesizer – was not at first too loud, it was raucous
head-banging stuff, the product of energy rather than
of musicianship. Zoë was an indifferent singer, but
encouraged by Grant put a lot of effort into aggressive-
sexy posturing. The lyrics, such as they were, were
difficult to hear properly; Hilly wasn't bothering to try,
but one chorus, repeated several times, caught her
attention:

> *You want your freedom, but I need my space.*
> *Don't breathe my air, just get out of my face.*
> *You can keep looking, but don't you look here.*
> *Nobody needs you, we don't want you near.*
> *Get back where you came from, this isn't your place.*
> *You're not a paid-up member of the human race.*

Only after this had pounded into her ears a few
times did Hilly recognize it for what it was.

By this time the headache could not be ignored
any longer, and she really was going to be sick unless
she lay down on her bed. She could hardly trust herself to walk through the clutter of leads and
equipment to the door, and the blessed solitude of
upstairs. 'Zoë! Not much longer, OK?' she managed.

'Yeah, yeah, don't make a fuss. We're only just
getting going,' Zoë said.

'I'm down to my last fag. Is that Paki shop down
the road still open?' she heard Pete, the guitarist,
remark behind her.

Hilly would not normally have let that pass, but her stomach was threatening to heave. She gave him a shrivelling look, and caught sight of something that disturbed her still farther.

Moments later she was retching into the toilet, thinking that if she'd thrown up over his feet it really wouldn't have been such a disaster. The involuntary heaving filled her eyes with tears, reinforced by an extra welling-up of self-pity and a childlike longing for attention: if Mum were here, she'd be soothing and patting, offering towels and sympathy. Left to cope on her own, Hilly gargled and washed her face, made her groggy way up to the attic, exchanged clothes for nightshirt, swallowed two more pills and lowered herself carefully into bed. All she could do now was give herself over to it, lie in the dusk with an arm over her face and wait for the now intense pain to go away. She could not bear the radio, couldn't even think properly; the sickness and disturbed vision made her thoughts seem to zoom and flash inside her head like splinters of light, bouncing off her skull, colliding with each other. The heavy bass thrumming was louder now, the amplifiers turned up, or was she imagining it? Valerie and Geoff next door must be getting it at full blast, too; Hilly was surprised Valerie hadn't come round to complain. But she couldn't do anything about it now.

She groaned, turned over, tried to arrange herself comfortably, waited. After what seemed a long while she began to drift into half-sleep, from which restless state she registered that the din downstairs went on and on and finally stopped, and that there was a lot of commotion by the front door as the band moved out, followed by shouting and revving outside, and then, at last, quiet. Zoë must have been making an effort to tidy up, as she did not come upstairs immediately. At last Hilly slept.

She woke early, surprised by the unfamiliar room. Early light filtered through the curtains; from the other bed she heard Zoë's soft, regular breathing. Zoë's mouth was open, hair strewn across the pillow; asleep, she looked about twelve. For a second, raising herself on one elbow, Hilly saw a much younger, sweeter Zoë; then everything about last night thumped back into her head. The nauseous feeling lingered, and a dull, background headache. Oh God, and there was so much to do. Mum and Dad and Heidigran would be here for lunch.

'Zoë! Zoë, you awake?'

Not a sound in reply.

Sensible Hilly will see to everything. Scatter-brained Zoë needn't lift a finger. That's what they'd all be assuming. But sensible Hilly felt like rolling over and going back to sleep.

Sitting up, she squinted at her alarm clock: ten past eight. She usually woke much earlier than this. She reached for her glasses, then for slippers and dressing gown. The stale ashiness of cigarette smoke reached her on the stairs; must get the windows open, and some air through. In the front room Hilly pulled back the curtains, then did a double-take at the sight of a blanket-shrouded figure asleep on the sofa. Only one, thankfully. But a gaze round the room revealed furniture still in disarray, an overflowing saucer of cigarette ends on the windowsill, ash trodden into the carpet. In the kitchen, a fly buzzed round a trail of spilled stickiness on the worktop, and the bin overflowed with beer cans.

Hilly stomped back upstairs and flung Zoë's duvet to the floor, leaving her exposed and bare, curled in sleep.

'Zoë! Wake up, *now!*'

Chapter Four

Leavings

> Dementia is progressive and incurable; it
> leads to a decline in the ability to
> remember, think and reason, and to
> changes in personality and behaviour
> which may turn a loved friend or relative
> into a fractious and increasingly
> dependent stranger.
>
> Robert T. Woods, *Alzheimer's Disease*

They're taking me away again, Heidi thought. I must
have done something bad.

Stiffly, she raised herself into a sitting position and
swung her feet to the floor. She sat for a few moments
looking at her bare feet, at the dry skin and dis-
coloured big toenails, beneath a hem of broderie
anglaise. Those can't be my feet, she thought. My feet
are smaller than that. Such neat little feet I remember
having. Quick, light feet, that could skip and dance
their way through squares marked on the pavement

for hopscotch. I liked those better. Where are they?

Someone was downstairs; she heard the clatter of dishes in the sink. Who was it? Frowning, she picked at the edge of her sheet. They had been here last night, both of them. Rose, and . . . and . . . Graham? No, no, Gavin, of course, how foolish. Gavin. She hoped Rose would bring a cup of tea in a moment. Her throat was dry, her mouth tasted sour; tea was what she needed. Carefully she stood: pushed back the curtains and looked out at her front garden, the late roses, the purple shrubby thing that brought the butterflies, and that plant with the grapey-mauve flowers she liked so much – what was its name? Pen – Pen – Penstemon, that was it.

When clarity returned it was like a picture coming into focus, like windscreen wipers sweeping away condensation, letting her see clearly. Penstemons, and the butterfly bush was buddleia – buddleja they'd started spelling it now in gardening magazines. Next to it were tall spires with ragged flowers limp on their stems but new buds still to open: evening primroses. She had planted them herself, watched the rosettes of leaves, flat to the ground, thrust up stems thick with buds that unfurled into primrose-yellow trumpet flowers, each lasting one day. And there was *Geranium macrorrhizum* 'Ingwersen's Variety', that spread itself and swamped everything near it if you didn't keep it under control, and left its strong musty smell on your hands when you pulled it up. The yellow clematis that scrambled over the trellis, already with some of the silvery tufts of old-man's-beard that followed the flowers, was *Clematis tangutica*. She was good at names.

That stair had always creaked, the second one from the top. Rose came in, dressed, carrying a cup and saucer.

'Mum, you're awake early! I didn't want to disturb you. Here. Why don't you get back into bed and drink this? There's no rush.'

Heidi sat, obedient. The cup rattled in its saucer as she took it from Rose's steady hand. She sipped the tea; not enough sugar. But the hot slide down her throat was soothing.

'I don't want to leave my garden,' she said. 'You know I'm perfectly capable. It's only first thing in the morning I'm a bit vague. Perhaps we should think again. Are you off to the gym?' she added, looking at Rose's lycra top and track pants, and her hair pulled back into a ponytail.

'No, Mum, I'm not going to the gym. We're taking you home with us, for a stay – you'll enjoy that.'

'Home?' Heidi said blankly.

'Home with us, Mum. Remember? We're all packed and ready, and the girls are cooking lunch. And don't worry about your garden – we'll come back and take care of it.'

'Is—?'

Rose looked at her. Heidi took another sip of tea, pretending she hadn't meant to speak. It had gone again, the name; how maddening! She had been about to ask if he was still here too, her son-in-law. She'd had it just now, but it had slithered out of her memory like an agile fish. G. She knew it began with a G. Puzzling over it, annoyed with herself for forgetting something so simple, she gazed around her room, noticing how strange it looked. The wardrobe was half-empty; someone had put out a pair of trousers and a shirt, on hangers against the door, ready to be worn. She didn't remember choosing those.

'Someone's stealing my clothes,' she said. And then the name came back: Gavin. How could she have forgotten? 'Is Gavin still here?'

'Yes, course he is. He's not up yet. We'll have breakfast, then we're all going back together.'

'Going back?' Heidi said. Her mind reeled. 'But there's nothing there. They've all gone.'

'Home. Home with us. Hilly and Zoë are there, getting our lunch.' Rose draped a plaid dressing gown on the bedside chair. 'Give me a shout when you're ready to get up.'

There was a purring rush, and Oscar arrived on Heidi's bed, trilling with pleasure, butting his head against her arm. Tea sloshed into the saucer. She stroked him, feeling the plumpness of his body, his warmth. His claws snagged on the bedspread.

'Poor Oscar,' she crooned, 'poor old fellow, poor old chap! What's going to happen to you? Who's going to look after you?' Her eyes filled with tears.

'Mum!' Rose said, putting out a pair of brown shoes. 'I've told you enough times! Oscar's coming with us.'

There was that other time. That other leaving.

She was buttoned into her best coat, which was

new last winter and still hardly worn. It was maroon, with a flared skirt, and had black fabric-covered buttons and a velvet collar; Mutti had bought her a velvet hat to match. When she'd first tried them on, the coat and the hat, and looked at herself in the mirror, she thought how grown-up she looked, how smart. 'My little princess,' said Mutti, standing behind so that both reflections smiled back at her. Mutti picked a stray hair off the velvet collar, and bent to kiss her cheek.

She had grown since then. The coat only just covered her knees. She wore clean white socks, and her lace-up shoes had been polished. It was a trick, dressing her up in her best clothes, making a game of packing her small suitcase. They were all pretending it was a special treat, an outing.

They don't want me any more. They don't love me, whatever lies they tell. Mutti can't be my real mother, or Vati my real father, or they wouldn't send me away.

Last night – her last night at home, in her own bed – she had cried and cried. She made herself carry on crying long after she could have stopped. I'll show them, she thought; I'll show them they can't do this to me. In the morning she would wake up very early and run away. She would live on her own in a forest, and eat berries and make fires, like people did in stories. She would find a hollow tree to sleep in, make herself a nest of grass and leaves, like a dormouse, and sleep there snug and warm. It would be an adventure.

But she had slept later than she meant to and it

was too late to run away. Her eyes felt red and hot, but if Mutti noticed she didn't say anything. She had made breakfast, coffee and warm rolls, as if it was a perfectly ordinary day. Her eyes looked red too, but she was only pretending. Vati wasn't even at home to say goodbye.

'Eat up your breakfast, there's a good girl,' said Mutti.

'I hate them,' Heidi said aloud, in the bedroom that didn't look like hers any more.

Chapter Five

Heidigran

Sisters, sisters, there were never such
devoted sisters.

Song lyric

'Zoë! Don't just lie there! Downstairs is a terrible mess
– shift yourself and do something about it!'

'Did it last night,' Zoë murmured, eyes closed.

'No, you didn't! And get rid of whoever's dossing
on the sofa.'

'Oh, for Christ's sake!' Sitting up, pushing tousled
hair out of her eyes, Zoë glared at her sister. 'Give it a
rest, can't you? You were a right pain yesterday.'

'*I* was a pain—!' Hilly began, about to broach the
subject that was more importantly on her mind than
mess. But lunch had to be cooked, and the house
made tidy and smoke-free before their parents and
grandmother arrived. Arguing would have to wait.

Hilly showered and dressed. When she went downstairs, Zoë, still wearing only the thin T-shirt she slept

in, was offering tea to the sofa-sleeper. 'Here you are, Clyde. You've got to go now. Hilly says.'

A blinking, bleary face emerged from under the blanket; a hand crept out for the mug. It was the unappealing square-faced boy, the one who'd been playing Hilly's piano. His eyes fastened on Zoë's bare legs, then, with far less pleasure, on Hilly. While Hilly straightened the furniture he sat up, put on his boots, downed the tea and got to his feet, reaching for his leather jacket. 'Ta. Catch you later.'

'I hope not,' Hilly said, in a mood to take exception to any harmless remark.

'Sorry about my grumpy sister,' Zoë said. She went with him to the front door.

'So,' Hilly said when she returned. 'Which one are you going out with – Prince Charming there, or the one you were snogging in the kitchen?'

'Grant, course.' Zoë started folding the blanket, sulky and defensive. 'Clyde doesn't like going home if he can help it, that's all.'

'Zoë, they're *awful*. All of them. Can't you see? They're ignorant, racist yobs. That guitarist, Pete – he's got a swastika on his jacket!'

'Oh, don't make such a stupid fuss! It's only a badge – lots of people wear them. And who are you calling ignorant?'

'Only a badge – who are you kidding? Christ, Zoë! And those song lyrics – don't you realize? How can you go along with it, joining their ghastly group? What are you going to do, perform at National Front rallies?'

'Don't be so stuffy! It's only a bit of fun. They're only words.'

'Stop saying *only*! *Only* this and *only* that! There's no *only* about it. You'll get yourself into trouble – please, do yourself a favour—'

'Get into trouble, will I?' Zoë stood, hands on hips. 'What you mean is, you'll tell Mum and Dad the minute they walk in the door. Good little Hilly with her shining halo, never does anything wrong. You're just jealous, it's so obvious! You're jealous of me.'

'Oh? And how d'you work that out?'

'Well!' Zoë tossed her head, throwing back her hair, with an unspoken invitation: Look at me, then look at yourself. 'You can't get a proper boyfriend, only Rubes. I mean, a gay boyfriend—' Her derisive huff of laughter made Hilly want to slap her face. 'How weird is that?'

'Don't start getting at Reuben! This is nothing to do with him.'

'No, it's you I'm getting at. I'll tell you why you hang around with a queer—'

'A *what*?'

'– it's because he's safe, that's why! You haven't got the guts to go out with a real bloke. Not that anyone's likely to fancy you, in your jumble-sale tat, with straggly hair and glasses – you wouldn't look too bad if you did something with yourself, but you can't be bothered. And with Rubes for a boyfriend, or nearest thing to one, you don't have to bother about sex, either.'

Hilly laughed. 'Setting yourself up as a psychiatrist now, are you?'

'That's what it comes down to, isn't it – that's why you're jealous! Because blokes fancy me, good-looking blokes like Grant, and they don't even look at you.'

'Zoë, I'm warning you – don't you ever call Reuben a queer again. And I'm not discussing me and Reuben, or my clothes or hair – I'm worried about *you*. Can't you see how they're affecting you, that lot?'

'You just want to stop me having a good time!' Zoë flung back.

'No. Listen! You called Heidigran a Nazi – don't you remember, at Dad's birthday lunch? So it's bad for Heidigran but OK for your yobby friends, because you happen to fancy Grant?'

'It doesn't mean anything!' Half-heartedly, Zoë arranged the sofa cushions. 'Don't go on and on at me – you're doing my head in.'

'Doesn't mean anything? Zoë, you've got a brain – for God's sake use it! Don't you read the papers? Watch the news?'

'What's that got to do with it?'

'*Oh—!*' Hilly raised both hands to her eyes. Where to start? This was going nowhere.

'I made tea for you as well.' Zoë, who moments earlier had looked about to flounce out of the room, changed her manner, tilting her head in little-girlish appeal. 'Are you going to tell Mum and Dad, then?'

Hilly recognized a strong bargaining position when she saw one. Fifteen minutes later Zoë, quiet and submissive, was washing up at the sink and preparing to peel a bowlful of potatoes. Hilly, who had decided to attempt a traditional Sunday lunch in Heidigran's honour, was consulting Delia Smith about the roasting of pork. Needing to weigh the joint, she opened the fridge door and stepped back with a piercing shriek that startled Zoë as well as herself.

Zoë turned warily from the sink. 'What?'

'My *cheese*cake, that's what! I don't believe it! Zoë, I'll kill you!'

It should have been waiting there, perfectly set, for her to dredge with icing sugar and add a few artistic touches with lemon slivers before presenting it at the table. Instead she was gazing at one thin slice and a scattering of crumbs.

'You gave them my cheesecake! I spent ages making that last night – now look at it!' she ranted. 'How could you? Don't you ever stop and think? You really are the limit! Now what are we going to have?'

'It wasn't my fault! Grant and Clyde got it out – they'd cut it up before I even noticed. I wouldn't have let them, honest, only by then it was too late. I'll go down to Sainsbury's and buy a new one if you like.'

'You bet you'll go to Sainsbury's,' Hilly stormed. 'And get the ingredients for another one. You'll just about have time to make it.'

'*Make* it! I don't know how!'

'Delia Smith does.' Hilly turned to the book's index. 'Get a pen, and make a new shopping list.'

'Look at Oscar,' Heidigran said. 'He's turning his back on us all.' The grey cat had settled himself in an armchair, on his own cushion. His litter tray was by the back door, food bowls in the kitchen, toys arranged temptingly on the carpet, but he maintained an offended indifference to his new surroundings.

Heidigran, at first, seemed completely herself; far more so than when Hilly had last seen her. That occasion was one Hilly would never forget. She, her mother and grandmother had been shopping in Banbury; Heidigran had slipped away from them in Boots, wandered off, and been discovered nearly two hours later sitting on the floor in Ottakar's bookshop, reading a picture book aloud to herself. A concerned sales assistant had approached her; Heidigran had been unable to give her address or even her name, and the police had been called. Hilly, searching with her mother, rushing from shop to car park and back again, went through a multiple-choice test of what might have happened. Heidigran could be lured away, mugged or murdered, or she might fall into the canal, or take herself down to the station and get on a train with no idea where she was going.

That had been the turning point: from then on they could not convince themselves that Heidigran was just a bit vague these days, a bit forgetful. It was clear that she could not safely continue to live alone. She might leave the gas turned on or let saucepans boil dry, or wander out of the house in the middle of the night. With the family about to leave for their holiday in France, hasty arrangements had been made for Heidigran to stay with Charles and Anita, the girls' uncle and aunt.

Zoë hadn't been in Banbury that day, and Hilly knew that she was still wondering what all the fuss was about. Heidigran ate with a good appetite, had an extra helping of the stuffed pork, and made normal conversation. 'Wonderful! What a delicious lunch! You are lucky, Rose, having these two to do the cooking.'

'Yes, they've done well. But don't let them fool you. This is a first.'

Hilly had seen her mother's suspicious glances; she was not taken in by her daughters' conspicuous politeness to each other. While Hilly cleared the plates, Zoë carried in the substitute cheesecake, to their father's feigned astonishment.

'What, there's more? And that doesn't look like it came out of a packet!'

'Cheesecake! I love cheesecake,' said Heidigran. 'Who made it?'

There was a slight pause. Hilly picked up a rumpled napkin.

'I did,' said Zoë, flushing slightly.

'What,' said Dad, 'my little Zoesie got herself organized in the kitchen?'

Zoë gave him a simpering look from under her eyelashes.

'Hey, I've got a pair of domesticated daughters . . . what a team, eh!'

'Don't overdo it, Dad,' said Hilly. 'We can turn our hand to cooking, like any capable person. Doesn't mean we're aiming to be domestic goddesses. We can do lots of things.' She passed Zoë the serving slice.

'The two of you remind me of that song,' said Heidigran. 'Anyone know the one I mean?'

'What song?'

Heidigran's forehead creased; then she started to sing, gathering volume as she remembered: '*Sisters, sisters, there were never such devoted sisters* ... The Beverley Sisters, was it?'

'I've heard it,' Mum said. 'I don't think we could really call these two devoted, though. Most of the time they just about manage to put up with each other. I'm amazed, though,' she added to the girls, 'to find such sisterly accord, after a morning cooped up in the kitchen together. Makes a nice change! I'd have expected you to be at each other's throats.'

Hilly caught Zoë's eye; the most furtive of smiles passed between them.

'Here, Gran.' Zoë passed a plate. 'Dad?'

'You bet.'

'Really,' Zoë said as they all began on the cheese-cake, 'it was Hilly's recipe. She showed me how to do it.'

'Delia Smith's,' Hilly corrected.

'Anyway, it's great!' Their father was eating rapidly, with appreciative sound-effects. 'Great work, both of you, *and* Delia. Are you offering seconds?'

'Hilly, you look pale,' said Mum. 'And you're hardly eating. Are you all right?'

'I'm OK,' Hilly said; spending all morning with food had not done much for her grogginess. 'Had a headache last night, but it's not so bad today.'

'Another headache? A bad one?'

'Last night it was.'

57

'You didn't tell me you had a headache,' Zoë said. Hilly toyed with her fork; neither of them wanted to start discussing last night.

'Hilly, I'm taking you to the doctor about these headaches,' their mother said. 'They're getting worse, aren't they?'

'That's funny. Rachel used to get bad headaches,' said Heidigran. 'Migraine, it's called. Had to go to the doctor.'

Everyone looked at her.

'Rachel?' said the girls' mother.

And now Heidigran seemed puzzled. Zoë looked at Hilly.

'You were talking about someone called Rachel,' Dad prompted. 'Who had bad headaches.'

'Rachel?' Heidigran's face clouded with uncertainty. 'Who's Rachel?'

Lunch was over; Heidi had enjoyed being waited on, and they wouldn't let her help with the clearing-up. She was pleasantly full of food but now her head was muzzed with tiredness. Rose steered her towards an armchair. 'Sit down and have a doze if you like, Mum. We'll make you a cup of tea.' She arranged cushions, brought a footstool.

Heidi's attention was caught by the piano. She had noticed it as soon as she came in. It was squat and rather ugly compared to the piano she knew, which was dark, lustrous rosewood, with a lace cloth and a candlestick on its lid. That one had a special stool, with an upholstered tapestry seat that could be lifted off to reveal a space inside where the music was kept, books and folded sheets. And always, always, the piano was kept polished, so that its wood seemed to glow; it reminded her of a groomed animal, or perhaps a fresh conker, a pleasure to touch and stroke. This one looked neglected, with rings and scrapes on the cheap-looking wood. Heidigran waited to see if someone was going to come and play, but no one did. The girl, the younger of the two, the pretty one with long fair hair, brought her a cup of tea. Such odd clothes they wore these days. Surely she must be cold, with all that middle showing.

'*Danke sehr*,' said Heidi.

The girl gave her an odd look and went away.

It was Rachel who played the piano, she remembered now. Where was Rachel? She looked round, but the kitchen was full of those other people, chattering and laughing the way they did, too quick for her to follow. She closed her eyes, and Rachel stepped out of her memory. Plain brown hair she had, clipped back from a middle parting; a quiet, serious face, a bit like this other girl, the one with glasses. Rachel lifted the lid of the piano stool and began sorting through the music stored inside. Then, finding what she wanted, she replaced the upholstered seat and settled herself comfortably, arranging the sheet music on its support. She paused, spreading her hands on the keys. And then the music.

Heidi's eyes filled with tears.

'Mum?' Rose, Rose, that was who it was, bent down to her. 'What is it?'

'That tune,' said Heidi, reaching for a tissue she did not have.

The time she went away on the train, she took her favourite book with her: *Heidi*, by Johanna Spyri. Mutti had been reading it aloud, a bit every bedtime. It had been a pleasure to look forward to at the end of each day, lying warm and snuggled in bed while Mutti's soft voice told the story. Sometimes the words and the pictures in her head had blurred into dreams. They had not finished the story, and she did not want it to finish, ever: she wanted to go on and on hearing about Heidi and the mountain hut and the old man and the goats. Now she would have to finish reading by herself, even though it was really too hard. No one in England would be able to read the German to her. She would have to imagine Mutti's voice reading, hear the words in her head.

At the station, the men in black uniform stopped the parents coming through to the platform. There were lots and lots of parents, some of them crying. Mutti did not cry, which proved she didn't care, not really. She smiled, though her eyes were red, and said, 'Be a good girl! We'll be with you as soon as we possibly can.' Then she waved as cheerfully as if they were only parting for a day or two. But they had never been parted before, ever, not even for one night. Why wasn't she sniffing into a handkerchief or openly crying, like the other mothers and even some of the fathers? And Vati was away on another of his business trips, and had not even bothered to come.

The train was full of children, some of them only toddlers, some as old as fourteen. All the bigger girls, any who looked older than eleven or so, had been put in charge of younger ones. Some looked excited, some bewildered, some ran through the carriages shouting about what they could see.

Mutti had told her it would be like this. The men in black, unsmiling, checked the tickets and the passes the children wore round their necks. They opened all the bags and cases and sometimes took things out. The journey went on and on, through sleeping, waking, reading her book, eating the sandwiches Mutti had made for her, and going – but not until she was quite desperate – to the small, smelly lavatory. It was hot on the train, far too hot to wear her winter coat, and she was bewildered by the changes of scenery. At one point, woken by cheering, she blinked and rubbed her eyes, wondering if they were in England already. 'We're in Holland!' someone told her, and now, instead of the black uniforms, there were smiling ladies handing out orange juice and chocolate, and soft white bread-and-butter, and it felt like a party. Then the Hook of Holland, the end of the train journey: all ships and masts and crates and yells and clanging. The ship waiting for them was enormous, and the sea, which she had never seen before, frightened her when they were out in the middle of it – shining, grey-green, muscular, with gulls planing over its surface. From the deck she saw foam creaming away from the ship's prow and the ripples spreading out for what seemed miles behind. The world was bigger than she had ever guessed. The sea and the sky made her feel so tiny that she could be buffeted right off the boat, swept away and lost, and no one would notice.

At last there was land. She had heard of the White Cliffs of Dover, and expected to see them rising sheer and white from the sea, like something built to keep her out, but the place they had reached was not called Dover but Harritsch, and had no cliffs. She did not think that sounded a very English name, until she saw the name on the station platform: Harwich, which she would have pronounced Harvick. Some of the children were to stay near here, at a holiday camp by the sea; she thought that sounded rather nice, but she was led, with the others who already had places, to another train. From a dusty-smelling carriage she saw a broad river estuary, fields of ripening corn, and cows grazing. Then London, a much bigger station, and here some of the children were claimed and taken away. The rest spent their first night in England in a building close by, called a hostel.

She cried, alone at last under her rough blanket, and heard other children crying too. One of the older girls, Helga, got out of her bed and went to the most distressed of the younger children and began to sing. A small hand crept out from under the blanket and curled its fingers round Helga's. At last a quiet of breathing, and only muffled sobbing, settled over the dormitory.

If it hadn't been dark, she would have read some more of her book. Although she didn't know yet how the story ended, she had started again from the beginning, because Heidi in the story was setting out just like this, to a new life. Heidi wasn't frightened of her strange grandfather, even though everyone else was.

The good thing about a story was that once you'd read it, it was inside your head and you could tell it to yourself when the pages were closed and night-time came. She had a small toy rabbit inside her case and she could have cuddled that, but she cuddled her book instead and wondered if there might be alps and goats where she was going.

Next day they were off again. Early in the morning they were roused and told to dress, given breakfast (sloppy stuff called porridge, and cooked bread, and tea so strong that it made her mouth hurt) and herded off through the streets to yet another station. Not all the children went this time, only a group of about fifteen, including Helga, for which she was grateful; Helga was the oldest of the group and looked sensible and kind. Perhaps a mistake had been made and they were being taken back to Harwich. Perhaps England didn't want them after all. Perhaps their parents *did* want them, wanted them sent back! But no, the man in charge said the train would take them to a place called Northampton. 'Noughthampson' was all her tongue could make of it when she tried to copy. There were no mountains in Harwich or London, but maybe Northampton was different. Maybe there would be alps and snowy peaks, and paths winding up the hillside to flowery meadows where goats grazed?

London was not much like Köln. It looked dirty, busy, with smoke-stained brick buildings, but she liked the red buses. She had been on so many trains now that she would rather have liked to go to Northampton on a red bus, but they were packed into a train compartment and she stared at the grubby backs of houses as the train pulled out. It was funny how trains seemed to creep in and out of cities through back entrances. She saw lines of washing, tiny gardens planted with beans and cabbages, a little boy waving from a shed roof. He wore baggy shorts, and socks that sagged round his ankles, and a cheeky grin. She waved back, watching his face blur as the train swept past. It cheered her to see a child of her own age who looked friendly, although he didn't know of course that she spoke a different language.

People in England didn't like Germans. Helga told her that. 'A lot of them don't understand. They won't like us. They'll call us names. They fought us in the war.'

Jerry. Kraut. Filthy Hun. Hitler-Lover. All those became familiar over the next few months, when the new war began. And the taunt that became her own: German Measle.

Chapter Six

Dangerous Corner

What most people mean by truth . . . is only half the real truth. It doesn't tell you all that went on inside everybody. It simply gives you a lot of facts that happened to have been hidden away and were perhaps a lot better hidden away. It's rather treacherous stuff.

J. B. Priestley, *Dangerous Corner*

'Fine, while it's the summer holidays,' said Annagran, on the phone. 'But how are you all going to manage once term starts?'

'I'm not sure,' said Hilly, who had been asking herself the same question. 'Mum goes to meetings, the Alzheimer's Support Group, and there's a carer called Josie who's going to come round once a week. And Mum can change her hours at the sports centre, swap with the other instructors to work evenings and weekends. We'll have to work something out.'

'It's good of Rose, but it puts a burden on the whole family. You and Zoë can't be expected to organize your lives around the needs of a seventy-two-year-old, even if she is your grandmother. It really needs a longer-term solution. I'll help whenever I can – come and keep her company, or take her out for a jaunt. You'll tell Rose, won't you? And there are day centres, even if she won't hear of residential care.'

'OK. Gran – Dad's here now. I'll pass you over.'

Hilly's father, just in from work, took the phone, loosening his tie with his spare hand. 'Hello, Ma. Yes, just got in.' While he listened he grabbed Hilly in a one-armed bear hug, pulling her off-balance; the way he still did, as if was a little kid. With ears muffled against his jacket she heard him say: 'Yes, brilliant! Deserved it, the way she worked. She's a great girl, my Hilly. I'm so proud of her.' Then Annagran's indistinct voice, on and on without a break, evidently going through the Heidigran conversation again. Hilly wriggled free and went upstairs.

Annagran, the girls' only other grandparent, was in fact six years older than Heidigran, but it was hard to believe this now that Heidigran was ill. The two grans were so different. Heidigran had always been rather conventional, dressing in tweedy skirts and cardigans and smart court shoes. Annagran, small, crop-haired, looking years younger than her age, wore denim and fleece and trainers, and was eminently capable. Heidigran, it was becoming increasingly clear, was not. At her better times, it was still possible to imagine there was nothing wrong; she would play Scrabble, weed and tidy the garden, take an interest in Hilly's and Zoë's comings and goings, comment on their clothes. But there was no predicting when she would drift into vagueness or, worse, a frustrated awareness of how little she could remember.

On Saturday afternoon, when Reuben came round for Hilly's piano lesson, Heidigran suddenly took against him, behaving as if he were an unwelcome stranger.

'Who's that?' She stared from her armchair, startled from the pages of her gardening magazine, while Oscar slept on her lap.

'It's Reuben, Gran!' said Hilly. 'You know Reuben!'

'Reuben,' Heidigran repeated slowly. She looked at the carpet and traced a circle with the toe of her slipper, then looked up at Reuben's face. 'And where did you get that name, young man?'

Hilly almost giggled; it seemed such a strange thing to say.

'My parents liked it,' Reuben said. 'I wish they'd thought of something else – *any*thing else. Everyone except Hilly calls me Ruby.'

'You know Reuben, Gran! You've met him dozens of times! And he was here yesterday – you knew him then—'

Heidigran looked at him again, shaking her head. 'No. No, I don't think so.'

'You do know him, course you do!' Hilly heard

herself using the bracing tone she had disliked when she heard nurses use it.

'I'll make you a cup of tea before we start. Want some, Reuben?'

'Thanks.' Reuben sat at the piano, opening the lid. He looked at Heidigran. 'OK if I—?'

'Good idea,' said Hilly. 'She might remember who you are, if you play.'

From the kitchen, filling the kettle and assembling mugs, Hilly heard a few warm-up fragments, then the first of the Gershwin preludes Reuben was practising for next week's concert with the youth orchestra. But after only a few moments the music stopped, and she heard conversation: Heidigran's voice, sounding agitated, and Reuben's, quiet and low. Hilly looked in to see the piano lid closed again, and Reuben facing her grandmother, who stared at him with a mixture of indignation and confusion.

'What's up?' Hilly said, still in the jollying-along voice that sounded false even to herself.

'Your gran says I shouldn't play without asking Rachel first. I said there isn't a Rachel here, but she's not having that. Who's Rachel?'

'Who's Rachel, Gran?' Hilly asked gently.

'It's Rachel's piano,' said Heidigran, in a tone that suggested everyone ought to know. 'She's the only one who plays it.'

'And Rachel is . . . ?' Hilly tried.

But suddenly Heidigran's face wore the defeated look Hilly had seen before. 'Can't remember.' For a second she looked likely to lapse into tears. Hilly went over and hugged her; Oscar made a protesting remark and shifted his position.

'Never mind, Gran. It'll come to you, I expect.'

'It's all right, I won't play,' Reuben said, though Hilly could tell his fingers were itching with Gershwin. He didn't have a piano at home, only an electronic keyboard which he said wasn't the same at all. 'Let's hope she won't take offence if *you* do.'

But Heidigran fell asleep in her chair, leaving her tea to go cold; she did not stir throughout the lesson, nor afterwards when Hilly and Reuben went outside to sit on the grass, nor when Reuben left for his concert rehearsal. She did not wake until Rose came in from the gym; then she blinked a few times, fixed a disapproving stare on Hilly, and told her: 'You shouldn't associate with that young man, you know. It'll get you into trouble.'

'Oh? What young man's this?' Rose teased, un-lacing her trainers.

'What on earth do you mean, Gran?' said Hilly, thinking for a second that Heidigran was confusing her with Zoë. 'Oh – you mean Reuben again?'

'Did you know she's had a young man here while you've been out at work?' Heidigran said waspishly to Rose.

'Has Reuben been round? Sorry I missed him,' said Rose, who was fond of Reuben.

'Gran, he's my friend, has been for years and years—'

'You shouldn't let her,' Heidigran told Rose. 'Jewish, isn't he?'

Hilly caught her breath. She saw her mother's expression as she looked up guardedly: not so much surprised as resigned.

It was Hilly who answered: 'No, Gran. Reuben isn't Jewish. What if he was?'

'Tell her, Rose,' said Heidigran sharply. 'You should have put a stop to this long ago.'

'Mum, Reuben's Hilly's best friend. We all know him well. He's not going to make trouble! As Hilly says, he isn't Jewish, and if he was, it wouldn't make the slightest difference. I really don't see why you've suddenly taken against him.'

'He's got a Jewish name,' Heidigran said, sounding like Zoë in a sulk.

'Lots of names sound Jewish,' said Hilly. 'Gran, you mustn't say things like this!'

'I know what I know,' Heidigran said obstinately. She looked at Rose, and a cunning look came over her face. 'And so do you. What about that woman Gavin had his fling with, that tarty piece? He was all set to leave you and move in with her, at one time. She was Jewish, wasn't she? What was her name—?'

'Who? What woman?' cried Hilly. 'Mum, what's she talking about?'

'Nothing,' said her mother, too quickly. 'She's getting confused, that's all. Mum, I think we'd better change the subject. Let me put the TV on for you – one of your videos – d'you want to choose one? Hilly, take no notice.'

'S. I know it began with S.' Heidigran, once her mind latched onto something, would not be diverted. 'Sophie, Sonia – Stella! That was it, Stella!'

Rose had her back to them, turning on the TV, looking for a video. 'How about this one – *The Camomile Lawn?* Do you want your knitting?'

'Yes please, dear,' Heidigran said, as if her last remarks were quite forgotten. 'I'll be needing more wool. Can you get it for me tomorrow?' she asked Hilly.

Hilly hadn't moved. 'Mum!' she appealed.

'Forget it. It's nothing,' her mother said, not meeting her eye as she went through to the kitchen. Hilly followed, closing the door behind her.

'What did she mean? Mum! It's not nothing, is it? I can tell by your face!'

Her mother was busying herself in the bottom of the cupboard, banging saucepans about. 'It's only something that happened years and years ago. I'm not dragging it up now. What kind of pasta would you like?'

'Stuff the pasta! I want to *know*. Dad had an affair, is that what Gran's saying?'

Rose straightened, holding the largest saucepan. 'Hilly, can you please stop this? Just forget it. I promise you, it would be much better left. And it really doesn't matter.'

'Then why are you so uptight?'

'I'm not!'

'Yes, you are. Look at you – you're shaking!'

Rose filled the kettle, taking slow, deep breaths to calm herself. 'I'm angry with her,' she said after a few moments. 'With Mum. Her selective memory is turning out to be a bit awkward. There was no need for you to know. But since you *must* know, I want you to promise not to tell Zoë. I don't want an even bigger upset.'

'OK, I promise. But tell Zoë what?' Hilly prompted.

Her mother looked straight at her. 'Yes, your father did have an affair. Yes, he did almost leave us. You were three at the time, and Zoë was two.' She huffed a laugh. 'This is going to sound like the plot of *Brookside* or something. Stella was someone he met through work – a sales rep. I suppose I'd let myself get completely wrapped up with you two – I was exhausted half the time, my life revolving round playgroup and meals and keeping you amused. He'd come home and there'd be toys all over the floor and I'd have baby food down my jumper and fall asleep as soon as I'd got the two of you settled for the night. Stella was younger, glamorous, more fun. He was – tempted, I suppose.'

'Dad!'

'It happens,' Rose said curtly.

'Yes, I know, but – to Dad! He was really going to abandon you, with us kids to look after!' The idea dizzied her; she clutched at the worktop for support. *But Dad loves us*, she wanted to say. *I know he does. All of us, all three! There must be some mistake.* 'And you took him back! Why?'

'Because I love him,' her mother said simply. 'Because I was faced with a choice – have him back and get over it, or struggle as a single parent. I chose him. And when it came down to it, he couldn't bear to leave you and Zoë. He thinks the world of you, Hilly, both of you – you know he does.'

Not enough, Hilly thought, with a sense of something hardening inside her. 'He was going to abandon us!'

'But he didn't. Thinking about something isn't the same as actually doing it.'

'How did you find out?' Hilly said in a flat voice. 'How does Heidigran know?'

'Oh, he told me.' Rose reached for a packet of spaghetti. 'Unburdened himself. It didn't suit him, being devious. And your gran – she saw them together in a restaurant, and, being Heidigran, told me as soon as she could, and I – I told her all the rest. I don't know about Stella being Jewish, whether she was or wasn't. That was the last thing that bothered me at the time. I don't know why Heidigran got hold of that idea. Or why she's suddenly got this thing about Reuben.'

'Did he love her – Stella?' Hilly said. The name had meant nothing five minutes ago; now she could hardly bring herself to say it. 'Or was it just sex?'

'I don't know.' Rose reached for a packet of spaghetti. 'Which would be better? Which would be worse? To give him his due, there's never been anyone else.'

'I should hope not!'

'Hilly – look, I know I can't tell you to forget all about it, but we're over it. Have been for years. We're fine, Dad and me – you know that. I don't want it to change the way you feel about Dad! We're adults. These things happen.'

But, Hilly thought, how can it not change things? She said, 'OK, Mum. I'll try.' She stepped out into the garden and felt herself trembling on the edge of tears. The garden smelled of cut grass; beyond the block of shadow cast by the house, the sunlight was still warm. Hilly went to the end, where a peachy-coloured rose grew over the fence; she leaned close, smelling its musky scent. The pressure in her nose and behind her eyes made her want to find a corner and have a good blub, but she'd have to go back indoors sooner or later, and her mother would know. So would Heidigran, if she were in a mood to notice.

The rose needed dead-heading; she crumpled a withered bloom in her fingers, scattering petals to the ground. Dad would be home from the shop, any minute now, and Mum was cooking spaghetti, and they'd all be expected to sit down and have a Happy Family meal. Happy Family was what she had thought they were, give or take the odd outbreak of sisterly sparring. Her parents loved each other, anyone could see that: she thought of them holding hands as they walked down the street, Dad kissing Mum when he got in from work, their cuddles on the sofa that so offended Zoë. Everyone else's parents had problems or had separated or found new partners – Tessa's, Reuben's – but the security of her own family was something Hilly had always taken for granted. They'll never split up, not my Mum and Dad. They're constant. They wouldn't even think of—

But now Dad had been proved not constant. He was fickle. Disloyal. A seducer. An adulterer. He was not the person she had always known. The roses blurred in front of her; she found a tissue in her jeans pocket. Who am I crying for? she wondered. For Mum, for myself, for the Dad I thought he was? What am I going to say . . . how am I going to look at him?

She went back indoors. 'Mum, I'm going round to Reuben's, OK? I don't want anything to eat.'

'Oh, Hilly—'

Only when she was some way down the street did Hilly remember that Reuben had gone to his rehearsal; how long ago had that been? She had lost all sense of time. She hesitated for a moment at the street corner. A motorbike was turning left into her road; she saw the rider looking at her, then pulling over to the kerb. He pulled off his helmet and tucked it under one arm, then ruffled his hair with his free hand, grinning at her. 'Thought it was you!'

Grant. Zoë's obnoxious boyfriend, in leather biker gear, sleekly black. 'You OK?' He was looking at her expectantly.

She was surprised he'd bothered to stop. He was the last person she felt like making conversation with, and would have thought the feeling was mutual. His manner was as matey as if they'd parted on the best of terms last weekend.

'Fine, thanks,' Hilly said, aware that she must look anything but fine, in her tear-streaked agitation – much as she'd appeared last time, in fact. How pathetic he must think her! – not, she amended quickly, that she gave a toss what *he* thought.

'Where you off to, then?'

As if it was any of his business! 'Out,' Hilly said, unsmiling. 'You?'

'On my way to see Zoë. But I'll give you a lift, first, if you want. Wherever you're going.'

Could he be serious? He sat loosely astride the big, powerful machine, letting the engine idle. It was all black and gleaming chrome, polished to a high shine. She hesitated, and knew that he had seen her hesitate. He really expected her to climb on behind him, put herself in his power?

'No, thanks.'

'Go on!' He gestured with his head; turned his hand on the accelerator and made the engine roar throatily. 'Hop on behind.'

'I said no. Thanks.'

He smiled. 'Whatever.' Hilly saw what he was up to, now: he was the sort of boy who was so confident of his power to charm that he had to test it on every female he met. And, while she was thinking this, she found herself mesmerized by the glare of his attention; she looked at his tousled fair hair, at his attractively crooked teeth, most of all at his eyes, such a penetrating blue, with their level, steady gaze. She could not be sure she wasn't blushing.

'Zoë's not allowed on motorbikes,' she said, turning away.

Grant replaced his helmet, revved the engine and pulled out from the kerb. 'Zoë's not allowed to do lots of things. Doesn't seem to stop her. You want to ease up a bit, let yourself have some fun.'

'I'm not sure,' she said over her shoulder, walking

on, 'whether your idea of fun would be the same as mine.'

He laughed; it seemed impossible to offend him. 'Catch you later!' he called, accelerating away.

It was Reuben's mother who opened the door to Hilly.

'Hi, is Reuben here?' Hilly asked, before registering the boom of orchestral music from above that confirmed he was.

'Communing with Rachmaninov,' said his mum. 'Go on up.'

Hilly recognized the second piano concerto – Rach Two, as Reuben called it. It was his favourite, his personal Everest; his ambition was to play it at the Festival Hall. She went up. Reuben was sprawled on his bed, listening with eyes closed, absorbing himself in the music in a way Hilly envied. When he heard her come in, he gave a not-quite-in-this-world smile and put out an arm to welcome her, not speaking. She kicked off her shoes and sat on the bed beside him, immediately comforted by his presence, and by the familiar rhythms of the Rachmaninov, which surrounded her so powerfully from strategically placed speakers that she felt it pulsing through her.

This bedroom was as familiar to Hilly as her own – more so, since she'd been dislodged. She knew Reuben's posters, his curtains, his shelf crammed with music scores, his mess, his habit of stuffing everything under his desk instead of tidying up. She knew that he had a stash of music manuscripts – his piano compositions – in his sock drawer. She knew that his ancient portable TV set had to be thumped on top when it went fuzzy. She knew that his bed had a wonky leg that needed jolting back into position every so often, especially when two people sat on it, or, on cold winter evenings, *in* it, huddling together under the duvet.

'Hey,' Reuben had said once, 'I can truthfully say that I've been to bed with a girl, if ever I need a cover-up!'

'And,' Hilly said, 'you're the only boy I've ever been in bed with. The only one I'm likely to, as far as I can see.' It was nice being on or in bed with Reuben: warm, companionable, easy. If she closed her eyes, and Reuben wasn't talking, she could pretend that the body snuggled close to hers wasn't his but Someone's – but that was OK, because she guessed that Reuben pretended too. She could make her heart beat faster and her skin tingle just by imagining herself and Someone together. But Someone remained obstinately faceless, even if she could go as far as imagining a body, and her own body's responses.

Now her father had spoiled even the secret indulgence of imagining. She could only see him adulterously coupled with Stella, who in her imagination had become a sultry temptress, perfumed and voluptuous. Stella had lured Dad away and mesmerized him with sex. How could he be so easily led – a grown man, a father? How could he push his wife and his daughters out of his thoughts when he was in bed with Stella? How could anyone be trusted, if feelings could be so quickly switched from one person to another?

The slow movement was making her sniffy again. Noticing, Reuben asked what was wrong; she told him. It wasn't really breaking her promise: Mum had said not to tell Zoë, but had not specified Reuben. Hilly had no secrets from Reuben, her best listener, consoler, adviser, hugger and cheerer.

'He's still your dad,' Reuben said, when she had finished, and lapsed into sorry sniffing. 'And if he and your mum have got over it, years ago, you'd better not stir things up. It's not as if he's a serial bimbo-chaser, is it? Anyone can make a mistake.'

'You're right – in theory. But I can't pretend not to know! How am I going to speak to him normally? And as if that's not enough,' she added, 'I've got a racist for a grandmother! Zoë says she's a Nazi, and I thought she was being stupid – but she's got a point. Heidigran's got this stupid thing about Jews being dangerous to know, like she's back in Germany in the Hitler time, or something.'

'I can't get this straight,' Reuben said. 'She was born in Germany, and stayed there all through the war, right—'

Hilly nodded. 'Cologne, yes.'

'– but came over here when it was all over? Why here of all places, when her parents had been bombed by our lot? You'd have thought England was the last place a German would want to come. To the enemy.'

'Mm, but she was an orphan – she wouldn't have had much choice. There couldn't have been any

German relations who could take her. She came to live with friends of the family – I've no idea how they were friends. Besides, she was only about twelve or thirteen.'

'Too young to be a Nazi, then!'

'Yes, but maybe her parents were Nazis, or at least anti-Jewish, and brought her up to think the same? She never talks about her life in Germany.'

'That's not surprising, if her parents were killed.'

'I've tried,' Hilly said, 'when we did it in history. I had a go at a proper interview with her, recording it, but she'd hardly tell me anything. Only the things I already knew from lessons and TV. It was all so long ago. Another life. That's all she'll say.'

'What about this Rachel she was on about? Rachel could be a Jewish name. I bet Rachel was her best friend, and when all the bad stuff started her parents made her give Rachel up.'

'Hmm. Could be. I don't suppose we'll ever find out, the way her memory is. Things pop up, then disappear again. And she gets the most peculiar ideas, like suddenly deciding you're Jewish after she's known you for – what? Ten years?'

'Tell her my folks are from Cornwall, with a bit of Welsh and Irish thrown in. No Jewish that I know of,' Reuben said. He listened intently to the music. 'Just a minute.' He turned up the volume, then leaned back against the wall with his eyes closed; Hilly knew better than to talk through the climax to the concerto, the cadenza, which showed off the pianist's virtuosity. Reuben's fingers twitched, and Hilly imagined him, wild-haired and passionate, playing a Steinway in the Festival Hall. He was lost in the music, his absorption carrying Hilly too with the great rolling swell and fall of the orchestra. They both sat in silence after the last notes had faded.

When a respectful few moments had passed, Reuben glanced at his watch. 'I've got to go out.'

'Oh?' Hilly said, guessing that he meant to Settlers, the coffee bar in town where Saeed worked four nights a week.

Reuben smiled.

'Don't let me stand in the way of young love.' She got to her feet and reached for her jacket.

'Come with me!' said Reuben, catching her arm. 'I can talk to you while Si's dashing about.'

'What, play gooseberry while you gaze into each other's eyes? No thanks.'

'Don't be daft! You're my favourite gooseberry – green and hairy. Si won't mind, he'll be busy anyway. I just like being near him. But I can still talk to you. And you can talk to me. And we can both talk to him.'

'Well – I suppose – OK, then. If you're sure.'

Reuben looked at her. 'Better not let your gran know I'm gay,' he said, half-flippant. 'She'll definitely think I'm a corrupting influence if she finds that out. Homos were there in the concentration camps, weren't they, along with gypsies and Communists and everyone else the Nazis didn't like?'

Chapter Seven

Hello, Goodbye

4th May 1939

Mr and Mrs Thornton,
12 Shoe Lane,
Northampton

Dear Sir and Madam,
  We are writing to thank you for
your very kind offer to take into
your home a refugee child. We would
like to inform you . . .

She did not want the train to stop at Northampton.
She had got used to the other children, the ones who
were left; among them Helga, who was so big and
sensible that she seemed almost grown-up. Why can't
I go with Helga? she wondered. Helga knew a little
English; it would be much easier if they could stay
together. But the children would be split up into ones
and twos, and she was to be a One. All alone in this

strange country. At her sponsors' house she would not even be able to ask for what she wanted. The only English words she knew were *Hello* and *Goodbye*, *Yes* and *No*, and *thank you*.

Apart from the German group, only two other people got off the train: a boy in short trousers who whistled tunelessly, and a smart woman in a belted coat. Both looked curiously at the German children, who clustered uncertainly on the platform. The guard whistled and the train pulled out, leaving space for a raw wind to slice between the station buildings. It felt much colder here than in London. The children and their attendant passed through the barrier, and a woman who seemed in charge of a group of adults waiting in the booking hall came up to introduce herself, speaking in English. After a brief conversation the attendant, who spoke both languages, took out a list of names clipped to a board. As he read out each name, a boy or girl stepped forward to be claimed. Which would be hers? she wondered, staring at the grownups. They all looked rather plain, she thought, drab, in their brown and grey clothes.

As her surname began with R, she was almost the last to be called. 'Come along – you're going with Mr and Mrs Thornton.'

Two of the remaining four adults came forward. The woman smiled and held out a hand. She was a lot older than Mutti and not nearly as pretty, in fact not pretty at all, with hair severely parted in the middle and pulled back in a bun. The man, who had a thin face and bushy eyebrows like caterpillars crawling to meet each other, looked uncomfortable, as if it hadn't been his idea to be involved in this.

The woman leaned down and put a hand on her shoulder, then said something, crouched, and took both her hands. In spite of her scraped-back hair and her big plain face, she looked kind. Then the man held out a hand and shook hers, which seemed a very English thing to do. The man smelled of tobacco, the woman of sweet perfume. She knew nothing of them except that their name was Thornton, Mr and Mrs Thornton, and that she was going to live with them.

The only word she had understood was her own name. Sarah. Sarah Reubens.

Two days later, in the front room of 12 Shoe Lane, Sarah was writing a letter home. Mrs Thornton sat her at the table with writing paper and a pencil. The table was square, with four chairs round it, dominating the small room. It had a cloth of green velvet that was worn flat in places. At meal times, Mrs Thornton spread a checked cotton tablecloth over the velvet.

Dear Mutti and Vati [Sarah wrote, forming the letters carefully],

I am here in Northampton. Mr and Mrs Thorton are kind.
Their house is not as big as ours. They have a grown-up son Erich
he is in the army so I have not seen him only a photo. I do not like
the food made. They say to tell you I am well and looked after.

Sarah could have written much more, but did not consider that Mutti and Vati deserved a proper letter.

They were still at home, without her. It is not a very nice house, she could have written. It is much smaller than ours and made of ugly brick. There are rows of houses exactly the same on both sides of the street, all jammed together. The front doors open straight onto the pavement. They call the meals by funny names too. In the middle of the day we have dinner. In the evening we have tea. Tea is not just to drink, it is bread and butter and cheese and cake. I have already learned some new English words. They have given me a room to myself, but it is really Eric's. They want me to call them Auntie and Uncle because I'm going to stay here a long time. Auntie Enid and Uncle Donald. How long am I going to stay here?

A brown box radio was playing cheerful music that made Sarah think of people dancing, men and women whirling around a crowded floor as they smiled into each other's faces. Mutti and Vati, glad to be together, rid of her. Mutti dancing looked young and graceful, with her slim legs and her swirling skirt. Her feet in high-heeled shoes would be light and precise, moving to the pulse of the music, and everyone would turn to look at her and her partner; such good waltzers they were, so happy together. Mrs Thornton was ironing in the kitchen, humming with the music. Sarah heard the hiss and thump of the steam iron, and smelled warm cotton. It reminded her of home so strongly – being tucked up in bed between clean sheets fresh from the laundry – that her nose became tickly with tears. But she wasn't going to cry any more. That was what Mutti and Vati wanted. They would be pleased to know she was crying and lonely in a strange country where no one could understand what she said. They would waltz on and on, free of her.

She slid down from her chair and held out her letter to Mrs Thornton to show that it was finished. Mrs Thornton, poking the nose of her iron between buttons on a shirt-front, looked in surprise at the careful writing. She stood the iron on its base, said a lot of English words, then gestured with her hands to show Sarah that she had expected more. Sarah shook her head, but pointed at the writing desk to try to show that she wanted another piece of paper.

'All right, lovey.'

Sarah understood *lovey*. It was a sort of new name, and sounded nice. It was like the German *Liebling*.

Mrs Thornton opened the desk, which had a scroll top that rolled back to reveal shelves and drawers inside. In it there were things like balls of string, used envelopes, sharpened pencils in a glass, and bundles of letters. The writing paper was lined and rough. Sarah realized that her new aunt thought she was going to start all over again and write a much longer letter.

Sarah sat at the table, resting her feet on the rung of the chair, and picked up the pencil stub. When Mrs Thornton had gone back to her ironing, she cradled her left arm round the paper. She breathed hard as she wrote, forming each letter carefully.

Dear Rachel,

I didn't mean it what I said.

I really didn't mean it.

Chapter Eight

Doppelgänger

Doppelgänger, *n*. German.
Literally: *double-goer*.

Chambers English Dictionary

Hilly and Reuben were sitting at a corner table in Settlers, Hilly facing the mirrored back wall, Reuben opposite with his seat angled towards the counter, positioned for the best view of Saeed as he moved among the tables.

'You can't take your eyes off him, can you?' Hilly said, in slight exasperation.

Reuben grinned. 'Something in the way he moves,' he said, misquoting one of his favourite George Harrison songs.

Hilly could see for herself that Saeed's unself-conscious grace made every movement watchable. He was slim and fine-featured, with eyes the colour of the darkest dark chocolate, full and expressive. Every so often he would glance in Reuben's direction, see

Reuben watching him and smile his quick dazzling smile that transformed his otherwise passive face. Hilly saw this, tried not to feel left out, and envied Reuben for finding his Someone. Where's mine, she thought, the person who'll share little secret looks with me? No, don't be so stupid – whoever would? She glanced behind her at the big plate-glass window, as if Someone might chance to look in at that precise moment, searching for her.

And instead she saw two of the boys who had come to the house last Saturday night: both in leathers like Grant's, one of them clutching a crash helmet. It was the one called Tuck, with the swastika on his jacket, and the greasy-skinned one with the multi-pierced ear. They shoved their faces against the window, leering, and Tuck thumped on the glass; they both made obscene gestures at Saeed. They did not recognize Hilly, did not even look in her direction.

Behind the counter, Saeed pretended not to notice. Reuben sprang to his feet, but the older boys had already moved on, laughing. Hilly glanced around the bar. Saeed, manning the espresso machine and the till, was the only member of staff visible, apart from a girl who appeared occasionally from the kitchen with pizzas or baguettes; only two other tables were occupied, one of them by a middle-aged couple who had just settled themselves. Saeed busied himself with the foam nozzle and a canister of flaked chocolate, but when he carried over two cappuccinos to the new customers Hilly saw that his hands were trembling, making the heavy cups clink in their saucers. 'Hooligans,' said the man, shaking his head; Saeed gave a small, rueful grin. He came over to the corner table, and Reuben put a hand on his arm.

'Do you know those morons?' Hilly asked.

'I've seen them before. They've been in, with some others. Late, and they stay ages making a lot of noise.' From habit, Saeed starting clearing the cups and a torn sugar wrapper. 'They're enough to put other people off coming in.'

'Leave that, Si. Sit down for a minute,' said Reuben, pulling him towards a spare seat. 'Do they bad-mouth you?'

Saeed met his gaze, then pulled back the chair and sat down. 'They have ways.'

'Ways of . . . ?'

'Of letting me know they think I'm scum. You know. Looks. Saying things I can't quite hear. Saying things I *can* hear. Making a mess just so I'll have to clear it up. Barging past me like I don't exist.'

Hilly glanced at the street outside. The coffee bar was warmly lit, the furnishings and décor chosen to give the feel of the American West in the 1930s, but she thought how conspicuous Saeed must feel, on view to any passer-by. OK by day, not so comfortable at night. 'Isn't there anyone you can call on if there's trouble?' she asked him.

'The manager's here quite a lot of the time. Stuart. There's Tracy in the kitchen and sometimes Doug, and there's a panic button if things get out of hand.'

'Stuart ought to know,' said Hilly, reluctant to interfere. 'If you feel vulnerable on your own.'

Saeed shook his head. 'I'm all right. Not really on my own.'

'Have you seen a tall guy with them – short fair hair, bright blue eyes?' she asked.

Reuben looked at her. 'Who's that?'

'Not sure,' Saeed said, thinking. 'I don't exactly gaze into their eyes. Why, do you know them?'

'My sister does.' Hilly glanced at Reuben; she had told him about last Saturday night, though not about meeting Grant earlier this evening. 'The tall guy's her boyfriend. Fingers crossed it won't last.'

'There was a girl with them a few nights ago,' said Saeed. 'Last time they came in. Young, sexy – nothing like you.'

'Thanks a lot!'

'No, I didn't mean—' said Saeed, in some confusion. 'I mean I'd never have thought she was your sister. Taller than you. Long blonde hair. Trying to act hard, I thought. The bloke she was with could be the one you're on about. They were all over each other.'

'I can imagine,' Hilly said drily.

'That's her, then, your sister?'

'Yes. Unfortunately. What can I say? I'm really sorry if she's been mouthy.'

Saeed shrugged. 'Not your fault.'

'She's heading for trouble. How can such a bright girl be so stupid? She's the sort of person, my sister,' she explained to Saeed, 'who gets all A grades at school without seeming to do any work at all. Compared to her I'm just your average plodder. This time next year she'll have done her GCSEs and it'll be all A stars. Unless she decides to throw all her chances out the window, that is. Which is what she looks like doing at the moment.'

'Looks and brains,' said Reuben. 'She's lucky.'

Hilly sighed. 'Looks, brains and mouth.'

'I remember the guy now.' Saeed glanced at the window. 'He called me Mustafa.'

Hilly looked down, crumpling a sugar wrapper, recalling that earlier, by the roadside, everything she knew and disliked about Grant had gone right out of her head, in the flattering glow of his attention.

'Si, you mustn't put up with it,' said Reuben. 'Racist cretins. Promise me you'll call the police if they come back?'

Arriving home, Hilly found her parents waiting up for Zoë. The downstairs rooms were in darkness, but the lights were on upstairs. She looked into her parents' bedroom to say hello. Her mother was in her dressing gown, about to make a phone call; her father was still dressed, sitting on the bed with his shoes off, flicking through a colour supplement. 'Hello, love,' he said. 'Had a good evening?'

'Fine, thanks,' Hilly said curtly, not looking at him.

'Thought you were Zoë, coming in,' her mother said. 'I don't worry about you, knowing you're with Reuben.'

'No, *I'm* not likely to get in any trouble, am I?' Hilly said, but her mother, preoccupied with Zoë, didn't notice her spiky tone.

'It's gone eleven – she knows she's supposed to be in by now.'

Her parents, Hilly knew, had been led to believe that Zoë was spending the evening with Nadine, her friend from school. 'She'll be all right. I wouldn't bother waiting up.'

Her mother – caught, Hilly saw, between annoyance and anxiety – pressed a key on the handset, listened, then put down the phone. 'Her mobile's not switched on. She knows I'll be trying to get her, that's why. I'm going to ring Nadine's parents. Can you pass me my address book, love? In my bag there, by your feet.'

'It's a bit late,' Hilly said, foreseeing trouble; but her mother held out her hand. Hilly found the notebook and passed it over; she could have gone upstairs to bed at that point, but curiosity made her wait.

'Hello, it's Rose Craig, Zoë's mum. I know it's late, sorry, but I wondered if Zoë was there, or if they've rung you?' She listened intently, her expression changing. 'Oh. Oh. I see. Well, sorry again for disturbing you. Bye.' She looked at her husband, then at Hilly. 'Nadine's already in bed. Zoë didn't go out with her tonight – it's Nadine's grandparents' golden wedding and they've had a family party at home. But Zoë wasn't there. She lied to us!'

'Hmm,' said Hilly, heading for the attic stairs, but her mother called her back.

'Do you know who she's with?'

Oh well, Hilly thought, if she can't cover her tracks

better than this she can hardly blame me. 'She's got a new boyfriend,' she said guardedly.

'Who?'

'No one you'd know.'

'Have you met him?'

Hilly paused; saw both parents registering her hesitation. 'Just briefly.'

'And?' prompted her father.

She shrugged, Zoë-fashion. 'And nothing. Ask Zoë to introduce you if you're interested.' She turned away, hearing him call 'Hilly!' after her, hurt and puzzled. Fine, she thought, in spite of what she'd agreed with Reuben. Let him be hurt. Zoë isn't the only liar in the family.

Lying awake in bed nearly an hour later, Hilly became aware of a commotion outside: revving engines, raised voices, laughter. It took her a few moments to connect the disturbance with Zoë, but then the shouting came closer and eventually the front door slammed. Hilly heard one of her parents crossing the landing. She listened for the inevitable row.

'What time of night do you think this is?' Dad's voice.

'Oh, is it late? I lost track of time.'

'Why didn't you let us know?'

'Just told you, didn't I? Didn't realize it was late.'

Now more footsteps, and Mum joining in: 'Shhh! Heidigran's asleep, so's Hilly. Zoë, we know you weren't with Nadine. Where've you been, and who with?'

'Friends.' Hilly could picture the jutting chin, the haughty expression.

'With motorbikes? Did you come home on a motorbike? There was enough noise to wake the whole street—'

'What if I did?'

'Zoë, we don't ask much.' That was Dad doing the Reasonable Parent bit. 'Just that you let us know where you're going and who with. And get home at the agreed time so we don't have to sit up worrying—'

'Oh, don't make such a fuss! I'm not a little kid—'

'– and we're not happy about you getting lifts on motorbikes. You're not to do it again, Zoë.'

'For God's sake why not?'

Hilly had to strain her ears to hear Mum's next remark: 'Have you any idea how many people kill themselves in biking accidents?'

'No, and I couldn't care less!' (No effort required to hear Zoë.) 'You're not bothered about them either. You only want to stop me having fun!'

'And who's this new boyfriend?'

'Who said anything about a new boyfriend?'

'Shh, Zoë. Who are these friends?'

'Just people. OK if I have friends, is it? Or would you be happier if I signed up for a nunnery?'

'Oh, this is pointless,' said Dad's voice. 'And we can't stand here shouting on the landing. Go to bed – we'll talk about this in the morning.'

'Not if I can help it,' Hilly heard Zoë grumble to herself as she clomped up the wooden stairs to the attic. Taking the cop-out of pretending to be asleep, Hilly rolled over and tugged the duvet around her ears. But Zoë didn't care whether she was asleep or not. She turned on both lights and banged her wardrobe door.

'Thanks, thanks a lot!' she fired at Hilly.

Hilly turned over slowly, feigning dopiness. 'What for?'

'Dumping me in it. Why'd you have to tell them about Grant? I thought you promised!'

'What am I supposed to say, if you lie about going out with Nadine? All I said was you were seeing someone. I didn't actually tell them you're hanging round with a bunch of yobs. Where were you tonight, anyway?'

'We had a band practice – not that it's any of your business. We're doing our first gig in two weeks.'

'Right, the famous Doppelgänger. Where's this happening, then? National Front rally? Meeting of the British National Party?'

'Why d'you have to be so snidey? It's a perfectly ordinary gig, that's all. At a club.'

'Oh, good. Mum and Dad and I can come and support you.'

Zoë huffed a laugh. 'Yeah, right.'

'Why not be straight with them, instead of lying about Nadine, then turning up so late you're bound to be sussed? Or have you got something to hide?'

Zoë didn't answer. She pulled off her shoes, sitting on the bed with her back pointedly turned.

'Anyone would think you were ashamed of Grant and Co.,' Hilly said.

'You're just jealous 'cos I've got a boyfriend and you haven't.'

'Don't flatter yourself! And, Zoë – I know about you going into Settlers the other night and giving the boy who works there a hard time. That's awful.'

'What boy?' Zoë was on the alert.

'Saeed, the Palestinian boy who works there.'

'Didn't know you knew him! Didn't know he was Palestinian, either.'

'Well, I do. And he is.'

'It was only messing about.' Zoë sat on her bed, back to Hilly, undressing.

'Not for him it wasn't. Can't you imagine what it's like being on the receiving end? On your own, out-numbered, at the mercy of any racist morons who happen to walk in? Christ, Zoë – and there you were, joining in and making it worse!'

'You don't have to make a big thing about it. Like I said, it was only a joke – he ought to be able to have a laugh with customers, not act like he can't lower himself to even talk to us. And how was I supposed to know you know him?'

'That's not the point, whether I know him or not! You know it isn't.' Hilly was too hot now, hot and exasperated; she pushed the duvet away. 'And *stop* talking about jokes and messing about. It's frighten-ing, the way you can't see what you're doing – if you go along with them, you're as bad. Do you really want to be part of that?'

'Give it a rest, will you? You're like a worn-out record. God, if I'd known it'd be like this, sharing a room with you—'

'It wasn't my choice!'

'Well, I can tell you it wasn't mine,' said Zoë, pulling her T-shirt over her head. She got into bed and turned her back on Hilly. Within five minutes Hilly heard soft regular breathing; Zoë was asleep. Hilly lay awake for a long time more, wakeful and fidgety, thinking of all the things she could have said.

Chapter Nine

Gone Away

Alterations to domestic arrangements are likely to involve the whole family, and should therefore be given careful consideration. The decision to remove an Alzheimer's sufferer from his or her own home, though often inevitable, is likely to cause further distress and confusion.

Denise Lombard, *Living with Alzheimer's*

Hilly was in the passenger seat of the car, staring moodily at the dual carriageway ahead. This hadn't been her idea. Her mother was teaching fitness classes, Zoë had been left in charge of Heidigran, and Hilly and her father were on their way to Heidigran's house in Banbury to collect the mail, mow the lawn and tidy the garden, and to bring back extra clothes and belongings. No, Mum had said, it wouldn't be a good idea to take Heidigran too; she'd think she was home to stay, and would get confused when it was time to come back. Which left Hilly with the prospect of spending almost the whole of Sunday alone with her father.

She could barely bring herself to speak to him. After his attempts at conversation had received curt answers, he drummed his fingers on the steering wheel and lapsed into silence for several miles. They were well clear of town before he said, 'Hilly, love, please don't freeze me out. I know what this is all about.'

'Do you?'

'I think so. Will you let me explain?'

'If you think it'll make the slightest difference.'

He glanced at her. 'Rose told me about the conversation you had. After your gran dropped the bombshell about me and – and Stella.'

Hilly gave an aloof little nod.

'I don't blame you for being upset,' he said. 'I'm just sorry you had to hear about it. It's not something I'm proud of.'

'But you did it. You had an affair.'

'Yes, I did. And I'm not making excuses – I don't expect you to make allowances for me.'

'Why, then? Dad, how could you?'

'I don't know. Don't know how to explain it. Only the obvious things – Stella was there, she was gorgeous, she was sexy, she wanted me—'

'And Mum didn't? Mum wasn't enough for you? And what about *us*, Zoë and me? You were going to leave us – betray us all for some tarty woman, just for sex!' Hilly's voice rose, quavered. 'You didn't even love her!'

After a moment, her father said, 'I did love her. I thought I did.'

'That's even worse,' Hilly said, though she wasn't sure whether it was or not. If love could switch its focus so suddenly, what was the point of it? How could you possibly trust it, and how it made you behave?

'I honestly don't know what came over me, Hill – it was a kind of madness while it lasted. I'd have done anything.'

'What stopped you?' Hilly said coldly.

'When it came to it, to leaving, I just couldn't.'

'You bottled out?'

'No – no, it wasn't a matter of bottle. It was like something had carried me along so far – this kind of reckless feeling – like nothing mattered so much as me and my wants. Just in time I realized what I was about to throw away. And Rose took me back, Hilly – I'd treated her appallingly, but she took me back.'

'Yes.'

'I'll never forget that. And you know what? She didn't hold it over me for ever after. Never made it a bargaining point. Didn't drag it up whenever we had a disagreement. She forgave me.'

Hilly was silent, recognizing the implicit question. Her father pulled out to overtake a Volvo estate full of a family apparently sharing a joke – parents, a couple of boys, a tailwaggy golden retriever clambering over the back seat to join in the fun. By comparison the Craig car was a capsule of hurt restraint.

'All I can say,' her dad offered, 'is – however much I hurt your mother, I hurt myself just as much.'

'Good,' said Hilly.

'And now you.'

They had reached the turn-off for the country road towards Banbury. At the roundabout, he took an abrupt turn into the Little Chef, pulled into one of the marked bays in the car park, and turned off the ignition.

'Do you need the loo or something?' Hilly asked.

'No. I just need to take a moment.'

He wasn't looking at her but she registered the catch in his voice, the rapid blinking. She realized that he was struggling to hold back tears. Never, never had she seen that before. Not her father.

'Dad . . .' she said, in dismay.

'Sorry, Hilly, sorry,' he whispered. 'The worst thing of all is that you think less of me than you did. I can't bear that. And it's all my own fault—' His voice wavered out of control; he put a hand over his eyes.

'It's OK. It's OK.' Shaken as Hilly was, the urge to comfort and soothe was stronger.

'Have you got a tissue?' He touched the corner of one eye, then the other.

She rummaged in her patchwork bag, found a crumpled one and passed it over. Her father blew his nose loudly, sniffed a couple of times; looked at himself in the driver's mirror, and took a deep breath.

'Shall we get ourselves a coffee now we're here?' he said.

* * *

No one had exactly said so, but it was understood that Heidigran would never live in her house again; not alone. The house would stay empty until a decision was made. Meanwhile, Heidigran's possessions and furniture looked forlorn and unused: the mantelpiece clock ticking to an empty room, Oscar's favourite chair with the cushion indented to the shape of his curled body, a calendar that already showed the wrong month. There was a pile of mail in the porch, most of it junk, and free papers. 'We'll have to do something about this,' Hilly's father said; 'get the post redirected, ask one of the neighbours to come in every couple of days and get rid of the papers. It's too obvious she's gone away.'

Gone away, gone away. The words sang in Hilly's head while she found a roll of bin liners. It was too appropriate; Heidigran had gone away in more ways than one. Part of Hilly's childhood was being shut up and tidied with this house and garden. If it were sold, all those memories would go with it. For as long as she could remember, Grandad had grown onions, runner beans and lettuces in the vegetable plot beyond a low privet hedge; as children she and Zoë had made an obstacle course round the garden, using canes and buckets and sacks. In her memory it always seemed to be either summer or Christmas. Most of her Christmases had happened here, too; she thought of Dad mulling wine in the kitchen, herself and Zoë arranging presents round the tree, and waking up early and excited in the tiny box room where there was only just room for their two camp beds.

But Zoë wasn't an excitable little girl any more. Grandad was in the cemetery. Heidigran was becoming an unpredictable stranger. And Dad—

Hilly and her father moved round each other carefully, going about their jobs, being too considerate, a little too polite. They opened up the shed; Hilly took secateurs and a wheelbarrow and dead-headed the roses, her father got out the electric lawnmower. Afterwards they raked and composted, and Hilly trimmed the edges with long-handled shears. It was a large garden, both longer and wider than their own; it would take a lot of effort to keep it tidy. Too much effort, perhaps. The house would have to be sold or let; it was a waste to keep it standing empty. The money it brought in could go towards a carer for Heidigran, taking the pressure off the family. But to put the house on the market would be to make an irreversible change, to acknowledge that nothing would ever be the same again. Easier to mow and trim and rake, and pretend that a bit of tidying up was all that was needed.

At lunch time, while her dad went out to fetch fish and chips, Hilly went indoors with the list of items she'd been asked to bring back. Heidigran's bag of knitting patterns, her address book; lily-of-the-valley talcum powder from the bathroom cabinet, and some interlock vests. Hilly's mother had told her where to find it all.

Heidigran's bedroom looked sadly uncluttered, abnormally tidy, with no personal possessions on view. Hilly found the knitting bag in the bottom of the wardrobe, then turned to the underwear. Heidigran had an old-fashioned dressing table with an upholstered stool, and a three-piece mirror angled so that someone brushing her hair could view herself from the sides as well as from the front. It made Hilly think of a glamorous woman in an ancient film, Betty Grable or Ingrid Bergman or one of that generation, dressing for dinner in slinky black, putting on pearls and leaning to the mirror making strange mouths while she applied lipstick. On the polished but now dusty surface there was a set of three lace mats, a crystal perfume bottle (empty – Hilly pulled out the glass stopper and got a waft of something musky and lavendery) and a photograph of Hilly's mother at about twenty, in an ornate silver frame.

Feeling like an intruder, Hilly slid back the lefthand drawer. A sweet powdery smell rose from it; it contained only make-up, a gold compact and a range of lipsticks and eyeshadows, all rather old and caked. The next drawer down contained scarves and handkerchiefs. Underwear was in the deeper bottom drawer. Hilly looked at the items inside, neatly folded and stacked. Big knickers in pink or white, otherwise identical; she took them out carefully, placing them in a carrier bag. Her nose was attuning itself to a range of scents, this time from lily-of-the-valley lining paper that slid under her fingers as she reached the bottom layer. As she took out four lace-trimmed vests, she realized that she had felt something under the thin paper; the edges of a piece of card. She lifted the lining, revealing a small square photograph, black and white, yellowed at the edges.

A girl. A girl of about her own age: thin-faced, dark hair parted in the centre and arranged in plaited whorls around her ears. A girl in round glasses, gazing up and to one side in slightly angelic fashion; but she looked self-conscious, as if someone had asked her to pose like that. The background was of draped curtain, perhaps in a photographer's studio. She wore a dark-coloured lacy cardigan with a bow at the neck. She wasn't Heidigran, Hilly was sure of that.

She turned over the photograph. '*Rachel*' was written in pencil on the back, in a looping hand.

The front door opened and slammed shut. 'Hilly?' her father called. 'I'm back!'

'Coming!' she answered. She slid the photograph back into its hiding place; then changed her mind. Retrieving it, she slipped it into the breast pocket of her shirt.

Today, with her mind working as if it had been oiled and serviced, Heidi felt good. Perfectly clear-headed. Such a fuss they all made, treating her like an old lady, when all she needed was a bit of rest! She'd be right as rain now; she knew what was going on. Rose was at the gym, Hilly and Gavin had gone home to check things, and Zoë was indoors. There had been a row last night; she had heard the raised voices and the shushing and knew that Zoë was in trouble about coming home on the back of a motorbike. Zoë. Heidi smiled fondly. Troublesome, that one was, rushing headlong into arguments, never stopping to think. Wanted it all at once, that was her problem.

Heidi sat in a garden chair in the shade of the apple tree, with Oscar washing himself by her feet. Her fingers worked at her knitting; the steady quiet clicking of needles accompanied her thoughts. She could hear starlings on the roof, chattering in that way they did that always made her think they must be happy, though how could you tell with a bird? What was happiness to a starling? Warm sun and enough to eat, that would be enough. So she was the same, needing no more than a starling. She'd been parked here by Zoë, out of the way, she knew that, though Zoë had made beans on toast at lunch time and had just brought out a mug of tea, not as strong as she liked it but still tea, and she'd put plenty of sugar in. She saw Zoë walking from room to room, talking all the while into her mobile telephone the way they did these days.

If she felt like stirring herself later she might do a bit more in the garden. The globe thistles were sagging; they'd collapse over the grass at this rate. They should have been staked long before this. And there was bindweed twining itself round the stems of a rose. She would spike her hands on the rose's thorns, pulling it off, but still she'd have to make the effort. She couldn't stand bindweed, the way it strangled and choked; once it got a hold there was no stopping it, its roots went so deep. You'd pull it out in handfuls and it would come straight back from its hold deep underground. She'd told Gavin to get a systemic herbicide, but he wouldn't have it. No sprays, no pesticides. No good complaining then if his hostas were eaten into tatters by slugs, and his roses smothered in greenfly and bindweed.

She finished a row of her knitting and left it on her lap for a moment. It made her hands ache after a while, that was the trouble. Her finger-joints seemed to get knotted up. She smoothed out the rows of maroon plain and purl, wondering. She had left her pattern indoors and couldn't now remember what stage she was at, whether this was the front or the back or whether it had long or short sleeves. It was for Rachel, she knew that. Maroon was Rachel's favourite colour: the colour of plums, of dark cherries, of the dahlias that grew in their garden in the autumn. It would suit her.

Zoë came out, still jabbering away into the phone she held clamped to her ear. She didn't look Heidi's way but walked slowly across the grass, kicking at a small apple that had fallen off the tree too soon. Such a tall girl she was now, Heidi thought, looking at her long legs in jeans, her slim waist, the fall of hair. Like a young racehorse, glossy and lithe. She could be one of those fashion models if she wanted. What must it be like to be so young and so careless, so untouched?

Zoë laughed. 'Right, then,' she said into her phone. 'My mum and dad'll go ballistic, but that's too bad. See you later!' She almost sang it: *See you la-ter.*

'Where's Rachel?' Heidi asked her. She pushed on the seat-arms and rose stiffly to her feet, tipping the knitting and wool to the grass; the cat, with a syllable of protest, walked away, tail high. 'When's she coming? When will she get here?'

'There's no one here called Rachel,' said Zoë. 'Shall I make you another cup of tea?'

Chapter Ten

Games

WE DONT WANT YOU HEAR
FILTHY GERMAN SWINE.
GO BACK TO KRAUT LAND.

Sarah was glad that Helga's foster family lived nearby. Helga was bigger and cleverer and knew how to do things. Although she was two years older, she went to the same school, and the two would always meet at play-times and dinner-times and speak German together. Other than this, Sarah spoke English. She was learning fast. Sometimes she stopped and wondered which language she was thinking in.

One summer dinner-time Sarah and Helga were playing together, a counting-and-sorting game with painted wooden cubes and a small ball. They were in a corner of the sports field; the grass had been mown for running races and the tracks marked out in white paint. The sky was blue and full of summer. Sarah had been picking daisies; they lay limp and wilting in her lap.

Absorbed in the complicated scoring of their

game, they did not notice the boys coming across the field until four of them grouped close, blocking the sun. They were big boys from the top year, grinning and confident. Sarah recognized the stocky freckle-faced one who was good at football. Some of the girls in her class were silly about him.

One of them spat. A gobbet of saliva made an arc in the air and dropped into the grass near Sarah's hands. Another boy laughed. Helga looked up at them, shielding her eyes. 'What do you want?'

'We don't want *you*,' said the ginger boy, the one who had spat. 'Filthy Germans. Go back where you came from.'

The freckle-faced boy pinched his nose between thumb and finger and made a disgusted expression. 'Phaw, what's that awful smell? Can anyone else smell it? Are we near a pig farm? Oh, no.' He pretended to notice the girls. 'Smelly Huns, that's what it is!'

Helga stood up and faced them. 'You're stupid! Stupid ignorant beasts, that's all you are!' Fury made her German accent more noticeable than usual.

'Ooh, she speaks English. Marvellous how you can train them, isn't it?'

'Heil Hitler!' The boys made Nazi salutes and one of them put a straight finger under his nose to represent a moustache.

'Come on, Sarah.' Helga stooped to pick up the wooden cubes and the ball. 'We don't have to take any notice of ignorant bullies.'

She walked across the grass, straight and dignified. Sarah, more frightened than angry, scurried after. She did not have to ask Helga, not any more, why the boys didn't like them. People were saying there was going to be a war. Another war, like The War she had seen in photos. Germany was going to be the enemy again. Always, it seemed, Germany and England were enemies.

Later, changing her shoes after PT, she found a screwed-up piece of paper tucked into one of her brown lace-ups. Unfolding it, she read: *We dont want you hear filthy German swine. Go back to Kraut Land.*

'They don't understand,' was what Helga always said when other children said spiteful things. But now it was Sarah who didn't understand. Germany didn't want her and England didn't either. Who did? She was wrong and bad wherever she went. If she made people hate her simply by being, how could things ever be different?

It was the end of the day and she was supposed to go back into the classroom with the others to put chairs up on tables, say the going-home prayer and be dismissed, but she waited for the others to go back to Mrs Milner, then slipped through the side door that led to the girls' toilets outside. Hearing the voices of older boys by the bike sheds, she hurried away fast towards the playing field and the alleyway that led home. Footsteps were pounding after her. She did not look round but was relieved it was only one pair of feet; she was afraid it might be the gang of boys from lunch time.

'Oi, wait!'

She stopped, turned. It was one of them, a fair-haired

boy whose name she didn't know. He seemed to tag along with the others, she thought; he hadn't spat or shouted insults. His tie was loose round his neck and his sleeves were rolled up; he had slowed to a jog. She thought of running away, but knew he would be faster.

He was smiling as he caught up. 'Look, I'm sorry about what happened at dinner time,' he told her. 'It was mean.'

'You were there though,' Sarah said, remembering the Nazi salute, the finger-moustache.

'I know, but it's the others,' he said. 'It's just a game to them, a bit of fun. Don't take any notice. They don't mean it.'

Sarah was silent. The taunting had seemed real enough to her.

'Anyway,' the boy went on, falling into step beside her as if he knew which way she was going. 'Sorry. Will you make up?'

'Maybe,' Sarah said, not sure what it meant.

'Friends?' He stuck out a hand, which he evidently expected her to shake, in the English way of introductions. She did, managing to smile back. She noticed what a handsome boy he was, with a smiley mouth and light blue-grey eyes that looked straight at her. The other girls in her class would be impressed, she knew, if they saw an older boy, and such a nice-looking one, taking notice of her.

'My name's Kenneth,' he said. 'And you're Sarah, aren't you?'

She nodded. 'How do you know?'

'I know, that's all. Will you marry me?'

'Will I – marry?'

'Will you marry me? Go on, say yes. To prove we're really friends.'

They had reached the alleyway, bordered by a garden fence on each side. She gazed at him, wondering if she had misunderstood. But Kenneth took hold of her hand, her left hand, and drew an imaginary ring on her finger. Was this the way things were done in England? Did boys and girls really promise to marry each other while they were still at junior school?

She noticed that Kenneth had gone pink in the face. Suddenly, he moved even closer to her and bent to kiss her on the cheek. She made a sound of protest and squirmed away, but he held her tightly by the shoulders and brought his face to hers and kissed her again, on the lips. Curiosity made her stand still and accept it. She felt the soft press of his mouth on hers, then he made a spluttering noise and pushed her away so hard that she fell against the fence.

Jeers and yells broke out from the edge of the playing field and suddenly the alleyway was full of boys – jostling and pushing each other, collapsing with laughter, the freckle-faced one and the ginger one and the others. Kenneth's friends. Kenneth, not friendly and smiling any more but one of his gang, pretended to stagger backwards, wiping his mouth. 'Yeurrgh! Bring me some disinfectant! I've been contaminated by a horrible slimy German Jew!'

'What was it like, Ken? Mind you haven't caught fleas—'

'Don't come near me – I don't want your German germs!'

'Heil Hitler!'

'Did you get my note?' Kenneth yelled at Sarah. 'My love-letter, in your shoe?'

Sarah ran: gasping, choking, tears streaming back from her eyes into her ears and her hair. She ran all the way to the end of Shoe Lane, then slowed to a walk, wiped her eyes and nose on her dress, and pushed her hair back behind her ears. When her breathing was properly under control she knocked on the front door of number 12.

Auntie Enid let her in, with hands floury from pastry-making. 'Hello, lovey! Had a good day?'

'Yes, thank you,' said Sarah. She went straight up to her room, Eric's room.

'I'm making jam tarts!' Auntie Enid called up the stairs. 'Come and help?'

'In a minute.' Sarah prised off her shoes, climbed onto the bed and took *Heidi* from the shelf. She had read it so many times now that she hardly needed the words in front of her to conjure the mountains and the wooden hut, the goats and the wild flowers. She opened the book at random and curled against her pillow with her thumb in her mouth.

The evening sun shone rosily on the mountains she read, and she kept turning round to look at them, for they lay behind her as she climbed. Everything seemed even more beautiful than she had expected. The twin peaks of Falkniss, snow-covered Scesaplana, the pasture land, and the valley below were all red and gold, and there were little pink clouds floating in the sky. It was so lovely, Heidi stood with tears pouring down her cheeks, and thanked God for letting her come home to it again. She could find no words to express her feelings, but lingered until the light began to fade and then ran on.

Everyone in the story loved Heidi: her grandfather, Peter's family, the people in Frankfurt. Everyone wanted to be with her. Everyone missed her when she was gone. Heidi did not have to do anything except be herself.

But Heidi was not German. Heidi was not Jewish.

Sarah put down the book and gazed at Eric's photograph on the mantelpiece. Eric's clothes shared the wardrobe with Sarah's, his books were on the shelf, his photograph looked at her. She hadn't met Eric, though she thought he looked nice, and Auntie Enid had told her about the naughty things he did when he was a boy. He was in the army at a place called Salisbury Plain, never at home. Now people were saying there would be a war, and Eric would be in it. He would be fighting the Germans. Germany was the enemy; Germans were nasty and dangerous. They were spies or traitors or they were filthy vermin.

Climbing down from the bed, Sarah put her shoes back on and tied the laces. She needed to see Helga. It was time to do something about Rachel, and Helga would know how.

Chapter Eleven

Letters to Rachel

Dear Rachel,

I am sorry I haven't been writing to you but you haven't written to me either, not once. Mutti says you have gone on a holiday. I and Helga are finding a place for you to come here. There you will know I mean when I said I am sorry.

At Lansdowne Terrace, Helga shared a bedroom with the Lewins' daughter, Amy, who was sixteen and had a job in an office. Helga's parents had been very concerned that she should go to a Jewish family. Entering, Sarah saw familiar objects: the nine-branched candlestick on the mantelpiece, and a plate decorated with a gold Star of David. The Lewins kept the Sabbath and all the Jewish festivals; they went to the synagogue on Saturday mornings and Helga attended classes in Hebrew. Helga thought Sarah ought to do these things, and had been deeply shocked when she discovered that Sarah now went to Sunday school and ate pig-meat: ham and sausages and bacon. Sarah hadn't really meant to, and – though she knew she should have asked what it was, and explained what she could and couldn't eat – she had tasted pig-meat several times before she realized. The sausages were delicious, herby and peppery. And what was the point of learning Hebrew, Sarah thought, when the language they spoke every day was English?

'Jews are bad. Everyone hates us, even here in England. Why must we still do Jewish things?' Sarah had argued.

'No, we are not bad. You must never believe that!' Helga said. 'And it's not true either that everyone hates us. We must keep the faith. We must keep faith with our parents.'

Sarah went silent whenever Helga talked about parents. She received a letter once a week, from Mutti. Vati did not even bother to sign his name. The letters always finished 'my darling Sarah, from your loving Mutti', but Sarah knew she was not really Mutti's darling. The letters were short and did not say much. Mutti wrote about the weather and about the trees in the park. At first Sarah had kept the letters, but now she tore them into pieces as soon as she had read them. They weren't proper letters anyway, not like Helga's parents wrote, pages and pages, full of news and gossip. Sarah would rather have read Helga's letters than her own. Helga sometimes read out little bits to her, and kept all the letters carefully in a drawer with her handkerchiefs. Already they made a thick wad.

Now Helga's parents were coming to England. Helga announced this to Sarah with great pride. Every evening, when Sarah had gone home to the Thorntons', Helga had walked the streets of Northampton – the smarter streets by the park, where the big houses were. After knocking on many doors she found an elderly couple who could offer work to her parents as housekeeper and gardener; work, and a place to live. Permits, passports and tickets were being organized, and Helga's parents should be here within weeks.

'Now I know where the rich people live,' Helga said, 'we find work for your mother and father and bring them also.'

Sarah shook her head. Her mother had never gone out to work, and would never think of being someone else's housekeeper. Mutti had promised that one day soon they would all be together, but she had not said anything about coming to England to work, especially not as a servant. And her last letter had said that Vati was away from home on a business trip. He was a prosperous tailor in Cologne, even though there had been that bad time just before Sarah came away, when the shop windows had all been smashed, and the suits and trousers and rolls of cloth thrown out on the street. He wouldn't swap his tailoring for being someone's gardener. What could Helga be thinking of?

'My sister, though,' Sarah said. 'Could we find a place for my sister?'

They were sitting facing each other: Sarah on

Helga's bed, Helga on Amy's. Helga stared.

'Your sister? What sister?'

'Rachel,' Sarah said. 'She's much older than me. Eighteen.'

'Why ever haven't you ever told me about her?'

Because, Sarah thought. Because.

Helga was full of ideas. The summer holidays began a few days later and there was lots of time for going round the streets of Northampton, knocking on doors, ringing bells. Sarah had never known there were so many kinds of knockers or that doorbells could chime in so many different ways. Sometimes a dog would yap, or a child indoors start crying. It was usually a lady who opened the door. Helga did most of the talking, as her English was better and she knew what to say. But some of the ladies would hardly listen; they just shook their heads and closed the door. Others were sympathetic, but still said no.

'Perhaps it's because Rachel's an in-between sort of age,' Helga said. They were sitting by the lake in the park, having tired of calling from house to house. 'She's practically grown up, not a child. But not old enough to be a proper housekeeper, like Mutti. What work could she do? Can she sew or cook, or type letters?'

Sarah thought. 'She can play the piano. She's good at that.'

'Music teacher?' Helga suggested. 'We might find someone who wants a music teacher for their children? I could ask at the synagogue.'

'But music teachers don't usually move in,' Sarah

said, remembering Frau Mayer, Rachel's piano teacher, who lived in a smart street close to theirs; Rachel went there for an hour every Sunday. It would have been ridiculous to have Frau Mayer living with them, however keen Rachel was and however many hours she spent practising.

'I know!' Helga got to her feet. 'The telephone directory. We'll look up Reubens. If we find someone with the same name, they're probably Jewish. More likely to say yes.'

* * *

'She lied to me,' Heidi said to Zoë in the garden, settled again with her knitting. 'Mutti told me a lie. Lots of lies. It wasn't a business trip.'

'Gran, I haven't a clue what you're on about,' said Zoë, flicking a page of her magazine.

* * *

Dear Rachel

I hope you are back from holiday.

You know I told you about our plan, mine and Helga's, well it has worked. You can come to England if you want to. We found people in the telephone book called Reulenstein, nearest we could find to Reubens, and they will be Auntie and Uncle for you just like mine. Only yours will be called Mr and Mrs Reulenstein, won't that be funny! We did not tell grown-ups, it was our secret. We went to find their houses one day after school. Helga can understand what people say back so she did all the talking.

The first lady was not nice she send us away, I think she thought we were beggars but the other one listened a long time and say yes she would help us. Helga said all we have to do now is tell the Refugee Committee and they get a permit and then you can come. Now we can be together. I will send you more news when it comes.

Love from Sarah

* * *

Everyone must listen to the wireless, Auntie Enid said. Sarah thought it was a bit like going to the synagogue, waiting for the rabbi's address. Auntie Enid and Uncle Donald were at the table, very solemn and straight, facing each other; Sarah was on the floor, kneeling on the carpet, close to the big mesh-covered speaker that stood on the sideboard. The voice that came out of it, filling the room, belonged to the Prime Minister of England, who had flown out to Munich to meet Herr Hitler a year ago. 'This morning the British ambassador in Berlin handed the German government a final note stating that unless we heard from them by eleven o'clock that they were prepared at once to withdraw their troops from Poland, a state of war would exist between us,' he said. Sarah did not understand all the words, but she knew from the tone of his very English voice that the news must be bad. 'I have to tell you now that no such undertaking has been received,' he went on, 'and that consequently this country is at war with Germany.'

His words fell into a silence. Sarah traced the worn

pattern on the carpet with her finger. Uncle Donald gave a big sigh. 'That's it, then. Just like the last lot.' He nodded towards the mantelpiece and a faded photograph of himself in uniform, a much younger man. Sarah knew that he was talking about what people had always called The War. Now there was war again. In the last one, her own father had fought for the Germans and had been given a medal, the Iron Cross. She wondered whether Uncle Donald and Vati had ever come across each other on a battlefield. She had only the haziest idea what a battlefield would be like. Like a giant game of chess, she supposed, with the two sides lined up facing each other, and the taken pieces toppled on the ground.

Auntie Enid bent down and pulled her over and gave her a big hug. 'Oh, lovey! Your poor mum and dad—' She smelled of eau de Cologne, which she kept in a glass bottle on her dressing table and dabbed on her neck and wrists every morning. Sometimes she just called it cologne. How funny, Sarah thought; I live – no, I used to live – in a town whose name, to an English person, means perfume. Perhaps Auntie Enid wouldn't be allowed to use it, now there was a war. She would have to use English perfume.

Sarah didn't want to think about Mutti and Vati. It was months and months now since she'd seen them. She wrote to them once a week, on Sundays: 'Auntie Enid says I am getting much better at English now. I speak it nearly all the time. I am reading English books at school.' But Mutti had not kept her promise and Sarah knew that now she would not. They were not to be trusted. 'We'll be together again soon, just as soon as we can' – that was what Mutti had told her, back in Köln, the day before Sarah left what she used to call Home. They couldn't have tried properly. They had sent her away and had only pretended they were going to follow. Helga's parents were due to arrive here this week; it had taken a long time, the whole of the summer holiday, for them to organize all the permission documents they needed to leave Germany, but they would be here at the station on Monday night. Her own parents couldn't have wanted to come or they would have got the documents too. Mutti had only been pretending.

And now war.

'Will Vati and Uncle Donald have to be soldiers again?' she asked.

'No, lovey,' said Auntie Enid. 'They're too old now. Eric's turn, this time.'

Sarah was glad that girls didn't have to fight. If the war went on a very long time, she might be old enough. But which side would she be on, if she was a boy and had to be a soldier?

England's side. Yes. England had taken her in when Germany had not wanted her. Germany was bad and all Germans were bad – the children at school made sure she knew that. She was a Hun, a Jerry.

There was no Sunday school today. Sarah liked Sunday school: the stories about people in the Bible, the pictures, the pretty young woman who gathered the children round her and spoke in a gentle voice. Most of the stories were about Jesus. Jesus sounded nice, Sarah thought. But when she told Helga some of the stories, about Jesus being the Son of God and a dove coming down from heaven when he was baptized in the river Jordan, and about Jesus healing the sick and raising Jairus' daughter from the dead, Helga said that Jesus was really Yeshu and not the son of God as Christians believed, only a prophet like Elijah and Isaiah. Perhaps Helga was right. People said prayers to Jesus and asked him to do things for them, and last week at Sunday school they had all prayed that there wouldn't be a war, but Jesus hadn't been able to stop it.

'Can I go and see Helga?' she asked.

'All right, lovey. Straight there and straight back, and don't be long. Dinner's at one o'clock sharp. Take care.'

Sarah closed the front door behind her and looked at the quiet Sunday street, the long pavement, the rows of brick terraced houses each side, and wondered what difference being At War would make. On the way to Lansdowne Terrace she saw an army truck driving past the end of the street. Perhaps the town would soon be full of marching soldiers.

I'd better not speak German any more, she decided. Germany is the enemy.

She found Helga in tears, and Mrs Lewin quite unable to comfort her.

'They won't get here now,' Helga sobbed. 'They should have come weeks ago. Why did it take so long? Now it's too late, too late!'

'Shh, shh.' Mrs Lewin stroked her hair. 'Maybe

they're already on their way. Maybe they'll get through.'

'They won't! I know it,' Helga wailed. 'I'll never see them again, I know I won't!'

Sarah stood by in dismay. She had never seen Helga cry before; Helga was always the sensible one, the one who knew what to do.

Dear Rachel Sarah wrote that evening,

I am very sorry the plan will not after all work because we are at War. And now there is War Helga says is not possible. We were too slow. We will try and think of a new plan. Also Mutti and Vati must leave Germany if not too late even to be servants in England. I will write and tell them and you must please tell them too.

Love from Sarah

Chapter Twelve

Preludes

Reuben Jones is a promising and versatile
young musician who plays clarinet with
the youth orchestra but whose main
instrument is piano. He enjoys playing jazz
and his own compositions as well as
extending his classical repertoire.

Programme notes

'I keep having a nightmare,' Reuben said. 'The same
one. I walk out on the stage and sit down at the piano.
Then there's this great awful silence. My mind's gone
blank. Can't remember a note. Can't even remember
what I'm supposed to be playing.' He was sitting at
Hilly's piano, playing irritable arpeggios, unable to
settle.

'What you must do,' said Hilly, 'in your dream, is
take the score with you. You can make things happen
in dreams if you really concentrate.'

Reuben shook his head. 'I've tried that. Doesn't

work. Either it's the wrong score, "Three Blind Mice" or "O Come All Ye Faithful" or something, else it's the right one but I can't read it. The more I stare, the more the notes blur into fog.'

Hilly didn't wonder at that. She had seen the score, much annotated by Reuben in pencil, and had marvelled that marks on paper could represent so free and exuberant a sound. All three pieces were liberally scattered with sharps, flats, accidentals, blue-notes and runs of triplets that she knew she would never, ever be able to get her brain round, let alone her fingers. When she stood ready to turn the page for Reuben while he practised, her eyes could hardly travel over the bars fast enough to keep up.

'You'll be all right,' Hilly said. 'You'll be brilliant. You've played in front of an audience lots of times before.'

'Yes, but not at the Derngate. A proper concert hall!'

'Good practice for the Festival Hall and your solo career,' Hilly said briskly. 'And it'd be worse *not* to be nervous, wouldn't it? You ought to be nervous.'

'I suppose.'

Reuben began to play properly; not the Gershwin preludes for Saturday but a Chopin étude that was one of Hilly's favourites. Sometimes she thought she loved Reuben most when he was playing the piano. She loved his complete absorption, his reverent stoop over the keyboard, his clever fingers, his frown of concentration. At the piano he was transformed from ordinary boy into artist, conjuror, musical athlete.

Hilly never tired of watching and listening to him.

He broke off and turned to look at her, stretching and pulling at his fingers. 'I wish Saeed could come.'

'I know you do.'

'I hardly see him,' Reuben grumbled, 'he works so hard. Some summer holiday.'

'You'll have to make do with me,' Hilly said lightly. 'And you'll soon be back at college, then you'll see him all day.' She glanced out of the window to the back garden, where Heidigran was trimming the edges of the lawn with hand-shears. Heidigran was in good form today; she had recognized Reuben, understood when Hilly had told her about Saturday's concert, and wished him luck.

Reuben started to play again, with his eyes closed. Hilly crept out, ran up both flights of stairs and fetched the photograph she had found in her grandmother's underwear drawer. She hadn't shown it to Zoë or her parents, nor even to Reuben; it was hidden inside the cover of her French dictionary.

Heidigran, on her knees, humming to herself, was pushing cut grass into a pile, and did not notice Hilly coming across the lawn.

'You'll get backache, Gran, if you're not careful,' Hilly said. 'Don't try to do the whole lot in one go!'

Crouching, Heidigran moved her kneeler pad farther along. 'I'm all right. I know you think I'm decrepit, but I'm not ready for my Zimmer frame, not yet!'

'Heidigran—' Hilly was not sure how to broach the subject.

'Yes, lovey?'

'I was wondering about Rachel. You know you sometimes talk about Rachel? Well, when I went home with Dad and got your stuff for you, I found this in your drawer.'

'What's that?' Heidigran leaned over and looked. She pulled off her gardening gloves, took the photograph and studied it closely for several moments. 'No.' She handed it back. 'I've no idea who that is. Never seen her before.'

'Are you sure, Gran? It says "Rachel" on the back. That's not your writing, is it? Do you know whose it is?'

Heidigran frowned. 'Could be. Not sure. Things get left in drawers, hidden for years and years. Could be anyone's writing.'

'Have you got any more? Any more photos?'

'There's the album, under the TV. But I don't suppose you'll find anything like that in there.'

Hilly knew. For as long as she could remember, the padded white album had been on the low shelf with the *Radio Times* and old magazines. When she was little, Hilly had loved to leaf through it, with Heidigran by her side: 'That's your mum at the fair. That's Charles on his first bike.' Hilly would turn the pages that chronicled her mother's upbringing: her brother, Uncle Charles, and her progress through fashions, hairstyles and several boyfriends, then Hilly's father – impossibly boyish and long-haired – and several pages of wedding photos, followed shortly by Hilly's own arrival, tiny, swathed in white.

'Why isn't Rachel in the album?' Hilly said, watching her grandmother narrowly.

Heidigran gave her an *it's obvious* look. 'Well, I only saw her once.'

Once? That made nonsense of Reuben's suggestion that Rachel might have been a childhood friend. 'When was that, Gran?' Hilly asked.

'Oh, years and years ago. Years and years and years.'

'So you *do* know!'

Heidigran let the photograph drop from her fingers to fall face-down on the grass. 'No,' she said. 'Don't remember.'

You do, Hilly thought, who was learning to distinguish genuine lapses from forgetfulness feigned, a convenient let-out. *I know you do.* She picked up the dropped photograph and looked again at the girl, the elusive Rachel, who gazed back at her, posed, self-conscious, almost smiling.

'Why do you talk about her so much, Gran?' she prompted. 'Was she your friend in Cologne? What happened to her?'

'I don't know what you mean.' Heidigran's face became obstinate. 'Please leave me alone. Don't be cross with me.' Her voice took on a childish wheedling note. She turned her back on Hilly and continued trimming. Hilly saw the shake in her hands as she tried to manipulate the hand-shears.

'No one's cross, Gran. I'm just trying to solve the mystery.'

'What mystery?' Heidigran said, sharp again.

'There's no mystery. The only mystery I can see is why you've been rummaging through my drawers.'

'But you know you—'

'Aren't I entitled to any privacy? You young people don't seem to care about anything. What in the world would your mother say about you stealing my things?'

'No! I only borrowed—'

'And is that young man still here? You know I don't like him.'

'Oh, Gran! Yes, that's Reuben at the piano. What have you got against him, all of a sudden? You've known him for years.'

'Why does he come here all the time? Can't you send him away?' Heidigran said plaintively. 'Reubens? I don't like that name.'

'Why not, Gran? Do you know someone called Reuben?'

'No,' said Heidigran. 'Now go away and leave me in peace, for goodness' sake.'

Later that afternoon, when Reuben had left, Hilly's mother decided to take Heidigran to the garden centre. 'Feel like coming?' she asked Hilly. 'Actually, it'd be a help to have you with me – you could sit with her in the back seat. I'm a bit afraid she might try to jump out of the car or do something daft.'

The garden centre was a huge one, with a large indoor display of garden furniture, barbecue equipment and tools, and extensive rows of plants and trees outside, divided by screens of trellis. Dismissing all the paraphernalia, Heidigran made straight for the plants.

'Penstemons. I want to look at the penstemons,' she announced, making purposefully for Hardy Perennials. 'Husker's Red, that's the one I want. It'll look nice in my front bed by the holly. Ken likes those.'

No one liked to tell her that she was unlikely to return home, or to remind her that Ken – her husband, Hilly's grandfather – was dead. But how odd, Hilly thought, that she could still name a herbaceous perennial at twenty paces, yet often struggled to identify her granddaughters and son-in-law.

'Shall we choose something for that untidy bit by our shed?' Hilly's mother suggested. 'You've done such a good job weeding it. I could buy something new to put there.'

'Well, what would you like?' Heidigran prepared to take charge. 'A hardy geranium, perhaps – or how about a shrub, for winter colour? You haven't got much for winter. One of those lovely pyracanthas, with yellow berries? Or a mahonia? They're lovely in December and January when there's not much else.'

This was a good idea of Mum's, Hilly thought, wandering ahead, not much interested in plants. It showed Heidigran at her best: knowledgeable and enthusiastic. But when the shrub was chosen and they went to the café for a cup of tea, Heidigran's mood changed abruptly. They sat at a pine table, with a pot of tea to share and a plate of flapjacks. Heidigran lapsed into silence while she ate, dabbing up every last crumb with her forefinger. Then she launched her attack.

'Why are you keeping me here?' Her voice was loud, attracting attention from people at the other tables. 'Why won't you let me go home?'

'Shh, Mum!' said Rose. 'We'll go home in a minute. Have you had enough?'

'I want to go home! I want to go back to Northampton!'

'Mum, we're *in* Northampton. This *is* Northampton.'

'No.' Heidigran looked down at her empty plate, frowning. 'No! No! The other one. Where I used to live.'

Hilly and her mother glanced at each other.

'You don't care about me!' Heidigran burst out. 'Why can't I go back to Charles? I liked it there.'

'Did you, Mum?' Rose soothed. 'Tell us what you did when you were staying with Charles and Anita.'

'Anita? I don't know Anita. Do I? All I'm asking is why you're keeping me here, like a prisoner!'

'Shh, shh! We're looking after you, Mum, you're our guest, not a prisoner!'

'That's what you say.' Heidigran folded her arms and kicked the table leg. 'It was different with Charles. He's a good boy. I like staying with Charles. So does Ken. It's not fair, the way you treat me!'

By now the other customers in the café were trying not to look, ostentatiously pretending not to notice, having animated conversations of their own. Hilly stayed silent, unequal to the embarrassment of being in public with a grown woman who was behaving like a six-year-old.

Heidigran changed her tack, leaning across the table to speak confidentially to Rose. 'I hope you know she's been stealing my things, this girl here! Rummaging through my drawers, she's been, helping herself.'

'Oh, now Mum, don't be ridiculous!' Rose reproved. 'You know Hilly went to get some of your things you asked for.'

Reluctant to mention the photograph to her mother, not yet, Hilly was saved from having to when Heidigran went on: 'Like that plumber came to do my radiators. Not Eddie, my usual, this one was a darkie. Took money from my purse, I swear he did! A ten-pound note went missing. I phoned Eddie and told him, only he wouldn't have it, said it must have been my mistake. I said to him, don't you send that darkie round again—'

'*Shhh!*'

'Told Eddie, he's not setting foot in my house, not him or his sort,' Heidigran went on loudly. 'I don't like blacks. You can't trust any of them.'

'Gran, *please!*' Hilly wanted to crawl under the table, aware of the black girl behind the counter.

'What? Twenty pounds went missing and I know it was that darkie took it—'

Rose got abruptly to her feet. 'Let's talk about this later. Not here.'

Following, Hilly smiled apologetically at the waitress, who surely must have heard, but she looked down, unresponsive.

'Now, Mum,' said Rose, in the car. 'About this

missing money. You really need to be sure of yourself before you start accusing people. How much was it?'

'How much was what?' Heidigran was fumbling with her seat belt.

'The money you said the plumber stole.'

'Oh, no.' Heidigran looked at her with wide-eyed innocence. 'He never stole it after all. I found it in my other purse.'

Rose caught Hilly's eye in the driver's mirror. Neither dared speak for a few moments; then Rose began, 'Mum, you're going to have to be more careful what you say in public.'

'Yes, dear, I know. I'm sorry,' said Heidigran, contrite and reasonable.

'But Gran,' said Hilly, 'don't you realize—?'

'Realize what, dear?' Heidigran turned with one of her most charming smiles.

Hilly gave up. It was impossible to know what her grandmother remembered or understood.

Back at home, Heidigran got out of the car with complete composure, looked around her, and remarked: 'You know, I really enjoyed that. Pity Ken couldn't have come too. I must get home soon, he'll be wanting his dinner.'

Reuben grew more and more agitated as Saturday approached. 'You'll be there, won't you?' he asked Hilly, for the fourth time.

'Course I will! Wouldn't miss it for anything.'

Now the William Watkins Birthday Concert, which had loomed for so many weeks, was tonight. Feeling that a special effort was required to mark Reuben's solo performance, Hilly had bought what she hoped was a sophisticated outfit from the Oxfam shop: a dark-green blouse with lace sleeves that fitted closely to her wrists, and a slim black skirt. Together they produced a rather Edwardian effect, which she tried to match by pinning her hair up and back. She frowned at herself in the bathroom mirror. Her glasses marred the elegance she was hoping for, but it would have to do.

'Wow!' said Tessa, meeting her in the Derngate foyer. 'Ready for a surprise appearance on stage? Guest slot with the Three Tenors or something?'

'Hey, look at you!' Reuben, immaculate in a dinner jacket, held Hilly at arm's length to give her a full scrutiny.

'You too! Not the grungy slob we know and love.'

'I feel like a penguin,' Reuben complained, tugging at his bow-tie.

'Good luck. Not that you'll need it.'

Reuben went backstage to join the other musicians, and Tessa and Hilly, with Reuben's mum and stepdad, found their way to the box seats reserved for them. 'Come on then,' Tessa prompted. 'Who are you trying to impress? Hunky horn player, is it? Fabulous flutist?'

'You mean flautist,' said Hilly. 'And no! Not even a dreamy drummer or a sexy saxophonist. Thought you were supposed to be a feminist? Can't I dress up a bit just for myself – or for Reuben, on his special night?'

'Hmm.' Tessa didn't look convinced. 'We've got a

good view, anyway. Who do you fancy?' She leaned forward to look at the members of the youth orchestra, who were taking their seats – the girls rainbow-coloured and gorgeous in bare-shouldered dresses, the boys smart in dinner jackets and bow ties. Hilly watched with interest as they settled themselves, exchanging comments and smiles, placing their sheet music on stands. Reuben, who was playing clarinet in the orchestra for the first half, looked at Hilly and smiled, holding up both hands and pretending to shake uncontrollably.

'I always feel like a wimp, don't you?' Hilly said. 'Not being able to play.'

'Never wanted to. All that practising. Hey, he's not bad – see the percussionist? D'you know him?'

'Only by sight,' said Hilly, glancing. How odd, she thought, that you could take one look at someone and think, well, he may be nice, funny, friendly, but he's not my Someone. Whereas – her gaze travelled along the third row, and settled on an unfamiliar face that did attract her. Bony, alert, it went with a rangy body – he would be tall when he stood up – and a highly polished French horn. He wasn't one of the regulars.

Tess nudged her. 'Who're you looking at?'

'Hunky horn player, like you said. Not the ginger-haired one. On his right.'

'Oh, yeah.' Tess sounded disappointed. 'I wouldn't call him hunky. D'you need stronger glasses? And who's this William Watkins bloke anyway?'

'Look at your programme,' Hilly said. 'He was the founder of the youth orchestra. It's his seventieth birthday, and the Gershwin Reuben's playing is his special favourite. I think that must be him, over there.' She indicated a box opposite, where a small man in a dark suit sat between the mayor, in his chain of office, and a plump woman in a tangerine-coloured dress. William Watkins – if it was him – had a tanned face and silvery hair, and was talking animatedly, gesticulating with his programme. 'It's this week, the birthday,' she continued, ''cos otherwise it'd be an odd time to put on a concert, in the summer holidays, with lots of people away. That's why some of the musicians look a bit too old for the youth orchestra. They've been drafted in to fill the gaps.'

'Well, your horn player's certainly one of those. You always do fancy older men.'

'Shh!' went Reuben's stepdad. A hush fell, followed by applause as the conductor stepped out onto the stage and turned to face the audience. Hilly watched Reuben, who sat with his clarinet across his knees, not needed yet. Over the years of their friendship, Hilly had been to many concerts and recitals, though none as grand as this. The town mayor and various dignitaries sat with Mr William Watkins in a box opposite Hilly's. In the Derngate, the boxes weren't only for special guests or the holders of the most expensive tickets, but for a sizeable proportion of the audience. Hilly hadn't sat in one since coming with her parents and Zoë to see *Aladdin*, years ago when she'd been in primary school. The imposing setting added to her apprehension for Reuben. How would it feel to walk out in front of such an audience, sit down at the piano and start to play? If it were me, she thought, my fingers would turn into bunches of bananas, and I wouldn't be able to breathe, let alone remember what I was supposed to be playing.

In spite of her anxiety, Hilly found her attention wandering, all through Bernstein's *Candide* overture, and two solo items. She could rarely give her full concentration to music, the way Reuben did, and she found herself dwelling on the conversation with Heidigran in the garden, puzzling over every nuance of Gran's disjointed remarks. *I don't like that name*, she had said, about Reuben; and what about Reuben's suggestion that Rachel had been a Jewish friend of Gran's, back in Cologne? Rachel Reubens? Was Gran trying to blot out something horrible from the past? Had Rachel died in the Holocaust? And if so, why would Gran have decided to dislike Jewish people?

Could she ask Heidigran directly?

Hilly's mind veered away from the concert hall and back to Natzwiller: to the punishment block, where cold had struck even in the heat of midday, where she had sensed – or thought she had sensed – lingering evil in the air, in the dust, in every atom of the place. Could Gran, she thought, feel guilty for what happened to Rachel? Could she have betrayed her in some way? But no, surely not. Gran had been, what, thirteen when she left Germany at the end of the war . . .

An outburst of clapping startled her back to the warmth and comfort of her seat, the packed audience beneath her, the lit stage, the musicians standing to the applause. 'That was marvellous, wasn't it?' said Reuben's mother, beside her.

'Yes,' said Hilly, who had hardly registered. No, she was thinking, it doesn't make sense at all: Heidigran said she had seen Rachel only once. But in that case, why had she kept the photograph?

'The interval now. Shall we go down for a drink?'

The bar was downstairs, in the spacious, open-plan entrance. Hilly thought of Reuben, minutes away from his solo in the second half; he was probably hiding in the loo, feeling awful. Sipping her drink, Hilly noticed the rangy horn player being kissed by a girl with sleek red-gold hair. He didn't look so interesting closer up, either. Oh well. It was only a game, imagining you could pick and choose as if from shelves in a supermarket.

As the audience began to drift back to the auditorium, Hilly saw a slight, dark-haired figure come in from the street door and go to the ticket window. Saeed! Reuben would have his supporter, after all, the one he really wanted. Saeed came away from the hatch with a ticket in one hand, pocketing his change with the other. He looked hesitant, unsure where to go. Hilly pushed through the crowd towards him, and was rewarded with one of his shy smiles, radiant with relief.

'Si! You made it after all!'

'I'm skiving,' Saeed explained. 'Tracy said she'd cover for me – Doug's there and it's not that busy tonight. I'll go straight back after Reuben's slot.'

They looked at the number on his ticket, which

directed him to the stalls, on the opposite side of the auditorium. 'See you after, maybe?' Hilly said, not sure what Reuben's plans were. Saeed nodded and went to find his place, and Hilly returned to hers.

The grand piano had been moved out on the stage during the interval. Throughout the Brandenburg Concerto which opened the second half, Hilly gazed at it. Playing in the orchestra, in the safety of the massed ranks, was one thing; performing a piano solo quite another. In her fidgety agitation she could only see it as a blood sport, like cock-fighting or bull-fighting: everyone gawping in relish while someone (Reuben) sweated and laboured, pitching himself against the challenge of the music, hurtling towards the traps that waited to catch him out. To perform in public was to offer yourself to the audience for approval or disdain; to risk failure, even humiliation.

But Reuben looked composed and professional as he stepped out onto the stage for the Gershwin. Hilly hoped he wasn't remembering his nightmare: his mind blank, the music forgotten. Three short pieces – seven minutes at most – and it would all be over, the performance he had practised and practised for.

Calmly, he seated himself on the stool, spread his hands over the keys and launched into the playful opening phrases of the first prelude. As the jazzy rhythm followed, the sweeping runs of notes in the right hand accomplished without a fault, she allowed herself to breathe; Reuben seemed to be fully in control, playing with all the exuberance the piece required. You need to be a real show-off to play it, he had told her. It made Hilly think of an acrobat, a tumbler – spring-heeled, energetic and daring, throwing in extra twists and somersaults just for the fun of it. The second prelude, the slow one, brought a change of pace: dreamlike, measured, almost soporific. Then back to *Allegro ben ritmato e deciso* for the giddy rush of the final piece, showy and demanding, which contained Reuben's downfall in practice – a run of triplets where he had to think very fast if he wasn't to find himself short of fingers. Hilly was hardly able to watch, trying not to think of the number of times in practice he had crashed to a standstill, swearing fiercely; but the moment was past, no hint of a wobble, and he was hurtling towards the finish. After the final triumphant flourish he lifted both hands and sprang from the stool like a jockey dismounting from a winning racehorse.

Applause was like the breaking of waves; someone whooped from the audience, others got to their feet, William Watkins among them. Hilly felt herself swelling with pride and relief. She wanted Reuben to look up at her, just a glance, an acknowledgement that she was there, but as he straightened from his bow he was gazing out into the stalls. Had he seen Saeed? He stood, flushed and smiling, for a few seconds, and Hilly thought he was going to play an encore; then he turned and marched off to the wings. Now Saeed slipped along the side aisle and out to the foyer. The conductor returned to centre stage for the final big piece, Bizet's Symphony in C; the orchestra came to attention; coughs and chatter from the audience subsided with his raised baton.

Hilly wondered if this was how it would be, in years to come. Her imagination soared, picturing Reuben as Young Musician of the Year, winning the Leeds Piano Competition, travelling the world, playing the big concertos, with herself and Saeed (or whoever) in attendance. Why not? Anything was possible.

Reuben had suggested that Hilly and Tessa might go on afterwards to the party at someone's house. 'What do you think?' Hilly asked, as the audience spilled out into the dusk.

'Mm, not sure,' said Tessa. 'We'd feel out of it, wouldn't we, with all those musical types? They'll all be on a high, and we'd just be hangers-on. I'd rather go into town.'

'OK. Shall we go to Settlers?'

'What, and make eyes at Reuben's beautiful boy over the latte machine?'

'You never know who else might be there. Anyway, I wouldn't be surprised if Reuben turned up.'

'Ah, isn't love sweet!' Tessa made a soppy expression.

'I wouldn't know.'

'Me neither. I wasn't speaking from experience. You know me,' Tessa said airily. 'I'm far too self-centred.'

'Yes, I've always thought that.'

'Cow!' Tessa aimed a genial swipe. 'Besides, a woman needs a man like a fish needs a bicycle. Have you heard that? It's one of my mum's sayings.'

Hilly giggled. 'If you were a fish, you'd spend an

awful lot of time goggling at bikes on the riverbank.'

'Goggling's fine. Window-shopping. You can look – no obligation to buy.'

'Bicycle voyeur! I've heard about people like you.'

'Hill, you're off your trolley, you are!'

Settlers was busy, every table occupied, but there was no sign of Saeed. 'No, he hasn't come back,' said Tracy, busy operating levers amidst hissing steam. 'Said he'd only be half an hour, but it's hardly worth his while showing up now. Stuart'll do his nut if he finds out.'

'He's gone off somewhere with Reuben, I bet,' said Tessa in an undertone to Hilly. 'They want to be alone.' She struck a film-starrish pose.

'Leaving us standing here like a pair of wallies.'

'Well, it was your idea. Hey,' said Tessa, suddenly alert, 'you're jealous!'

'No, I'm not! Jealous of who?'

'Of Saeed – coming between you and Reuben.'

'That's rubbish! I don't own Reuben. But it's a bit odd,' Hilly added, 'Si not being here, after we saw him leave. Wouldn't he have stayed to the end if he was going off with Reuben? Anyway, he told me he had to come straight back.'

'Let's have a coffee anyway, and see what happens.' Tessa slid onto a bar stool. Hilly sat too, watching the door, expecting at any moment Saeed to come in, flustered and apologetic, or Saeed with Reuben. After a few minutes she took out her mobile and tried phoning Reuben, but got only voice-mail. She left a quick message: 'Hi, it's me.

We're at Settlers, but no Saeed – is he with you?'

'Don't worry about it,' Tessa said, looking at the menu. 'P'raps he felt ill or something and went straight home. God, I'm starving – how much dosh have you got?'

'That you, Zoë?' Hilly's mother called, as she let herself in.

'No, it's me.'

Hilly went quietly up the stairs and glanced through the open door of her parents' room. They were both in bed; her mother's reading lamp was on, though all Hilly could see of her father was a hummock of duvet and the fingers of one hand.

'You didn't double-lock the front door, did you?' her mother asked. 'She's late again.'

'Amazing,' Hilly said drily.

'And after last week! I wonder how she expects me to get any sleep at all. How was the concert?'

'Good, thanks—' Hilly broke off, hearing the unmistakable sound of a powerful motorbike coming towards the house. They both listened. It stopped outside, the engine idling. Zoë's voice called, 'See you later!' and then her key turned in the lock.

'Oh, dear,' said their mother. 'After we told her! She'll get herself grounded if she goes on like this.'

Hmm, fundamental mistake, Hilly thought: imagining that merely telling Zoë something was likely to make the slightest difference. Didn't parents ever learn? 'Oh well, at least she's not *very* late. I'm going to bed.'

'Just as well Dad's not awake! I'm too tired to argue all over again.'

So was Hilly. She heard Zoë going through to the kitchen, and a tap running. 'Night, Mum,' Hilly said hurriedly, and went upstairs to undress.

She was lying awake, though with the lights turned off, when Zoë came up to the attic. Uncharacteristically, Zoë tiptoed around in the darkness, avoided slamming doors or drawers, and got into bed with barely a creak of her mattress.

Chapter Thirteen

Encounters

'We're very concerned about this unpleasant outbreak of hooliganism,' Councillor James Raymond, the Town Mayor, said yesterday. 'It's a disgrace to the town and its people, and risks making the town centre a no-go area at night, especially for those from ethnic minorities.'

Chronicle and Echo

'Hilly! You awake?'

For a few seconds, her father's voice was part of a confused dream; then Hilly came to, registering closed curtains and Zoë's sleepy murmur of protest.

'Reuben's on the phone.' Her father was calling up from the middle landing.

'Coming.' Hilly pushed back her duvet and padded barefoot down the stairs, slowly remembering last night, and Saeed's non-appearance at Settlers. Her dad, still in his dressing gown, handed her the receiver.

'Hi!' she said to Reuben. 'What time d'you call this? Have you been to bed yet?'

'Hilly, Saeed's in hospital. I've only just heard. He was attacked last night.'

'Attacked—?'

'Beaten up by racist yobs. How sick is that?'

'God, no! Is he badly hurt?'

'Concussed, black eye, cut face, possible broken ribs.'

'How'd you find out?'

'Rashid just phoned from the hospital.'

'Are you going?'

'Right away. I had no idea, Hilly – I was at the party, for Christ's sake! While Si was lying half unconscious in A and E—'

'Well, how could you have known?' A thought struck her. 'Saeed was at the Derngate – in time for your Gershwin – he came specially. Did you know?'

'Yeah, saw him in the audience. I was well chuffed. But that's when he got mugged, on his way back—'

'What—?'

'Yeah. It was my fault he was walking about on his own.'

'Don't be daft! How bad is he?'

'Bad enough, from what Rashid said.'

'Did the police arrest anyone?' Hilly asked, with a horrible suspicion forming.

'I bloody hope so!'

'Shall I meet you at the hospital?'

'Would you?'

'Course. What's the ward?'

Reuben gave details; they agreed to meet at the main entrance in half an hour. As soon as she had replaced the receiver, Hilly bounded up both flights of stairs. Zoë was still sprawled in bed, face up, blinking as Hilly yanked back the curtains.

'Don't! Whassup?'

'Zoë, where were you last night?'

'Oh, not the Spanish Bloody Inquisition again!' Zoë said, tugging at her duvet. 'What are you, my prison warder?'

'Come on, I need to know. Where were you?'

'Band practice, as if it's your business.'

'You do a lot of practising,' Hilly said neutrally.

'We need to. You complaining?'

'Where was it, this band practice?'

'Someone's house. Why're you going on about it?'

'Were you in town?'

Zoë rubbed sleep from her eyes and blinked at Hilly. 'No. What's this all for?'

'Saeed was attacked last night,' Hilly said, watching her sister carefully. 'He's in hospital, injured.'

'Saeed? Who's Saeed?' Zoë said, yawning.

'You know. The young guy from Settlers. I told you about him the other day!'

'Oh, right. I get it!' Zoë sat up abruptly, hugging the duvet to her chest. 'The guy's been mugged, so naturally you jump to the conclusion it was me that did it. I mean, I'm a known criminal – mugger of old ladies and snatcher of bags.' She held out both hands, wrists turned up. 'Got your handcuffs handy? Want to see me safely behind bars?'

'Don't be stupid, Zoë – course I didn't think it was you.' Hilly felt wrong-footed, hardly knowing what she did think. 'I was just – well, you know how I feel about Grant and Co. – I wanted to find out if you knew anything, that's all!'

'Yeah, right. Well, I don't, OK? Happy now? You'll have to find another suspect.'

A little later, walking through the Sunday-quiet edge of town towards the hospital, Hilly felt bad about interrogating Zoë like that. For one thing, it would only make her even more prickly. And for another, Hilly had believed her when she said she knew nothing about the attack. Zoë was irritating, inconsiderate, maddening at times, but she wasn't an outright liar – not usually to Hilly, anyway – and she wouldn't stand and watch while someone was beaten up. Maybe it hadn't even been a racially motivated attack; maybe Reuben had jumped to that conclusion. Saeed could have been mugged for his money, or his mobile phone; attacks in the street weren't unheard-of.

Reuben was waiting at the hospital entrance, his hair tangled as if he'd just got out of bed, his face pale; dressed in a crumpled T-shirt and torn black jeans, he was unrecognizable as the dinner-jacketed concert pianist of last night.

'I'm so sorry,' Hilly said, touching his arm.

'Yeah.' He turned away.

'Is it OK to visit, this early?' Hilly said, as they entered a long corridor of polished lino.

'I don't think they're all that strict about it.

Rashid had just come from the ward when he phoned.'

Hilly registered newly-washed flooring, a lingering smell of disinfectant and a plethora of signs pointing in various directions: RESTAURANT, FRACTURE CLINIC, X-RAY, OUT-PATIENTS. A young woman in white tunic and trousers hurried past, clutching a clipboard. The hospital was like a small town, functioning independently of the world outside and with a sense of heightened importance, allowing visitors brief glimpses of its organized, focused routines.

They found the ward, and asked at the desk for Saeed. His bed was in a bay of four; his parents were sitting either side, his brother standing by their mother, who wore a black headscarf. Saeed was propped up against pillows, his face swollen and bruised, a dressing over his forehead and one eyebrow; he looked like a caricature of himself. Hilly felt a wrench of regret for the spoiling of his flawless good looks; she heard Reuben's sharp intake of breath, and knew that he was close to tears. But Saeed's father was standing, coming towards them, holding out a hand. 'You are Reuben? And—?'

'Hilly,' said Hilly.

'Muhammed Anwar,' said Saeed's father, shaking hands vigorously, 'and this is my wife Soraya, and our son Rashid. It's good of you both to come.'

Reuben stood with his eyes fixed on Saeed, who looked as if he would rather be anywhere than confined in bed like a butterfly in a chrysalis, the centre of this awkward social situation. Hilly saw that Reuben was going to be quite useless, at risk of giving himself away if he said anything at all. 'Saeed, how are you?' she asked.

'Oh, I'm great,' said Saeed, with a smile that twisted painfully. 'Never felt better in my life. Ready to run a marathon.'

'They're probably keeping him in another night,' said the brother, Rashid, 'because of the concussion. He'll be home tomorrow.'

'That's good,' Hilly said, in the falsely bracing tone she hated when she heard herself use it to Heidigran. What could she possibly see that was good? Saeed disfigured, the victim of mindless morons?

Saeed's mother smiled doubtfully at Hilly. 'You are Reuben's girlfriend? Or Saeed's?'

'Neither,' said Hilly; 'Hilly's with me,' said Reuben; 'Friend,' said Saeed – all at once, and rather too quickly.

Mrs Anwar looked puzzled, glancing from one to the other in the embarrassed silence that followed. 'We've guessed Saeed has a girlfriend, but he's so secretive about where he goes and who he sees. Are you sure there's no one you'd like me to call,' she asked him, with an indulgent smile; 'no one you'd like to come and visit?'

'I'm fine, thanks. Everyone's here,' said Saeed.

Hilly saw that Rashid was noticing everything, his expression wry, and wondered if he knew. But none of us, she thought, is saying what we want to say. *What happened? Where? Who was it? Did you recognize them? Did anyone help?* hung unasked in the air.

'Have the police been here?' she ventured.

Saeed nodded, and Rashid said, 'He's just been making a statement. It's tired him out, I think.'

His mother nodded. 'Very nice young lady, that WPC. But you must rest now, Saeed. Go to sleep.'

'I'm not tired,' said Saeed.

Rashid got to his feet. 'Come on, Mum, Dad. You need to get some rest. They've been here all night,' he added to Hilly and Reuben.

'Si,' Hilly said urgently, 'did you recognize them? The attackers?'

Saeed looked at her for a moment, knowing what she meant. 'I couldn't be sure, but I think so. Three of them.'

'Apparently they've bothered him before, in the coffee bar, these delinquents,' said his father. 'He doesn't know their names but he was able to give the police a good description.'

But I know their names, Hilly thought. Nicknames, anyway. *Wait till I get hold of Zoë . . .*

Mrs Anwar kissed Saeed carefully, and submitted to being led away by her elder son. 'Don't get over-tired, now – try to sleep. We'll be back later.'

Saeed had left the concert hall immediately after the Gershwin, he told Reuben and Hilly. Instead of going up by the Guildhall he had taken a shorter back route, cutting through the car park and a narrow alley. He saw no one until, approaching the back of Bridge Street, he heard voices, laughter, saw a lit fag-end in the dusk. Three blokes were standing by a skip;

something was passed from hand to hand. They were all bigger than him. He thought of turning back, but decided it was too late, not wanting to let them intimidate him. He gave as wide a berth as possible, swerving away towards the gap between two buildings.

'Oi, Abdul!' one of them yelled. 'Paki!'

One of the others stepped towards him, blocking his route. 'And what might you be doing out all on your own this time of night, Mohammed?'

'Scrotty little Towelhead sneaking round alleys at night – we don't like that. What you up to, eh?'

He saw leather jackets, shaven heads and hard faces, a silver badge that caught the light. ('Oh, God!' Hilly muttered. 'I knew it!')

'Fuck off!' he said, trying to sidestep.

'Ooh, mouthy! No one talks to me like that, Abdul.'

'Where's your boyfriend tonight, eh? Cleared off, has he? Got fed up of curried—'

('– I can't tell you their exact words,' Saeed said, with an embarrassed glance at Hilly, 'it's far too disgusting. Anyway, a lot more of that sort of thing.'

'We can imagine,' said Reuben. 'And then . . .?')

They had gradually closed round him, Saeed said, cutting off his escape. He looked around edgily. There was no one in sight, no one he could yell to for help. He stood for a few seconds weighing up the situation, then ducked and made a dash for it. But they were ready; a body blocked him, an arm went hard round his neck from behind, throttling him, and with a rough twisting pressure he was forced to bend forward. 'Think we'll let you get away that easy, Paki? No way. Haven't even started yet, have we?'

'Don't pretend you're not going to enjoy this, you pervy little git,' another voice said. For a second, then, clamped in a headlock, bent over and helpless, he thought they intended to rape him. He struggled and kicked, fighting for breath; his foot made contact with someone's shin, and he heard a grunt of pain. But their idea of fun was more straightforward.

First, a kick to the groin brought tears to his eyes and doubled him up. After that, he said, things got confusing. He was on the ground, trying to curl up to protect himself. A boot slammed into his ribs, another into the side of his head. He thought he was going to die, that they were going to kick and beat him to death.

His mouth twisted; he lay back against the pillows, eyes closed. 'Oh, Si!' said Reuben, grasping Saeed's hand, his eyes dark with compassion. 'I'll kill them, I swear I'll kill them!'

'No,' said Saeed, attempting to shake his head; 'no. I don't want you involved.'

'I *am* involved, aren't I? How can I not be, when the bastards did this to you?'

'Then what?' Hilly prompted. 'Who found you, called the ambulance?'

'I don't know.' Saeed opened his eyes and looked at her wearily. 'I must have passed out. Last thing I remember is someone's voice in my ear saying, *You don't know us, right? Never seen us in your life. But we know where you live, got that?* Next I knew, I was coming round in the ambulance, and I was one big mass of hurt.'

'Someone must have come along. Walked up from the car park,' said Reuben. He and Hilly exchanged glances. What if no one had come? Would Saeed have been left there, lying injured? Or worse?

'There weren't—' Hilly forced herself to say it. 'There weren't any girls with them? Nearby?'

'No,' said Saeed, understanding. 'Your sister wasn't there.'

Well, thank God for *that*, Hilly thought. She sat pondering, perched on the end of Saeed's bed. A nurse came round with the electronic equipment for measuring temperature and blood pressure; Hilly stood up and moved out of the way.

'I think I'll go for a coffee,' she said, when the nurse had done. 'Leave you two to talk. Back in about half an hour, OK?'

She bought herself what the hospital restaurant called cappuccino, and looked for somewhere to sit. There were plastic-topped tables, and screens of artificial greenery; a window looked out at a garden area with a bird table. A group of nurses sat at one table, and at another a family group that included a patient in a dressing gown. Hilly sat at the table nearest the window and stared gloomily out.

Zoë had lied, hadn't she? How could there have been a band practice, if half the members were beating up Saeed?

What must it be like, to face that sort of abuse and

violence whenever you went out on your own? To know that some people hated you merely because of your race, seeing only the colour of your skin? To know that prejudice could so easily take the form of blows and kicks, not just hostile words?

And while this was happening, Hilly thought, I was at the concert not a quarter of a mile away, listening to Bizet's Symphony in C, happy for Reuben, never suspecting. If only Saeed had stayed to the end; if he hadn't been so conscientious about returning promptly to Settlers . . .

'OK if I join you?'

She looked up and saw Saeed's brother, alone, with a cup of coffee and a Danish pastry on a tray.

She gestured towards the spare seat opposite. 'Thought you'd left.'

'I took Mum and Dad home – they've been here all night, like I said. Then came back to talk to Saeed on his own. Wanted to see if he could tell me a bit more about what happened.'

'So,' said Hilly, 'why aren't you in the ward?'

'Same reason as you, I guess,' said Rashid. 'Your friend Reuben is with him.'

'Ah,' Hilly said cautiously.

'I thought they'd appreciate a bit of privacy. As much privacy as you get in a public ward, anyway. I guessed, a while ago. Knew for sure when Si was desperate for me to phone Reuben. It's OK, I'll keep it to myself. Not a word to Mum and Dad.'

'I'm so sorry about what happened,' Hilly said.

'I know. But you don't need to apologize.'

Hilly was silent, wondering if she had in fact been apologizing: for having even an unwilling connection with Saeed's attackers; on behalf of her sister, for getting involved with such people.

'Hilly, did you say your name is?' said Rashid, breaking a piece off the Danish pastry. 'Here, have some of this?'

'Thanks,' said Hilly, realizing how hungry she was. 'That's right. Short for Hilary, only no one ever calls me that.' Back in the ward, she had only glanced at Rashid; now she had a better look. She felt in awe of him, remembering what little Reuben had told her: that he'd got straight As in his A levels, wanted to be a doctor, and had been away for nearly a year. 'You've only just come home, haven't you? Are you staying there now?'

'Not for long. I've just come back from my gap year. Well, actually I'm having two gap years. I start on applications now.'

'Oh, for . . . ?'

'Medicine, if I'm lucky. The competition's fierce.'

'What did you do in your gap year?' asked Hilly. 'The round-the-world thing?'

'No, I was in Palestine. The West Bank, near Jerusalem. That's where our family's from.'

Hilly nodded. 'Were you working out there?'

'Helped build a community health centre – builder's navvy, was what it came down to. What about you? Are you at college?'

'No, school. I start sixth form next month.'

'Doing what?'

'AS levels – History, English Lit., Business Studies, Biology.'

'And after that?'

She shrugged, smiled. 'Haven't a clue.'

Hilly wanted to ask more about Palestine, but wasn't sure how to phrase it. Whether or not there *was* a state of Palestine had been, she knew, the cause of dispute, but she was unsure what stage had been reached. She thought of news items, so regular that she took little notice except for something particularly startling – suicide bombers, tit-for-tat shootings, weeping mourners.

'It wasn't your first trip to Jerusalem, then?' she asked.

'I was born there. We lived for a while in Saudi, then Dubai, then Spain for two years. Here since I was twelve. But we've still got family in Jerusalem and in West Bank villages. Aunts and uncles, cousins.'

Hilly had lived all her life in one place, and felt that it would be a dull thing to admit to. 'What made your parents come to live in Northampton?'

'Dad's work – he's in international air freight.'

'But there's no airport!'

'The head office is out on the industrial estate.'

'Oh.' She felt silly; he must think her ignorant. She fiddled with her spoon. Rashid seemed quite at ease, looking at her while he sipped his coffee. 'Did you see anything of the – the troubles?' she ventured. 'In Jerusalem, I mean?'

'It would be impossible not to,' Rashid said, with a wry look that silenced her. 'There was one thing in particular,' he added after a moment, 'just before I came away.'

'Yes?' prompted Hilly.

'Someone was killed, someone I knew.' His glance flicked away from her, out of the window. 'Amos, a taxi driver. He used to come most days to a café run by a friend of my uncle, in a village not far from Jerusalem. He'd just ordered his breakfast as usual and he was sitting there in the sunshine. And next minute he was shot dead.'

'But why? Who—?'

'Extremists,' Rashid said.

'Why would they shoot a taxi driver?'

'Amos was Jewish. All the same he was friends with a lot of the Arab people in the village. He lived on the other side of the line, but he was in and out of the village all the time. He spoke fluent Arabic, he was from Libya. He was a kind man. Generous. Loved to chat. Used to tease me about wanting to be a doctor, used to ask me to come back with a cure for his wrinkles or his baldness. I didn't see – what happened, but I saw the bloodstain on the pavement.'

'How awful,' Hilly said, inadequately. 'You mean – he was shot by Palestinians? Or by Israelis?'

'No, not by Israelis,' Rashid said. 'Not this time. This was Palestinian extremists marking down someone who crossed the line. It's usually shootings and suicide bombs against the Israeli tanks and army and helicopters – a no-win situation. A cousin of mine – well, second cousin – was killed in the street a year ago, in an Israeli mortar attack. It was the day I flew out there, I was expecting to see him, he was the same age as me – instead I was in time for his funeral. The Israeli soldiers and the militants on our side, they'll carry on fighting, never mind the latest peace settlement. But the ordinary people don't necessarily hate each other, you see. Lines get crossed. Amos was Jewish, but he was our friend.'

Hilly nodded; Rashid looked bleakly out of the window.

'Now home, and this,' he added.

'Has it ever happened to you?' Hilly said. 'Being attacked, like Saeed?'

'Not as badly as this. I've never ended up in hospital. But every Muslim gets to hear the whole range of racist abuse. Sometimes, from other kids, it's meant in a semi-friendly way. Often it isn't. You get used to people looking at you with suspicion – even fear. Now, since the Iraq War, you can't walk down the street without someone staring at you and wondering if you're plotting something, or hiding explosives in your shoe,' said Rashid, adding: 'It hasn't done much for race relations.'

'What about where you live?' Hilly asked. 'I mean, gangs in the town centre is bad enough – you don't get trouble at home as well, do you?'

'Not much. But things need to change – we shouldn't keep ourselves apart. We live in a street that's mainly Asian, and all my mother's friends are Muslim women. My father meets a wider range of people, through business. That's the way it is for a lot of families. It's different for our generation. Which is a good thing, as far as I'm concerned.' He smiled, for the first time, and Hilly saw the resemblance to Saeed. He seemed more solid than his brother – more confident, more at ease with himself. Instead of Saeed's delicate beauty, he had instead a sort of robust attractiveness. 'Our parents would be happy if Saeed and I married nice Muslim girls, but they're likely to be disappointed.'

'Your mum thought I might be Saeed's girlfriend.'

'Yes,' said Rashid, his almost black eyes looking at her keenly; 'that was an interesting moment.'

'Would she mind if I was?'

'Nice Muslim girl would always be top choice. Non-Muslim girl would be a long way second,' said Rashid. 'But as for non-Muslim *boy* . . .' He shook his head. 'Let's not go there.'

'But if they found out?'

'I wouldn't want to be around,' said Rashid. 'Put it like that. And you?' he asked. 'Since Reuben and Saeed only have eyes for each other?'

'Me, what?'

'Is there someone for you?' said Rashid.

'No,' Hilly said lightly. She hesitated to ask, 'And you?' What had he said just now about his parents being disappointed? Was he hinting, perhaps, that he was gay too?

Well, she couldn't come straight out and ask *that*. She'd only just met him. She replaced her empty coffee cup on the tray. 'Shall we go back to the ward?

Chapter Fourteen

Hands Together

She was so far away, and . . . if she did not
go home for a long time, she might arrive
to find everything changed and her loved
ones gone for ever . . . And when she was
in bed, and all the well-loved scenes of
home came before her eyes, she cried and
cried, until her pillows were quite wet.

Johanna Spyri, *Heidi*

Sometimes I hate Heidi, Sarah thought. I used to
pretend she was my friend, but now she really annoys
me. Everything comes right for her in the end, every
single thing. And everyone loves her, because she's
always cheerful, with her rosy cheeks and her
sparkling eyes and the way she runs and skips to and
fro and makes everyone happy.

Perhaps people would like me too if I was always
happy. But I can't be cheerful and neither can Helga.

We'll never see them again, our families, and I was

horrible and mean to say what I said to Rachel. That's how she'll always remember me, shouting nasty, hurtful things at her.

I remember how she looked. Not angry but sad.

Why didn't she tell me? Why didn't they tell me the truth? I suppose they thought I wasn't old enough to know, but now I do know.

Everything now was to do with the war. Even things that apparently had nothing to do with it were only diversions, ways of pretending life went on as normal. At school there was a special assembly. Everyone trooped into the school hall, which smelled of floor polish and cooked potato and cabbage, to sit down in neat rows, cross-legged. Miss Munson clapped her hands. 'A special treat for us, today!' she said brightly. A small boy called Billy Watkins, from the year below, was playing the piano – what Miss Munson said was called a medley. 'A medley of English folk tunes,' she said, 'to cheer us in these dark days. William Watkins is going to play them for us.' And people shuffled and giggled, because it sounded so funny and grown-up, William Watkins, when everyone knew him as Billy. Afterwards Miss Munson asked the children what separate tunes they had recognized, and they put up their hands and said things like 'Greensleeves' and 'Early One Morning' and 'The British Grenadiers'. Sarah didn't know any of them.

He looked so funny, Billy, solemn and tiny at the big piano, but playing with such confidence. He sat perched on the stool, his feet not even reaching the pedals. But Sarah watched him with a big, choking lump in her throat, because listening to piano music – any piano music – reminded her of Rachel. Every day at home Rachel practised. Scales and exercises and boring things like that, but then she'd play proper music too. Sarah's favourite was called *Für Elise* and she knew it was by Ludwig van Beethoven. Last time Billy Watkins had played in assembly, it had been a piece from *A Little Notebook for Anna Magdalena Bach*, but Bach, like Beethoven, was a German composer, and Sarah supposed that no one wanted to hear German tunes now, because Germany was the enemy.

Für Elise was still her favourite, though, and she knew it so well that she could hear it in her head, even if she would never hear Rachel play it again.

She liked the way it started, as if leaning sadly into itself, falling into a run of deeper notes. The beginning bit was easy, Rachel said, and she even taught Sarah how to play it. Rachel had written the names of the notes above the line of music, and they'd play that bit together, Sarah perching on the stool to Rachel's right, carefully playing her nine notes: E D# E D# E B D (making sure to play the ordinary note, not the black one this time) C A. Her fingers weren't strong enough to give each note its proper weight, but Rachel didn't criticize. She only smiled, waiting to come in with the solemn, deeper voice of the left hand, then both hands together, and Sarah would move back until Rachel nodded and it was time to play the same nine notes again. They kept coming back.

Sarah would watch Rachel's clever hands, bouncing and rippling over the keys, as the music became difficult in the middle part: crashing and dramatic, the notes on the score clustering themselves in black clumps and climbing right above the staves where Sarah had no idea what their names were. But right at the end her own phrase repeated itself, as if it had been waiting all the time to calm down the fierceness and make it peaceful again. I'll be able to play the whole thing, Sarah thought, both hands together, when I'm as big as Rachel. All by myself.

All by myself. Now she *was* all by herself, and it wasn't what she had meant. Not what she had meant at all.

Sarah was trying to scream, but no scream could get through the tightness of her throat. She strained and strained, eventually producing a wailing noise that sounded as if someone else was making it.

And now someone was coming in, clicking the light switch, padding over to her bed: Aunt Enid, soft and cushiony in a candlewick dressing gown, smelling of talcum powder and face cream. 'Shh, shh, lovey!' she soothed, kneeling, clasping Sarah in a big cuddle. 'Whatever's wrong? Was it a bad dream?'

'Rachel. I – want – Rachel—' Sarah's sobs were like hiccups, stopping her from breathing properly.

'Who's Rachel, love? I don't know a Rachel.'

'Yes, you do!' Sarah shouted. 'Rachel's my sister and I want her here with me!'

'Say it in English, lovey, you know I can't understand.'

Sister. Sister. That was the word. Not so different from the German *Schwester*.

'Rachel is my sister,' Sarah said in her heavily accented English. Auntie Enid frowned, and began to rock her.

'No, no, lovey. You haven't got a sister. You must have been dreaming.'

'I have! I *have* got a sister!' Sarah struggled to free herself from the soft, suffocating clasp. 'She's left behind in Germany!'

'But—' Auntie Enid held her at arm's length and looked into her face. 'You never said anything about a sister! You told me you were the only child!'

'It was a secret,' Sarah mumbled, looking aside because the light hurt her eyes. 'When I first was here I didn't want Rachel to come. Then I did, but now too late.'

'Secret? Why would you keep something like that a secret?'

'I don't know.' Sarah pulled at frayed threads on her eiderdown. 'But I did.'

'How old is Rachel?' said Auntie, in a different, more serious voice that told Sarah she was beginning to believe her.

'Eighteen, much older than me. Look, I've got photos.' Sarah reached for the copy of *Heidi* on her bedside table. She kept them tucked into the back cover, the two black-and-white photographs Mutti had given her to put in her suitcase. For a long time Sarah had kept them hidden in the pouch compartment, but now that she'd told Helga about Rachel she kept them in her book, as a marker, to look at first thing each morning and at bed time. 'Rachel went specially to the photographer's studio to have this one taken,' she told Auntie Enid. 'It was her birthday.'

Mutti had done Rachel's hair in what she called earphones – parting it severely in the middle, making two long plaits, then winding them around Rachel's ears.

'Rachel hated it when she first got her glasses,' Sarah said. 'But she couldn't see properly without them. And she said it was awful sitting there feeling silly while the photographer took ages messing about with lenses and hoods. That cardigan was a birthday present. I helped Mutti choose it. You can't tell but it's a sort of dark maroon colour – like plums, not the golden ones, the little dark dark red ones, damsons.'

'In English, Sarah. Don't you know the English words?'

Sarah shook her head, giving up. There were too many words. She passed Auntie Enid the second photograph.

'This is Rachel and me in the garden at home,' she said in English. 'We're having a – a—' The word defeated her again.

'Picnic,' said Auntie Enid, 'it looks like.'

Sarah and Rachel were sitting each side of a table-cloth spread on the lawn, under the big plane tree with its distinctive bark. Picnics at home were always rather formal, since Mutti could not bear to do without plates, cutlery and linen napkins. Sarah sat cross-legged in her pink dress with the embroidered pocket, and was showing her knickers; Rachel was more poised and elegant, her legs folded to one side, like someone in a magazine picture.

'That must have been before she got her glasses. But Mutti's written on the back, look. That's Mutti's writing. *Rachel. Rachel and Sarah in the garden.*'

'And she stayed at home with your parents? She'd have been too old to come out, the way you did. Oh, lovey.' Auntie Enid began to rock her again, holding her tightly. 'My poor love, my poor little love. And you've kept it all to yourself, all this upset, you've never even said!'

Sarah tried to push her away. 'Mutti,' she wept, 'I want Mutti! And Vati. And Rachel.'

'I know, I know, my darling lovey, of course you do. And Mutti and Vati and Rachel want you too, more than anything in the world – believe me, they do.'

'I'll never see them again, will I?'

'Shh, shh, my love, don't say that. No good making yourself miserable about something that hasn't happened! Maybe things aren't as bad as they seem. Maybe you'll all be together again before long. Where was Rachel when you saw her last? Was she at home?'

Sarah shook her head. She could not tell Auntie Enid about that.

'Here,' said Auntie, taking a crumpled hanky from the pocket of her dressing gown. Gently she wiped the tears from Sarah's cheeks. 'Have a good blow as well.'

'Will Rachel be all right?' Sarah said. The tears

were still coming, quietly now, as fast as Auntie Enid could wipe them away, squeezing between her closed eyelids and running down the sides of her face, into her mouth. She could taste the salt, and that made her want to cry even more.

'We'll have to hope so. We must say our prayers for them. Every night you must pray to Jesus, and perhaps he will make everything all right. That's all we can do, love. Shall we do it now?'

Sarah had got used to saying prayers to Jesus at Sunday school. She thought of his kind face, in the picture where he carried a lamb under one arm and a lantern in the other hand. In the story he had searched and searched till he found the one lamb that was missing. That showed, said the teacher, that he cared about everyone. He looked like the sort of person who might bother himself to look after Rachel, especially if he really was the Son of God and could do miracles, as he did in some of the stories.

Stiffly, Auntie Enid got down to a kneeling position, facing the bed. She made her face solemn, put her hands together very neatly, fingers pointing up, and closed her eyes. Then she opened them again to look at Sarah and pat the floor beside her. 'You kneel with me, love. Then I'll say the words and you can just say *Amen*. Or join in if you want to.'

I'd better think it in English, Sarah thought, in case Jesus doesn't speak German. And what if he knew she was Jewish, and wasn't supposed to pray to him at all? It was better to let Auntie Enid do the talking. Auntie Enid asked Jesus to look after Sarah's parents and Rachel, and to take care of Eric and all the brave soldiers, and not let anyone be hurt. She finished with the Lord's Prayer. Sarah knew some of that, and joined in, in case Jesus thought she wasn't enthusiastic enough to have her prayers answered.

'*For Thine is the Kingdom, the power and the glory, for ever and ever, Amen,*' they finished together. It was like a chant when they said it at Sunday school, all the children reciting the words in an up-and-down rhythm, like a song without a tune. You could say the words without knowing what they meant.

'There, love, that'll make us both feel better.' Auntie Enid got awkwardly to her feet; she straightened Sarah's eiderdown and plumped the pillows into shape. 'Back into bed with you, now. I'll bring you some hot cocoa and a biscuit, and then you must try and settle back to sleep. Things'll seem different in the morning.'

Sarah's feet had got cold while she kneeled on the lino. She let Auntie Enid tuck her snugly between the sheets. While she waited for her cocoa, she thought: wouldn't it be easier to ask Jesus to stop the war? If he can do miracles, why doesn't he do that?

Where was Rachel when you saw her last? Was she at home?
Yes, she was.

Rachel wanted to read Sarah a bedtime story, the way she had when Sarah was little. '*Heidi?* Are you reading that again?' She picked up the book from Sarah's bedside table. 'I used to love *Heidi* when I was little.'

Rachel was like that sometimes. Wanting to be grown up. Making *Heidi* seem like a book only little children would read.

'It's mine,' Sarah said. She grabbed it and pushed it under the bedcovers. 'Is the door locked? We mustn't leave the door unlocked at night.'

'Yes, it's locked and bolted. Don't worry. Let me read to you!' Rachel sat on the bed beside her. 'A bed-time story. I'll read one of your favourite bits, if you show me where.'

'Want Mutti,' said Sarah. 'Go away.'

'Sarah, please! Just a little bit of story, just for the two of us!'

Sarah shook her head obstinately. 'Why are you pretending? I know you don't really care. You're staying with Mutti and Vati and you can't wait for me to be gone.'

The lenses of Rachel's glasses made her eyes look big and sad. And now shiny with tears. Sarah looked away.

'Oh, Sarah!' Rachel pleaded. 'I know it's hard for you to understand, but you must try. Mutti and Vati are sending you to England because it's safer there. If we could all go together, then we would, I promise.'

'*You're* not going.' Sarah stroked the cover of *Heidi* under the sheet. They like you better than me, she thought. They love you but they can't love me. They can send me away, across the sea to a strange country, but they're keeping you with them. How can I believe what they say?

There was a big lump in her throat, as if

she'd swallowed a whole hard-boiled egg, shell and all.

'I can't go to England,' Rachel said. 'I'm too old, or I'd go with you.'

'Are you sure the door's locked?' said Sarah. 'Those bad men won't come back, will they?'

'Yes, the door's locked. And there won't be any bad men in England.'

'But you're not going there!'

'No,' said Rachel, 'I shall be in France instead – won't that be exciting, you in England and me in France! I can think of it as a holiday, learn to speak French. And you'll learn to speak English! Next time we meet we can show off our new languages.' But Rachel's voice was thick with tears, not excited at all, and she pulled a lace-edged handkerchief from her pocket and turned her head to dab at one eye and then the other, as if she thought Sarah wouldn't notice.

You're part of it, Sarah thought. You know what's going on, and you think you can fool me by pretending it's all exciting. She moved away to the farthest side of her pillow, and gazed across the room at Berthe, the big doll who sat on her chair. Berthe had been a birthday present last year; Mutti had sewn a dress for her, with tiny buttons, and Sarah had plaited her hair. But Berthe was too big to go in the suitcase, Mutti said, and she had found a much smaller rag doll instead, one Sarah hadn't even looked at for months, with an ugly flat face and wonky sewn eyes that made her look as if she were squinting. Berthe had lovely golden hair and round blue eyes with real eyelashes.

Berthe was staying here with Rachel and Mutti and Vati, and Sarah was the only one leaving. I'm going to be like someone in a fairy tale, Sarah thought: the poor stepdaughter, the one no one wants.

'Don't hate me, Sarah, please don't,' said Rachel. There, she was as good as admitting it now. 'I'll think of you every single day. I promise I will.'

The lump in Sarah's throat was swelling, pushing itself up into her mouth, bursting, and what came out was anger. 'Go away! Go *away*!' she shouted. 'Leave me alone – I won't listen to any more of your stupid lies! I hate you!'

'You don't mean that.' Rachel was pale-faced, trembling.

'I do mean it! Get out of my room! I hate you and I don't care if I never see you again, ever!'

Rachel stood up. As she left the room, Sarah hurled *Heidi* after her; it missed, bounced off the wall and fell to the floor with its pages splayed. She heard Rachel weeping as she went slowly downstairs.

Chapter Fifteen

Shopped

shop, *v.* to lay information on which a
person is arrested; to deliberately get
(someone) into trouble.

*A Concise Dictionary of Slang and
Unconventional English*

'Fucking morons!' Reuben exploded as they left the
ward, getting a fierce *tut* and a *young people today* look
from a woman coming the other way with a pot
chrysanthemum wrapped in cellophane.

'Sorry – he's a bit upset,' Hilly explained, while
Reuben stomped on down the corridor.

'And your sister,' he fired at her as she caught up.
'Can't she see what those blokes are like? What's the
big attraction?'

'Sex! That's the attraction. But don't say I haven't
tried!' Hilly clung to the one shred of comfort: 'At
least she wasn't actually *there*. She might be besotted
with Golden Boy, but she's not completely out of her

mind. She wouldn't go along with something like that.'

'How d'you know she wouldn't?'

'I just know. And she wasn't there – Saeed said.'

But Zoë had lied. She said they were having a band practice. Hilly did not tell Reuben this. She was saving up for a mega-row with Zoë when she got home, and not looking forward to it. Maybe the police were already on to Grant and his friends, and Zoë would have to stop pretending that they spent their evenings harmlessly rehearsing songs.

Reuben kicked at a stone. 'What shall we do?'

For want of any sense of purpose, they wandered in the park, looked at the ducks, argued, talked, tried to console each other; they went over and over what had happened, all the what-ifs and why-dids, and the merits of castration versus community service as fit punishment for racist yobs. Later they went back to Reuben's, where he said he was ravenously hungry and made his speciality French bread pizza with olives, which they ate in his bedroom.

'Play something for me,' said Hilly, when their plates held only crumbs and olive stones. 'It'll take your mind off it.'

'I'm not in the mood,' Reuben grumped, but he switched on his electronic keyboard and sat on the stool. He crashed a few angry-sounding chords.

'Not like that!' said Hilly, from his bed. 'Chopin. Play Chopin.'

'I'm not in a Chopin mood.' Reuben doodled a tune on the keys with his right hand. He lingered on two notes for a moment, then launched into a sad little phrase that Hilly thought she knew.

'What's that?'

'*Für Elise.* Beethoven.'

'Go on, play the rest,' Hilly said.

'It won't sound right on this stupid thing,' Reuben complained, but played it anyway. Hilly listened closely, recognizing the simple, haunting phrase that kept returning after the interruptions of more excitable stuff in the middle.

'Lovely,' she said when Reuben had finished. 'I wonder who Elise was?'

'No idea. I learned this when I was doing Grade Four or Five. It's a standard test piece.'

'Oh, so you polished it off when you were about three, I suppose. It amazes me, all the music you carry about in your head!'

'I'm not sure it *is* in my head,' Reuben said, playing the first section again. 'It's my fingers that remember.'

'Wish I had fingers as clever as yours,' Hilly said, flexing hers.

'You could play it, you know – the beginning bit, anyway. It's quite easy, listen. Just a few simple chords in the left hand.' He demonstrated.

'Simple for you!'

'And for you. Come and try. If you like it I've got it in a book somewhere. You can practise for your next homework.' He nodded towards the shelf that ran above his bed, sagging in the middle under the weight of stacked music books and scores.

'If we can find it in that lot. I'm sure there'll be an avalanche one night and you'll be discovered in the morning crushed under a mountain of books. Battered by Beethoven ... bruised by Bach ... suffocated by – by Schubert—'

'Squashed by Scarlatti, mashed by Mozart, yeah, OK. Come on, stop putting it off. Sit down here and I'll show you.'

Concentrating hard for the next half hour or so, Hilly managed to produce a semblance of the first few bars. 'I can learn the different *bits* of it,' she complained, when both she and Reuben had had enough; 'it's putting it all *together* I just can't do. I don't think I've got a musical brain, like you have.'

Reuben turned off the switch at the socket. 'Bloody scrambled brain, at the moment. OK, you've made a start. Shall we go back to the hospital?'

'Sure you want me to come, this time?'

'Course. I bet his mum and dad'll be there anyway. You're useful camouflage. Unless you'd rather go home?'

Hilly pulled a face. 'No thanks.' Going home meant confronting Zoë, if she was in. Not yet. 'Camouflage it is, then.'

However, they found Saeed alone, propped up in bed listening to his Walkman. 'Is it still Sunday?' he said, with a wincing smile. 'I've lost track. It seems to have gone on for ever.'

'Are you tired?' Hilly said. 'Would you rather we left you alone?'

'No! Sit down.' Saeed moved his legs to one side; Hilly sat by his feet, Reuben next to him by the pillow, leaning close. 'That policewoman's here again,' Saeed continued. 'She's just gone to get a cup of tea – said she'll be back.'

'Any news?'

'No. If there was, she didn't say.'

'Si, who exactly did you recognize last night? Three of them, you said – which three?'

Saeed looked reluctant. 'I only *think* I recognized them. Couldn't be sure. Even if I was, I don't know names.'

'But I might. You said they were the ones who hassled you in the coffee bar?'

'I think so. Didn't have too much time to take in the details.'

'You gave a description to the policewoman, you said?'

'Yeah, but that wasn't much. Your sister's boyfriend – the tall one, cocky, tanned face—'

'Yes?'

'He definitely wasn't one of them,' said Saeed. 'There was one with the swastika and skull badges, leather jacket, ear-studs. I've seen him before. He was the one called me Abdul and Towelhead.'

Hilly nodded. 'Pete, that'd be.'

'Then there was this big ugly one – face like a shovel, big square chin.'

'Clyde,' said Hilly. She looked at Reuben. 'He's the one I told you about, who stayed the night. Stayed the night! In our house!'

Reuben grinned. 'You ever thought of playing Lady Macbeth?'

'Uh?'

'When she hears the king's been murdered, first thing she says is, *What? In our house?* – like it'd be quite OK for him to get bumped off anywhere else.'

'Well, you know what I mean,' Hilly said. 'All right, he's got to sleep *some*where, but I don't like the thought of our house being polluted. Anyway, Si? That's two.'

'Big greasy-looking one, shaved head.'

'Tuck,' said Hilly, 'could be.'

Saeed frowned. 'Don't know if I could identify them.'

'But you told all this to the police?'

Reuben looked doubtful. 'Not much to go on. There could be any number of blokes roaming the streets with swastika badges and leathers and pierced ears. It's not actually an offence.'

'They've probably been caught on CCTV, just before or just after – the policewoman was telling me,' said Saeed.

'But we know who they are,' said Hilly. 'And Zoë must know more.'

'Think she'll tell you?'

'She will when I get hold of her.' Hilly got to her feet, annoyed with herself for doing nothing constructive all day. 'You don't mind if I go now, do you? I need to make an urgent appointment with my sister.'

In the corridor, walking fast, she rounded a corner and almost collided with a young WPC coming the other way. Both smiled and apologized; then, as the WPC made to walk past, Hilly said: 'Are you visiting Saeed Anwar?'

'That's right,' said the policewoman, who looked little older than Hilly and was blonde and very pretty, with hair pinned back in a neat ponytail under her cap, and careful make-up. 'Are you a friend of his?'

'Yes – Hilly. Hilly Craig.'

'Hi! My name's Jo.'

'Have you got, er, any information – any names?'

'We're working on it. Saeed was able to give us quite good descriptions, and we're checking against CCTV.'

'He was just telling us. They go to the coffee bar sometimes – you know Settlers, where Saeed works? I was there once when they banged on the window and shouted insults. They're all members of a band my sister's in.'

'Just a minute.' WPC Jo pulled a notebook and pen from her pocket. 'Hilly Craig, you said? Can I have your details?'

On the front doorstep, Hilly paused, feeling for the key-ring in her pocket, hoping Zoë wouldn't be in. As she turned the key in the lock and opened the door she felt someone pushing from the other side, trying to stop her from entering.

'Gran! Heidigran! Is that you?' she called. 'It's only me, Hilly.'

Heidigran opened the door a fraction and peered round it. She smiled brightly, recognizing Hilly. 'Oh!'

she exclaimed. 'It's Hilly, isn't it! I didn't know you were coming today.'

'Let me in, Gran!' Hilly pushed, and sidled through. 'What's the matter?' she said, noticing her grandmother's teary eyes, and a shiny trail down one cheek.

Heidigran fixed her with a glance and raised a finger, turning in an instant from child to stern adult. 'You must lock the door. You must always keep the door locked,' she said. 'I keep telling that other girl but she won't take any notice.'

Hilly closed the door behind her; Heidigran pulled at her arm. 'No, no! The bolt and chain as well! You must always lock the door!'

'Gran, there isn't a bolt, and I can't lock and chain it or no one'll be able to get in. Mum's at the sports centre, isn't she? Is Dad here?'

'Lock the door.' Heidigran was fumbling now as if for a non-existent bolt. 'You must always lock the door.'

And now Zoë's feet were clumping down the stairs. 'Christ Almighty, is she still on about that? She's been driving me demented, banging on and on.'

'Gran,' Hilly said, trying to steer her grandmother through to the front room, 'it's only six o'clock. Not night-time. Why's she been crying?' she said over her shoulder to Zoë.

'Christ knows. She won't stop going on about the door.'

'Why did you leave her on her own down here?'

'That's right – have a go at me! It's not my fault she's ga-ga!'

'*Don't* say that in front of her! Don't say it at all!' Hilly said fiercely, then, in a louder voice, 'There, Gran, sit down in your chair. We'll make you a cup of tea.'

Zoë glowered, standing squarely in front of Heidigran's chair, hands on hips. 'Go on then, Saint Hilary. If you want to do your Florence Nightingale bit, you're welcome. I've been lumbered with her all afternoon. She's got a stuck record instead of a brain – something about men coming to the door.'

'Zoë's going to put the kettle on,' Hilly told her grandmother.

'Like a mug of tea's going to cure everything!' Zoë grumbled, but took the excuse to leave Hilly with their grandmother, and went into the kitchen.

'It's all right, Gran.' Hilly sat on the arm of the chair and stroked the knitted sleeve of Heidigran's cardigan, noticing that it was inside-out. 'What's all this about locking the door?'

'Bad men came,' said Heidigran, looking at her with round eyes.

'What bad men? When?'

Heidigran shook her head. A tear oozed from one eye; she raised stiff fingers and brushed at it. 'Lock the door. You must always lock the door. Lock the, lock the door.' Her voice became agitated; she made to get up again. 'Bolt it tight.'

'Shh, shh, Gran! It's all right. The door's locked – no one can get in, only Mum and Dad, with their keys.'

'Bad men came,' Heidigran insisted.

'What bad men? Did you have burglars, Gran? At home in Banbury?'

'At home.' Heidigran nodded earnestly. 'Home.'

'Did you have burglars?' Hilly repeated, pronouncing it clearly. Heidigran watched her, craning her neck, then her lips moved silently as she tried it for herself, like a child learning a new word. 'Burglars, Gran? Intruders?'

'They came in at night,' Heidigran said, in her little-girl voice. 'The door wasn't bolted and they came in. They took my daddy away.'

'Daddy?' Hilly said in astonishment.

'They took my daddy away.' Heidigran picked at the inside-out seam of her cardigan. 'It wasn't really a business trip. He didn't even come to the station. Never said goodbye! They smashed things and threw them out on the street!'

'Who did, Gran?'

'The bad men. You must lock the door. Keep it locked and bolted. Where's my tea?' Heidigran craned her neck to look past Hilly towards the kitchen door. 'That other girl said she was making tea.'

'Zoë, Gran. That's Zoë, your granddaughter. You know Zoë. Who am I?'

Heidigran stared at her and chuckled, as if they were playing a game. 'Rachel,' she said.

'No, I'm Hilly. Gran, who's Rachel?'

'You're Rachel. That's a funny thing to ask me!' Heidigran said plaintively. 'Why are you asking me?'

'Because you keep talking about her. I showed you the photo, do you remember?'

'Yes,' Heidigran said, in a troubled voice. 'I think so.'

The moment was broken by the sound of a key turning in the lock. Hilly stood, expecting Heidigran to panic, to rush to the front door, start worrying again about bad men and locks. But Heidigran sat back calmly, remarking, 'That'll be Rose, I expect.'

Hilly looked up with relief as her mother entered the room, in trainers, exercise shorts and a zipped lycra top.

'You'll catch your death, going about dressed like that!' Heidigran said sharply.

Hilly giggled, and her mother said, 'What? On a warm day in August? I thought you'd be out in the garden, Mum!'

'We're having tea,' said Heidigran. 'Zoë's making tea for us all.'

Just like Happy Families, Hilly thought, for the moment at any rate. It was a relief to let Heidigran's puzzling remarks take precedence over the inevitable row with Zoë. Hilly found Heidigran's knitting and tuned the radio to Classic FM, then followed her mother upstairs, knowing she'd be heading for the shower.

'Mum?'

'Mm?' Rose was in her bedroom, in a white towelling bathrobe, freeing her hair from the high ponytail she wore for exercise classes.

'Gran was saying the weirdest things. Something about bad men coming in. I thought at first she must have been frightened of burglars in Banbury, or something – but she's never been burgled, has she? And then she said something about bad men taking her daddy away, and I realized she meant back in Germany.'

'Oh, dear,' said Rose. 'She often rambles, but that's a new one.'

'Gran's never wanted to talk much about her life in Cologne,' said Hilly. 'Remember when I tried to interview her for my history project? She hardly told me anything – it was practically useless. But *bad men*? And something about it not really being a business trip and her dad not being at the station. And she called me Rachel again.'

'*Bad men*,' Rose said slowly. 'The bombers, did she mean? The RAF who bombed Cologne? She might think they deliberately killed her parents.'

'No, I don't think that's what she meant.' Hilly propped herself against the door-frame. 'She keeps going on about locking the door.'

'Oh, yes, she did that the other night,' said Rose. 'Didn't tell you, did I? Dad found her down in the hall at half-past two in the morning, saying the door wasn't locked. He had to show her five times, and she still went down again afterwards to check. I don't suppose we'll get any sense out of her. Maybe she meant looters? There'd have been looters, wouldn't there, raiding the bombed-out houses?'

'Mm. Maybe,' Hilly said doubtfully. She moved aside to let her mother through to the hall and the bathroom.

'It's a feature of Alzheimer's,' said Rose's voice

through the open bathroom door, 'not being able to remember what's happened in the last five minutes, but having clear memories from years and years ago. And it's going to get worse.'

But I want to *know*, Hilly thought; and there's only Gran to tell me. Once her memory goes completely, it'll all be lost, her past, and we'll never know what she meant; what's there, somewhere, tangled in her brain. Eventually, Heidigran will die of Alzheimer's – the part of Hilly's mind that knew this was able to contemplate it quite emotionlessly – and then everything will be gone for ever. We'll be left with a few pieces of jigsaw that no one else can possibly fit together.

I must go back to Gran's house, she decided; get Mum or Dad to take me, see if there are more pieces to be found.

Rose turned on the shower. 'Be a love, Hilly, and bring my tea up for me when it's ready?'

Hilly went downstairs; Gran was contentedly knitting, Zoë pouring tea in the kitchen. For all her resolve to open the conversation as tactfully as possible, to avoid Zoë flying into a rage, Hilly found herself saying waspishly: 'Nice of you to show such concern for Saeed. You knew I'd been at the hospital, didn't you? Doesn't it even cross your mind to ask how he is?'

'Oh, fine – start on that again, why don't you? What's it to me? I told you I wasn't there!'

'Thought you might just show a bit of concern – one human being to another, you know? But, right, it's nothing to you.'

Zoë slammed the fridge door. 'Bunch of blokes get into a fight? Happens every night of the week. Even you must know that.'

'Yes, except there was only one bunch. Bunch of your friends, and Saeed on his own. Not quite the same thing, is it – three yobs and one Arab boy? Now, about this band practice you were having. I'd be very interested to know how you could have been having a band practice, when three of the members were beating up Saeed in a back alley.'

'Oh, so I'm a liar now?'

'Just possibly.'

'I just don't get you. I'm a liar, but poxy little what's-his-face has got to be telling the truth, is that it? When it comes to choosing between your own sister and some slimy little poofter, you'll take the other side, won't you, every time? Every bloody time!'

'Zoë – did you tell your friends about Saeed and Reuben?'

Zoë flushed. 'What's to tell? Bloody obvious, isn't it?'

'So you did! D'you want Reuben beaten up, as well? Zoë, don't you know what they're like, your so-called friends?'

'I know what *you're* like. Don't I just – Miss Shining Halo, Miss Squeaky-Clean. Now get off my back, for God's sake!'

'Zoë, wait. I want to know about the band practice.'

'Yeah – well, get this. OK, there wasn't a band practice.'

'So you *were* lying?'

'It was better than a band practice. We were having sex, Grant and me – heaving, sweaty sex. Got that? Jealous, are you?'

'Jealous?' Hilly flung back, recovering. 'Of you having under-age sex with a racist moron?'

Zoë tossed her head. 'Don't suppose you'd understand – you'd rather hang round with queers for some peculiar reason—'

'You, young madam!' They both turned to see Heidigran standing in the doorway. 'You want your bottom smacked, talking like that!'

Zoë was shocked into silence for a few seconds, then she gave a spluttering laugh.

'And where's my tea?' Heidigran demanded. 'You're taking long enough. Are there any biscuits?'

'Go and sit down,' Zoë said. 'I'm just fetching it.' She pushed her grandmother back in the direction of her chair, and muttered to Hilly, 'Christ! How much do you think she heard? What if she tells Mum?' She picked up the tray.

'Well, if you choose to broadcast it at the top of your voice—'

The front doorbell shrilled. 'I'll get that,' Zoë said, plonking the tray down on the work surface, sloshing tea. Assimilating what Zoë had said – thinking of Grant's piercing blue eyes, his golden skin, his lean body, and wondering if she did, in fact, feel a tiny bit envious – Hilly mopped up the mess and found a packet of biscuits in the cupboard. She carried the tray through to the front room, and almost dropped the lot as she took in the scene.

Zoë, angry and scowling. Heidigran crouching behind her armchair, knitting wool and needles scattered over the floor. And a uniformed police-woman, WPC Jo, smiling uncertainly.

Chapter Sixteen

Snakes and Ladders

No one's meant to say defeatist things like this but you can't help what you think. I honestly don't see how we can win this war. They've overrun France, marched in and swarmed in and taken over, they've got us on the run. Dunkirk just about summed it up. It'll be us next.

Letter from Eric Thornton to his parents

Uncle Donald did firewatching at night, so he kept odd hours, going to bed at dawn and getting up in the afternoon. His meal times were upside-down and back to front, he said. When Sarah got home from school he would be reading the paper, his shirtsleeves rolled up. After tea, the two of them sometimes played board games together, Ludo or Snakes and Ladders. Occasionally Auntie Enid played too, more often just Uncle Donald and Sarah. All the games were kept in a cardboard box whose lid was battered from use, with split corners. It was called a Compendium of Games. Sarah was fascinated by the Snakes and Ladders board – the ladders that could carry you on a swift short-cut through eight or even ten rows, and the brightly coloured snakes, zigzag patterned, with grinning mouths and forked tongues, that waited to slither you down. There was one particularly vicious snake, thick and fat as if gorged on countless victims, that twined its way from nearly the top of the board to the very bottom row, back to the start.

Sarah liked looking at the board more than she liked playing. Playing made her feel anxious. It was too dangerous. No matter how diligently she worked her way up the numbered squares, moving her counter (always the red one) towards the winning corner, the next throw of the die could send her into the jaws of a lurking snake, and the dizziness of the slide right down to the bottom.

Die, dice. Auntie Enid called it a dice, but Uncle Donald said that was wrong, because *dice* meant two of them. If there was only one, it was called a die. The English language didn't seem to follow sensible rules, like German. If it was *die, dice*, why not *one pie, two pice* or *one lie, two lice*? That would make sense. But she always remembered *die*. Throw it and die. Throw the wrong number and the snake would swallow you.

The war was like Snakes and Ladders. Listening to

the news she heard good news followed by bad: the aircraft factories were turning out more and more Spitfires, but the Germans had reached Paris. The local paper showed Northampton army boys posing in uniform, ready to go and fight Jerry, but in France people were leaving their homes, carrying their belongings in wheelbarrows and handcarts. There were more snakes than ladders, Sarah thought.

'German Measle,' some of the children called her at school, the bullying boys. 'Slimy German Measle. Go back where you belong! We don't want you here.'

But I don't belong anywhere, Sarah thought, not now. Not in Germany, not in England. Only at Shoe Lane, where they never call me German or Measle, where I'm just Sarah or Lovey.

And now Dunkirk. The advancing German army was the hugest snake of all, obscenely fat. It had gulped and swallowed great bites of the British army, and sent the rest slithering and sliding all the way back to England. Sarah had seen a map in the newspaper with muscular black arrows snaking their way across France, pushing the feebler English arrows as far as the sea and then into it. The little ships had flocked to the rescue, to fetch soldiers from the Dunkirk beaches. Sarah knew that the sea was vast and green, but on the map it was a thin strip, so narrow between Dunkirk and Dover that it looked as if the German army could take one easy step across to England. The little pleasure boats and launches were like children's toys that had strayed into a war, the wireless said, and there were tales of heroism, of pluck, of last-minute rescue. The little boats were like frail matchstick ladders for the lucky few to cling to, escaping from the greedy German snakes.

And Rachel's ladder to safety had taken her to France and now to danger. She was somewhere among the black snakes that got fatter and fatter as they stretched. What would happen to her now?

Only time will tell, Auntie Enid said. We must pray for her, and for Mutti and Vati. Hope and pray that God will keep them safe. Maybe it isn't as bad as we think.

Heidi clambered out of her chair. There was only one of them, a woman, in black uniform. The bell had rung and straight away that silly girl had opened the door instead of bolting it, and had let her come in. Heidi expected more of them to follow, like last time, but the policewoman – hardly more than a teenager, she looked – was on her own. She stood there smiling. A trick, it would be.

Quick, hide! Heidi ducked behind her chair, clutching its velvet back. 'I told you!' she shouted at the girl. 'Told you to bolt the door, only you wouldn't listen! Don't let them come in! Shut them out!'

And now Rachel was here too, with a tray of tea, staring. She should have got away sooner, found somewhere to hide. It wasn't safe here.

'For Christ's sake, Gran!' said the blonde girl, the moody one.

'Please don't be alarmed, Mrs – Mrs Craig?' The policewoman came round the side of the chair and held out a hand, pretending to be friendly.

'No,' said Heidi, backing up against the sideboard. 'No!'

'You won't get any sense out of her,' said the girl. 'Not when she's in this mood. She's our grandmother, staying with us. Unfortunately.'

Rachel was scared, Heidi could see she was, but she put the tray down on the coffee table. 'Come on, Gran! It's all right – nothing to be worried about. Sit down, come on, sit back here.' She patted the seat of the chair, and picked up the knitting from the floor.

Now Heidi stood in confusion. It wasn't Rachel after all, her name was something else, and she was the kinder one. Gripping the chair-back, Heidi made her way round it and sat down carefully, her eyes fixed on the pretty face of the policewoman, who smiled back. Why had they sent a young girl round, a girl on her own, instead of the usual gang of thugs? She wasn't so stupid that she couldn't recognize a trick when she saw one.

'Please, have a seat. Would you like some tea?' the Rachel-girl asked the policewoman. Tea! Offering tea now!

'Thanks, Hilly, that'd be lovely.' The police girl sat on the sofa.

Hilly, yes, of course I know that name, Heidi thought, but I do wish she wouldn't keep pretending to be Rachel. It's not fair. And you can't trust anyone – why was she being nice to the policewoman, inviting her to stay? The two of them, those two strong girls, they should have bundled her out into the street and bolted the door behind her.

'I'm so sorry to have startled you,' the police girl said, still smiling. 'Mrs Craig, is it?'

'Mrs Craig's not here,' Heidi said loudly. 'She'll be back soon and then you'll be out on your ear. Barging in here!'

The blonde girl made a snorting noise. 'She thinks you want Mum,' she said. 'Gran's name's Richardson, not Craig.'

Heidi glared. 'Heidi Thornton. My name's Heidi Thornton. Heidi. Thornton. Don't you try to tell me what my name is!'

The policewoman looked at her and nodded. 'Thank you. Heidi – what a lovely name – like the story! I loved that when I was little, but I've never met anyone called Heidi before. Is it all right if I call you Heidi, then?'

'Heidi,' said Heidi, clutching the arms of her arm-chair. 'Heidi.' She had the feeling that her words were coming out much more loudly than she meant.

'Thornton was her name before she was married,' said Hilly. 'It's Richardson now.'

Married? thought Heidi, her mind blurring. Yes, I suppose I must be married. Where is he, where's Ken? He ought to be here.

'Actually, Heidi,' said the policewoman, 'it's your granddaughter I've come to see.' She looked at the younger girl. 'You're Zoë, are you?'

'Yeah?' said Zoë, with a *what's-it-to-you* lift of her chin.

'Is your mum or dad at home?'

'No!' Heidi shouted. 'It's no use looking for them – they're dead!'

Everyone turned and stared at her.

'No, no, Gran!' said the Hilly girl. 'You're getting confused again. Mum's upstairs in the shower, and I think Dad's playing squash,' she told the police-woman.

But now a strange sound was coming out of Heidi's head, and they were all gawping at her again. 'They *are* dead!' she wailed. Her mouth twisted and tears blurred her eyes. 'You don't know! They're dead and I'll never see them again! They shouldn't have sent me away—'

They were all talking at once. 'No, Gran, no one's sending you away—'

'Oh dear, I'm so sorry, I had no idea—'

'Take no notice, she's like this half the time, no one's got the faintest idea what she's on about—'

'What's going on?'

Heidi blinked, and brushed tears from her eyes. She wondered why she was crying; all this noise and fuss had pushed it out of her head. But now Rose was here in the doorway, dressed for some reason in a white dressing gown though surely it was late after-noon. Rose would know what to do.

'Oh, Rose dear, there you are,' Heidi said. 'It's lucky you've come, but why aren't you dressed yet? We seem to have got ourselves in a bit of a muddle – perhaps you can sort it out. This young lady's looking for Mrs Craig. Do we know a Mrs Craig? This is my daughter, Rose,' she told the policewoman. 'Now, what was it you wanted?' She picked up her knitting and started a new row of ribbing: knit two, purl two.

And was this the truth? Could you tell, with Zoë? Hilly listened intently as Zoë answered WPC Jo's questions.

The members of Doppelgänger had intended to have a band practice in the garage of Tuck's house in Radford Road, where he lived with his older brother; Zoë and Grant had got there at about eight, having met earlier in town. Clyde and Oz were late, and Grant realized that he'd left the sample CDs at home, so he and Zoë had gone on the motorbike to fetch them. Arriving at Grant's house in Duston, they had found it empty, his parents out, and had stayed there a while (Zoë glossed over this. 'Listening to music, just messing around,' was her phrasing; if WPC Jo guessed, she chose not to pursue it). When they got back to Tuck's, they found the door on the latch and a note on the kitchen table saying that the others had got fed up waiting and gone out for lager and a takeaway. It must have been just after ten, Zoë thought, when they came back with the Chinese food. No, they said nothing about any incident in town. No, they didn't look as if they'd been fighting.

'And the names of these boys?' WPC Jo's pen was poised.

'I don't know their real names. Just Tuck and Clyde and Oz.'

'But you do know the address? The house where Tuck lives with his brother? Radford Road, you said?'

'Number ten,' Zoë said sulkily. 'But that might be wrong.'

'And Grant, your boyfriend? You must know his surname?'

'Griffiths. Grant Griffiths. But he wasn't even there, I've told you – he was with me!'

'And his address?'

While this conversation was going on, Heidigran sat knitting calmly, with Oscar on her lap, but the girls' mother was intent and concerned, her eyes hardly leaving Zoë's face. When WPC Jo had left, she told Zoë: 'You're not to leave the house. Do you hear me? Dad'll be in soon and he'll be devastated to hear all this – as horrified as I am—'

'Hear *what*? Weren't you listening? It was nothing to do with me!'

'We don't like you hanging round with these people. I'm sure you've got more to tell us, and we'll hear it when Dad's here, we'll have a proper discussion. OK?'

'You've got nothing against them! Only because of what *she* said!' Zoë gave Hilly a venomous look. 'It's your fault that policewoman was here, isn't it? You grassed me up! What have you been saying?'

'All I told her,' Hilly said, 'was that I'd seen your friends hassling Saeed at the coffee bar. Don't tell me *that's* not true.'

Zoë flushed, and glanced edgily at her mother.

'I see,' said Rose, tight-lipped.

'– ninety-one, ninety-two,' said Heidigran, counting stitches. 'Can't we have the TV on?'

'For God's *sake*!' said Zoë.

Hilly decided it was time to retreat. She took refuge in the attic bedroom with a book, but was disturbed a few minutes later by Zoë clumping up the stairs.

'I hate you! I really hate you, d'you know that?'

'Oh, don't be so melodramatic!' Hilly said, not looking up.

'Melodramatic! You bring the police round here and make me shop my boyfriend, and you think it's melodramatic to complain! Can't you keep your mouth shut?'

'*That's* good, coming from you!'

'What have you got to go on? Come on, what makes you so sure it was them?'

'If it wasn't, there's no problem, is there?' Hilly said, knowing full well that the calmer she remained, the more Zoë would be infuriated. 'Grant wasn't even there. Which was only a bit of luck, as far as I can see, 'cos I bet he'd have thought it was a bit of a laugh, beating up Saeed. As for the others, bloody good job if they get arrested. Why d'you want to protect them?'

'I'm surprised you didn't make an announcement about the under-age sex as well! Did you forget? Want to go down and tell Mum? Run after your police-woman friend and put her right? I'm sure you can get Grant in trouble for that if you really try.'

Hilly turned a page.

'Now I've got to go through it all again, when Dad comes in! Thanks a lot!'

'You'll be all right,' Hilly said, looking up. 'You know how to get round Dad, don't you?'

'What's that supposed to mean?'

'Oh, you know – do your sweet little girly act, a bit of pouting and hair-flicking – be his cute little Zoesie—'

Zoë gave a humourless laugh. 'You're jealous!'

Stung into silence, Hilly remembered that Tessa had said the same thing – calling her jealous of Saeed and Reuben. Maybe I am, Hilly thought, staring at her book: jealous of everyone. Jealous, sour and crabby. Sometimes I don't much like myself.

'I'm sick of living here!' Zoë fumed, chucking clothes from her bed into a heap on the floor. 'Parents who don't trust me – Gran getting battier by the day – and to top it all, having to share my room with *you*. The last person in the world I want to be lumbered with, right now. My room, in case everyone's forgotten! God, I never get a minute's privacy in this house!'

'Me, on the other hand,' Hilly said, giving up, putting her book face down on the floor, 'I find it such a joy, your charming company. Your cheerful personality brightens every hour. Your consideration for others never fails to inspire me. Your radiant smiles—'

'Give it a rest!'

'Privacy, you want? Have it. I'm going out.'

'Thank God for that. Don't hurry back.'

Hilly turned at the stairs for one last attempt. 'There's no getting through to you, is there? What do

Grant's friends have to do – find another victim, kill someone, kick someone to death? Or would you find excuses even then? Just a game? Bit of a laugh?'

'You said you were going – get out! I can't stand the sight of you – scrawny, sexless cow!' Zoë hissed. 'Pathetic mummy's girl! Grungy saddo!'

'At least you could try to be original.' Hilly managed to have the last word, but found, going downstairs, that she was trembling.

Reuben. She had to talk to Reuben, tell him what had happened.

Her mobile was in the bag she'd dumped by the front door; she switched on, selected Reuben's number, but the only answer was voice-mail. 'Where are you? Give me a ring?' she asked it. Was he still at the hospital? She looked at her watch; it was a bit late to go there.

'I'm glad you've come back,' said Heidigran, through the open door to the front room. 'Play the piano for me, would you? I love to hear you play.'

Hilly remembered the *Für Elise* music Reuben had given her earlier; it was on the hall floor, under her bag. Was that really only today? She felt as if a week's worth had happened since this morning.

'For a few minutes, then, Gran,' she conceded. Playing the piano would be a soothing thing to do; or rather, it would produce its own frustrations, to push away the more pressing ones that nagged and nudged at her. She opened the book at *Für Elise*, did a few finger-limbering exercises and began to play. Only the opening, Reuben had said; concentrate on that and see if you can do it smoothly. Behind her halting notes, Hilly heard the music as it ought to be: simple, haunting.

After a few tries, she turned to see Gran sitting alertly on the edge of her chair, watching.

'Do you know this, Gran? Lovely, isn't it, if only I could play it properly?'

'Play the rest,' Gran commanded. 'The whole thing.'

'I can't, sorry! Wish I could.'

'Play the rest. The whole thing.'

'It's best if I learn the beginning first. It gets much harder after this.'

'Play the rest. The whole thing.'

'Gran, you've said that twice already.' Hilly went back to the beginning. Left hand only; she could manage that, if she concentrated hard. Right hand only, ditto. Maybe eventually she'd be able to put them together without her mind going blank. Out in the hall, her mobile rang.

'What's that?' said Gran. 'Is it the police again?'

It was Reuben. 'Hi! I'm at the hospital – they're letting Saeed go home. Rashid's coming for him in about fifteen minutes. Want to come?'

Copying Reuben, Hilly took off her shoes at the door, adding them to a row left by various family members. The Anwars lived in Weston Favell, on the east side of town; their house, a brick semi almost identical to the one Hilly lived in, was plushly furnished, with lots of midnight-blue upholstery and velvet cushions, and a framed Arabic text on the wall which Hilly assumed was taken from the Koran. Besides his parents and Rashid, there was an uncle, aunt and two young cousins, who apparently lived in the same road. Hilly and Reuben were welcomed warmly; a tray of sweet pastries was brought out from the kitchen, and coffee served in tiny, elegant cups. Saeed, still rather embarrassed, occupied centre stage on the sofa. Hilly felt rather impressed by the family's determination to make a celebration out of something as awful as a racist attack.

'We'd better go,' said Reuben, when Saeed had tired of the attention and looked on the point of falling asleep.

'It's lovely to see you both,' said Saeed's mother. 'Please come again, won't you?'

Rashid jingled his car keys. 'I'll take you.'

'Please!' Mrs Anwar raised a hand as Hilly began to say that she could easily get the bus. 'It's nearly dark, and I'd much rather you were seen safely to your doors. And besides, here is Rashid, eager to show off his new toy.'

'That's right,' said Rashid. 'I'm like a big kid.'

They wouldn't be so kind, Hilly thought, putting on her shoes by the front door, if they knew about Zoë. When she could speak to Saeed without his family around, she would tell him about WPC Jo and Zoë's statement, but not now. She followed Reuben and Rashid out to the car that stood in the driveway. Whether or not it called for special admiration, she had no idea.

'Where do you both live?' asked Rashid when they were all in and belted, Hilly in the front, Reuben in the back. 'Who shall I drop off first?'

Rose and the dad – G – G – no, gone again – had the television on, but Heidi couldn't concentrate. Things kept playing themselves in her head, she wasn't sure what; thoughts, memories or the TV. Fragments that came from nowhere, bits of nonsense. She had knitted and knitted until her fingers were stiff and bent. She held up the neat rows and saw that it was another sleeve, but she'd already done two, she was sure. She rummaged in her bag, took out the other pieces – yes, there were two of them; how could she have been so silly? – and smoothed them over her knees. Funny sort of pullover it was going to be, with three sleeves! She laughed, and turned it into a cough.

Unravel it all, she could do that, the sleeve she'd just knitted, but then the wool would get into a tangle if she wasn't careful. And she'd have to work out what she needed to knit instead. What did a jumper need? She frowned, puzzling over it. A front. A back. And two sleeves. Had she done the front and the back? Or was that years and years ago? That girl Hilly would help her, but she'd gone out when the phone rang. The other one had had a row with her mum and dad, a real humdinger that had left Rose in tears and the dad tensed with anger, and stomped off upstairs. The language that came out of her mouth! Heidi was amazed she even knew such words, let alone used them to shout at her parents. After she'd gone,

Rose and the man had settled down in front of the television as if nothing had happened.

Heidi kept glancing at the piano. Stuffing the knitted sleeves back in the bag, she got up and opened the lid. She sat carefully on the stool, running a finger along the white keys, too gently to make a sound. Rose and the man were on the sofa, both of them half-asleep; they didn't notice her.

It was funny how she still knew which note to start on, after all those years. She could remember that bit. The Hilly girl had been playing it earlier.

E D# E, she tried. She remembered their names. That sounded right. E D# E again, and then the rest followed: D# E B D# – no, the ordinary note this time, not the black one. Start again. Concentrating hard, she played the whole opening phrase without a mistake. Now it was time for Rachel to come in with the left hand. She looked at the lower notes, not knowing which ones were involved.

'Mm?' said Rose, propped sleepily on the sofa. She sat upright. 'Mum? Is that you playing? I thought it was Hilly. I never knew you could play!'

'Not really,' said Heidi. 'Only this.'

'Isn't that the tune Hilly was practising, before she went out?'

'*Für . . . Für . . .*' Heidi tried. She moved along the stool and patted it with her left hand, for Rachel to sit down. 'You come and play!'

'But Mum, you know I can't.'

'Come and play. Play the whole thing. Play all of it.'

'I haven't a clue how to. Wait till Hilly comes back.'

'Come and play. Play the whole thing.'

'*Mum—*'

I'm doing it again, Heidi thought, seeing Rose's gesture of exasperation, hearing herself asking the same question again and again. I hate the way that happens! I don't know I'm doing it and then I see them get annoyed, and I realize. Like a stuck record, I must be.

'Sorry! Sorry!' she said. 'I don't do it on purpose, you know.'

'I know, Mum,' said Rose. 'I know you don't. I didn't mean to be irritable.'

'Him, then,' Heidi said, pointing. 'That man there. Tell him to come and play. Play the whole thing.'

'No, Gavin can't play either, Mum. We're useless, aren't we?'

'You're unkind to me, do you know that?' Heidi's eyes filled with tears. 'If you cared about me at all, you'd do a simple little thing like that for me. It's always the same. I'm just a nuisance, aren't I? Why won't you let me go home?'

'Mum, of course you're not a nuisance. Come and sit down, and I'll make you some hot chocolate. Would you like that?'

'All right, all right! You don't have to treat me like a child, you know,' Heidi said, resisting Rose's attempts to lead her back to her chair. Then, in triumph: '*Für Elise!* That's what it was. Play it for me now! We used to play it together, you know.'

'Who did?'

'Me and Rachel,' said Heidi. A key turned in the front door; someone was in the hall, and a car pulling away outside. 'I hope it's not that policewoman again,' she told Rose. 'You didn't give her a key, did you? You must bolt the door.'

'No, it's only Hilly,' said the man. 'Hello, love! Was that a car outside? Did Reuben's dad bring you home?'

'No, it was Saeed's brother,' said the Hilly girl.

She looks pleased with herself, Heidi thought. Like that other one, the blonde one. Like a smug kitten, that young madam is. Altogether too full of herself. Heading for trouble.

'She wants her bottom smacked.' Everyone stared at her; she was surprised to realize that she had spoken out loud. 'The way she talks,' she explained. 'You shouldn't let her get away with it.'

'For goodness' sake, Hilly, sit down and play that piano tune for Gran,' said Rose. 'Then perhaps we can all have a minute's peace.'

'Where's my hot chocolate?' said Heidi. 'You promised me hot chocolate!'

Chapter Seventeen

Window Dressing

Three youths have been charged in
connection with a brutal attack on a
17-year-old boy close to the town centre
on Saturday night. The victim, from
Weston Favell, was admitted to hospital,
suffering from concussion, abrasions and
bruised ribs. Police say the attack was
racially motivated.

Chronicle and Echo

The shop window was Hilly's special pride. The first
time she had arranged it was when Velma had been ill;
Jean, the manager, was impressed, and had made it
one of Hilly's regular jobs. An eye-catching window display would bring customers in to browse, and most
browsers bought something, however small: if not
second-hand clothes it would be books or candles, gifts
or cards, pens. Some would pick up an Oxfam leaflet or
magazine, or put a few coins in the collecting box.

There were two mannequins in the window – both female, impossibly slender, with bland, haughty faces. Hilly's aim was that whatever garments they wore should sell within two days. One week she would dress them in party clothes; the next in streetwear, or in formal suits. Often she organized it all around one colour. Today's starting point was a long purple dress with embroidery round the hem and neck, which she would have coveted for herself if it hadn't been three sizes too large. She assembled a range of complementary garments: a white voile overshirt, a silky scarf in purples and blues, a beaded bag; for the other mannequin, a batik skirt, denim jacket and crochet hat. The dress and the jacket, she was sure, would sell by closing time, so she chose substitute garments to put ready. Now the rest of the window space. Cushions and mats, indigo, blue and white. Jugs and pots, a few draped scarves. Not bad, she thought, assessing the effect from outside.

Now books. Most of the books donated to the shop were fiction – romances, thrillers and children's books – but every so often someone would clear out a whole houseful, and bring in boxes and boxes of old hardbacks, a collection built up over years. Many of these were unsaleable and would end up being pulped, but it was worth looking through carefully. A batch that had arrived yesterday was piled in boxes in the storeroom at the back. Sorting, Hilly found illustrated art books, in good condition, with colour plates: the Impressionists, the Pre-Raphaelites, Wassily Kandinsky. Those would sell, for sure; she priced them and arranged them, open at the plates that best suited her colour scheme, in the front of the window.

'You going for lunch, Hilly?' called Velma.

'Just finish this first.'

It usually meant someone had died, when a whole private library was boxed up and brought in. *Reader's Digests*, book club special editions, gardening books, cookery, fiction, out-of-date reference books, everything. Jean usually looked through to see if there was anything valuable, and took stuff weekly to the antiquarian bookseller in Wellingborough Road. Most of the rest was worth only a pound or two, if it happened to catch the attention of a browsing customer. It was so sad, Hilly always thought, when a house was dismantled: a life reduced to jumble, strangers picking over the remains. Objects lost their meanings, stripped of context. A book lovingly inscribed as a birthday gift ended up in a recycling skip; a cherished photograph was worth less than its frame.

Eventually, Heidigran's house would have to be sold and cleared. There was no point keeping it on; it was a responsibility they could do without. But still no decision had been made, and Hilly had heard many conversations that went back and forth like tennis, her father and her mother, getting nowhere:

'Can't that what's-her-name, Josie, come round more often?'

'Yes, but she can't give twenty-four-hour support, can she?'

'What, then? Are we going on like this for ever?'

'What's the alternative? Have you got a magic wand?'

'Come on, love. You know what they say at your Alzheimer's group – you've got to find a workable solution that doesn't leave you worn to a frazzle and still feeling guilty. There are residential homes. Good ones. Bob's mother's in the one in Rushden, and he says—'

'No! I promised not to put her in a home.'

'Maybe you shouldn't have promised! Not when it affects all of us. You, most of all. Look at you, you're exhausted.'

'I *know* I'm exhausted! But I can't go back on it now. Who are we thinking of, here?'

'Your mum, obviously. But we've got to think of ourselves, too. And the girls. All of us.'

'A promise is a promise!'

Mum, Hilly thought, tweaking a scarf, draping a shoulder bag, can be just as obstinate as Heidigran. A promise is a promise: end of conversation. And she can't really be blamed for that. What was she supposed to say to Heidigran, otherwise? I was lying when I promised? You've turned out to be too much of a nuisance? We can't be bothered with you, now you're old?

Meanwhile, Hilly and Zoë were in a state of cold war: avoiding each other, maintaining a hostile silence, staggering their going to bed and getting up so that there was no need to speak. The chill in their attic bedroom was enough to form icicles on the rafters. Hilly couldn't suppress the thought that if

Heidigran went into a home she could have her own bedroom back, and her privacy. By now it seemed a long-ago luxury that she shouldn't have taken for granted.

She climbed between the plywood screens that divided the window from the shop, stepped down between the tie-rack and the trays of jewellery, and found herself face to face with Saeed's brother Rashid.

'Oh!'

'Saw you and tapped on the window,' he said, 'but you looked as if you were miles away.'

'Sorry, I – are you, I mean what are you—?'

'Just wandering about, really. Is it lunch time? What do you do?'

'For lunch?' Hilly looked at her watch. 'Sandwich in the back room, usually. But today I'm going to the library.'

'Shall we go together? I'm going that way.'

'OK,' Hilly said. She could see Jean and Velma looking at Rashid with keen interest, the way she'd noticed some middle-aged women did stare at attractive young men: practically goggling. Boyfriend? they were clearly speculating. I wish, Hilly thought, aware of a small warmth of pleasure that had entered the shop with Rashid and lodged itself somewhere in her chest. 'I'll just put these bits and pieces away first.'

'Your last week?' said Rashid, out on the street.

'That's right. I'm back at school tomorrow.' Hilly noticed that the magazine he held rolled in one hand was *The Big Issue*; there was usually someone selling them outside Waterstone's. Rashid wasn't the sort of person to sneer at her for working in an Oxfam shop. 'How's Saeed?' she asked. 'I don't suppose he'll be at college this week?'

'He's not too bad, thanks – no, rest at home till at least the weekend, the doctor said. But we've just heard from the police that three people have been charged – one with assault, two with GBH.'

'Oh?' Hilly said cautiously. 'Are they in custody?'

'They go to the magistrates' court tomorrow.'

'Will Saeed have to appear in court, when the case comes up?'

'That's what we've been talking about at home. There can't be a conviction unless he gives evidence. But then there's the fear of reprisals. That's how they get away with it, gangs like that. They know people are afraid to make a stand.'

'So do you think he should?' Hilly remembered what Saeed had told her and Reuben – that one of the attackers had threatened him with: *We know where you live.* What must that feel like? Going harmlessly about your business, to know you were being watched, targeted?

'I would, I think,' said Rashid. 'But I'm not Saeed. I don't live here. I don't work in town. I don't walk home alone at night.'

'At least the police know who they are now, those yobs.'

'I think they did before. They'd been pulled in, had verbal warnings, that sort of thing.'

'And what about your parents?' Hilly ventured. 'It must make them feel vulnerable, too.'

'They're upset, of course, very upset. That WPC's been round a couple of times to talk to them. And someone from Victim Support's coming tomorrow. There are people to call on,' said Rashid. 'All the same, I wish I wasn't leaving, just at the moment.'

'Leaving?'

'For Oxford, Friday. I've got a job there.'

Hilly tried not to let her disappointment show. 'What sort of job?'

'Painting, decorating. Doing up a whole house, with a mate of mine. Matt. His dad's bought the place, and Matt's going to live in it with some other students. I'm staying there too till I've made other plans.'

'It's daft, but I've never been to Oxford and done all the tourist stuff,' Hilly said. 'Even though it's only – what? Forty or fifty miles away?'

They had reached the Central Library. Hilly hesitated at the entrance, wondering whether Rashid was going to leave her here and go wherever he was going, but he looked at his watch and said, 'How long are you going to be? And what time do you have to be back? Is there time for a coffee and a sandwich somewhere?'

'Oh, I should think so. I'll be quick – I'm only getting a CD.'

Rashid came in with her and looked at the newspapers and magazines while she searched the racks of CDs. She was hoping to borrow a recording of *Für Elise*, but, finding only concertos and sonatas in the Beethoven section, she chose the 'Emperor' concerto instead.

'Are you another pianist?' said Rashid, taking

the CD while she put her library card back in her bag.

'No – well, I'm only a beginner. Reuben's the pianist. He's trying to teach me.'

'He seems a nice guy, Reuben. Have you known him long?'

'Oh yes, since we were at junior school. He's my best friend.'

'And,' said Rashid, as they emerged onto the busy pedestrian area, 'does Saeed get in the way of that?'

Hilly hesitated, not wanting to recall the feelings of resentment that had prickled her on the night of the concert. 'Maybe. Not sure, yet. It's all so new.'

'Settlers is on your way back,' said Rashid. 'Would that be OK?'

They sat at the only spare table, a small one in the corner, squeezing past shoppers and carrier bags to reach it. The weekday staff were strangers to Hilly: an unsmiling girl of photogenic appearance and an over-good-looking boy who couldn't resist checking himself in the wall mirror each time he passed with an order. Hilly saw Rashid noticing this, and they exchanged smiles.

'Will Saeed come back here?' Hilly asked.

'I hope so. If he doesn't, it's giving in to intimidation.'

Hilly thought about the time she had sat here and heard the thumping on the window, seen the leering faces and the crude gestures. Tuck and Pete, having a bit of fun. Marking out their victim. She told Rashid about this, and he nodded grimly.

'One good thing is, there's likely to be increased

police presence around the town. It's wrong if people are afraid to go out at night. But I don't think Saeed should walk through dark alleyways on his own.'

'Do you think,' Hilly said cautiously, 'it would be a good idea if Saeed came out about Reuben? Told your parents?'

'No,' he said emphatically. 'I don't.'

'Oh.' She felt rebuffed.

'I know you're probably thinking it's best to be open,' said Rashid. 'Not to have secrets.'

'Well – if he didn't have to worry about your parents finding out, or guessing – I mean, Reuben's told his mum and stepdad, and they're fine about it.'

'But it's different for us. Especially for my parents' generation, not so much for ours. It's just not acceptable to them, gay-ness. They see it as a wicked perversion. It'd be a disgrace to the family.'

'But they'll have to know sooner or later!'

'Will they?' Rashid looked at her steadily.

'How not? He can't tell lies all his life!'

'No, I mean . . .' Rashid's glance flicked down at the table, up again to her face. 'This thing with Reuben – it's fairly new, isn't it, like you said? It may not last.'

'I think it will, as far as Reuben's concerned. I mean, I know him. And if Saeed's gay, it'll be someone else if not Reuben.'

'But does he really know he's gay – Saeed, I mean? It's not as simple as people sometimes assume – one thing or the other. It could be just a temporary – infatuation. How sure is Reuben?'

'About himself? Oh, he's known for a couple of years at least. But, well, what would your parents *do*, if they found out about Saeed?'

Rashid frowned, shook his head. 'They'd be terribly upset, for a start. They'd put pressure on him. Stop him seeing Reuben, for sure. Keep him grounded.'

'So you think he should go on pretending?'

'I think he should wait till he's sure. Perhaps till he moves away from home. At least wait till he's eighteen, till he's more independent.'

'And you?' Hilly said. 'Do you think it's a disgrace to the family? Do you hope he'll settle down with a nice Muslim girl?'

'I'd prefer him not to be gay, yes. Not because I'm homophobic. I'm not as conservative as my parents. Not as Muslim, either. But Muslim enough not to want it for my brother. If he really *is* sure, then I'll have to accept it.'

'That sounds a bit grudging.'

'Maybe. But you don't see it the same way.'

'Obviously not,' said Hilly.

Rashid gave her one of his wry looks. 'I'd like Saeed to be happy. And that means not jumping feet first into trouble. But I can see you're not convinced.'

'I'm not sure. All I know is that Reuben was miles happier once his mum and stepdad knew, and stopped expecting him to have girlfriends. But then his parents aren't so – I mean they're more – more—'

'Tolerant,' said Rashid. 'I think that might be the word you're looking for.'

This *was* what Hilly meant, though she did not say so. The bored-looking girl brought their order, coffee and toasted sandwiches. Rashid passed the sugar bowl; Hilly shook her head. Sitting like this, facing him across the table, was providing a good opportunity to study him. Eyebrows, shapely and expressive. Intelligent dark eyes. A humorous mouth that smiled easily. Skin the colour of – she searched for a comparison. Strong coffee? Wet sand?

What would it be like to kiss him, be kissed by him? She found herself imagining it most powerfully, while he stirred his coffee; felt herself flushing. Oh, for goodness' sake – he's Saeed's brother! We're just having a conversation! But all the while they had been talking she had felt an unfamiliar sensation – of being flattered by his interest. He didn't have to come into the shop. Didn't have to suggest coming here. He must like me a bit. Mustn't he? But does he know—

'Look, Rashid,' she said. 'I think I'd better tell you about my sister.'

She talked, he listened. It took some while.

'I know,' he said when she had finished. 'Saeed told me.'

'Told you—?'

'About your sister and who she hangs out with. About them harassing him in here.'

'Ah.'

'Your sister,' said Rashid, 'sounds a right little cow. If you don't mind me saying so.'

'She's not really.' Hilly, who had called Zoë far

219

worse, felt a need to defend her. 'I mean, I'm not making excuses. This isn't really her. She's so besotted with this vile Grant character, she can't see what she's getting into.'

'And now?'

'Can she see now? I think so.' Hilly was less certain than she sounded. 'But we're not even on speaking terms, since I—' *Since I shopped her to WPC Jo,* was what she meant. But she did not want to say this to Rashid. 'Since,' she finished lamely.

He nodded, sipped his coffee. 'You put the police on to her, and she had to come up with names? Reuben guessed, when he heard your sister had made a statement.'

'Right. I grassed. Not good for sisterly harmony.'

'I imagine not.'

Hilly looked up at the clock. 'I ought to get back.'

'Yes, you ought,' said Rashid.

That's it, she thought. I've blown it. He's not likely to bother with a racist-fancier's sister, is he? I should have said more. Or maybe I should have said less. But I haven't told him anything he didn't already know, have I?

She stood up, reaching for the bill.

'I'll get this.' He snatched it from under her out-stretched fingers.

'Shall we split it?'

'No, let me.' He reached into the back pocket of his jeans. 'You can pay next time. I don't want to tread on any feminist principles.'

'Next time?'

'I'm hoping,' said Rashid, taking a note from his wallet, 'that there might be a next time?'

'What, in spite of my sister?'

Rashid looked at her. 'It's not your sister I'm interested in.'

'He said that?' said Tessa, on the phone. 'That's it, then. He's the one. Older than you, brainy, social conscience. What more can you want? Oh, and his own car—'

'You're leaving out the fact that he's about to move to Oxford. He'll meet all sorts of girls with social consciences and brains and looks as well. What hope have I got?'

'He wants to see you, doesn't he? Don't put yourself down. Is he as beautiful as Saeed, on top of everything else?'

'Fairly,' Hilly said, keeping a wary eye on the open door – phone calls were rarely uninterrupted. 'Well – he's one of those people you don't specially notice at first, you just think, He's OK, and then when you meet them again, and start to look properly, you think, Mmm, yes, he's lovely, why on earth haven't I thought so all along – d'you know what I mean?'

'I knew it!' said Tessa in triumph. 'You're in love.'

'Tess! I am not in love,' Hilly protested. 'Not after one cup of coffee.'

'*Two* cups of coffee! There was the one at the hospital. A hospital romance! Like something out of *Casualty*!'

'Can this be the girl who goes on about fish and bicycles?'

'Some bicycles are more interesting than others, obviously. So when are you seeing him again?'

'Sunday. We're going to do the Oxford tourist bit.'

'Dreaming spires? Punting on the river? And what does Reuben think of all this?'

'Er . . . Tessa, if you see Reuben before I do, don't say anything, OK?'

'What, you haven't told him? But Reuben knows what kind of conditioner you use and the exact date your next period's due. Why the secret?'

'It isn't a secret,' Hilly said uneasily. 'I just haven't told him yet, that's all.'

Chapter Eighteen

The Night of a Thousand Bombers

Meanwhile, [Sir Arthur] Harris was
impatient to test his techniques on a
major city. On May 30th, he assembled
every man and plane he could – including
half-trained crews and obsolete bombers –
and launched the R.A.F.'s first thousand-
bomber attack, against Cologne.
Reconnaissance reported that six hundred
acres of the city were devastated.

Angus Calder, *The People's War*

After more than two years of war, Sarah had almost
forgotten that there had ever been a time without it.
She had stopped expecting the war to end. It was the
way things were.

In the first few weeks it had seemed a bit like playing. There were trenches dug in the park and on the
big grass area called the Racecourse; people wore all
sorts of different uniforms and it seemed for a while

that being at war meant marching in the street and parading and holding inspections. Each week, the local paper had photographs: the Salvation Army, the Home Guard, the Women's Fire Service, all looking proud and self-conscious in their uniforms. There were underground shelters in the town, and lots of people built Anderson shelters in their back gardens. In Lansdowne Terrace and Shoe Lane, where the gardens were too small for Andersons, a line of brick shelters was built down the middle of the street.

At school, the children had to keep their gas masks with them always; there were gas practices and air-raid drills. More newcomers had arrived at the school, London children. They were called East Enders and they had a different way of talking from the Northampton accents Sarah had become used to. Miss Munson called them evacuees. With children newer than herself and marked out by the way they spoke, Sarah felt less conspicuous. I'm an evacuee too, she told herself. Not refugee. Evacuee sounded less pitiful, less hopeless; evacuees would, eventually, go back home. But do I want to go back home? Sarah wondered. This was home now: Northampton, and Shoe Lane, with Auntie Enid and Uncle Donald. Although she could remember what her own parents looked like, she could no longer recall their voices. Her ears were tuned to English.

Most of the boys at school were obsessed with aircraft. They pretended to be Spitfires in the playground; they fought off Messerschmitts, they engaged in furious dog-fights that invariably ended with the Messerschmitt plunging into the sea or bursting into flames. Often real aircraft were seen flying overhead. Lots of new airfields had been built around Northampton, Uncle Donald said, mostly for training. The main action was elsewhere. All through the first summer it had been farther south, in Kent and Sussex, the brave little Spitfires and Hurricanes fighting off the invaders. In autumn and winter the Luftwaffe changed its tactics, and bombed London. Coventry was bombed too, and Exeter, but mainly London. People spoke in shocked voices of the East End on fire, of St Paul's Cathedral rising above the flames. Would the Luftwaffe reduce the whole city to rubble? Then what?

'Your lot'll be here soon,' Frank Surman yelled at Sarah in the playground. 'We'll all have to speak Kraut.'

But if the Germans came here—

'They must not come! There would be another Kristallnacht, an English one,' Helga predicted. 'And we will be refugees again – no! It must not happen!'

Sarah knew now that Kristallnacht, the night of breaking glass, was the name for that night that loomed so horribly in her mind, the night the bad men had come into the flat and taken her father away. Sometimes still she had dreams about them, the men in black uniforms who had stomped up the stairs and stood there looking around with disdain. One of them had swept his arm along the mantelpiece, knocking all the ornaments to the floor, and while Mutti had cried out with indignation the men had only laughed.

Home, Sarah's home, where she had lived all her life, was suddenly as fragile as a doll's house, to be smashed by these cruel men for amusement. She had thought at the time that it was only her own home and those of her neighbours, but she knew now that it had been a terrible night of smashing and beating and burning. On that night, Helga had told her, the Jews of Germany knew that Herr Hitler and the Third Reich thought of them as less than human. 'To them we were rats. Vermin,' Helga said. 'That is all we were. But here we are people again.'

Sarah had been lucky. Her father had come home again, a few days later. She saw the change in him – he looked smaller, shrunken, with eyes that stared and jumped in his head. 'Where did you go? Where did they take you?' Sarah had pestered him, but all he would say was that it was a business matter. The SS had wanted to see him about a business matter. And a short while after, they had come for him a second time, wanting to do more business, and Sarah had never seen him again.

She understood now that Mutti had kept the truth from her, thinking she was too young. Where was Mutti now? Vati? Where was Rachel? Where was safety?

It wasn't in France, she knew that. The German army was there now, and France was an extension of Germany. Rachel's flight had not been far enough. Auntie Enid and Uncle Donald stopped talking about Rachel.

Sarah had decided to make herself invisible. Luckily, Sarah wasn't a name that drew attention to itself in England – unlike Helga. She worked hard at losing her German accent. She copied the local children's sayings, listened to the way they pronounced their words; seasoned her language with Cockney. She could make Auntie Enid and Uncle Donald laugh by coming out with an almost perfect bit of gor'blimey, overheard in the playground and practised in her bedroom.

Helga had gone up to the seniors now. Sarah had a new friend, a girl called Patsy in her own class, and although she saw Helga sometimes she no longer regarded her as her best friend. Helga was too Jewish, too German. 'Speak in German!' Helga urged, when Sarah obstinately spoke only English. 'We must speak German! Yes, it is the language of Herr Hitler, but it is also *our* language. How are we going to speak to our mothers and fathers when we see them again, if we no longer speak the same language?'

'Will we see them again? You said we wouldn't,' Sarah pointed out.

'We must hope. We must always hope. We must not abandon them. We must keep the faith.'

Sarah didn't know what faith was. To have faith meant to be disappointed.

Meanwhile there were the air-raid sirens and the bombings. 'Don't you worry. Northampton's not important enough for them to bother with,' Uncle Donald said confidently. 'I bet we'll hardly use those shelters.' But there were nights spent huddled with the neighbours in the narrow brick buildings, listening to the ominous pause before an explosion, and wondering how much nearer it could get before the whole of Shoe Lane was smashed to rubble.

Duston was hit, and a school in Rushden (a school! That provoked a thrill of could-have-been-me excitement, especially when the local paper reported that seven children had been killed) and St Andrew's Hospital partially demolished. In the summer there was great excitement when a Stirling bomber crashed in Gold Street – at night, fortunately – smashing several shop fronts and leaving a trail of debris. The pilot was killed, but the rest of the crew baled out successfully. Patsy's uncle, cycling home after his fire-watching shift, fractured a leg when he was blown sideways by the blast; amazingly, he was the only civilian casualty. 'Pity it weren't one of Jerry's kites,' grumbled the boys in Sarah's class. 'I'd like a bit off a Messerschmitt or a Dornier.'

Sarah wondered how all the boys were suddenly so expert in aircraft recognition. To her all aeroplanes were dangerous, especially if even Allied planes could plough without warning into town streets. She imagined the men who flew them – whether boys in blue or members of the more sinister Luftwaffe – as strong-jawed heroic types like the ones in the boys' comic books, until Philip Baines's brother came into school to give a talk, and stood in the assembly hall looking nervous and very young in his new uniform. He twisted his cap in his hands all the while he was talking, and had a slight stammer. By the end of his talk, Patsy was in love with him and said she was going to give all her pocket money to the Air Force Fund.

Uncle Donald spoke proudly of someone called Bomber Harris. 'He'll turn the tables on Jerry, wait and see if he don't. All these bombers aren't being built for nothing.'

First there were the Dam Busters. Then the Thousand Bomber Raid.

The target was Cologne. Köln. Home.

BOMBER COMMAND VICTORY, COLOGNE IN FLAMES, said the stands outside the newsagent's. THE NIGHT OF A THOUSAND BOMBERS.

Weeping inside, Sarah went to school exactly as usual. She said nothing to anyone, not even to Patsy. At playtime she went and cried secretly in the outside toilets, which smelled of wee and disinfectant. When she came back to the classroom she pretended that it was hay fever making her eyes red and her nose runny.

Cologne. Köln. Home. What hope was there for Mutti and Vati? Bullied by Hitler's SS, now threatened from the sky by the RAF. Sarah pictured the night sky full of bombers, patterning the darkness, wing-tip almost touching wing-tip. They would have dropped their bombs like spawning fish: deadly spawn that ignited fires and turned whole streets to rubble. How could anyone survive? She thought of her road, Lindenstrasse, named for its tall lime trees that filled the air with intoxicating scent in July. The lime flowers brought bees in such numbers that she liked to pretend the whole tree was humming. Once, she and Rachel had exclaimed over bees that lay drunk on the pavement, sated with nectar. She thought of the baker's shop in Königstrasse, where Frau Klemper handed over breakfast rolls still warm from the oven. She thought of the cathedral, the market with its gaily-coloured stalls, the school two streets from home which she had attended until the new law said that Jewish children must go to separate schools. What was left? Any of it? None of it?

'Oh, love.' Auntie Enid understood why Sarah was downcast, refusing to speak. 'Perhaps they're not in Cologne, your mum and dad. Perhaps they're somewhere else.'

Somewhere else. Not somewhere safe, because nowhere in Germany was safe. And nowhere in France was safe for Rachel.

We are refugees after all, Sarah thought, clutching a sodden hankie. All of us. Mutti, Vati, Rachel, me. Scattered in our different countries. Evacuees might go back, but not us. Where is there to go back to?

'We must never give up hope,' Helga said, with what was beginning to sound like obstinacy. 'We must keep the faith, and then the faith will keep us.'

Every time, though, every time Sarah admitted to the smallest stirring of hope, it was squashed by some new development, like a beetle under an SS boot. It was safer not to hope at all. Not to think.

The only indulgence she allowed herself was to look at the photographs kept in the drawer of her bedside table. Rachel. Rachel and Sarah in the garden. The smiling faces came from another life, one she might have dreamed about, filled with gardens and picnics and humming bees, and skies empty of bombers.

Chapter Nineteen

Looking for Rachel

Memory behaves strangely in the mind of
a person with Alzheimer's. Some may
seem to have lost their power of recall, but
just as frequently an Alzheimer's sufferer
may be quite overwhelmed by memories.

Denise Lombard, *Living with Alzheimer's*

'So how does it feel,' Rose said in the car, 'being in the
sixth form?'

'OK. Much the same as before, only it's nice to
have smaller classes and free periods,' said Hilly.

'Remind me to fill in that form for you when we
get in,' said Rose, 'about the history trip to Berlin.
That sounds fascinating, I must say.'

'Yes – it's ages to wait though, not till next
Easter.' Hilly waited for her mother to pull out at
the busy Sixfields roundabout before remarking, 'I
thought Dad wanted you to have a complete break
today? Go out and enjoy yourself. Get away from

everything at home. This isn't what he meant.'

'But it needs doing,' said her mother. 'I'll feel better if we've at least made a start. We can't put it off for ever.'

Making a start meant beginning to sort out Heidigran's house in Banbury; today was the first step, bagging up things for the Oxfam shop. Unwanted clothes, books, clutter. 'It'll make it easier,' said Rose, 'when we eventually do clear the place for selling, if we've already got rid of redundant stuff.'

There was a lot of money tied up in the house, Hilly knew – money that could, possibly, be spent on a bigger one for themselves, with enough bedrooms for everyone. But it wasn't simply a matter of house-room. With Zoë and Hilly back at school, their mother had to take almost all the responsibility of looking after Heidigran, fitting her own part-time work at the sports centre around everyone else's hours. The strain was beginning to show.

'Even though I seem to be dashing about all the time, trying to fit everything in,' she had told Hilly, 'I feel as if my whole life has slowed down to creeping pace. Creeping slowly towards the inevitable.'

She was referring, Hilly knew, to Heidigran's further decline and death. How long? How long are we talking about? Hilly wanted to ask, but it seemed callous – almost impatient, as if she were saying, *Come on, let's get on with it, if we must.* Heidigran's life was being measured out slowly, in cups of tea and rows of knitting, in trips to the shops or garden centre, in small treats and pleasures. She could not be left alone, and it was a blessing if she slept through the night without going downstairs to check the front door. Early on Wednesday morning, Rose, going to the bathroom, had checked Heidigran's room and found the bed empty. The front door stood wide open. In a panic, Rose roused the whole family to search the streets; Heidigran was brought back in state in the milkman's float, having been found in her nightgown and slippers three streets away. Now, the door was kept Chubb-locked from the inside, the key hidden where everyone but Heidigran knew where to find it. It felt uncomfortably like keeping her imprisoned.

Hilly looked out of the car window at bleached, late-summer fields, at a landscape patched into wheat, grass, wheat, stubble; at copses of trees not yet beginning to show the approach of autumn. 'Couldn't Heidigran go to stay with Uncle Charlie and Aunt Anita for a week or two?' she ventured, already knowing the answer; she had heard her parents discussing it.

'They've offered,' said Rose, 'but we think it would only unsettle her – moving off again, another house, another bedroom. And it's a burden for them.'

'It's a burden for you!'

'I know, but she's my mum. I can fit round her. Charlie and Anita both work full-time – they can't keep taking days off. You know that time in the garden centre, when Mum kept saying she wanted to go back to Charlie's? Do you know what he said, when I told him?'

'No, what?'

'They took her out to Bourton-on-the-Water one

afternoon, and she made a scene in a teashop – kept saying she wanted to be with me. "Why won't you let me go to Rose's? You know you don't really want me. I'll be much happier at Rose's." That sort of thing. Then when they got home she said what a lovely time she'd had.'

'It must be awful to be so confused.'

Rose pulled out to overtake a removal van. 'Yes, but you know – I think most of it washes over her. She says something one minute and then it's forgotten. *We're* the ones who remember everything. We're the ones who get upset.'

'But then she remembers things from years ago,' Hilly said, 'like Rachel playing the piano. Who do you think Rachel was?'

Her mother shrugged. 'Could be anyone. A friend from school?'

'In England or in Germany? Rachel could be a Jewish name. Do you think Rachel was a Jewish friend, who died?'

Rose shook her head. 'Could be. I've no way of knowing. She's never mentioned anything like that at all.'

'And if she had a friend who was Jewish,' said Hilly, 'what's made her decide she doesn't like Jewish people?'

Rose shook her head. They lapsed into silence for a few moments; then: 'I've never really understood,' Hilly said, 'why Heidigran came to England after the war. Wasn't that a bit odd? I know she was an orphan, but you'd have thought England was the last country a

German orphan would be sent to. And it must have been difficult for her, mustn't it? Having a German accent. Not speaking much English. Being from the enemy country. Did she talk much about it, when you were little?'

'Hardly ever,' said Rose. 'She always called Gran and Grandad her parents. Actually it was my dad who told me they weren't – till then I had no idea Mum was German. We were all together, I remember that – it was Mum's birthday tea. Dad let slip something about Mum being born in Cologne. She was furious, I remember that! I must have been about ten at the time. We were having birthday cake, but she wouldn't even speak to Dad, or answer our questions. Of course I tried to get it out of Dad later, but he'd clammed up too – only said Mum would tell us all she wanted us to know. He'd never talk about it again, it was always "Ask Mum". Later she did tell me – about her parents being killed in a bombing raid in Cologne – but in a way that meant she didn't want to talk about it. Losing both parents at such a young age – it was obviously a terrible shock, and I think she'd never really got over it. Gran and Grandad adopted her – well, you know that. I mean my gran and grandad Thornton. At least, I always called them Gran and Grandad, though of course they're no relation, really. She was Heidi Thornton before she married my dad. I think they were friends of the family from before the war, or distant relations, or something. I'm a bit vague about it myself.'

'It must be so odd for you, knowing next to

nothing about your German grandparents, your real ones.'

'Mm. As far as I was concerned, Gran and Grandad Thornton *were* my grandparents.'

As children, Hilly and Zoë had been fascinated by Heidigran's other identity in Germany. 'Who were you, Gran?' they would ask her. 'Tell us your German name.'

'Heidi Schmidt,' she would say, and explain that Schmidt was the same as Smith in English.

'So you were Heidi Schmidt, then Heidi Thornton, then Heidi Richardson when you married Grandad. What a lot of names!'

'I know,' Heidigran used to joke. 'You know, I sometimes have to stop and remind myself who I am!'

When Hilly was about seven, Gran had given her *Heidi* for her birthday – an illustrated version, with coloured pictures of mountain chalets, wild flowers and pretty goats. Heidi herself was round-cheeked and curly-haired, given to rushing around impulsively, consuming quantities of milk and goat's cheese, and gathering alpine flowers in her pinafore. Hilly had been enchanted.

'Did your mum and dad give you your name because of this Heidi, Gran?' she had asked.

'Yes, they did! Because I was always such a happy little girl, you know. Always cheerful and smiling.'

'But how did they know that, when you were still only a baby?' Hilly had objected.

'Oh, they knew.'

As a child, Hilly had confused Heidigran with

Heidi in the book to the extent that she thought her grandmother had actually lived in a mountain hut in the Alps with the fierce but loving Grandpa, and that her early years had been spent clambering around hilly slopes with Peter the goatherd.

'Haven't you got any photos of when you were a little girl?' seven-year-old Hilly demanded.

'No, no photos,' said Gran. 'Everything was lost in the bombing. Lost and left behind.'

Though she said nothing to her mother, Hilly knew that at some point in the day she was going to search through Heidigran's dressing table. Perhaps her mum was right, and there was no way of finding out who Rachel was – other than from Gran herself – but Hilly intended to try.

The air in the house felt undisturbed since her last visit, with Dad. A neighbour had piled a heap of post – mainly junk mail – on the hall table, that was all. Hilly thought of prospective buyers being shown round by an estate agent: 'It needs some redecoration, of course, but the rooms are all good-sized. The bathroom could do with modernizing . . .' She thought of a new family coming to view, young parents with a toddler, and an eye on the spare room for a nursery for an imminent baby. Heidigran had been taking up too much space here, space that could be exploited by a younger generation. 'An old lady lived here alone, but she couldn't cope any more,' said Hilly's imaginary estate agent. And the young couple would mentally strip the wallpaper as they looked around, seeing it all redone in aqua, or sage-green, or whatever was fashionable. 'Oh, but look at this!' they would say in the garden, deciding on the far corner for a child's swing and sandpit. Gran's garden, Hilly thought, was the saddest thing of all. For years Heidigran had weeded and tended and pruned, knowing all the plants by name; it was probably the best thing she had made, her work, her signature. Soon the plants she had nurtured for so long would be dug up and replaced with decking or gravel or paving, according to the recommendations of TV gardening programmes. And then where would Heidigran be? For she was surely not the neatly dressed woman who had got meekly into the back seat of Annagran's car this morning, to be taken by Dad and his mother to visit a local garden. The real Heidigran was lost somewhere in her own mind.

'I'll sort the post, first,' Rose said, 'then I've got to find all the paperwork to do with her bank accounts and phone bills – I should have sorted that out ages ago. Here, I've brought plenty of bin bags, and there's cardboard boxes in the boot. Are you going to start on the books?'

Hilly went upstairs, but not to the spare room where most of the books were shelved. Instead she went to her grandmother's bedroom. She sat on the upholstered stool in front of the dressing table, and looked at herself reflected three times in the angled mirrors. She did not hesitate for long enough to feel guilty, nor to allow a build-up to potential disappointment. But she held her breath as she reached into the bottom drawer, lifted out the underwear stacked inside, and took out the lavender-scented paper.

Nothing. The inside of the drawer was bare, grainy and unvarnished, unlike the lacquered veneer of the dressing table's outer surfaces. There was a coin, an old tenpenny piece, that was all.

Hilly replaced the drawer's contents, then sat for a moment, numbed by the room's silence.

Where would you expect to find a photograph? In a photograph album. Where was Heidigran's photograph album? On the shelf under the TV, downstairs. Hilly knew what was in there, or thought she knew. But how long since she had looked, properly looked? And she had not been alert to glimpses of Rachel, then.

She ran downstairs; there it was, underneath *Gardeners' World* magazine and an outdated copy of the *Radio Times*. Through the open door to the dining room she saw her mother sitting at the table with a pile of letters and catalogues. 'Oh dear,' Rose remarked, not looking up. 'It looks like we missed an appointment at the clinic. And her TV licence should have been renewed. Still, I suppose that hardly matters now.'

'No.' Surreptitiously Hilly slid the photograph album under her arm, and went back upstairs. She had no idea why she was being so furtive; she could easily have sat with her mother at the table and said, 'I'm looking through Gran's photos.' Instead she sat on the old-fashioned quilted bedspread that covered the bed – the big double bed that had once been

Heidigran's and Grandad's – and opened the album.

There they were, the pictures she knew would be there. With Heidigran's typical neatness, each was fixed in place on thick black paper, and captioned in white pen. The album began with Hilly's uncle, Charlie, as a baby; Heidigran was a pretty young woman, with permed wavy hair clipped back from her face. The infant Charlie kicked and beamed, became a bottom-heavy toddler, took his first steps, and was joined by a new white-swathed bundle, baby Rose. Hilly flicked through the familiar images to the blank pages at the end. There was nothing that pre-dated Charlie's birth, not one image. Not even a picture of Heidigran's and Grandad's wedding.

'There must be more,' Hilly muttered. Another album, an older one? She closed the book and stood, gazing around the room. More from frustration than for any other reason, she slid open the door of the cupboard space above Heidigran's wardrobe.

With a slithering rush, the contents poured out. She raised her arms to protect her face, and was almost knocked aside by a heavy torrent of paper and card. The separate pieces slid against her head and shoulders and arms, snagged in her hair; they cascaded to the floor, landing in an untidy heap.

Slowly, Hilly lowered her arms and looked incredulously at the pile at her feet. Photographs. Images and images, hundreds of them, black and white, colour, matt, shiny, faces, places, various sizes. A jumbled archive of family life.

She had been hoping for a single stray photograph! Overwhelmed by the unexpected choice, she got down on her knees to examine the lucky dip.

'Hilly? What was that?' Her mother's voice came up the stairs.

'Nothing!' Hilly called back.

But Rose was coming up; Hilly almost panicked. She considered sweeping all the photographs under the bed, but there was no time for that.

'What's going on?' said her mother. 'I thought you were in the spare room!'

'I – was looking for something,' Hilly faltered.

And now Rose was in the doorway, staring at the heap of photographs, then at Hilly. 'Where did you find all those?'

'In Gran's cupboard, up there.' Hilly indicated the slid-back door; Rose shook her head, doing a double-take.

'What, just like that? Loose, ready to tip out like an avalanche? Not in boxes or anything?'

Hilly nodded. They both knew how completely unlike Heidigran it was to shove things into cupboards, in disarray. All her other cupboards and drawers were meticulously neat, everything ordered. Hilly fetched the bedside chair and stood on it to peer inside the storage space. 'There are still more! More photos, and some boxes, at the back.' She pulled them out. 'Empty. See?' There were three of them: lidded, each labelled in Heidigran's writing: '*Photographs, various*'. They did not look capacious enough to hold the heap on the floor.

They looked at each other. 'She must have been

going through them for some reason,' said Rose. 'Recently, since she's – become ill. She must have got tired, or confused, or cross, to stuff them all back like that. I wonder what she was looking for?'

'And whether she found it?' With a sweep of her arm Hilly brushed out the remaining photographs, then climbed down and replaced the chair.

Kneeling, Rose picked up one picture, then another. 'What you still haven't explained,' she said, glancing at Hilly, 'is what you were doing.'

'No,' said Hilly.

'Go on, then!' Rose looked up at her, exasperated.

'I was looking for something. I was looking for Rachel.'

'Rachel again! I'm beginning to think Mum's not the only one with a bee in her bonnet about this mysterious Rachel!'

'I want to know! And I feel it's up to me to find out. *I'm* Rachel, according to Gran – you know how often she calls me Rachel! And Rachel played the piano. And I found a photograph, last time I was here – just one, with '*Rachel*' on the back.'

'You didn't tell me!'

'No, I . . .' Hilly went to the window and looked out. The Rachel quest was not her only secret. There was Rashid, and tomorrow. She hadn't yet said anything about that, either – not to her mother, nor to Reuben. What's the matter with me? she wondered. I'm not used to being devious. 'I don't really know why not.'

'Well,' said her mother, settling cross-legged on

the floor, 'we may as well sort through this lot, now you've side-tracked us.'

Hilly said nothing, reluctant to let her mother join her private quest. She began to pick up one photograph after another. There were holidays, Christmases, weddings, people she could not begin to recognize. 'Oh, look!' said Rose, from time to time. 'This is me in my horse-riding craze,' or, 'This was on holiday in Devon.' Once, 'This is me at about fifteen, look, when my hair was long. Don't you think I look like Zoë?'

'Yes,' Hilly agreed, seeing the almost uncanny resemblance; the haughty, I-want-my-own-way expression that made her wonder if her mother had been a right little pain, Zoë-style. 'You don't look like me. I don't look like you. But I don't look much like Dad, either.' She snatched up a photograph at random, beginning to indulge in a fantasy of being a changeling, an orphan, the child of unknown parents, the fruit of a mysterious liaison. But that was stupid. The evidence was there in Gran's album that she was the first-born of Rose and Gavin; she had just seen it. 'The person I look like is Rachel,' she said.

'Hilly! What's got into you, with this Rachel business?'

'Oh, nothing. What are we going to do with these? Shouldn't we be putting them in some sort of order?'

Rose threw up both hands. 'But how to start? I think we should throw away most of them, the ones we can't recognize. Just choose a few to keep.'

'But you can't throw photos away!'

'Start saying that and we'll never get rid of anything. We'll be just as cluttered as when we started! Look, we'll use Mum's boxes – divide them into three. Keep, throw out, undecided. Shall I do it while you start on the books? I have a feeling you're not going to be nearly ruthless enough.'

'No,' Hilly said sharply. 'No. You do the books. I'll do this.'

'Well, OK,' Rose said, getting to her feet. 'I'll fetch some bin bags.'

'And go easy on the books,' Hilly called after her.

She resumed her sorting, more urgently, looking for black-and-white, for the older pictures, the ones that were browned at the edges, or cracked or dog-eared, or concealed in a studio's paper slip-case. Heidigran and Grandad, young and smiling, hand-in-hand on a seaside promenade, in ridiculous clothes. Heidigran in her wedding dress, with a bridesmaid. An even younger Grandad – Hilly supposed it was him – in some sort of cadet's uniform. Those must be kept. Unknown people at another wedding; passport-style pictures of Grandad, a strip of them; young Rose gazing at a birthday cake lit with candles.

And two girls in a garden, having a picnic.

A tablecloth spread on a lawn; a low, spreading tree. A rather formal picnic it looked, with knives and forks set out on the spread cloth, food on plates. Hilly stared at the older of the two girls, her senses quickening. Rachel. She knew this was Rachel. The girl smiling out of the photograph was not wearing her glasses this time, and looked more relaxed than in the studio portrait; she was leaning on one hand,

244

her legs folded to one side, her feet in bar shoes. She wore a dark-coloured cardigan and a blouse with a small bow at the neck. Her hair, as before, was parted in the middle and plaited into neat coils over her ears.

Hilly turned over the photograph. '*Rachel und Sarah im Garten*' was written on the back in pencil, in – she thought – the same handwriting as the Rachel portrait. Rachel and Sarah in the garden. That gave it a time and a place. Germany (Cologne?), before or during the war. The other girl, the younger one, looked excited, as if she was only just managing to sit still for the camera. Her face was rounder than Rachel's, her hair a shade lighter, wavier. She sat cross-legged, showing white knickers.

Rachel and Sarah. Sisters? Hilly peered closer. It was possible; the younger girl's round cheeks and general chubbiness might have matured into something more like the slimmer Rachel. Jewish sisters? What had happened to them?

Had Heidigran been at the picnic?

Hilly put the photograph carefully aside. There might be more.

'Coffee, Hilly?' her mother yelled up the stairs.

'No, thanks,' Hilly shouted back.

She knew she was not going to show her mother what she had found. A careful search through the remaining photographs revealed nothing more; not another glimpse of Rachel, nothing that seemed to be from Germany.

What had Heidigran been looking for, when she'd

stuffed the photographs back in the cupboard? For Rachel, or for something else? Had she found it, or given up in frustration?

I'll see, Hilly thought, when I show her this. When? It's got to be when there's no one else around. Not tonight, then. But tomorrow is Rashid – she remembered with a rush of warmth and nervousness – so not then either.

She put the photograph into her patchwork bag and went downstairs.

'Mum,' she began, 'I forgot to say – it's all right if I'm out all day tomorrow, isn't it? With Tess?'

Annagran's car was parked outside the house. They were having tea in the garden, Dad and the two grandmothers.

'We had such a lovely time!' said Heidigran. 'Where did we go?'

'Coton Manor,' Annagran supplied.

'Yes, that was it. Wonderful gardens, Rose, I'm surprised you haven't been to see them! And I bought that *Geranium renardii* I've always wanted. It was a shame Ken couldn't come, though. He'd have loved it.'

The usually tireless Annagran looked somewhat frazzled. 'How was she?' asked Rose, a little later, when Heidigran had wandered off to water the hanging baskets.

Annagran flopped back in her garden chair. 'Rose, you must be a saint. I'm worn out after a few hours – and Gavin says this was one of her good days! *Ken, Ken,* it's been *Ken* non-stop. *Where is he? When's he coming? Will he know the way?* She even wanted to go back and wait at the entrance, so's he wouldn't miss us. I explained to her, Gavin explained – *No, Heidi, don't you remember, Ken died? Don't you remember the funeral?* She nodded and seemed to understand, and then straight away it was: *Where's Ken? When's Ken coming?*

Hilly remembered something, and went up to the attic. Zoë was there, lying face-up on the bed. No radio or CD playing, no Walkman.

'What's up with you?' Hilly said. 'Aren't you well?'

'Nothing,' said Zoë.

'Why don't you come down? We're all in the garden.'

'Don't want to.'

Sulking, Hilly thought: since WPC Jo's visit, Zoë had been grounded. The problem was that a grounded Zoë was never out of the house, and always where Hilly didn't want her to be. Giving up, she went to the section of cupboard space that was designated hers. She hid the Sarah and Rachel photograph under her sweaters, then went to the shoe box in which she kept cassettes and CDs.

'I've got bad news for you,' Zoë said tonelessly.

'Oh, what?'

'Those three blokes that were arrested – it wasn't Grant's friends. Nothing to do with them. They were at the Chinese takeaway at the exact time what's-his-face was being mugged, so there's no way it could have been them.'

'Oh—!'

'But you had to stick your oar in, naturally, and get me into all this trouble. And all that police hassle for my friends. You're not their favourite person, let me tell you.'

'Have you told Mum and Dad? It might make things better.'

'Not yet.'

Hilly faltered, 'Well, I'm—' *No!* She wasn't going to say she was sorry. How could she be sorry? She had only told WPC Jo what she'd seen at Settlers, and she was definite about that. Even if Zoë's friends weren't muggers, they were still unpleasant racists. She stared at Zoë, puzzled by her mood – instead of being triumphant, angry or self-righteous, as Hilly would have expected, she was lying back with her eyes closed.

'So what's wrong? Aren't you well?' Hilly repeated.

Zoë rolled over, turning her face away. 'I'm fine,' she mumbled. 'Leave me alone, for Christ's sake. You're not my favourite person, either.'

Hilly shrugged, and turned back to the cupboard, unable to remember for a moment what she'd been looking for. She pushed the new information to the back of her mind; she would think about the implications later. First, the cassette. She hadn't recorded over it, had she? – no, here it was, a C90 cassette with *Heidigran's War* written on the spine in her own handwriting.

The recording, Hilly and her grandmother, had been made two years ago for a GCSE History project. Two years ago was before Heidigran had Alzheimer's. The interview had not been a success. Heidigran hadn't wanted to do it: 'All that was years and years ago! Why drag it all up again? And my memory's so bad, you know . . .' She had said little that Hilly didn't already know from her history lessons or from TV documentaries, and none of it had gone into the project. But this time Hilly wanted to listen for a different reason. Heidigran was her project now.

She took her small radio/cassette player down to Heidigran's room, inserted the tape and pressed PLAY. Immediately her own voice spoke. (God, do I really sound like that? she thought, telling herself that it was two years ago, that she didn't now sound quite so high-pitched and girly.)

HILLY:	I'm talking to Mrs Heidi Richardson, my grandmother. She was born in Cologne in 1931, and lived there until the end of the war. Heidigran, what was it like in Cologne when you knew the war was coming?
HEIDIGRAN:	Oh, there were all sorts of preparations, you know. Sandbags everywhere, trenches being dug, shelters made. People made shelters in their back gardens.
HILLY:	Like the Anderson shelters over here?
HEIDIGRAN:	(*pause*): Andersons, that's right.
HILLY:	Things had been getting harder and harder for Jewish people in Germany for a few years before the

	war, hadn't they? Did you see any of that – did you have any Jewish friends?
HEIDIGRAN:	No.
HILLY:	None at all?
HEIDIGRAN:	No, there were no Jews living near us. If there were I didn't know them.
HILLY:	You were only a little girl at the time, but when the Jews were rounded up and taken away did you realize what was going on?
HEIDIGRAN:	No.
HILLY:	But at the end of the war you must have realized?
HEIDIGRAN:	No.
HILLY:	So when did you realize what had been happening – I mean the concentration camps?
HEIDIGRAN:	I can't remember. It was all so long ago.
HILLY:	All right, let's talk about something else. Was it like in England, with ration books?
HEIDIGRAN:	Rationing, that's right. I can remember there was an enormous queue for tomatoes at the market. Because tomatoes weren't rationed, you see.
HILLY:	What did you mainly eat, then?
HEIDIGRAN:	Mmm . . . I can't really remember. Not much of anything. We had to make do.

HILLY: What was it like when the bombing
            raids started? Did people panic?

HEIDIGRAN: No, there wasn't much panic.
            Because we weren't in the main
            bombing area, you see.

HILLY: Oh, but wasn't there the Thousand
            Bomber Raid on Cologne?

HEIDIGRAN: (*pause*): Yes. Yes, there was.

HILLY: So people didn't panic even then?
            It must have been terrifying.

HEIDIGRAN: I can't remember.

HILLY: (*hesitantly*): Can you remember the
            raid when your parents were killed?
            It wasn't that one, was it – it was
            later? Have I got that right?

HEIDIGRAN: No, I can't remember anything
            about it. (*Pause – laughs*) I'm not
            much use to you, am I? My memory's
            not what it was. I tell you one thing
            I *do* remember though. There was a
            bomber crashed in the street – right
            in the middle of town! Left a trail of
            devastation, it did.

HILLY: How awful! Were a lot of people
            killed?

HEIDIGRAN: No – only the pilot. The rest of the
            crew had baled out. And it was in a
            shopping area at night, so there
            weren't many people about. One
            man broke his leg, I remember that
            – got blown right off his bike!

HILLY: Was it a German bomber? Or one of ours? (*In confusion*) – I mean, what was it?

HEIDIGRAN: A Stirling. The boys at school were keen to get souvenirs – you know, bits of fuselage, whatever they could find. But they'd have preferred a Messerschmitt.

HILLY: (*pause*): Oh, why? I'd have thought German boys would be more excited to get bits off a British plane.

HEIDIGRAN: Oh – yes, yes. (*Laughs*) I'm getting myself confused. I expect I've got it all wrong.

HILLY: What was it like coming to England after the war, Gran? That must have been weird. Did you speak English?

HEIDIGRAN: You learn quickly as a child. You know, I've forgotten nearly all my German. If I were to go back there now I wouldn't be able to speak to anyone!

HILLY: I expect it'd come back to you. Haven't you ever been back to Germany?

HEIDIGRAN: No.

HILLY: Haven't you ever wanted to?

HEIDIGRAN: No.

HILLY: Because of your parents?
(*No answer*)

HILLY: How did you meet Grandad, er, Ken

Richardson?

HEIDIGRAN: Oh, Ken was one of the boys at my school. Horrible, he was at first! Teased me something rotten. Worse than teasing. But later on he was sorry for it and told me he'd only gone along with the other boys. Lovely-looking boy he was, really handsome. Even when he bullied me I thought that.

HILLY: Grandad bullied you?

HEIDIGRAN: Oh, not when we were married! Just when he was a boy at school. They were only having a bit of fun.

HILLY: Fun! What sort of fun? How did they bully you?

HEIDIGRAN: Called me names.

HILLY: What names?

HEIDIGRAN: German Measle. And . . .

HILLY: Mm?

HEIDIGRAN: No. Can't remember.

HILLY: So you forgave him?

HEIDIGRAN: Oh yes. Well you see I had a new life.

HILLY: How do you mean, Gran?

(*No answer*)

HILLY: Your new life in England? Is that what you mean?

HEIDIGRAN: (*laughs*): Sorry, love. I'm getting myself in a bit of a muddle, aren't I? Do you mind if we finish now?

Chapter Twenty

Heidi Thornton

... I expect you've seen it by now
on the newsreels or in the papers.
It was hell. And I'm not
exaggerating, believe me.
We could see these wire
enclosures, like some kind of
animals were kept there. And the
stink. It was ~~xxxxxx~~ carried on the wind.
Someone made a joke about it,
but that was the last joke we heard
for a long ~~time~~ while.
As we got closer we saw faces
behind the wire. I'll never forget
those faces, honest to God I won't.

The bodies were shrunk like
skeletons, they were skeletons with
faces.
You wouldn't have believed a human
being could be so starved and still
not be dead. Children and all,
little kids. Big eyes staring at us,
hands stretching. Help us. Help us.
Only who could save them from what
had already happened? Batesy threw up.
Jackson started raving, on and on, about,
'they deserve slow torture, whoever did this.'
And the rest of us was moving about
like in a trance. Like we was

in a nightmare we couldn't wake
up from. Couldn't believe what we
was seeing, just couldn't believe it.
And then there was the dead ones.
It was hell.

Letter from Eric Thornton to his parents, April 1945

Whatever happens now, Sarah thought, I needn't be afraid any more, because the worst has happened. The very worst I could ever have imagined. Nothing can ever be as bad as this.

Rachel, Mutti, Vati, gone. Swept up like leaves for a bonfire. The ashes blown across the plains of Germany.

'We don't *know*,' Auntie Enid kept saying, pleading with Sarah to believe her. 'We can't know for certain. We mustn't give up hope.'

But Sarah felt that hope had gone long ago. It would have been better not to hope. It was better not to be like Helga, who was crying, raging, weeping, praying, repeating the same useless phrases over and over again. Helga kept coming round to the house to be with Sarah. Sarah listened to her, but did not join in. She could not find tears, only a numbness in her mind that got in the way of thinking, and a dryness in her throat that stopped her from speaking.

For three whole days she did not speak at all. She stayed in her bedroom – Eric's room – and read *Heidi.* So simple it seemed now, Heidi's story! Heidi was good and cheerful and she lived in the mountains where the sun shone and the goats bleated and there was good bread and cheese to eat, and people were kind. Sometimes there was sadness in Heidi's story but there was no horror to compare with now. There was no Bergen-Belsen, no skeleton-dead and skeleton-living. Soon the war would be over and Eric would be coming home, bringing his horrible memories with him. Talking about them. Sarah did not want to hear.

Concentration camps, they were called. Buchenwald was the first; Bergen-Belsen a few days later. Then Auschwitz. Ravensbrück. Theresienstadt. Mauthausen. Treblinka. They were scattered over Germany and Poland. The armies – Russian, British, American – were 'liberating' them. Liberating the dead, and the living dead. To what? To drift back over the plains and cities like dead leaves, ghosts of themselves?

I would have been there too, Sarah thought. I was a Jew. That's where they would have taken me. With Mutti and Vati, with Rachel.

'We don't know,' said Auntie Enid. 'We don't know anything for certain. We can write letters – the Red Cross – they'll be trying to trace people.'

Sarah didn't answer. After three days of silence Auntie Enid thought she must be ill, and took her to the doctor, who stared down her throat and poked his stethoscope into her chest and swiped his hand in front of her eyes. There was nothing physically wrong with her, he said.

On the fourth day Sarah ripped all the pages out of her *Heidi* book, and tore them up into tiny pieces, which she sprinkled on the floor. They fell singly and in drifts, like leaves, pale leaves that could be blown and scattered on the wind.

'Oh, lovey!' said Auntie Enid, coming into the room with a mug of Ovaltine. Sarah was twelve now, nearly thirteen, but Auntie Enid still treated her like a little girl. 'What have you gone and done that for?' She stooped and picked up the cover, the empty hard cover; she turned it over and looked. 'It's *Heidi*! Your favourite!'

'I don't want it any more,' said Sarah. 'It's only a story for little children. And it's German. I don't want German.'

It was the first time she had spoken. Auntie Enid clucked and fussed, put a hand on her forehead. 'Feeling better now, lovey? Got your voice back? Won't you come down now and have something to eat? I've got a nice bit of fish for our tea.'

Sarah had hardly eaten for three days, but now she ate hungrily. She ate every last scrap of fish, and mopped her plate with a bread crust to get every oily smear. With food rationed, you were supposed to chew each mouthful slowly, so that you tricked your stomach into thinking it had had more; so that you got as much eating as possible from the meagre plateful in front of you. But today Sarah ate fast, greedily, her eyes on the spare crust of bread on the board in the middle of the table. Eating was a way of proving she was alive. Eating was a way of widening the gap between herself and the skeletal figures behind the wire.

'I'm an orphan now, aren't I?' she said matter-of-factly.

'But we don't *know*—'

'*I* do. I know. I haven't got a Mutti or a Vati any more. I've only got you. Will you adopt me?'

'Lovey, it's too early to talk about that. Much too early. If the time comes – well, we'll talk about it then.'

In May the war ended, at least the European part of the war. Hitler was dead. Dead, the Führer! He had shot himself in a bunker, and Eva Braun with him, when the various armies had converged on Berlin – the American, the Russians, the British. The Germans were defeated. Or perhaps Germany had defeated itself.

There was flag-waving and celebration, there were parties in the street, there were victory parades. It was like having ten birthdays rolled into one, Uncle Donald said: the best present possible. He and Auntie Enid were happy because they knew that, in time, Eric would come home. Sarah felt like someone who had sneaked her way into a party she had no right to attend. If she stayed around the edges, no one would notice her.

It was better than being like Helga. Helga was pale-faced and tearful. There was an air of reproach about her, of martyrdom. She will never let me forget, Sarah thought, as long as I am friends with her. She will never let me forget that I am German and Jewish. She wants to drag me back.

Sarah went into town with Patsy instead, and waved a Union Jack flag and went to the victory parade in the Market Square. Helga was too old now, anyway. She was sixteen and much taller than Sarah. She wore heeled shoes, and dresses nipped in at the waist to show her grown-up figure. She was courting Daniel, a boy she had met at the synagogue. As soon as the war was properly over, she said, she was going back to Germany to look for her parents.

Look? Look where? In the smoke from the chimneys? In the dust on the ground? In the ashes of the ovens?

Never. Never. I shall never go back, Sarah thought.

'When Auntie and Uncle adopt me properly, I shall have a new name,' she told Patsy, as they walked home from town.

'Sarah Thornton?' Patsy tried.

Sarah shook her head. 'No. I don't want Sarah any more. I want a completely new name.'

'Can you really choose your own name?' said Patsy, round-eyed. 'Does that mean you could have anything you like?'

They were overwhelmed by the enormity of choice. Sarah thought of trying on different names, like dresses, to see which she liked best. It had to be a happy name. Sarah Reubens was an announcement of Jewishness, a confession of a tragic past. It was time to leave all that behind. There was nothing left of it, anyway. Nearly all the houses they passed had V-signs or flags draped in their front windows. No more need for the shelters, the sirens, the gas masks. *The war's over. The war's over.* In town, people had been linking arms, singing the wartime songs as if they didn't want to let go of them. *Run, rabbit, run, rabbit, run, run, run. There'll be bluebirds over the white cliffs of Dover. Pack up your troubles in your old kit bag.*

'You could be Elizabeth! Or Margaret! Like one of the princesses!' suggested Patsy. 'Or Veronica! Bette! Loretta! Like a film star!'

It felt like being in a sweet shop, looking at the rows of jars and packets, with money to spend on anything she wanted. She would not hurry over the choosing, because for as long as she was undecided, the possibilities were limitless. Her new self would grow into a young lady like Helga, like the older girls Sarah saw about the town. She would wear lipstick and nylons; she would perm her hair. She would be a happy, untroubled person with a mum and dad at home. Could she call them Mum and Dad?

She could not sleep for the excitement of the victory celebrations and the new mood that was everywhere. Still awake in the early dawn, she heard birds singing outside and knew that her new name would be Heidi. Of course. She had been jealous of Heidi, but now she need be jealous no more. In her new post-war life she would be as happy and as lucky as Heidi had been. The name Heidi would account for the German accent she could not completely hide, but Heidi wasn't a Jewish name. No one need know.

'How can you?' said Helga, when Sarah/Heidi told her. 'How can you betray them like that? What are your parents going to say, if they come looking for you, and find you're ashamed of being Jewish? Of your Jewish name? You're betraying us all. Those of us who escaped, and all the hundreds of thousands who died!'

Helga had not got that quite right, Sarah/Heidi was to realize later. It was calculated that six million had died. But six million was such a huge figure that it was almost comforting in its meaninglessness. Her brain wasn't capable of imagining six million.

'That's stupid!' she told Helga. 'It's only a name.'

It was so typical of Rachel to come back to her in a dream, refusing to be locked in the past. Rachel was staring at her through a wire fence, her eyes pleading. She was pushing her hands through, stretching them towards Sarah. And the odd thing was that while everyone else behind the fence was pale and naked and skeletal, Rachel was the same as she always had been, her hair plaited into earphones, her clothes neat, her shoes polished. 'Go away!' Sarah shouted, though her throat was constricted in sleep. She had to force out the words. 'It's your own fault! Why didn't you get away properly?' Rachel said nothing, but her eyes were huge and dark, pulling Sarah dizzily, irresistibly towards her. Sarah tried to dig in her heels, but the dream-ground was soft and gripless. 'Stop it! Stop it!' she tried to yell. 'I told you before, I hate you! I hope I never see you again!'

Chapter Twenty-one

Secrets

I'm just a jealous guy.

John Lennon, song lyric

'So,' said Tessa, as she and Hilly boarded the bus on Monday morning. 'Tell me all!'

'You can have edited highlights.'

'No, everything,' Tessa insisted.

'What's this, the Spanish Inquisition?' said Hilly, just like Zoë. They made their way to their usual seats at the back.

'First things first.' Tessa settled herself comfortably. 'Is it Lurve?'

'Well – if I were twelve years old I'd be writing his name all over my pencil case.' Hilly was conscious of a silent and possibly eavesdropping woman in the seat in front. 'In fact I might, anyway—'

'So it *is*! You'll be hoarding all his text messages next. Come on! I want the unexpurgated version.'

Hilly gazed out of the window. Today was

appropriately wet-Mondayish, damp and drizzly, turning yesterday into a sunlit dream of crowds and privacy, of city streets and river solitude. It still felt like the after-effects of some hallucinatory high: she was smiling, floating on her thoughts. Because it must have been a hallucination, surely? This sort of thing didn't happen to her.

'I'm not telling the whole bus,' Hilly protested.

'Well, whisper then.' Tessa huddled close.

'OK. We went to an art gallery. And we went to the park. That was nice.'

The Museum of Modern Art – white walls, cool spaces and minimalist exhibits – could have been arranged for her satisfaction. The university park, where people threw balls for enthusiastic dogs and the river Cherwell rippled through a tunnel of willows, seemed to have made a special effort to present itself at its most appealing.

'Then what?'

'We bought sandwiches to eat by the river.'

'And after that?'

'It was so nice and warm, we stayed there talking for a long while.'

'Just talking?'

'You've got sex on the brain!'

'*Who's* got sex on the brain?' Tessa accused. 'Never mentioned the word, did I? So, come on, what did you find out about him?'

'Lots of things, thank you.'

'So, you talked in the park, then what? Did he entice you back to his place?' Tessa raised her eyebrows suggestively.

'No. Saw it though, the place where he's staying while he does the decorating job. We passed it on the way to the cinema.'

'What was the film? Did you sit in the back row?'

'It was *Les Enfants du Paradis*. French, with subtitles. In a nice little cinema in a back-street.'

'Ah, so that's what it's like going out with an intellectual. A bit different from the scrum at Sixfields and a bucket of popcorn. So, no snogging in the back row, then?'

'Tessa! It was more romantic than that.'

'Romantic – now we're getting somewhere. Come on, tell.'

'I can't. It's private.' In her imagination Hilly was back in the darkness of the cinema, all her senses tuned to Rashid beside her, and the small distance between them that might be bridged if only he would lean close or reach for her hand. It had been hard to concentrate on the film, to read the subtitles. After a while he did lean closer and said into her ear, 'It's one of my favourites, this. I must have seen it six times.' She had not known that it could be so *sexy*, the vibration of a low voice close to her ear, the stir and tickle of his breath. And she felt an obligation to like the film as much as he did, since he had chosen to share his favourite.

Tessa puffed out her breath. 'I give up! You're like a clam, you are. Are you seeing him again, then? Can you bear to reveal that much?'

'Yes,' said Hilly. 'Yes.'

'When? Where?' But the bus was slowing at the

school entrance; Tessa was getting to her feet. 'You're mean, you are! Told you all about being groped by Jason Wilde, didn't I?'

'More than I wanted to know, thanks!'

'And you get yourself a real *man*, and can't be bothered to tell me a single thing about him!'

'I will if you ring me later,' said Hilly, shouldering her bag.

They joined the drift into school. Kids in uniform, as well as sixth form not in uniform, were lingering in huddles, regardless of the thin rain.

'See you in the common room,' Tessa said. 'I've got to hand in my geography.' She hurried off, head down. Hilly saw Zoë, huddled by wet shrubbery, in animated conversation with Nadine. Having been silent and withdrawn all weekend – to judge by what little Hilly had seen of her – Zoë was making up for it now. Her face was serious, intent.

Hilly felt uneasy about the matter of Zoë's friends and the police, unable to think that she'd come out of it well. She had jumped to a conclusion – the wrong conclusion – and not only jumped, but acted on it by telling WPC Jo. If other people did that, she knew, in other circumstances, she'd be quick to label them prejudiced. Though she still had no reason to like Grant or the others, she had to admit that Zoë's accusations had some point.

But she didn't want to think about Zoë. She wanted to think about Rashid. The way he could look so darkly brooding one moment, then, when he smiled, so much at ease. The way he made her feel.

With him she had seemed transformed into a different person: not her quiet, cautious self, but someone buoyed up on a strange new confidence and hope. Never in her life had she felt so attractive, so *interesting*, as Rashid made her feel. She might have been the only girl in the whole of Oxford, so completely did he give his attention to her.

She found that she was smiling as she walked slowly up the driveway. She could retreat to yesterday whenever she wanted, smug inside herself.

What do I know?

That he's nineteen, nearly twenty.

He speaks three languages fluently and two passably.

He's working on his application to study medicine, preparing for interviews. There, in Oxford, if he's lucky and gets his first choice.

He likes cricket and motor-racing.

He's Muslim through habit ('and laziness') rather than through conviction. If he's at home on a Friday he goes to the mosque to please his father.

He chose grilled chicken sandwiches with salad, and mineral water, fizzy not still.

He was arrested by Israeli soldiers in a mass round-up of Palestinians and held for six hours in hot sun without food or water.

He's had one serious girlfriend, while he was at school; she met someone else at university, but they're still friends.

He knows a lot about films, not much about music.

And, she thought, unexpected, unbelievable, unsettling though it is: He likes me. Me! Why?

His expression had become serious when he told her about the West Bank, the Occupied Territories; about Israeli road blocks, tanks in the streets, curfews and restrictions. He talked about the massacre at the Jenin refugee camp, of houses bulldozed, helicopters firing on civilians, people bleeding to death while the Israeli soldiers refused to let ambulances near; of the rage that turned susceptible young Palestinians into suicide bombers. He had seen for himself how easy it was for young men to be drawn into the cycle of hatred and retribution. Again he spoke about his second cousin, killed in a mortar attack in the streets of Hebron; another cousin had been a member of one of the resistance groups. 'Didn't you want to stay there?' Hilly had ventured. He shook his head firmly. 'No. No. It'd be different if I'd been brought up there. It'd be too easy to get sucked in. To see the struggle for freedom as my whole purpose in life, the way so many do.' He was determined to study medicine, to return as a doctor, if at all; to pick up the pieces, not help in the destruction. But he had left the country with mixed feelings: glad to leave the bitterness and the suffering behind, but with a pull of guilt for returning to a life of freedom others couldn't share. 'And when I got back to England, the tabloids were all full of who'd won some stupid contest on TV.'

When he spoke like this, Hilly felt boringly inadequate, aware of the huge gulf between his experiences and hers. What could *she* know of any of

this, having spent all her life in Northampton?
Mentally she transplanted Rashid into scenes familiar
from the TV news: chaos and terror in a busy street,
people clustering round the wreckage of a car, angry
young men threatening revenge, relatives weeping.
She hardly knew what to say, what questions to ask.
What could he possibly see in her, with her comfortable middle-class life, her complete lack of
involvement in any political situation – let alone one
like this, that stirred the most passionate of feelings?
What must it be like to live in a country where any day
not scarred by violence must seem like an ominous
waiting for the next explosion?

'What about you?' he said. 'After college?'

She could only shrug and say that she didn't know
yet. 'Travel,' she added, as feebly as a Miss World
contestant. 'I'd like to travel.' And then, turning the
conversation back to him, 'I suppose that's one thing
about being a doctor. You could go anywhere you
wanted.'

The film, to her relief, was not dark or political,
but whimsical and charming and set in Paris. After
Rashid leaned close to speak into her ear, she lost
concentration altogether. All her senses were keenly
aware of his body, warm and breathing in the semi-
darkness, his foot close to hers, their shoulders just
touching. His hand, the one nearest her, was resting
loosely on his thigh. More than anything she wanted
to hold and stroke that hand. Why shouldn't I? she
thought. He wouldn't mind, I know he wouldn't. I
don't have to sit here passively, waiting. Oh, this is

laughable. Other people behave like this, think like this. Not me. Her hand seemed to be tingling with an electrical charge that any moment was going to make it reach out of its own accord, tangling her fingers with his; she was unable to think of anything else. He glanced at her, and in a moment their hands had moved together and were touching. His skin was warm and smooth, brushing hers. His fingertips and her fingertips moved gently, touching, exploring. Her whole self felt gathered and concentrated in one hand. Fingers moving against palm and knuckle and wrist. Fingers stroking, tickling, caressing.

Afterwards they had walked back to his car in the dusk, first discussing the film, then falling silent. They walked slightly apart, not touching; holding hands now, Hilly thought, would seem too complacent, too possessive. When they reached the parking place in a side-street, he came round to the passenger side. He stood looking at her. For a second she thought he was going to ask if he could kiss her, but he did not. His hesitation asked the question; her move towards him gave the answer.

Now, sidestepping a huddle of Year Nines who were obstructing the steps to the main entrance, Hilly felt stirred all over again from remembering. How different one kiss could be from another! Hilly's kissing encounters had been limited to the slobbery, tongue-thrusting embraces of boys her own age – experimental, meaning nothing. She could not have described this first kiss to Tess, though she recalled every detail. It had been a brushing of lips, soft, darting touches: experimental in a different way, a sampling of each other, an approach, each offering more if the other wanted to respond. Tentative, almost teasing.

Her mother had seen straight through the bluff and vagueness when Hilly arrived home. 'So,' she said, when Hilly came in, rather late; 'Tess has learned to drive now, has she?'

Hilly felt herself flushing: another kiss had just been exchanged in the car outside, and it had been hard to breeze straight in as if nothing unusual had happened. 'That wasn't Tessa. I've spent today with Rashid. Saeed's brother.'

There was a small but noticeable pause – a registering, a stiffening – before Rose spoke. Then: 'Oh? So why lie about it? That's Zoë's province. Why didn't you tell me the truth? I knew you were hiding something.'

Hilly still didn't know; nor did she know why, when Reuben phoned at morning break, she found herself preparing to lie again.

'Where've you been?' he demanded. 'I've hardly seen you the last few days!'

'Sorry! I've been busy all weekend. Look, why don't you come round this evening?'

Even then, when she and Reuben were together up in the attic, she could not bring herself to say it. 'I was with Rashid yesterday. And I'm seeing him again at the weekend.' A simple enough combination of words, but she could not get them past her lips. Not to Reuben.

As Zoë had been allowed to go round to Nadine's, they had the room to themselves. Reuben threw down his bag and lay on Hilly's bed, arms folded behind his head, gazing up at the skylight. 'I like this. Better view than your old room.'

'Only when Zoë's not here. When she is, the only view's of her sulky face. Course, she's got it in for me worse than ever, now.'

'Oh, since it came out about her yobby friends being in the clear?'

Hilly nodded. 'She thinks I grassed on them just to stir things up. Well, perhaps I shouldn't have done that, but I honestly thought . . . Now I think she'll be quite happy if they do me over, one dark night, to get their own back.'

Reuben raised his head. 'You serious?'

'Not really. It's not a nice feeling, though, that there are people out there with a grudge against me. Or to know they're not the only gang of racist yobs in town. Anyway, let's not talk about them.' Hilly picked up the cassette tape from her bedside table. 'I want you to listen to this. Remember I interviewed Gran two years ago for history? I played it again the other day. She says she didn't know any Jewish people. Says that more than once. But what I noticed this time was the way she says it, too quickly, like she's covering something up. See what you think.'

She slotted in the tape and pressed PLAY. Reuben closed his eyes while the two voices talked, and after a few moments Hilly thought he had fallen asleep. But when she clicked PAUSE, he said at once, 'Yeah, I see what you mean. She knows more than she's saying.'

'Knew *then* – that was two years ago. I wonder how much she still knows now?' Hilly pressed EJECT, but Reuben sat up and said, 'No, play the rest. There might be something else.'

'There isn't, nothing interesting. I listened the other day,' Hilly said, but she re-started the tape. Reuben sat up, elbows on knees, and listened intently.

'*Your new life in England? Is that what you mean?*' asked Hilly's voice from the cassette player, and Heidigran laughed. '*Sorry, love. I'm getting myself in a bit of a muddle, aren't I? Do you mind if we finish now?*'

'Getting herself in a muddle,' Hilly repeated, pressing STOP. 'That was two years ago. We didn't know, then, it was the start of the Big A. I mean, when do you know? Everyone gets confused sometimes.'

Reuben was frowning. 'There's something odd.'

'How d'you mean? About the fact that she hardly said anything at all?'

'You hear about that, don't you? – German people of the time saying, *No, no, we had no idea what was going on.*'

'With the Jews?' said Hilly. 'But Gran was only a girl – only about thirteen at the end of the war.'

'Old enough to know things. See things. Hear things. Neighbours taken away, things like that – she must have done, surely! You could hardly not!'

Rachel, Hilly thought. And Sarah. She had not told Reuben yet about her latest find, her prize exhibit. 'There's something else.' She moved towards her section of the wardrobe, where the *Rachel und*

273

Sarah im Garten photo was hidden, tucked inside her French dictionary.

'Hey! I meant to tell you,' Reuben remarked while she pushed a hand under her folded sweaters, 'Si thinks Rashid's got a mystery girlfriend. He came all the way back from Oxford last night, when he's only just gone down there. And when Si asked why, he did the non-answering thing, just like your gran. What's the big secret, d'you reckon?'

Her back to him, Hilly felt the rush of blood to her cheeks. Slowly, with the French dictionary in her hand, she turned.

'Reuben – it's – it's me. I spent yesterday with Rashid. I've been wanting to tell you.'

Reuben's expression was almost comical: mouth falling open in a cartoonish wordless gape, eyebrows arrowing upward. 'Uh?' came from somewhere in his throat. Hilly nodded; Reuben found his voice. 'You're going out with him?'

'I hope so. We spent yesterday together and we're going out again next weekend.'

'But—'

'What do you mean, *but*? It's OK, isn't it?'

'Well, it's . . .'

'What?' Hilly sat on Zoë's bed, facing him. 'Is it so unbelievable that someone asks me out?'

'No, but is it – I mean, is it . . .' Reuben looked down at the floor, up at her face again: 'Are you keen on him, then?'

'Keen! Well, course. Why would I go out with him

otherwise? You know I don't go out with boys unless
I—'

'Unless you what?'

'Unless I really like them,' Hilly said lamely.

'So you do,' Reuben said, in a strange, flat voice.

'Yes! I really like Rashid! I think he's lovely, if you
want to know. Is there something wrong with that?'

Reuben didn't answer; Hilly felt irritation rise.
'Why can't you be pleased for me?'

'I didn't say I wasn't pleased,' he said sulkily.

'But just look at you! I don't make a fuss about you
and Saeed, do I? You want it all one way, is that what
you're saying? I can be your camouflage when you
need it, go with you to the hospital, go to Saeed's, be
around whenever you need me, but when I want something for myself you don't want to know? Was I
supposed to ask your permission then, or what?
I thought you were my friend – more than my friend!'

'Don't be stupid! That's not going to change. It
takes a bit of getting used to, that's all.'

'You're saying you want to choose who I see, apart
from you?' Hilly flared at him. 'I can't have other
friends?'

'We're not talking about *friends*, are we? You don't
want Rashid as a friend. You want—'

'Don't tell me what I want! What do you know?
What's the matter with everyone? Mum was a bit off
about it too, when she found out—'

'Maybe she shouldn't have had to find out,'
Reuben said. 'Maybe you could have told her. Perhaps
you could have told *me*.'

'Well, now I have.' I don't believe this, a part of her mind said; I'm quarrelling with Reuben. With *Reuben*!

'Thanks a lot,' said Reuben, getting to his feet, looking round for his jacket. 'Hope it wasn't too much effort. Look, I've got to go.'

'But aren't we having a piano lesson?'

'Ask Rashid to teach you,' Reuben said curtly.

'*Oh!*' Hilly rolled her eyes up at the rafters. '*Now* who's being stupid?'

'OK,' Reuben said, with an indifferent shrug. 'If you say so.'

'Just listen to yourself! And now you're walking out on me! Let's at least talk about it, now you know!'

'What's there to talk about?'

He was as distant as a stranger. Not looking at her, he pulled on his jacket and made for the stairs. With a final, non-committal 'See you', he stomped down to the landing. Hilly picked up one of Zoë's slippers and chucked it after him; it hit the stair-rail and fell limply back on the mat.

'Of all the *stupid*, obstinate, ridiculous, unreasonable—'

Hilly paced to her own end of the room, yanked her duvet straight where Reuben had been lying, pummelled the pillows into shape. I could run after him, she thought; but why should I? He's the one who's behaved like a prat. But replaying the conversation in her mind, over and over, she heard her own voice, prickly, defensive. OK, Reuben was out of order, but I got it all wrong too, she told herself. Her eyes filled with tears. She could not remember quarrelling with Reuben, ever. Never before had he walked off and left her; never before had she seen him cold and aloof. She reached for a tissue as her eyes blurred.

Feet were clomping up the stairs. Her senses quickened in anticipation; she wiped her face, got up and went to the stair-well: he was coming back to say he was sorry. *Me, too!* she would say. *Let's start that conversation all over again, shall we?* But it was Zoë, not Reuben. One hand on the rail, she hauled herself up, with weary, laborious steps, not even noticing Hilly till she reached the top stair. They stared at each other, tear-stained face to tear-stained face.

'What's the matter with you?' Zoë said.

'Nothing. What's the matter with you?'

'Nothing.' Zoë barged past. 'Can't I have my room to myself for five minutes?'

Chapter Twenty-two

Dumped

Dump, *noun*: a pile or heap of refuse, etc.,
dumped or thrown down; a dull, abrupt
blow; a thud; a bump
      verb: deposit; throw down in a
lump or mass (rubbish); drop down with
a thud
Dumps, *noun pl.*: depression, melancholy.

The Oxford English Dictionary

The front door was wide open. For a moment Hilly
thought Reuben had left it like that, but then she saw
Heidigran outside with a garden trug, dead-heading
the roses beside the path. Hearing Hilly's tread on the
doorstep, Heidigran looked round.

'What's going on?' She rubbed the small of her
back. 'People stamping out, people stamping in!
What's upset your young man?'

'He isn't my young man!'

'Had a tiff? I expect it'll blow over. And what's the

278

matter with Zoë?' Heidigran, evidently in one of her more lucid states, gave Hilly a sharp look.

'No idea!' Hilly felt full of fidgets. The rain had cleared, and the late afternoon was bright and cloud-scuddy. It was tempting, after all, to go in pursuit of Reuben – indoors there was Zoë in one of her moods, and now Gran asking questions, and probably Mum had heard Reuben stropping off too, and would want to know why. Hilly pulled on her jacket, told Gran she wouldn't be long, and was almost at the park before she realized that Reuben would quite likely have gone straight to see Saeed. Her mobile phone was at home in her bag, so she couldn't ring him to find out.

Exasperated, deciding it wasn't dignified to chase after him – he was the one who'd stormed out! – she walked all the way home again. Heidigran had finished her gardening and the front door was closed; Hilly, with no key, had to ring. Her mother answered, looking puzzled. 'What's going on?'

'Why does everyone keep wanting to know what's going on? I'd like to come in, if that's all right!'

'Where's your key?'

'Here, in my bag!' Hilly pointed to the rucksack on the floor. 'I didn't take it with me, OK?'

Rose gave her a straight look, then, with the slightest of shrugs, went back to the kitchen. Hilly felt hemmed in with questions and trivia, and still annoyed with her mother for that slightest of slight pauses, that tiny frown, when Rashid's name had been mentioned last night. In the early hours of the morning, Hilly had lain wide awake, thinking of that brief hesitation. *But he's—* That, Hilly felt, was what was implied. Was Mum, for all her apparent fair-mindedness, a closet racist? Did it take something like this to bring it out?

I seem to be annoyed with everyone, Hilly thought, hardly recognizing herself. Is this what Lurve does to you? Rashid! I want to talk to Rashid! But he'll be working now, it'll have to wait till later, and anyway what can I say to him? *My mum seems to be racist and Reuben's gone into Deep Huff at the mere mention of your name?*

She grabbed her mobile phone and checked the messages: at once there was the loud bleep of a new arrival. U HAVE RMAIL. That was all: RMAIL meant an e-mail from Reuben.

OK, so he'd made the first move – unless his e-mail consisted of more reproaches. She'd better check before ringing him. Only snag, that meant going up to the computer, and Zoë was there. Resignedly, she went up both flights of stairs. Zoë was lying face-down on her bed, apparently asleep, one arm trailing to the floor. Good – Zoë asleep was at least tolerable.

She reached under the table to plug in the computer, and dialled up the internet connection. Reuben's message appeared in the inbox, with :-(as the title:

> Hilly,
>   Sorry sorry sorry! What a gallumphing great eejit. Me, I mean. Can't believe I did that – behaved like a five-year-old in a tantrum.

But I do know why. Like John Lennon said, I'm just a jealous guy. Does that sound daft? I know it's stupid and it was bound to happen sooner or later, that you'd find someone, I mean. And you've been great about Si, so I was well out of order. Like you said, I ought to be pleased for you.

I don't want things to change, that's what I'm saying. You and me. I can't imagine not having you around. But why wouldn't you be around? You're only going out with someone, not clearing out of my life for ever. Why do I mind that it's Rashid? I honestly don't know! Because he's Si's brother? Dunno. I mean, I like Rashid (LIKE, I said, not fancy!). Maybe I'd be jealous of anyone you went out with. If that's stupid, I'm sorry. I'll do my best, honest. I'll try to be happy for you and I really hope it works out. I mean, he's OK. More than OK. And because I know you, and from what I know of him, it's going to be the Real Thing, I bet. He's right for you.

Only, make sure you leave time for me! Kiss and make up? x x x (just in case) But there's another reason I'm sending this. It's about that tape with your gran.

I knew there was something weird about it and when I got home I realized what. It's that bit about the plane crashing in the street, a Stirling. The pilot killed, she said, and some bloke broke his leg when he got blown off his bike. Well, I knew I'd heard that before. So I looked up some books Dad's got, and checked it out.

And there it is. Northampton. Gold Street. 1941. I'll show you when you come round. But on the tape she was talking about Cologne.

Coincidence or what? Or not?

Have you forgiven me? Mail me back if you have. Piano lesson tomorrow? Go and practise!

Your more-than-friend R x x x (again)

Dear MTF Hilly typed in return,

How stupid are you? Stupid to think the Rashid thing will make the slightest difference to me and you, I mean. Yes, you're my more-than-friend, and I can't even begin to imagine not having you around, and hope I never have to find out what it'd be like.

I'm sorry too.

To be honest, I've had the jealous twinges about you and Saeed. And wondered how I'd feel if you went out with girls. That'd be harder. So that's what it must be like for you. I should have told you before, and I don't know why I didn't. I'll do better from now on, promise! Only DON'T walk out on me like that again, please! Don't think I could stand it.

See you tomorrow then, same time, same place only NOT same mood?

I love you, you prat. Don't you know? And that's for always.

Hilly x x x

SEND: her message disappeared from the outbox. Now, after all her agitation, she felt soothed, restored. All was well. But the outburst had shown how much Reuben meant to her; and how much she meant to him. *I love you.* She had never told him that before; had never needed to; but it was true. Will I ever say that to anyone else? she wondered: to Rashid? Will anyone (no, will he) ever say it to me?

It's going to be the Real Thing, Reuben had said. Tess assumed the same. How could they be so sure? Hilly re-read Reuben's message, noticing the last section properly this time.

She began a new reply:

P.S. That IS weird about the plane crashing in Gold Street. But I suppose planes must have been crashing all over the place in wartime. Or else maybe Gran read about it, and got mixed up?

Till tomorrow, another x, Hilly.

SEND again, the message vanished from her outbox, and now she noticed that Zoë was not asleep but staring at the ceiling, shiny-eyed.

'Oh – you're awake!'

'Don't mind me,' Zoë said, in a voice thick with tears. 'You just carry on.'

'Is something the matter?'

'You could say that.'

'Want to tell me?' Hilly turned off the computer and moved round to her own bed, where she sat facing Zoë's.

'No! You'll only rub my face in it.'

'I won't! Come on – if there's something really bothering you, tell me. Perhaps I can help!'

Zoë gave a grimacing smile. '*You* help! You're the last person I'd ask for help. Anyway, you can't!' Her eyes swam with fresh tears; her lower lip trembled. She struggled for a few moments before giving way. She sat up, knees to chin, head down to hide her face, her shoulders heaving with sobs.

'Zoë!' Hilly kneeled, put an arm round her, pulled strands of loose hair away from the hot, damp face. 'Tell me what's happened!'

She reached for a tissue and pushed it into Zoë's hand; Zoë snatched it and dabbed furiously at her eyes and nose. 'It's – Grant, he's – he's . . .'

'He's what?' Hilly said, with a sense of foreboding.

'Dumped me.' Zoë buried her head in her arms.

'Oh.' Hilly assimilated this; Zoë raised her head, glaring with wet, angry eyes.

'Go on – gloat! Tell me you're pleased! Tell me it's what I deserve! You can't pretend to be sorry!'

'I'm sorry he's upset you,' Hilly conceded. 'Do you want to tell me about it?'

'Found this other girl, hasn't he?' Zoë said through gritted teeth. 'This other girl singer. Justine. A bit older, a lot sexier. Great voice, miles better than me . . .' Her voice wavered. 'I hate her! So she's lead singer for Doppelgänger now. And being Grant's girl-friend goes with the job, so I lose out both ways. And there's the stuff about me giving names to the police. That's down to you – not that you care! Either way, I'm out. Ditched. Dumped. He's had enough of me—'

'Don't say dumped!' Hilly hated the word – it made her think of rubbish tips, detritus, scraps and fragments left to be picked over by scavengers.

'What d'you want me to say? What difference does it make?' Zoë's voice was muffled in her arms. 'And that's not even all . . .'

'What, then?'

'Promise you won't tell Mum and Dad? Promise not to tell anyone?'

'OK, I promise,' Hilly said uneasily.

Zoë's crying now took on a different tone – no longer hot and angry, but a quiet weeping that worried Hilly far more. She smoothed Zoë's hair and shoulder, waiting. 'Come on, Zoesie! Please tell me!'

'I'm late with my period,' Zoë managed to get out. 'A few days. It's never happened before.'

'Oh, God—'

'Right! Oh God. Only *he's* not going to help, is he? If there was such a person. He'd be pleased I've got my come-uppance, just like you are—'

'Zoë! I'm not. Please believe me! Are you sure – sure you haven't got the dates wrong – I mean, a few days late wouldn't necessarily mean—'

'Course I haven't got the dates wrong! I've checked and checked! Don't lecture me, for Christ's sake – what do you know about it?'

'Not as much as you, and you know a bit too much, if you ask me! But weren't you careful? Didn't you use—?'

'Yes, course!' Zoë flared. 'How stupid do you think I am?'

Better not answer that – there had been enough quarrelling for one day. 'Shh – don't yell at me! Mum'll hear and want to know what's going on—'

'You won't tell her, will you? You promised.' Zoë began to weep quietly again. 'Oh, Hill, what am I going to do?'

'It's too early to be sure,' Hilly soothed. 'But if you have to tell Mum and Dad, if—'

'I can't!' Zoë wailed. 'They'll kill me, they'll absolutely *kill* me!'

'Course they won't – wouldn't. They'd want to help – do the best for you. Are you sure about dates and things? When were you due?'

'Last – last Friday.' Zoë put both hands on her abdomen, over her jeans, and pressed gently with her fingers. 'What's going on in there? God, I can't be pregnant! There, now I've said it. First time I've used the word out loud.' She fingered her tissue, a tight, sodden ball; she chucked it at the bin and reached for another.

'Three days late? It's not that long.'

'It is for me! And – OK, Hill, I was an idiot. I might as well tell you. It was Bank Holiday Monday. We haven't done it that many times, honest! And all the other times Grant did use a condom. It's so unlucky! That day he'd run out, and we were – you know, well into it, and he just said, *Don't worry, I'll be careful, it'll be all right.* Only he wasn't – wasn't careful enough! And it's not him who's got to—'

'The bastard,' Hilly said fiercely. 'I wish it was him who had to go through this.'

Zoë began to giggle and weep at the same time. 'Can you imagine? Counting the days since his last period! Making sure he's got plenty of Tampax, just in case! Wondering if he's getting PMT! It's not *fair*, is it? Honest, Hill, I've never wanted it so much, that awful cramp, the zits, the moods, the whole bit! I keep trying to bring it on by imagining it!'

'Come on, daft.' Hilly gave her a hug. 'Try and think about something else, then p'raps it'll happen. If Mum and Dad notice you've been crying, tell them you've split up with Grant – that'll help get things back to normal, at any rate. Let's go down and see what's for tea.'

Everyone was in the kitchen: their father had just come in, Rose was washing salad, Heidigran making a pot of tea. Zoë, being Zoë, was able to throw off her despairing mood so convincingly that Hilly gazed at her once or twice wondering whether she had imagined the entire conversation. It was as if, by talking about it, Zoe had passed the burden over. What if . . . what if . . . what if? Hilly kept thinking, all through the meal and the washing-up. For Zoë to be pregnant would be bad enough; to be pregnant by Grant would be complete disaster. Zoë was well rid of him, Hilly considered, but he'd offer no support whatsoever. There could be no question of Zoë going through with a pregnancy, could there? . . . she wasn't even sixteen yet . . . but the alternative was hardly more acceptable. Oh Zoë, you stupid bloody idiot!

'You're quiet tonight, Hilly,' said their father, getting out cups for coffee. 'What's on your mind?'

Hilly shook her head. 'Oh, nothing.'

Chapter Twenty-three

Sarah Reubens

The night of 9th November 1938 has come to be known as Kristallnacht. In Germany and Austria, Jews were targeted in acts of violence – businesses and homes were ransacked, synagogues set on fire, and Jewish individuals arrested, attacked and killed. It became impossible for German and Austrian Jews to remain unaware of the danger they were in, simply by virtue of being Jewish.

Great Britain offered entry visas to ten thousand unaccompanied Jewish children from Germany, Austria and Czechoslovakia. The trains carrying these children to safety, and the whole operation concerned with the children's removal from Nazi-controlled territory, have become known as the Kindertransports. Some of these youngsters were eventually reunited with their families; most were not.

Marta Rubenstein, *Exodus*

Home from school, Hilly registered stiffness and tension in the back of her neck, the beginnings of pressure above her eyes: the early signs of migraine. The sick grogginess would be next.

Well, she decided, I haven't got time for a headache; Reuben's coming. I'll just ignore it and hope it goes away. She looked at the wipe-clean message board on the side of the fridge.

Gavin - shop, 8.30-6
Zoë - school
Hilly - school
Rose - here till 5.45, Day Centre meeting 6-8
Hilly's turn to cook

Her mother had made a new house rule that everyone's comings and goings each day must be written here. It was mainly for Heidigran's benefit, so that she could check if she became alarmed about who was looking after her, or even if she forgot the names of the people who lived here. My turn to cook – it *would* be, Hilly thought, wondering whether to take her headache pills now or wait till later. If Zoë were here she'd ask if they could swap cooking duties, but Zoë was round at Nadine's. Their mother was going out shortly, to one of her meetings at the Alzheimer's Support Group, where carers shared experiences and discussed ways of dealing with problems. It was from the last meeting that Rose got the idea of the message board.

Hilly made tea for Heidigran and was looking in

the fridge and freezer when Reuben arrived. As soon as she opened the door, he kissed her cheek and looked at her closely. 'That's for yesterday. OK? Are we definitely OK now?'

Hilly touched his arm. 'Course! All forgotten.'

'You don't mean that,' Reuben said sternly.

'No, you're right.' She reconsidered; what had happened was too important to be forgotten. 'Explained, then. Cleared of clutter.'

'A one-off.'

'A blip.'

'A temporary interference.' Reuben followed Hilly to the piano. It was a still, warm afternoon; the patio doors were open. In the relief of seeing Reuben, Hilly almost found herself launching into her new worry, Zoë's dilemma, which had preoccupied her all through school and reduced her to silence during a seminar on *The Great Gatsby* which she would normally have enjoyed. Another secret from Reuben! But she had promised to tell no one.

'Where's your gran?' Reuben asked.

Hilly gestured towards the garden, and Heidigran in her lounger seat with *House Beautiful* magazine.

'Got something to show you.' Reuben reached into the battered canvas bag he used for his files, folders and sheet music, and brought out a hard-backed book: *Northampton's War Years*. They sat side by side on the piano stool. 'The book I was telling you about. It's Dad's. He's got all sorts of stuff like this.' He flipped it open at a page marked with a Post-It, found the place, jabbed a finger at the text. 'Here. Read this.'

Although Northamptonshire escaped the worst of the bombing raids [Hilly read], there were occasional incidents. Albert Street School in Rushden was bombed in October 1940, with the loss of 11 lives. In July 1941, a Stirling bomber crashed in Gold Street, causing considerable damage to shops and businesses. Casualties were surprisingly slight; most of the crew had baled out successfully, and only the pilot was killed, his body being found later several streets away. The only civilian casualty was a firewatcher cycling home from his spell of duty, whose leg was broken when he was thrown off his bicycle by the blast. Parts from the shattered plane were avidly collected as trophies by local schoolboys.

'How odd!' Hilly gave him a sideways look. 'It's exactly what she said, every detail – the Stirling, the man breaking his leg. But on the tape she was talking about Cologne.'

'Coincidence? Muddle?' he asked. 'What d'you reckon?'

Hilly thought. 'She could have read about this and got confused. Here' – she indicated the page – 'or in some other book. Or people might have been talking about it when she came here at the end of the war. Maybe something like it happened in Cologne too, and she got the two crashes mixed up. That's the most likely explanation, isn't it?'

'Is it?' said Reuben. 'Your gran's always had you believe she came here after the war, but – what if she came earlier? What if she slipped up in that interview, and talked about something that happened here *during* the war?'

'But what would have—?'

'Couple of weeks ago,' Reuben said, 'you were telling me how odd it was for her to come here after the war. To the enemy country.'

'That's right, yes. Mum says her adopted grand-parents were friends of the family. She had nowhere else to go.'

'Just imagine it,' Reuben said slowly, 'the other way round. End of the war, you're an English child, orphaned, both parents killed by German bombs. How likely is it you'd go to live in Germany?'

'I know, it'd be the last place you'd want to go. But if there was no choice?' Hilly looked at him. 'What are you getting at?'

Reuben said nothing, waiting for her to assimilate what he had said. Her head reeled sickly; the migraine wasn't going to let itself be ignored. Pills, Hilly thought, I must take the pills. Her thoughts flew to her bedside cabinet, the pills in the top drawer, and, on top, the *Rachel und Sarah im Garten* photo face-down underneath *The Great Gatsby*, out of Zoë's sight but ready to show Reuben. 'I still haven't shown you the photo, have I? The new one I found—'

'Shh!' Reuben nudged her with his elbow. She turned to see Heidigran at the patio doors, supporting herself with one hand on the frame.

'Thought I heard voices,' Heidigran said. She looked at Reuben, then at Hilly. 'Patched up your quarrel, have you? Where's Rose?'

'Upstairs, Gran, getting changed.'

'You going to play the piano?' Heidigran said, with a touch of sharpness.

'We're having a lesson,' said Hilly, 'nothing very interesting. Scales and stuff.'

Heidigran nodded, gave them a rather disapproving look, and went back outside, but stayed on the patio, picking off wilted flowers from the planted tubs. Hilly watched her, really wanting to continue her conversation with Reuben; but Heidigran hovered, evidently to keep an eye on them.

'Lesson first, then?' Hilly said to Reuben. 'But I've hardly touched *Für Elise*, the last few days.'

'Too many distractions?' He gave her a suggestive glance, meaning, she supposed, Rashid.

Rashid! The name – the mere thought of his name – was enough to make her blood rush and her skin tingle. He had said he would phone tonight. And Zoë – what had today brought, for her? Relief, or a sharpening of worry?

'Distraction,' she said lightly, 'tell me about it!'

She looked at the opening of *Für Elise*, with the sense of meeting it after an immensely long absence. Maybe her fingers remembered. Reuben made her practise the scales and arpeggios first, then the easy beginner's piece from her tutor book. When he was satisfied, he removed the book from the stand, centred the Beethoven and looked at her expectantly.

She held her breath and began: the lightest of touch, almost trembling on the opening E and D sharp, then leaning into the surer weight of the deep notes in the left hand, feeling herself caught almost immediately in the spell, the simple, yearning beauty that could not be obscured by the fumbling uncertainty of her fingers. If only her hands were as clever as Reuben's, and could caress the keys, transmit the music instead of hampering it! She played as well as her limited capability allowed: for Reuben, for herself, for Heidigran. A wrong note here, an uncertainty there. Tantalizingly Beethoven, frustratingly Hilly.

'That's it.' She looked at Reuben for approval. 'As far as I can go.'

'OK, not bad. You've obviously practised it a bit. I'll do the left hand this time, so you only have to worry about the fingering in the right.'

Hilly concentrated hard, managing at least to play the notes in the right order.

'You're doing some awkward fingering we can straighten out. Here, try this –' He took a pencil from his bag and wrote 5, 4, 3, above a run of notes – 'then you've got a better reach with your thumb for the C.'

'It's all so *practical*,' Hilly said. 'I mean, you'd think it was all about getting into the heart and soul of the music. What it actually comes down to is getting your fingers organized.'

'Well, it's both. Start again – still right hand only.'

'Hang on a minute.' Hilly rubbed the back of her neck, feeling the one-sided pain tightening its grip. 'I'll just go upstairs first.'

As she mounted the stairs – what an effort two flights seemed, once the grogginess set in! – she heard Reuben start on the Scriabin he was learning now, a restless, agitated piece she didn't much like. Thinking about the book he had brought round, about Heidigran's muddle, she remembered the photograph. She took it from underneath *The Great Gatsby*, glanced at it, read the writing on the back.

Only when she got to the bottom of the stairs, registering that Reuben had stopped playing and seemed to be arguing with Heidigran, did she realize that she'd forgotten the pills she went up for.

Heidi had been feeling perfectly content. She had all she wanted: the late-afternoon sunshine still warm, a mug of tea, a magazine to flick through, and a comfortable seat. Shame there weren't any biscuits, some of those nutty chocolate-chip ones would have been nice, but she really oughtn't to eat between meals, and someone would start cooking soon. Hilly was here, yes, Hilly, and Rose was upstairs getting changed. That meant someone would be here, all through the evening, and again tomorrow morning. There were butterflies on the buddleia tree, spreading their wings on the purple flowers: Red Admirals, tortoiseshells, peacocks, she knew their names. People said there weren't the butterflies about nowadays, but they came flocking when the buddleia was in flower. One Painted Lady, she'd seen earlier, sunning itself. She had a buddleia just like that in her own garden; Ken had planted it for her, one birthday. And the boy was here too; she knew his name if only she could think of it. Anyway, she'd seen him often enough, the thin boy with the sharp, intelligent face, Hilly's special friend. Friend, not boyfriend, Hilly always insisted, though they certainly spent a lot of time together and Hilly had been almost beside herself yesterday, when they'd quarrelled about something or other. He'd look better, in Heidi's opinion, if he did something about that curly mop of hair, got it cut neatly, but there was no telling the young how they should present themselves.

Reuben, that was it. The name made her feel edgy. There was really no need for it. It wasn't safe to say it out loud.

And they really oughtn't to play Rachel's piano without asking. Rachel wouldn't like that. She and Rachel sometimes played together, but otherwise no one else touched the keys. Now Rachel's fingerprints would be smudged all over with Hilly's and the boy's.

She went to check what they were doing, then noticed that Rose really wasn't looking after her garden pots very well – those regal pelargoniums would carry on flowering for another month or two if you kept dead-heading them. Her back was stiff as she bent to tweak off the withered blooms.

Scales, exercises, over and over again, nothing worth listening to. Then a pause, and – she tilted her head to listen more intently – the tune she remembered better than any other. Her tune, Rachel's tune! Had Rachel come, at last?

Heidi let the dried petals fall from her fingers. Her soft-soled shoes made no sound as she crept back to see. Disappointment was like a gnawing at her insides, a weeping hollow. Not Rachel, but these two again.

They were playing together, left hand and right hand, the way she and Rachel used to. Who had taught them to do that?

She steadied herself with a hand on the door frame, watching them. Two people making music together, both of them focused and attentive: it was like loving. Their hands moving, each giving to the other.

'Again,' said the boy.

The beginning bit was easy; *I* used to play that, Heidi thought. She flexed her fingers, wondering if they still knew how. But only the beginning. Not far in, the music got darker and rumblier, the manuscript clotted with notes, and Rachel had to take over both hands. These two kept going over and over the opening bars, never reaching the deep growlings that waited inside the piano.

'Play the whole thing,' she was about to say – but just then the girl said something and went out of the room. The boy, left on his own, started to play a quite different piece, modern and discordant. His hands were strong and sure on the keys. Like Rachel's.

Heidi stood, listening, thinking of that other, long-ago room that smelled of sun-warmed carpet. Rachel's feet on the pedals were neat and small, in plum-coloured bar shoes that were fastened by little round buttons covered in the same plum leather. The piano stool stood squarely on a patterned rug, and if you moved it you could see the worn flattened indentations its feet had made in the pile, with dust and carpet-fluff pressed in. It was a world of feet down there. She looked at the boy's feet. They were large, considering how skinny he was, in scuffed black boots that trampled all over Rachel's pedals.

When Sarah was very small she had liked to shelter under the piano by Rachel's legs, watching her clever feet. Sometimes she would press one of the pedals with both hands and listen to the difference it made. One of them made the sound swell and boom from the heart of the piano, the other made it linger in the air, like when Sarah had been allowed to play the cymbals once at school and she had felt the sound, a golden wave in the air, that tingled against her ears and slowly receded. She would have liked to sit down by the pedals now, in the cave of sound, but she was too stiff to get down to the floor, and getting up again was even more difficult.

Reuben. She looked at the back of his neck, at his head bent intently over the keyboard, at his tangle of hair. He was Reuben, she felt quite sure of that. Someone ought to tell him.

'You know you don't have to keep it,' she said loudly, approaching from behind.

He stopped playing abruptly, swivelling round to look up at her. 'Oh – you made me jump!'

'You can change it,' she repeated.

'You don't like this?' said Reuben. 'Shall I play something else?'

'Change it. It's safer that way.'

Now he was looking at her in complete bafflement. Didn't he understand?

'Safer? Sorry, change what?'

'Your name. That's what I did.'

'You changed your name? What, when you got married, you mean?'

'No – no!' She heard the frustration in her voice. How could she make him see? 'Change it. No one need know.'

The Hilly girl was back, silent and staring in the doorway. The boy looked at her; they both looked at Heidi.

'What do you mean, Gran?' said the girl. 'No one need know what?'

'What his real name is.' Heidi looked at her. 'What's that you're holding?'

A glance passed between the girl and the boy. Too many secrets, those two had. Then the girl, suddenly decisive, held out a photograph. 'I found this, Gran. This picture of Rachel.'

Heidi took it, smiled in recognition, looked and looked. 'Now wherever did you get this? Thought I'd lost it!'

'In your cupboard,' said the girl.

Heidi giggled. 'Mutti ought to have told me my knickers were showing! It's not nice!'

'No, that can't be you – it says Sarah—'

'It *is* me,' Heidi said, and her voice came out as Sarah's.

'Can I see?' said the boy.

Slowly, reluctantly, Heidi passed it to him; he examined it closely, turned it over and read the writing on the back.

'Sarah?' he said, looking at her in a way that showed he understood. For a moment she felt cold with panic. What had she told him? 'You changed your name from Sarah?' he repeated.

'Changed—' The girl's face produced a comical range of expressions, ending up all Os – round eyes, mouth open. She swallowed, said something incoherent, then tried again. 'Gran? *You're* Sarah?'

'I might have been, once,' Heidi said; then, more cheerfully: 'I remember that picnic!'

'This is you, Gran, in the photo – are you sure?'

Heidi nodded. 'Under the tree in our garden. The bobble tree, we called it, but that wasn't its real name. What was it, now – p, p—'

'Never mind the tree, Gran—'

'D'you mean a plane tree?' said the boy. 'There's one outside our house.'

Heidi nodded. 'Wasps kept coming after the lemonade. There was Battenburg cake. I liked that. It was someone's birthday, not mine. Now, whose was it?' She felt happy now, remembering. But a strange hush had settled over Hilly and the boy. Of course, they hadn't been there.

'Heidigran,' said the girl, and her voice came out hoarse and strange, 'you're really saying this is you – you're Sarah? And Rachel's—'

'My sister, that's right,' Heidi said proudly. 'She'll be here soon, I expect. Are we having a picnic? There are more chairs in the shed, aren't there. Shall I put them out, ready, or shall we sit on the grass? Whose birthday is it?'

She looked from one face to another. They seemed oddly trapped in stillness, as if they daren't make any sudden movement. There was that play-ground game where you had to creep up on someone without them noticing. What was it called? – Yes, grandmother's footsteps! That's funny, she thought, because I am a grandmother, aren't I? That's why they call me Gran. She gave a splutter of laughter, but could tell from their faces that they hadn't seen the joke.

'Er – Heidigran,' said the boy slowly. 'What was your other name? Your surname? Rachel and Sarah—'

'Oh, it was – yes, I know that.' Heidi thought for a moment, puzzled, looking at her feet. 'R – R – now what is it? I used to know. Oh, of course!' she said, brightening. 'It's Reubens, same as yours!'

What were they staring at now? It was funny about names, how they came and they went. She was certain now that she must have been called Sarah Reubens once, but that wasn't her name now and she had no idea why she'd changed it.

'Can we have Battenburg cake?' she asked. 'Rachel likes that.'

Hilly felt as if the whole world had gone blurry; nothing quite in focus, nothing quite as she expected it to be. She stood in the patio doorway, while Heidigran arranged garden chairs on the lawn. 'Schmidt!' she told Reuben, with an effort of memory. 'But her German name was Heidi Schmidt!'

'While you were out of the room,' Reuben said, 'she as good as told me she'd changed her name. Why would a German girl called Sarah Reubens want to change her name?'

'Because it's a Jewish name?' Shutters closed in Hilly's mind – impossible.

'Sarah Reubens sounds Jewish. Heidi Schmidt doesn't. That's why she changed, or her family changed it for her. That's why she wants me to change *my* name. She thinks we're back in Nazi Germany.'

'She changed her name in case people thought she was Jewish?'

'No,' Reuben said. 'I think she changed her name because she *was* Jewish. That's why she came to England. That's why—'

'You're saying Gran's Jewish? Sarah Reubens – German and Jewish? No, how can she be? – have been? The things she says – you've heard her! She's just confused. Seeing that photograph has muddled her – she thinks it's her, when really it's someone else, someone called Sarah Reubens.'

Reuben shook his head. 'There's too much that makes sense. Like the crashed bomber in town. She was here during the war, like I said. She couldn't have stayed in Cologne – not if she really *is* Sarah Reubens. She must have been one of the children who came here as refugees – we watched a documentary about it in history. If her parents stayed behind—'

'God! And Rachel? What could have happened to Rachel?' Hilly's head was reeling.

'Rachel might have been too old – she looks about eighteen, would you say? The Kindertransports were only for children, weren't they?'

'Stop. Stop now.' Hilly covered her eyes with her hands, pressing with her fingertips. She could not grasp one coherent thought from the swirl inside her head.

Reuben put a hand on her arm. 'I know, it's . . .'

Cautiously, Hilly opened her eyes and looked out at Heidigran in the garden, unable to make the adjustment. Heidigran was Heidi, of course, and had always been! The present was all there was to get hold of. The rest was a spider's web of what-ifs and supposings. 'Hang on, though! Wait,' she told Reuben. 'What about the other photo of Rachel, the first one? When I showed it to Gran, she didn't even recognize her—'

'Could have been pretending,' Reuben pointed out.

'Yes, I know, and I think she does pretend, sometimes, but what she said was, "I only saw her once." Only saw her once? Her own sister? That doesn't make sense at all. We must have got this all wrong. Rachel can't be her sister! But then why does she go on about her so much?'

'There's only one person who knows,' said Reuben.

Heidi was looking forward to the party. There would be nice things to eat, and games, and presents. Should she have bought a present? Only she couldn't now remember whose birthday it was. Not Rachel's, she knew Rachel's – March 15th, and it wasn't March now, it must be – oh, August, or September, something like that.

There were four chairs, which she arranged in a square; then she went indoors to find out what to do next. 'Do you think four chairs is enough?' she asked the Hilly girl, who for some reason was standing in the doorway next to the boy, instead of helping. 'Only I can't remember who's coming.'

'Heidigran,' said the girl. 'We need to ask you something.'

'You ask an awful lot of questions!' Heidi said, bored with their conversation. Shouldn't the others be here by now?

'It's important, though. Are you sure Rachel's your sister?'

Heidi laughed. 'Do you think I don't know who my own sister is?'

'Gran – what happened to her? Did she come to England as well?'

'No. She stayed behind with Mutti and Vati. Then she went to France, but that was no good. She ended up in that place, you know—'

'What place?'

'You know. In another country. Where hundreds of them went and never came back. On the trains. Oz – oz – no, ow—'

'Do you mean Auschwitz?' said the boy, who seemed rather good at guessing what she wanted to say.

'Yes, that's it!' she said, pleased.

'And your parents?'

'They were taken, too. One of the other places.' Now Heidi felt her face doing strange things – her mouth screwing up as if she were sucking a lemon, her eyes smarting. She took the photograph out of her cardigan pocket and gazed at it.

And now everything was happening at once. Feet trod briskly down the stairs and at the same time someone opened the front door with a key. The blonde girl came into the room, Zara, no, Zoë, with a face like a wet weekend as usual. And behind her, from upstairs, came Rose, dressed in a skirt and jacket and smart shoes.

'Oh, Rose dear, you look nice,' Heidi said sadly. She noticed that everyone seemed to be staring at everyone else. She dropped the photograph on the floor, face-up; the Hilly girl just gazed at it. A telephone rang in the hall. 'Your mobile, Hilly,' said Zoë, her voice flat and dull.

'What's this?' Rose asked, bending to pick up the photograph.

Chapter Twenty-four

Survivor

A few fragments of diaries, letters and
scribbled messages do survive. But in the
main, others must bear witness to what
was done to the millions who could never
tell their own story.

Martin Gilbert, *The Holocaust:
The Jewish Tragedy*

'Hilly? It's me, Rashid.'

Hilly walked slowly upstairs, clamping the phone to her ear. 'Oh – hi.'

'Where are you? OK to talk?'

'Fine, thanks. I'm at home. Only there's quite a lot going on—'

'Shall I ring back later?'

'No – no, it's all right.'

Rashid's was the voice she had longed to hear for two days, but now she heard the tone of her own: brusque, offhand, not at all the way she wanted to sound. Her headache was intensifying; she'd been stupid not to take the pills as soon as she felt it coming. She hauled herself up to the landing and leaned against the wall. The migraine brought with it a debilitating feebleness, the sense that everything was too much.

'Sure?' said Rashid. She heard his uncertainty.

'I've just got a headache, that's all.' It sounded the lamest of excuses. 'I get them quite badly. Perhaps it'd be better to talk later. I'll call you back, shall I?'

'OK, but I'm going out about seven,' Rashid said. 'Sorry you're not well – go and look after yourself.'

Hilly rang off, and stood for a few moments more, flooded with disappointment. She had wanted to say, *How are you? What have you been doing? Tell me all about your day!* Even, jealously: *Where are you going tonight? Who with?* She had said none of it – hadn't managed to sound even mildly interested. Serve her right if he went out and met someone else tonight.

But it was one problem too many, for the moment. Embarking on the second flight of stairs, she plodded up like a pack pony. She found the pills, and made herself gulp down two, without water; it was too much effort to drag herself all the way downstairs again. As she lay down on the bed, she felt it tilt and lurch in the way it did when grogginess took over her mind and body. She closed her eyes against the painful sunlight, but the inside of her head was no more restful. Patterns played on the inside of her eyelids, thoughts surged like currents, whizzing about her brain, bouncing off each other, clamouring for attention . . .

Rachel died in Auschwitz. My relation, my – what is she? – great-aunt? And my great-grandparents. Killed, murdered. I'd have gone too, if I'd been there, we all would, Mum, Heidigran, Zoë, me – I'm part-Jewish, one-quarter of me—

I knew! Did I? In the concentration camp – the hot sun and the butterflies, the stillness – the photographs – yellow stars and stricken faces – something in the air, something lingering – Only a visitor in the palace of death *– yes, but—*

Reuben's still here, downstairs, and Mum saw the photograph –

Poor Heidigran, poor Sarah – she lost them all, she lost herself—

Rashid, I didn't mean – it's all too much to explain – too much to take in –

The tracks – those railway tracks, leading in – the gates looming, slamming shut – ARBEIT MACHT FREI . . .

As the pain above her eyes receded to background dullness, and the thoughts blurred and mingled, she was aware of drifting into sleep: letting go, letting herself be taken. She was inside, where she belonged, where she had known she belonged. Her hands were on the bars of the gates, her wrists thin and feeble. *Let me out! It's a mistake –* And the guards laughing, jeering: *No, you're staying here, you'll never get out.* Outside, free, in the sunshine, her father walked away, not looking back. Don't leave me! Her throat was tight, she had to force out the words, making only the thinnest, feeblest sound. *It's a mistake! An awful mistake!* But *– No,* said the guard, lighting a cigarette, *there's no mistake. You're the one who's been mistaken—*

Her eyelids flew open: she was lying on her back, staring up at the sloping ceiling. Pain returned with a relentless surge. Someone was coming up the stairs. She groaned, and rolled over onto her side.

'Hilly?' said Reuben's voice. 'Are you OK?'

'No.' She moved her legs aside to make room for him to sit.

'Poor Hilly. Where does it hurt?'

'My brain.' She gave a pathetic whimper. Reuben touched her forehead with two fingertips, drawing slow circles – which, somehow, helped.

'What's happening downstairs?' she asked him.

'I told them. Your mum picked up the photograph, so I didn't see what else to do. Your dad's here now and I told all of them.'

'And now?'

'They're trying to believe it. Your mum and dad and Zoë. Your gran seemed quite oblivious – she was back in her magazine!'

'*I'm* trying to believe it. No, I *do* believe it. But Gran – she's lied to us, all these years!'

Reuben nodded. 'Made up a different version, perhaps. She didn't like the real one. Maybe, after so long, she *believes* the alternative version.'

'But all the anti-Jewish things she comes out with! Zoë even calls her a Nazi.'

'Camouflage,' Reuben said. 'Could be, couldn't it? If you spent most of your childhood hearing how Jews are bad, Jews are evil, Jews are dirty, Jews aren't wanted here, wouldn't you want to distance yourself from it? And one way of distancing yourself is to be anti-Jewish yourself. Maybe it's not even pretending, after so long.'

'Mmn.' Hilly let herself be soothed by Reuben's voice, his massaging fingers.

'You need time to absorb all this.'

'Time!' Hilly's eyes flew open; she gazed at Reuben's face. 'I've got time! Like the rest of my life – the rest of Gran's life! But how long is that going to be? When she goes, it'll be lost – her past, the truth – it's already half-buried!'

'But the point is,' said Reuben, 'that it's *been* buried, all these years – even your mum had no idea – and we're only just beginning to see what's under the surface.'

'I've read books and pamphlets and stuff about Alzheimer's,' Hilly said, 'and they all say more or less the same – people can remember things that happened years and years ago, amazingly clearly, even though they can't remember what happened yester-day, or five minutes ago – *oh!*'

'What?'

'You know I told you about Gran having this obsession with checking the front door was locked? Over and over. *Bad men'll come*, she said. I thought her house must've been burgled or something, and that's what she was worried about. But when I tried to ask her, she said, "They took my daddy away." I thought – I thought she was talking about the bombing, you know how people say someone's *gone* when they've died, or *passed away* – but of course—'

Reuben nodded, understanding.

Hilly shook her head. 'I can't take this in. All this

past, all this stuff. It used to be history. Now it's Gran's history – my family's history – *my* history!'

'I know.'

'At school last year,' Hilly said slowly, 'we watched a documentary about that conference in Potsdam, the one where Eichmann and the others sat round a table and worked out the Final Solution. You know? They had figures and charts, working out how many Jews would have to be disposed of, how it could be done – and just like everyone else, I thought how awful, only I had no idea – Gran's parents, then – Mum's German grandparents, my great-grandparents – they died, didn't they? – only not in the bombing like I've always thought, they—'

No! her brain jibbed. Don't make me go there!

'Are you OK?' said Reuben in concern.

She took slow, deliberate breaths, trying to repel a wave of nausea. No, it wouldn't be put off, there was no time to explain. She scrambled to her feet, clamping a hand to her mouth; bolted for the stairs, as the need to throw up demanded her attention. She made it to the bathroom just in time.

On her knees, retching into the toilet again and again till there was nothing left to heave up, she was aware of Reuben bending over her, holding back her hair, making soothing noises. When she had finished he helped her to her feet, tore off loo roll for her to wipe her mouth, flushed the toilet and put the lid down for her to sit, while she leaned over the sink to brush her teeth.

'God, God, I'm sorry.' The shock of throwing

up had squeezed tears from her eyes, tears of childish self-pity; her toothbrush was shaking in her hand. 'What a state!' She ran water to wash her face.

'Don't worry. Why didn't you tell me? Come on, let's get you back to bed.'

'Rachel used to get migraines. Heidigran said. Rachel's my great-aunt – it runs in the family! I keep thinking of things—'

'Don't think. You need to sleep.'

'Ever thought of changing your name to Florence?' Hilly said, allowing him to steady her as they went back upstairs.

'I think we've had enough name-changing to be going on with. Lie down, go on, and try to stop thinking about it all.'

'Next time I get one of these, I want you on standby. Will you marry me?'

'Only if I can wear white and have five pink bridesmaids,' said Reuben. He arranged her pillows, pulled the curtains, fetched her a glass of water. 'I'd better go now, but I'll phone you later, OK? And stay home tomorrow if you're not well.'

When Reuben left, her attempts to settle were disturbed by one visitor after another. First, her mother, on tiptoe: 'Oh, love! We never did get you to the doctor, did we? I'm making you an appointment for next week. Don't worry about anything else – I'm not going to my meeting after all, so you don't have to come down again if you'd rather sleep.'

Then, a little later, Zoë: 'Are you OK? Reuben said

313

you threw up.' She smiled wryly. 'You're not joining the club too, are you?'

Hilly raised her head. 'Oh, Zoë, so there's no change?'

'No such luck. I've bought myself one of those pregnancy test kits – well, to be honest, I got Nads to go in and buy it for me. But I don't dare try. I'm dreading it!'

Zoë's mouth formed a helpless grimace; Hilly saw how near she was to crying, glimpsed the frightened little girl just beneath the surface.

'Don't, yet,' Hilly said, too wearied to contemplate the possible result. 'Wait till tomorrow.'

'You'll help me, Hilly, won't you?'

'Yes, course I will,' said Hilly, closing her eyes again to visions of family conferences, baby bottles, baby nappies, baby-sitting. No! It couldn't happen. She switched her mental image to one of Zoë sitting up in a hospital bed, pale and brave, awaiting an abortion . . . the images slammed against her eye-sockets, bright and insistent.

When Zoë went away, Hilly turned and turned in an effort to evade the pain that felt like something drilling through her skull. At last she began to doze, feeling herself sink back into the dream – the shut gates, her hands on the bars, the laughing guards; her father walking away without her, not turning back . . . And now heavy footsteps were clumping towards her. She gripped the bars, feeling her limbs heavy and weighted, her strength fading, her will to escape more feeble by the moment . . .

'Hilly?'

She opened her eyes to evening light filtered through curtains, and remembered why she was here.

'Hilly? Are you awake?' her father called again, his voice soft. 'Just came to see if you need anything.' He sat beside her on the bed, where Reuben had sat.

'I was dreaming,' she said, still dopey. 'I dreamed you were leaving me. Walking away.'

'Oh, love!' He looked aghast. 'I'd never do that, never. You're precious to me – you know that – more than I can tell you—' He wasn't used to making this sort of declaration; he fidgeted with her duvet, tucking it around her neck. 'You've had a shock – we all have.'

'You mean about Gran?' In Hilly's mind-fuddled state, she thought for a moment he was talking about Zoë.

'It's – unbelievable, isn't it? But it has to be true. Reuben's convinced us – shown us the photo, shown us how everything adds up. It's a lot for us to take in, all of us – your mum, especially. We're talking and talking about it, you can imagine.'

'And Gran?' Hilly said, reaching for her glass of water.

'Oh, she's quite oblivious – watching *Neighbours*! Are you OK here on your own?'

'Yes – no – stand back—'

Another dash for the bathroom, this time with her dad in pursuit and support. He ran hot water, fetched a clean towel, waited. She heaved and spluttered, her eyes streaming tears. It felt as if poison had invaded her, her body responding with this violent purging. Some ten minutes later, spent and hollow, she made her way back to bed.

'Why don't you get properly undressed this time?' her father urged. 'I'll fetch a bowl – don't want to risk you falling downstairs – what about pills? Should you take some more now? Try to eat something?'

'God, no! Just have to wait for it to go.'

He fetched the bowl, fussed around for a bit, tuned her radio to soothing music when she decided it might help her to sleep.

'Call me,' he said, 'if you need anything. Anything at all. I'm here.'

The next arrival was Oscar, pleased to find someone in bed at an unexpected time; he swept his tail against Hilly's face, clawed at the duvet and trod a nesting circle behind her head, where he settled. At last, soothed by his purring warmth, her brain slowed from its fast-spin, and the pain in her head subsided to a tolerable level.

Now she became aware of someone on the floor below – in Gran's room, her old room. It sounded as if Gran – or someone – was searching through cupboards, sliding doors open and closed, shutting drawers. A while later, someone could be heard slowly mounting the attic stairs, breathing hard.

'Gran?' Hilly sat up in bed, offending Oscar, who jumped to the floor and began washing himself. Heidigran had never come up here before.

With her eyes fixed on Hilly's face, Heidigran

moved slowly across to the bed. She offered Hilly a small, floral-covered notebook.

'What's this?' Hilly took it, seeing that it was an address book – old, well-filled, with dog-eared indexed pages. 'Why are you giving me this, Gran? D'you want to write to someone?'

'No,' Heidigran said, in her little-girl voice. 'You write.'

'Who to? Who d'you want me to write to?'

Heidigran took back the address book and fumbled through the pages; she dropped it on the floor, Hilly reached down for it and handed it back; she started again. Eventually she found what she wanted and thrust the open book at Hilly, pointing.

Fastened with a paperclip to the last spare page at the back was a torn piece of card, written in a different hand from Heidigran's neat, looped, pre-Alzheimer's writing:

Rachel Schönfeld,
4 Ben Gurion House,
Hadolphin Street.
Tel Aviv,
Israel.
Rschonfeld@adsl.net.il

Hilly's eyes swam; her mind reeled. She read, read again, staring at the marks on paper that jumbled and jangled themselves into nonsense.

'Rachel? Israel?' Her throat was dry. 'E-mail?'

Heidigran was nodding and smiling.

'*Your* Rachel? Your sister Rachel? But she died in Auschwitz!'

'No. No.' Confusion flickered over Heidigran's face. 'Didn't say that, did I? She went there. Yes. She came out. She isn't dead. Survived.' She pointed to the clipping. 'She sent me a card, a . . . b – b—'

'Birthday card?' Hilly prompted.

'Yes, when I was seven – seven – seventy. Wanted me to write back. I don't think I . . .' Heidigran's face creased into a frown. 'Don't think I did. Don't remember. But I kept it just in case.' She pointed to the e-mail address. 'Don't know what that means. Do you?'

'Yes, Gran.' Hilly lay back limply on the pillow. 'Yes, I do.'

Chapter Twenty-five

Out of the Blue

When you're unhappy you laugh, and
when you're hungry you sing.

Jewish saying

Dear Rachel [Hilly typed],

I'm sorry if this gives you a shock. I'm not
sure if you even know I exist. Probably not.

My name is Hilly Craig, and I believe you are
my grandmother's sister. My mother, Rose, I
think is your niece – she is the daughter of
Sarah Reubens, who changed her name to
Heidi when she came to live in England. My
grandmother showed me your address and
e-mail in the birthday card you sent her. Till the
last couple of weeks, I had no idea you existed.
We knew nothing of Gran's real past, only the
version she made up to hide the truth, which is
what we've always believed. And we're not sure
how much we know now. We didn't know she

was Sarah Reubens, and had a sister. We didn't know she had come to England as a refugee before the war. We found some photos and she started talking about Rachel — you — and that's how it started to come out. But it was only yesterday I found out you're, well, alive, and in Israel. After all the wondering and puzzling we've done, it's hard to believe you could get this as soon as I press SEND.

Sadly, Gran has Alzheimer's, and has come to live with us now. She's getting more and more forgetful. This means that everything will soon be lost, and you're the only one who can fill in the gaps for us. I hope you don't mind me asking . . .

* * *

'Sarah – Heidi! Open the door! I've made you some nice toast and dripping.'

She gave no answer. A hand outside turned the knob and rattled the door against the chair she had rammed against it. She didn't answer to Sarah; Auntie Enid ought to know that!

Her name was Heidi now. It was on her adoption papers – Heidi Thornton. Everyone was supposed to have new names, because Auntie Enid and Uncle Donald had decided that really she ought to call them Mum and Dad, since she had no other parents. Sometimes she remembered, but more usually she thought of them as Auntie Enid and Uncle Donald.

'Heidi, don't be silly! Let me in!'

Sometimes they just didn't understand! They really expected her to be delighted with the news. Instead she had retreated into silence, just as firmly as she had when the first reports came from Bergen-Belsen. More than a year had passed since then, and she never wanted to think about that again. No one was allowed to remind her that she was Jewish – not Patsy, not the Thorntons, not Kenneth, who met her each afternoon after school. He held her hand and carried her bag for her, and sometimes she let him kiss her cheek: not every day, not enough for him to take it for granted, but as a special favour. At first he had tried to apologize for being so mean to her, back in the junior school. She had put a hand over his mouth, insisting that she didn't remember him ever being horrible.

Sometimes she believed her own story: that she had somehow, carelessly, lost her parents and come to live with her aunt and uncle; that her new life had begun on the date shown on her adoption papers; that she remembered nothing before then.

The letter, addressed to Auntie Enid, had looked harmless enough when Heidi picked it up off the doormat, with two others. But she should know by now that letters usually brought bad news, like the one from the Red Cross that said Mutti's and Vati's names were on a list of people sent to the gas chambers at Chelmno.

As usual, Auntie Enid put the mail for Uncle Donald beside his place at the table, for him to open when he came in at tea time. Her own envelope she slit carefully with a knife. She gave a small gasp as she read it; glanced at Heidi, looked back at the typed page.

'No – no!' said Auntie Enid, holding the letter close, then at arm's length. 'I don't believe it! Sa— Heidi, it's the most amazing news . . .'

'What?' said Heidi, feeling her heart thud in her chest as mad supposings took her over.

'It's about Rachel – your sister! She's alive – oh, Heidi, it says she was in Aushwick, one of those dreadful places, but she was one of the survivors – oh, the poor love, losing her mum and dad, and going through all that – But, Heidi, this is from the Refugee Committee – it seems she wrote to them to find out where you are, and—'

'She's coming here?' In one instant Rachel had been changed from someone dead, burnt to ashes, into someone who threatened Heidi's stability.

'No, but she *is* coming to England! To London. Yes, really! Wants us to go down and meet her there. Oh, lovey, what a marvellous surprise for you! I don't wonder the cat's got your tongue. It's too much to take in, isn't it?'

'Let me see.' Heidi reached out for the letter. 'Will she come and live with us? I don't want to share my room,' she said, in a sullen voice. Eric, obligingly, had got married to a dull girl called Violet soon after being discharged from the army, and had gone to live with her at her parents' house in Rushden. It would be inconvenient if Rachel wanted to move in.

Auntie Enid gave her a shrewd look. 'You're

shocked – I'm not surprised. You sit there and let me make you a nice mug of hot sweet tea. Oh, but isn't it exciting! I don't suppose she's thinking of coming to live here. But you're going to have so much to tell each other – so much to catch up on!'

She made it sound as if Rachel had been on holiday. Heidi finished reading, folded the letter back in its envelope and sat tracing the pattern on the tablecloth with her forefinger while Auntie Enid bustled about, chatting all the while. 'You needn't rush, I'll write a note to explain why you're late for school—'

'No! You mustn't – I don't want anyone to know!' It burst out of her, angrily. 'I won't be late. It's just a normal day.'

Auntie Enid stood with arms folded, head on one side, scrutinizing her. 'I'm wondering if you ought to go to school at all. It's a big shock. For me, let alone you. And we'll need to make plans . . .' She looked back at the letter. 'Saturday week, it is. Can you tell them at the shop, take Saturday off? I'll have to see about train tickets . . .'

Heidi had not been to London since her first arrival in England. The war years, London's battering by German bombs, put a buffer between Heidi now and Sarah Reubens then. The news about Rachel was dragging her back, making her behave like a child again – a grumpy, sulky child who kicked her feet at the table leg and pushed out her lower lip and wouldn't look at anyone.

But I'm fourteen now, she thought. It's too late for

going back. Far too late. And she was frightened of Rachel. She imagined an ash-grey, skeletal figure, with twiggy arms and legs sticking out from those pyjama-like garments they wore in the photographs, the nearly-dead people who had reached out to the soldiers and begged silently. Eyes would be black holes in a skull-like face, there would be wisps of dead hair. Her parents had gone there, where Heidi's mind would not go. And now Rachel was coming to drag her back to them.

Auntie Enid was cutting bread, her back turned. Heidi turned and ran up the stairs to her room, and wedged the chair against the door. She flung herself on the bed, face pressed into the pillow. She stayed there all day, ignoring Auntie Enid's pleading, sneaking out only for the toilet. She spoke to no one.

* * *

Dear Hilly,

I cannot tell you how much tremendous surprise to receive your e-mail. You must please excuse my English, it is not my first language nor my second.

I had given up hope of ever hearing from my sister Sarah. Around the time of her seventieth birthday a friend showed me news of a reuniting of the Kindertransport children, all in their seventies as they are now (the Kinder, they call them) and of a book written about them. Now there is e-mail and the internet, it makes contacting people so much easier. Sarah would never wish to be part of a reuniting, but the organizer was able to give me her address and new name, which I think the Thorntons have passed on at the time of her marriage. I sent the card with my address and e-mail thinking that after so long she might contact me, but she did not.

It is only from you that I know of my English family. You will not know that you have family here too in Israel. I have not spoken to Sarah, or heard a word of her, since October of 1946 on my one visit to England. That was not a happy meeting. She did not wish to be remembered of the past . . .

* * *

For the next week, the Singer sewing machine had whirred late into the night as Auntie Enid worked at the dress she was making for Heidi, with fabric bought from the market. Heidi tried to remember how old Rachel would be. In her mind Rachel was always eighteen, not that much older than Heidi was now. The real Rachel, the Rachel resurrected from the dead, hauled back from behind the wire, would be twenty-four, grown up. I won't know her, Heidi thought: don't want to.

Auntie Enid and Uncle Donald dressed for the occasion as if they were going to a wedding. At Charing Cross Station, self-conscious in the green dress that gave her a new shape, Heidi scanned the faces of people hurrying to and from the platforms.

Trains. Always trains, carrying her out of her old life, carrying her parents to the extermination camp; now a train was bringing her dead sister to her. The rattling of train wheels punctuated her life. When I'm grown up, she thought, when I get married, I'll go everywhere by car, and then I need never go on a train again.

Auntie Enid and Uncle Donald, she thought, looked out of place in London, as if they'd strayed here by accident and weren't quite sure how to behave. They had arranged to meet Rachel by the newspaper stall, but they couldn't help being in everyone's way. People tutted, swerved, knocked against them. 'She'll soon be here, lovey, don't you fret,' said Auntie Enid, looking at her watch yet again, squeezing Heidi's hand.

Heidi didn't think Auntie Enid would ever stop treating her as a child. But I'm nearly grown up, she thought, making herself taller, pushing her breasts against the green fabric of her dress. I shall leave school next year. I shall have a job. In a few years I shall get married and have babies, English babies with an English father. No one can decide for me, no one can make me go anywhere I don't want to go. I'm not going back, ever.

'Sarah? Mr and Mrs Thornton?' said a gentle, accented voice behind them.

* * *

. . . She could not hide the shock of seeing me. Partly I expected that. I had put on flesh since being freed from Auschwitz, but the three years I was there had taken from my ableness to recover. You would not know now, but then you could not help but see. The kind foster-parents, Mrs and Mr Thornton, they quickly cover up. Sarah did not try to cover, did not get over her look of revolution [Hilly puzzled over this before realizing that Rachel must have meant *revulsion*] the whole of the time we were together. I disgusted her. This I saw in her face, and it was hard. It was not, after all, my own choice to be prisoner in that terrible place, to be ill, cold, famished, loused, to be brought to such desperation that there was hardly any spark of life still in me. I truly believe these two things kept me alive. One was the far possibility that my parents might be brought here where I was. That did not happen. Two was knowing my little sister was safe in England and that if I live, some day I may find her again . . .

*   *   *

It was Auntie Enid who talked to Rachel as they made their way to Lyons Corner House in the Strand. 'This is unbelievable – like a miracle!' she kept saying. Heidi walked on the other side of Uncle Donald, as far from Rachel as possible, looking down at the pavement. In the café, they found a spare table near the back. Auntie Enid motioned Rachel to sit, and Heidi opposite; she summoned a waitress.

'Choose whatever you like – here.' She pushed a ten-shilling note into Heidi's hand.

'You are going?' said Rachel.

'I think we'll leave you girls to talk on your own for a bit. You must have so much to say to each other!' said Auntie Enid, smiling indulgently. 'We'll be back in an hour.' Heidi gave her a beseeching look – don't leave me with *her*! – but it went unnoticed. With a wave of her hand, Auntie Enid followed Uncle Donald out towards the street.

Now Heidi had nowhere to look but at Rachel's face. It was not quite like the living skeleton of her dreams, but never had she seen a person whose skull was so close to the surface, whose eyes were sunk deep in their sockets yet looked out at her, bright and expectant. Rachel's wrists looked too frail to support her hands. She wore a jacket and skirt of navy fabric with a dark red thread in it, a neat white blouse underneath. Her hair – much thinner and less luxuriant than Heidi's – was brushed and looped back into a bun; she wore small gold earrings. She was making the best of herself. But, Heidi thought, it's like decking winter twigs with false blossom. Everyone looking at us will see what she is. They will know. They will smell the ashy smell of death she brings with her. They will move away, to avoid breathing the air she breathes.

'Sarah, please!' Rachel said in German. 'Look at me – I've come all this way to see you! We are together at last, after so many years!'

She reached across the table for Heidi's hand. Heidi withdrew quickly, folding her arms, tucking both hands out of reach. 'Talk in English,' she said. 'I don't speak German any more. And my name's Heidi now. You must call me Heidi like everyone else.'

'But to me you are Sarah! And my English is not good. You must speak German, or we will never understand each other! You cannot have forgotten!'

Heidi thought she had, and was dismayed how easily the sounds flowed into her brain. A waitress came to the table, pad and pencil poised. 'Tea for two, please,' Heidi said, in English as correct and un-accented as she could possibly make it. 'And a selection of cakes.' I can pay, she thought, with Auntie Enid's ten-shilling note. I want Rachel to see that I've got money and I can pay.

'I am only here in London for three nights,' Rachel said. 'Since the war ended I have been living and working in Poland. But soon I shall be moving on again. I'm going to Palestine. And – in two weeks I shall be married. So you see, life does begin again.'

'Married!'

'Yes. His name is Aaron Schönfeld. I can see what you're thinking, Sarah – you're wondering how any-one can want to marry such a scrawny scarecrow as you see opposite you. But Aaron does. We understand each other. What we have been through, you see, we have both been through.'

'What's he like?'

'He is a little older than me. He is also from Köln. He was in Auschwitz, though we did not know each other there. We were both young and fit, so we were chosen for work. That is what saved us. We met later, through a kind Polish family who helped us when we were released. I have found work in an organization in Krakow concerned with the resettlement of survivors.

Earlier this summer Aaron and I travelled back together to Köln to see if we could find out what happened to our families. We found nothing, neither Aaron nor I. All gone. Our flat, Sarah, our garden – there are other people living there. It is as if we never were.'

Be quiet. Be *quiet*! Heidi willed her. Rachel would talk on and on, she would say terrible things in her gentle, matter-of-fact voice. She would say what she had seen: the things Eric had described, the things of the radio broadcast. Only worse, because those things had been Rachel's world. Her entire world.

Rachel looked down at her hands. 'Many letters, many visits, many searching through lists, it took before I found out what happened to Mutti and Vati. Do you know?'

'Yes. They were gassed,' Heidi said, in an offhand voice.

'Yes. They were deported from Köln to the Lodz ghetto, and from there to Chelmno. Not until I had the facts did I give up hope. Aaron's parents also, killed at Sachsenhausen – they fled Köln only to be caught and imprisoned. But even then we were not alone, because we had found each other. And I had thoughts of you.'

Heidi looked away.

'I knew then, when I returned to Köln, that I could never stay in Germany. All the while, I was afraid. Someone would see us, know we were Jewish, hand us over. I could not forget that fear, not for one second. Things have changed now, but my skin and my blood and my nerves could never believe it was so. And

Aaron the same – we must for ever be watchful, for ever afraid. That's what made us decide that our new life together will be in Palestine, in the new Jewish homeland. We will feel safe there.'

The waitress brought cakes on a tiered plate, teapot, milk jug, cups and saucers.

'Why have you come?' Heidi asked.

'Oh, Sarah, is there any need for you to ask that?'

Heidi busied herself with the teapot and strainer, pouring two cups of tea. 'Have some cake.' She took an éclair and started eating it. Rachel looked sadly at the abundance of cakes, and took one shortbread finger, which she left untouched on her plate. Suddenly, for Heidi, it became important to eat hungrily: to show Rachel. *Look, I'm alive, I'm healthy, I'm eating. This is what it's like. I am plump and well fed.*

A silence fell between them. Heidi ate; Rachel looked at the walls, at the waitress, at the other customers.

'So,' Heidi said, finishing the éclair. She took a madeleine, and licked flakes of coconut off her fingers. 'You're marrying a Jewish boy, and you're going to live in Palestine. You'll have Jewish children. We're so different now. The Thorntons aren't Jewish, you realize that? And neither am I.'

'Yes, I know. You have become less Jewish, and I have become more so. In the camp, we kept the faith. We kept the traditions, as best we could. We said the prayers, we kept the Sabbath. It helped keep us alive – gave us some sense of purpose, of continuity, of belonging to each other. The Nazis could destroy everything, our homes, our families, could even destroy us whenever they chose, shoot us, torture us, send us to the gas chambers, but the one thing they could not destroy was our faith. And through this my faith was strengthened. You have to understand that!'

'Yes,' Heidi said, with a faint shrug. 'I don't see how it affects me, though. What do you want from me?'

'We belong to each other, too,' Rachel said. 'We are still sisters.'

Their eyes met across the table. Heidi remembered last time: *I hate you! I hope I never see you again!* She had regretted it, then, almost immediately. But now she was thinking it again, without compassion: she was willing Rachel to know it, to read it in her eyes.

'You just told me,' she said. 'It's as if we never were.'

* * *

Afterwards I knew that she was frightened of me, but at the time I saw only disgust. No longer could I stand it. The years of separation, the hoping, the journey, and for this I had been waiting! I got up and left, walked out of the café without a goodbye, I did not even wait the return of the kind Thorntons, who must have been so disappointed with the lovely day they planned. I returned to my lodgings the Refugee Committee had arranged for me. I was meant to stay one night more but I collected my bag and caught the next train back to Dover. That same night I left England and have never returned.

So, Hilly, that is the last time I have seen

my sister. I do not blame her for it. I do not blame myself. I blame events. But, you say, she has not forgotten me – in her confusion she asks questions? Perhaps Sarah Reubens is still there inside her? Perhaps she remembers that once we were sisters?

Can you please tell her I do not blame her?

* * *

Heidi sat alone at the table with tears burning her eyes. For a moment, bleakness and emptiness threatened to overwhelm her. She would not cry; she was utterly determined not to cry. People were looking; they had heard the German conversation, they had seen Rachel shove back her chair and walk out, they knew there had been an argument. Heidi was not going to add to the spectacle by sitting there in tears. She blinked rapidly, smiled at a lady in a feathered hat at the next table, and took a butterfly cake from the plate. What was the point in crying? She was Heidi Thornton, a Northampton girl in London for the day. She had English parents who loved her, and a house to live in, with a room of her own. She was an only child, and happy with that.

'Oh, where's Rachel?' asked Auntie Enid, returning, looking around. 'Has she gone to the Ladies'?'

'She had to leave,' Heidi said.

* * *

As you will know, there are those who attempt to deny the Holocaust, who say it has been exaggerated, even that it did not happen. Those like myself who bear the scars (yes, the number tattooed on my arm, and other scars you cannot see) find that our witness is not acceptable. We find that we were too closely involved to be believed. We are not objective enough. We cannot be relied on to tell the truth. This I cannot understand. It is why I have written about my experiences for those who collect such accounts. It is my testament. If you are interested to read what I have written I will send it to you.

Aaron and I were married and came to live in Palestine, now Israel. As you will know from the television and newspapers, it is not the safe homeland we hoped. We came here with optimism and hopes, but again we find ourselves in a country on the edge of war. Israel is seen as the bully, with its tanks and helicopters and army. But there is atrociosity on both sides, suicide bombers come into cafés and buses, to kill at random, to terrify. Bitterness and blame reach back to before the time of our coming. The holy places of three great religions are trampled and fought over.

But it is our home, and I shall never leave. We have a saying, When you're unhappy you laugh, and when you're hungry you sing. If there is one thing I have learned, it is be happy when you can. Love the blessings life gives you. Aaron and I had each other, and soon we had children: son Daniel, daughter Sarah. And we have fine grandchildren, four: Samuel, Esther, Ruth, Chava. Samuel is a soldier in the Israeli army, Ruth is a teacher. Chava is the youngest, still at school, she is seventeen, the same age as you. And, can you believe that I am a great-grandmother, as my dear Esther has a beautiful baby boy, David. A next generation!

I am eighty-two years old now, and not in good health (this is the damage of my time in Auschwitz, come back in my old age). Alas, this means I am unable again to travel to England so I fear I will never see my dear sister once more.

But in Yiddish we have a word *beschert*, which means meant to be. How much was meant to be and how much was not, I cannot know. But maybe it was *beschert* that before I die I should receive your message and know of my sister, and that she has been happy in her family life, and that you exist. Israel is not at present a welcoming place to travel, but if you or your family could make the journey it will be the delight of us all.

This is a very long message and I have tired myself struggling with my memory and my dictionary. I have waited more than fifty years to send it. Thank you from the bottom of my heart for making it possible.

G—d is good.

Blessings,

Your Great-Aunt Rachel

Chapter Twenty-six

Long Shadows

HOW TO GET TO ISRAEL
By air: Ben-Gurion Airport, between Tel
Aviv and Jerusalem, is Israel's international airport. There are daily flights from
Heathrow. Those intending to travel
should be aware that security is extremely
rigorous. The situation in the Middle East
is still extremely volatile, and travel for non-
essential purposes has been discouraged.
Passengers should consult their tourist
office for up-to-date information before
booking.

The Holy Land – travel brochure

'No, you can't possibly go!' said Rose. 'Who in their
right mind would let their daughter go to Tel Aviv?
Now, in the middle of all this violence?'

Hilly had hidden today's newspaper, which carried
news of another suicide bombing on a bus full of

commuters, and ominous statements by represent-
atives of both sides. 'But I've *got* to go,' she pleaded.
'And soon! If I don't – if one of us doesn't – we'll never
see Rachel!' She glanced at her grandmother, who
had pushed her chair back from the table and was
examining her knitting pattern. 'There's no way
Heidigran can go, nor you, Mum, while you're looking
after her – even if you wanted to. And there's no
chance of Rachel coming here. We can't just forget
about it!'

Her mother shook her head. 'If it were anywhere
else, I'd agree with you.'

'Dad?' Hilly pleaded. 'Please, think about it, at
least!'

He said nothing, glancing at Rose. They had
finished eating, but no one had moved to start clearing away the dishes.

'I don't see why you're suddenly making a big
thing about this,' said Zoë. She leaned over to look at
the pasta left on Hilly's plate. 'If you're not eating that,
can I have it?'

'Sure.' Hilly passed over half a plate of pasta; the
sickness had left her with a dodgy stomach. Zoë, at
least, had a healthy appetite – was that a good or a bad
sign?

'After all,' said Zoë, digging in with her fork, 'we
never even knew Rachel existed, two days ago. Doesn't
mean you have to jump on a plane, not when you've
got e-mail. Why should it change everything?'

'Because it does!' Hilly looked at her in mild
exasperation. 'E-mail's not the same as actually *meeting*

337

someone. And it's not just Rachel – it's all of them. Our relations! A whole branch of the family we didn't even know we had!'

'You've sprung it on us very suddenly, this idea,' said their father. 'We'll have to give it a lot of careful thought.'

'I *have* given it thought,' Rose said sharply. 'And it's a definite no, as far as I'm concerned—'

'I needn't miss school! I'll go in the Christmas holidays—'

'It's not school that's bothering me! It's much too dangerous out there. And going on your own? I'd never have a second's peace, worrying about you—'

'I'll promise to be careful! Never to get on a bus, or go into busy streets!' Hilly tried. 'We don't even know exactly where Rachel's house is, do we? She lives there, she doesn't sound as if she's terrified, every minute of her life! I expect we get a distorted picture here – we only hear about the violence, not about ordinary life.'

'There are lots of questions to be asked. Lots of things we'll need to find out, before we decide,' said her father.

Hilly gave him an encouraging smile. 'I've already done some internet searches about flights and stuff.'

'And, yes, I can understand why you're desperate to go. If you don't, if you miss this chance, you'll always regret it, the rest of your life.'

'Thanks, Dad!'

'Wait!' said Rose. 'Nothing's decided yet. How

much is the air fare? Where'd the money come from? Even *if* we get to the stage of agreeing, which I'm certainly not ready to do yet. We're already paying for your history trip to Berlin.'

Hilly was silent, knowing that her savings wouldn't begin to cover the cost of travel.

'We'll find it, somehow,' said her father.

'I can pay,' said Heidigran, unexpectedly.

Everyone turned to look at her. She had shown no interest in the conversation till now.

'Pay, Mum?'

'You thought I wasn't listening, didn't you?' she said, looking triumphantly round the table. 'But I was. Hilly wants to go on holiday and she needs a plane ticket. Why can't I buy it for her, if she wants it? I've got money sitting in the bank, doing nothing.'

'Are you serious?' said Reuben on the phone. 'Yes, course you are. How's Rashid going to take all this?'

'It'll be fine,' Hilly said. 'He'll understand.'

Afterwards, Hilly thought: I should have known. I should have been more careful. Now I've blown it. How did I honestly think he'd react? He's a Palestinian; he's lived out there. What did I expect?

All week, with all its upheavals and adjustments, she had been counting first the days, then the hours till Rashid came back from Oxford on Friday evening. She had tried to summon him in her thoughts: his voice, the exact colour of his skin, the way he threw back his head when he laughed; the way he had looked at her just before they kissed for the first time.

He was to pick her up at the bus station. While she waited, she continued reading a book she had found in the school library: *On Being Jewish*, by Julia Neuberger. It was more than relevant; the opening chapters described Julia Neuberger's grandmother receiving children from the Kindertransports, before the war. Hilly had only meant to pass the time, keeping an eye on the clock and looking out for Rashid, but he surprised her by arriving early, finding her completely absorbed in reading. 'I thought we might go the country park, then get something to eat later. OK?'

'Great!' Hilly put the book away in her bag, saw Rashid looking at it, at the black cover embossed with a Star of David in gold; she saw his puzzled expression, but neither of them made any comment, not yet. Maybe he thought she was reading it for a history assignment.

Later, she realized that his reaction to seeing the Star of David must have been similar to hers on seeing Pete's swastika badge. To him, it was the Israeli flag, the symbol of oppression.

Yet, for the first half hour or so, everything was better than she could have wished. Rashid parked the car within view of the lake; they kissed, clung to each other without speaking, smiled into each other's eyes; they had the whole evening, and, as Rashid was staying with his family, the whole weekend. Arms round each other's waists, they walked slowly along the edge of the lake, skirting white dollops of goose-droppings. The sun was going down behind them, its reflection gilding the lake's surface. A raucous quacking, like coarse laughter, sounded from the reed-fringed island.

Then Hilly told Rashid everything that had happened, and the idyll came to an abrupt end.

He became increasingly silent as she talked, his expression withdrawn. 'So,' he said at last, 'you're Jewish now. Is that what you're saying?'

Their shadows on the grass were distinct and separate.

'It's not for me to decide, is it? I *am*. A quarter of me, anyway. Can you imagine how weird that is? Suddenly you're not quite who you always thought you were?'

'And that changes everything, does it?'

'Yes – in a way it does. No, not everything!' Not you and me, she wanted to say; but Rashid had become aloof and unapproachable. He turned away from her, looking across the water. Lights were being switched on in the yachting clubhouse.

'Quite a week you've had, one way and another,' he remarked.

'You could say that!'

'And it'll take a lot of getting used to. That much I can see. What I don't see is why you need to throw yourself into it. It doesn't have to change who you are, does it? Only if you let it! That book you've got—'

'I'm curious!' Hilly said. 'That's not hard to understand, is it?'

'No, but – On *Being* Jewish—'

'It was the Nazis who wanted to stop people reading books! It's a free country – I'll read what I like!'

They were walking again, aimlessly; Rashid kicked at a dried head of sorrel. 'It's not just reading, is it? You want it all, the whole Jewish thing.'

'I want to find out. I want to understand. God is good, Rachel said. She can still think that! After all that's happened to her! I want to *know*. I want to see things from her point of view.'

'She's an Auschwitz survivor. You think you can understand what that feels like? You want to? As for this sudden plan to go to Israel – don't you watch the news? Don't you know what's going on out there?'

'Course I do – well,' Hilly conceded, 'not as much as I ought to know. I've watched the news every day since – since I've known you.'

'And why are you the only one? It's the same for your mum and sister, isn't it? – they've found out all this, just like you have? They're not dropping everything to fly nearly three thousand miles, are they?'

'Neither am I dropping everything! It's not till Christmas. And then only if it seems safe.'

Rashid gave a humourless laugh. 'Safe? Forget it, in that case. You'll never go.'

'Three thousand miles is a travellable distance. I thought Rachel was dead! Wouldn't you want to go, if you'd just found out you've got a whole family there you never even knew about? Cousins – well, second cousins, one of them my own age – they're like the other half of us, of my own family! We could have *been* them, if things had turned out differently. I've just got to meet them, it's a way of – of – trying to put things right. And Rachel – I've got to meet her, and she's eighty-two and not well enough to travel – how much time is there? We can't all go. We've talked about it – Mum can't, with Heidigran to look after—'

'One of your cousins is in the *army*! What do you think they'd say, your Jewish relations, what do you think *he'd* say, if he knew you were seeing a Palestinian Arab? That's if we *are* seeing each other, if that's not assuming too much—'

'I haven't even met him yet! Why should that affect the way I—'

'It will, wait and see!' You don't know how racist they are. An Israeli soldier sees a Palestinian like me, he sees either a terrorist, or the idiot who sweeps the street in Tel Aviv. He doesn't see a human being. Believe me, I know!'

'But you can't know that he's like that!' Hilly flared. 'Anyway, what would your lot say? I'm hardly a nice Muslim girl, am I? I don't see that it's for anyone else to decide – only us.'

Rashid looked away. He picked up a stone from the path, turned to throw it, and sent it skimming across the water. Hilly had the fatalistic sense of everything going wrong. I can't do this, she thought: I can't manage all the different strands of my life. When one goes right, another gets messed up.

'So,' she said, 'you're saying it changes everything, now that you know I've got a Jewish grandmother?'

He shook his head. 'That's not what I—'

'Doesn't that make *you* a racist?'

'Now you're just distorting what I've said.'

'What about that taxi driver? Your uncle's friend, the one who was shot? You didn't hate him for being Jewish, did you? Why's this different?'

'Look,' Rashid said, not looking at her. 'It's a big change, that's all I'm saying. Half an hour ago, I had no idea you had a connection with – now you're all set to go out there. It needs some taking in – not because of what you've found out, but because of how you're reacting. You had Jewish relatives in Germany – but that was then, and this is now. You don't have to turn into a Zionist sympathizer! And you will, if you go out there. They'll tell you Israel's got a sacred right to their Promised Land, and the Arabs are a fanatical bunch of killers. Hilly, I've just come back from there! Israel's the enemy. I hate them. I don't want to, don't want to hate, but I can't tell you how much I hate them. Can you begin to imagine what it's like to live under occupation? Curfews, road blocks, rules telling you where you can and can't go? Soldiers killed my cousin, killed him in the street! Can't you see where that puts us? It's like – it's like – I can't even think of another example – no, it's like I tell you my grandad was an SS Kommandant or something. Only this is happening *now*.'

'So what are you saying?' Hilly scuffed her shoe on a patch of mud rutted hard by bike tyres. 'If I go out there, forget about you and me? Or – is it all off anyway?'

'I don't know what I'm saying. Just telling you how it seems. I'm not telling you what to do and what not to do – why should I? In your position I'd probably want to do the same. But it does change things, can't you see that? Puts us on different sides.'

'I'm not on anyone's side! I'm just trying to make sense of what I've found out!'

'Wait till you get out there, wait till you start reading Israeli newspapers and watching Israeli TV, then see if you can be neutral!'

'Perhaps I'm not so gullible! It's not as if I don't know *you*—'

'You don't understand,' Rashid said flatly. 'You just don't understand. I think— Oh, forget it.'

He stopped walking and stood, arms folded, looking out across the water. Hilly touched his shoulder. 'Forget what? Don't go all silent!'

He turned, not looking her in the eye. 'Look – I think we'd better call off tomorrow. You need time to think about all this, sort it out in your head. So do I. I'll ring Matt and tell him I'll work tomorrow after all, he can use the help. I'll drive you home now if that's OK, then go straight back. Anyway,' he added with what Hilly considered unnecessary sarcasm, 'shouldn't you be keeping the Sabbath?'

In the car, Hilly hardly looked at him. It was like Monday's argument with Reuben all over again – bleakness and sorriness conflicting with a stubborn refusal to make any move to put things right. He's using this, she thought miserably, as an excuse to – to dump me, Zoë would say. I'm being dumped. I've built the whole thing up into more than it is; I've been deluding myself.

They were close to the town centre. 'Stop! Stop here,' she said, in a tight voice. 'I'll get out here, thanks.'

'Sure?'

'I'm going to see Reuben.'

'Oh yes, Reuben,' Rashid said, with a look on his face she could not fathom. 'See you, then.'

'Possibly,' Hilly said coldly.

She got as far as the window of Settlers, looked in, saw Saeed but no Reuben, and turned away again. She walked away between rows of shops, hardly aware of her surroundings, unsure, now, whether she wanted to see even Reuben. But she couldn't go home yet either; they'd been expecting her to be out all evening, and would ask questions she didn't feel like answering.

Veering away from the town centre, she took the road to the park between her house and Reuben's. Another park, another lake, and the round pond where they so often met. This time she could be alone there; she could think about what had happened. It's all my own fault, she thought one moment; then, immediately, no! It was his fault. He didn't have to react like that, did he? But underlying her annoyance was the thought that no, she did not understand. She had not been to the Middle East. Had not seen what happened on the streets. Had not experienced the anger and hatred on both sides. But the whole point, she thought, is that I want to find out! I'm making an effort, aren't I?

Disappointment dragged at her steps; the weariness of having been misunderstood; the heaviness of loss, the feeling that a promise had been made between them that would not now be kept.

Voices behind her broke into her thoughts: young male voices. She heard a whooping call, loud laughter. Turning, she saw three boys, tall, large, filling the alley, shoving and joshing each other. Unsure whether she recognized them in the fading light, she walked on faster towards the open space of the park.

Grant! Was it? The tallest one could be Grant; she didn't want to turn again for a better look. Grant, with Clyde and Tuck! And if it was, had they seen her – stupidly walking alone into the shadows of the park – recognized her, seen their chance for revenge?

She was ahead of them, walking fast: but at what point did a brisk walk stop looking confident, and become a frightened scuttle?

Reaching open grass, the slope down towards the lake, she looked around hoping to see pairs of lovers, dog-walkers, even druggies – but the park was quiet, no one in sight at all. Instinctively, Hilly turned towards the round pond, and the sanctuary of her meeting place with Reuben. It was tempting to break into a run, but she didn't want to display her fear so openly. A glance back showed the boys taking the same path, behind her. She quickened her pace, felt her heartbeat quicken, the pulse swooshing in her ears. There was no one she could yell to for help. Spasmodic traffic on the road moved smoothly behind a screen of trees – no one would see if they—

Reaching the hedge that bordered the pond, she

risked a look round before deciding which way to go. The boys had left the path, spilling out across the grass, running down to the lake. One of them waved at her. Not Grant, not his friends, but three boys she knew vaguely from school, Year Thirteen. Stuart Adams, the one who had waved. The other two started a mock fight by the edge of the lake, threatening to wrestle each other into the water. Hilly returned the wave, stupid with relief.

Turning her key in the lock, she had the sense that her family was not quite the family she knew, not any more. Nothing was quite the same; no one was who she had thought. The doormat, the hall table with a shaded lamp on it, the pegs for coats, looked almost jarringly ordinary, but the floor no longer felt quite solid under her feet. Heidigran was not Heidigran. And Mum, Zoë, me, Hilly thought . . . we've all shifted our identity. Even Dad isn't the same, since I found out about Stella . . .

She went upstairs, not wanting to explain to her parents why she'd come back early. In their attic room, Zoë was getting ready to go out; she turned from the mirror, smiling, radiant, a mascara wand in her hand.

'Hilly! Everything's OK – look!' She pointed to the open packet of Tampax on her bed. 'Started this afternoon. Isn't it great?'

'Oh, Zoë—' Hilly found herself enveloped in a hug, whirled between the beds in a mad caper.

'Isn't it fantastic? I've got a stonking great period pain but I've never been so glad in my life! I wouldn't care if it went on for a fortnight! Periods are great! I'm so lucky. Now Gloopy Grant can get stuffed, I don't have to think about him again, ever—'

'You've put mascara all over my sleeve,' Hilly pointed out, detaching herself.

'Oh, it's only one of your crummy Oxfam jobs. It'll wash out. I never even had to use the pregnancy kit!' Zoë said, giggling. 'What shall I do? Throw it away or save it for another time?'

'Please,' Hilly said feelingly, 'don't put me through this again. I don't think I could stand it.'

'*You* couldn't stand it? What about me? That's just typical of you – you're so self-centred!'

Hilly laughed, sitting on her bed, pushing off her shoes, toe against heel. 'So we're back to normal, are we?' How typical of Zoë, she thought, exasperation mixing with affection. Trust her to bounce back, full of herself and bolshie as ever, after a scare like this!

'Do you think I really *was* pregnant, and lost it?' Zoë was back at the mirror with her hairbrush. 'Or is it just my period was late?'

'Late, I should think. All sorts of things can cause that – like being upset,' Hilly said.

'Honestly, I don't even know what I saw in Grant now – he's vile, and as for his friends—'

'I do,' said Hilly.

'You what?'

'I do see what you saw in Grant.'

Zoë stared. 'But I thought you hated him!'

'I don't like him,' Hilly said, 'not at all, but he's – well, sex on legs. Anyone can see that.'

'You thought so?' said Zoë, with a disbelieving laugh.

'Even I thought so, yes. Trouble is, it can sort of mesmerize you – make you do stupid things.'

'Hilly! You don't mean *you've*— This bloke you've met – you mean him? I didn't realize you'd—'

'Well, you were right,' said Hilly. 'You're ahead of me there. And it's not going to happen now. All off.'

'Oh, too bad.' Zoë was too preoccupied with her own relief to show much interest. 'The thing was with Grant, he made me feel good about myself. That's all it was.'

'But Zoë, you've got all sorts of reasons to feel good about yourself! You don't need an arrogant yob to tell you who you are. For God's sake, if you want a boyfriend, find someone who's worth the effort! Where are you off to, anyway?' she added.

'Out with Nads.' Zoë took a sleeveless top from her wardrobe, then another. 'Which, do you think?'

'Mm – the red one.'

Zoë held it against herself, posing for the mirror. 'Yes, I'm in a red mood, red's my favourite colour!'

'Just be careful how you celebrate,' Hilly said.

Downstairs, Heidigran was watching a comedy on television, with the vacant expression she often wore nowadays; she looked vaguely, blearily at Hilly as she passed.

'Thought you were going out?' Rose said, in the kitchen. She was writing in felt tip on the message board.

'I did go out. Now I'm back.'

Rose looked at her for an explanation; when none came, she turned back to the board where she had written '*Saturday*'. Now, underneath, she wrote: '*Rose, Gavin, Heidi – Fairlawns, 11*'.

'Fairlawns? The residential home?'

'Yes,' Rose said – slightly defensively, Hilly thought. 'Just to have a look. Josie's arranged it. The idea is we start taking Mum there one day a week, and see how things go from there. When she's used to it, we can arrange longer stays – a few days, even a whole week, if we want to go away, or if we just need a break. I know I've always said I'd never put her in a home,' she said, as if Hilly had accused her of betrayal, 'but one of the most important things I've learned from Josie and the group is that guilty feelings are no use to anyone. And after all, we're not planning to dump her there, abandon her. I honestly don't think it's going to make much difference to her, once she feels safe there – look how all these revelations have washed over her! We have to make a situation we can all live with.'

'It's hard for you, Mum,' Hilly said.

'Hard for all of us.' Rose wrote '*Hilly*' on the board. 'You could come with us, if you wanted – or are you working?'

'No, I'm doing Wednesday afternoons now and late Thursday,' said Hilly. The Saturday she had kept free for Rashid now loomed emptily ahead. 'I *could* come, or . . .'

'Mm?' said her mother, pen poised.

'No, on second thoughts I might go to Oxford. Have we got a bus timetable?'

'In the drawer, I think.' Rose looked at her with eyebrows raised. 'Oxford? Rashid?'

'Yes,' Hilly said, with a hint of defiance.

'Perhaps you'd like to bring him home, next time he's back in Northampton? Invite him round for a meal?'

A conciliatory move: shame it was probably too late.

'Thanks,' Hilly said. 'I'm not sure if it's on or off, to be honest.'

Her mother looked at her. 'But you want it to be on?'

Hilly nodded, not trusting herself to speak, looking in the drawer for the timetable leaflet.

'OK. Let me know how tomorrow turns out.' Rose wrote '*Oxford*' beside Hilly's name on the board.

There. It's definite now, Hilly thought – timetabled, in writing. No chickening out.

Chapter Twenty-seven

Catch 22

Love, *n*. a warm affection, strong
emotional attachment; sexual passion or
desire. **Fall in love (with)** begin to feel
passionate attachment (for); **make love**
express sexual desire, usually physically.

The Oxford English Dictionary

In Walton Street, Hilly's feet began to drag. She couldn't be sure she hadn't passed the turning, let alone make up her mind whether this was a stupid thing to do.

Last night it had seemed the *only* thing to do. Either come and find Rashid, or let whatever they had between them fade away to nothing. That would be pathetic, wouldn't it? *A*pathetic. She had to try. *If there is one thing I have learned*, Rachel had said in her e-mail, *it is be happy when you can. Love the blessings life gives you.*

And what had she herself said to Zoë? *If you want*

a boyfriend, for God's sake find someone who's worth the effort. Well, wasn't Rashid?

And against these thoughts were ranged all the common-sense arguments Hilly didn't want to hear: *You've only been out with him one and half times. One day and half an evening. Why are you making it into such a big thing? Do you really think he cares about you this much? Anyway, he's working today, he said he doesn't want to see you, he'll think you're an idiot, coming all this way for nothing* . . . And, making her stop and gaze absently at ridiculously overpriced dresses in a shop window, Zoë's words about Grant: *He made me feel good about myself, that was all.*

Rashid makes me feel good about myself, Hilly thought. Is that all? How could she possibly tell? He made her feel unusual, intelligent, fascinating, attractive. Unused to feeling any of these things, she was intoxicated. Mesmerized? Wasn't that what she'd said to Zoë? And how could you trust such feelings? Look what happened to Dad—

Wouldn't it be simpler to go out with some sixth-form boy with nothing in his head but football and mates and having a good time?

Simpler, yes – but I want Rashid, and no one else will do. I want to see and touch him. I want his dark, dark chocolate-brown eyes looking at me, and the solid warmth of his body, and his voice, and his obstinacy and his separateness, I want it all now, and I want more and more and more—

Yes, she was going the right way; she saw the Picture House cinema and a bike shop on her left, the Jericho Café on her right, and now it was only a short distance farther, along a residential road. Well, it was too late to turn back now. She could, if she were really feeble, go back to the city centre and wander round the shops or do more Oxford sightseeing before catching the bus home; but then how would she put up with herself?

This was the house, she knew, coming to a halt: no curtains at the downstairs windows, a front garden full of brambles and nettles, the gate propped open. She stood on the cracked path, looking up at the bay window. Rashid was on a stepladder, working at the ceiling with a paint-roller. Hilly stood, indecisive with anticipation. He was here, and she only had to knock on the door, or wave, to get his attention.

It was a kind of madness, Dad had said that time in the car – wanting Stella so much that it made him forget everything else. But I'm not mad, Hilly thought: I'm too cautious for that, too careful. As she hesitated, a young man in paint-stained navy overalls came to the window with a scraper in his hand, saw her, and gestured that he was going to the door. There was no going back.

'Yeah?'

'Can I come in? I've come to see Rashid.'

'Sure.' Matt, presumably, stubble-jawed and spiky-haired, led the way over a dust-sheeted floor and into the large front room. Rashid looked down from ceiling height and gave Hilly a startled look, almost dropping the roller. He clumped down the steps.

'See if you can cheer him up.' Matt took a pack of

Players and a lighter from his dungarees pocket, took out a cigarette and offered one to Hilly, who shook her head. The interior smelled cleanly of new emulsion.

Hilly and Rashid looked at each other awkwardly. Both began speaking at once. 'How did you—?'

'Sorry to barge in—'

'No problem—'

'Got the bus. Just thought I'd—'

Matt sat back against the windowsill, unlit cigarette in his hand, watching them with mild interest.

With deliberate slowness, Rashid put down his roller on the edge of a paint tray; carefully, it seemed to her, he kept his distance. 'Well, this is it,' he said, indicating the freshly creamed walls. The room was high-ceilinged, with a fireplace swathed in a dust sheet, a radio on the windowsill, trays and tins of paint on the floor. 'Work. Home, for now. And this is Matt. Matt, Hilly.'

I'm embarrassing him, she thought: he doesn't want me here.

'Might as well have a break,' Matt said, 'since we've stopped anyway. My dad does his nut if I smoke in here.'

'I'll show you downstairs,' Rashid said to Hilly. 'Where we live.'

'See you later,' Matt called from the front door, leaving it open.

Stairs led down to a narrow hallway, a kitchen and two bedrooms. 'That's Matt's room,' Rashid said, leading the way past a half-open door. 'This is mine. I haven't done much to it, yet.' A roughly made bed-cum-sofa, shelves with books and folders, a CD player, a hanging space with a few clothes in it half-concealed by a curtain, a desk with a reading lamp. His room was at the front of the house, a half-basement, with a high window showing the green tangle of the front garden.

'It's a lovely house,' she said, looking at him, uncertain.

'Yes. I wouldn't mind staying on here, if I get my place at the John Radcliffe.' He laughed suddenly. 'Next time you appear from nowhere like that, make it when I'm not balancing on a stepladder. Thought I was hallucinating! I was thinking about you, and suddenly there you were.'

'I didn't mean to stop you working,' she said. 'No – I *did* mean to stop you working—'

'You have.'

'Sorry if I've annoyed you—'

'Hilly. I am not annoyed.'

'You said you didn't want to see me today—'

'Well, I do.'

'You do? In spite of yesterday?'

'*Because* of yesterday.'

'What do you mean?' she said, in confusion.

'It was a shock, what you told me. Takes a bit of getting used to. But I'm trying.'

'And I'm trying.' Hilly launched into her prepared speech. 'What I came to say was – one of the things – I *am* going to Israel, even if you don't like it, because I want to. But you don't have to react like you did. It's to see it from both sides, see for myself. Not to sign up

for the Israeli army. Yes, I'm going because I want to
meet Rachel, and her family, and find out about her.
But because I want to know more about *you*, too.
Where you come from, where your relations are, how
they have to live. After all, if two people can't be
together, two people in England, two people who –
really like each other, what hope is there?'

'I know. I know. It was stupid, a – a gut feeling.
But—'

'Mm?'

'I'll get used to it. There are more important gut
feelings.'

Hilly looked at him, uncertain. They had not yet
touched; now Rashid moved close and put both arms
around her. Hers went around him; she closed her
eyes, breathed his warmth and his painty smell.
Her head was afloat with relief: everything was going
to be all right.

'What were the other things you were going to
say?' His voice tickled her ear.

'Can't remember. It can wait.'

'Good.' He kissed her hair, her neck, her mouth,
held her close; her hands roved over his back, at first
over and then inside his T-shirt, feeling the blades of
his shoulders, the ridges of his spine, the suppleness
and strength of his body. She lost her balance, swayed;
after a moment when they both seemed to totter
drunkenly, locked together, she found they were on
the bed, half-sitting, half-lying.

Rashid removed her glasses and placed them on
the windowsill. 'They get in the way.'

'I can still see you without them. I'm hopelessly short-sighted.'

'I like the way you look in your glasses. Serious.'

'Like an old-fashioned schoolmarm, Zoë says.'

'Don't listen to her. You're lovely, with or without them.'

'Rashid, there must be plenty of opticians in Oxford. You'd better book yourself an appointment.'

Rashid shook his head. 'I'm not letting anyone put you down. Not your sister – not you, either.'

Stillness, fitful sunlight through the greenery at the window, and looking and smiling, and then Rashid pushed her gently back against the pillow and his weight over her, and now they were touching and exploring, stroking and smoothing, moving against each other, wanting and wanting, pulses pulsing, breathy breathing, temperature rising, his hand cupping her breast, his knee parting her legs, her hand fumbling at the button of his jeans, and she thought, Oh, this is what it's like, this is what I've imagined, only more, because it's him, not some vague Someone – this isn't playing, isn't pretending, it's real! Her body knew what to do, how to respond; the heat and swell she could feel through his jeans was answered by a thrill and a deep ache of longing that cried, *Oh, please, I love you, I want you* . . . The thought came into her head that there was nothing to stop them, no disapproving adult, no one about to barge in, nothing apart from . . .

'Hilly,' Rashid said into her ear, suddenly still. 'We can't. I haven't, you know, got anything.'

'Oh.' Hilly was shocked into realizing that this urgent practical matter had not entered her thoughts. 'Sorry, I didn't think – I mean, I didn't plan this—'

'And I certainly didn't—'

'No—'

'I'm sorry,' Hilly said again.

Rashid lay back against the pillow, eyes closed, breathing rapidly. 'Oh, f—' Then he looked at her and laughed, and pulled her against him. 'Matt'll be back any minute, and his dad's coming round to see how we're getting on. Time and place not quite right. But nearly. Cold shower, anyone?'

Hilly giggled. 'But I'm glad neither of us planned it. That would have seemed a bit – calculating.'

He began to re-fasten the fiddly loop and button arrangement on the front of her cheesecloth shirt. 'If it just happens, that would be nice. But it can't, unless you're prepared. And if you do prepare, then it hasn't just happened.'

'Perhaps,' Hilly said, 'for future reference, what we need is a bit of – of pre-arranged spur-of-the-momentness.'

'Contrived spontaneity,' said Rashid. 'Safe recklessness.'

'Perfect.'

Rashid clasped her hand; they both looked down at their interlaced fingers, hers pale, his darker. 'It would have been the first time,' she said.

'I know.'

'You know?'

'Well, I thought. So we must get it right, the

time and the place. It might take a bit of invisible organizing.'

'Surreptitious scheming.'

'I still can't believe this,' said Rashid. 'You turning up here.'

'Must have been *beschert*. Do you think? That's a Yiddish word Rachel told me for *meant to be*.'

'What did I tell you? You're learning Yiddish already.'

'But I'll learn Arabic as well, if you teach me.'

He spoke rapidly and incomprehensibly into her ear.

'What's that mean?'

'I'll write it down for you,' said Rashid.

Chapter Twenty-eight

Going . . .

When she went indoors again she found
her grandfather had made her a lovely
sweet-smelling bed, with hay which had
not long been gathered in, and had covered
it completely with clean linen sheets. When
she lay down in it a little later, she slept as
she had not done all the time she had been
away.

Johanna Spyri, *Heidi*

Oscar was lying flat on his side on a sunlit patch of
carpet, purring. Everything was all right when Oscar
purred. Heidi was at the dining table, helping Rose
sort photographs, though she couldn't remember
why. Rose had a cardboard box full of photos and she
was sorting them into piles and choosing some to put
in one of those – what was the word? Al— ali— alibi –
no, gone. She was writing words on sticky labels to go
with them.

Heidi remembered some of those photos, though she didn't know who all the people were, but sorting and labelling them meant they were fixed in one place and she could look at them again if she wanted. From time to time Rose would say something like, 'Here, Mum. Here's a nice one of Charles, in his school uniform,' or 'Here's you and Dad – Brighton Pavilion, isn't it?'

She did remember the man called Dad. That was Ken, dear Ken. But surely he was older than that? She hadn't seen him for a while now, but perhaps he'd turn up.

'Are we going to that place again?' she asked.

'Brighton Pavilion?' asked Rose.

'No.' Heidi shook her head, smiling. It was hard to get through to Rose sometimes. 'That – that other place. The yesterday place.'

'Oh, you mean Fairlawns!' said Rose. 'The residential home. Yes, we'll go there again on Wednesday, again on Friday. Every Wednesday and Friday from now on. Did you like it there?'

'Like it?' Heidi considered. It was hard to remember. Chrysanthemums in a vase, there had been, that lovely bronze colour, her favourite. And a chair with a fringed cushion. Faces, she didn't know the names of those, but she hadn't minded that because there was a big tabby cat that had chosen her lap to sit on. Out of lots of laps. Rose was still looking at her for an answer, but what was the question? 'What?' she asked.

'I asked if you liked it at Fairlawns yesterday.'

'Oh yes, I liked it. Are we going there again?'

'Yes, Mum. Wednesdays and Fridays. I've written it on the message board in the kitchen, so you can look there if you forget.'

Heidi nodded. 'Is it nearly lunch time?'

'Mum! We've had lunch, more than two hours ago.'

'So is it lunch time then?'

'No. No, it's not.'

She could hear laughter upstairs. They seemed happy today, those girls, both of them. The blonde one – Heidi could never remember her name – she was a lovely-looking girl once she got that scowl off her face. Shame about the other one, but she could do more with herself if she made a bit of an effort. Often at it hammer and tongs, the two of them were, but today they seemed almost friendly. Were they sisters? I think I might have had a sister, once, Heidi thought, frowning. I wonder what happened to her?

'Mum!' one of them yelled from upstairs. 'Mum?'

Rose went to see what was the matter, and Heidi pulled the photo book over to her and flipped back through. It was new, bought specially, made of transparent pages you slid the pictures into. The first page had two pictures of the girl Heidi knew was called Rachel. Someone had said that the other girl at the picnic – the one showing her knickers – was her, but she couldn't remember it. '*Rachel, Heidi's sister*', Rose had written for the first one; and under the second, '*Rachel and Sarah (Heidi) in their garden in Cologne, 1937/8 (?)*'

'Do you remember, Gran?'

She hadn't realized the girl had come into the room, the older one, the one that played the piano not very well; sneaking up behind her, fit to make her jump out her skin. 'Remember?' she said. 'I remember Cologne. Eau de Cologne, in a nice bottle. I like the smell of that. Have I got some?'

'It's not your fault, Gran. Rachel wants you to know that it's not your fault.'

'Well, of course it's not my fault!' Heidi said crossly. What was the girl talking about? 'Aren't you Rachel?'

'No, Gran. I'm Hilly.'

'Are you?' Heidi said, puzzled.

The front doorbell rang. 'Oh, that's for me!' said the Hilly-girl, brightening. 'See you later, Gran.' She gave Heidi a quick kiss, and was gone. Then Rose's voice in the hall, and a deep male voice, in conversation, before the door closed.

'Mind the corners,' Heidi said, wondering what that could possibly mean. She got up stiffly from the table and went to the front window. The girl who had been here just now was walking down the path with a dark-haired boy, his arm round her shoulders, hers round his waist. Heidi peered at the car parked outside. There were two other boys in the back: one of them she knew was the boy who came here to play the piano, though she couldn't remember his name, and the other she didn't recognize.

Rose came back into the room. 'All right, Mum?'

'She's gone off with three boys,' said Heidi. 'The one that comes here, but I don't know the other two.'

'Reuben, Mum. You know Reuben! One of the others is Reuben's, er, friend, and the one who came to the door's called Rashid. Hilly's boyfriend – he seems very nice.'

'What are they – Indians?' said Heidi. 'Are you happy to let her go round with Indians? And *three* boys – isn't one enough for her? She'll get herself into trouble, she will, the way she carries on.'

'Oh, Mum,' said Rose, laughing. 'Come on, let's get back to the album.'

Album! That was the word she'd been looking for.

Chapter Twenty-nine

Gone

... Two and a half weeks seems an unbearably long time to be away from you. I nearly changed my mind, saying goodbye at Heathrow. As soon as I got through to departures I took out that piece of paper you wrote on in Arabic, and I can look at it whenever I want, which is approximately every two minutes. I've kept it in my wallet ever since you gave it to me, and you've only just told me what it means! Now it's even more precious.

And you'll have had your Oxford interview by the time I come back. Don't worry about it — you'll be brilliant. If they don't think so, somewhere else will.

It was sad too saying goodbye to Heidigran. She's slipping away from herself so fast now that I'm not sure how much of her will be left when I get back in January. I tried to explain where I'm going and why, but I don't think it got through to her at all. She's talked to Rachel on the phone a few times, but I don't think she understands who Rachel is. But, for Rachel, it's the nearest thing to a reconciliation. At least they've heard each other's voices.

I keep thinking about my map of the world — how it's changed, and still changing. It's bigger and it's smaller than it used to be. Bigger, because new bits of it are opening up — your bits, Rachel's bits, the parts that used to be (if I'm honest) just this vague Bible area where people were killing each other all the time. Smaller, because bits I thought were just faraway countries now have something to do with me, with my own personal history. Germany! There's the history trip to Berlin next Easter. That's going to be strange, to say the least. But I do want to go.

Now, in mid-flight (we're over Austria, though there's only cloud to be seen) I'm beginning to feel really nervous about meeting Rachel. And all these aunts and uncles and cousins! (I know they're really second cousins, etc., but that's too much of a mouthful to keep saying) It's going to be weird meeting Chava, the one who's the same age as me — because I keep thinking that I could have been her, and she could have been me, if things had turned out

differently. Or there could have been none of
us. Rachel and Heidigran could so easily have
been among the six million. And yet Rachel will
be meeting me at the airport in a few
hours' time!

I wonder if you'll ever meet her?
Wouldn't that be great?

I've been reading On Being Jewish again,
the bit about the Seder, the special
Passover meal, and realizing what it means.
Originally it was about the Jews escaping
from persecution in Egypt, to the Promised
Land — grief for those who died, joy for
the new life of the ones who escaped to
freedom. But of course the Holocaust has
added a new meaning. I know what you'll
say — the story of the Promised Land gives
the Jews a false reason for believing
Israel is theirs. But I'm thinking of a personal meaning, not political. How so much of
Jewishness is about survival, new life. When
Heidigran left Nazi Germany — when her
parents sent her away — it made my life
possible, and the lives of any children and
grandchildren I might have, years and
years into the future. It has to make me
think my life means something, doesn't it?
It's for something? Beschert.

Being two miles high is going to my head,
so let me tell you about the airline food.

We've just had another meal, and the vege-
tarian option was definitely the best, judging
by the plastic-looking stuff the person next
to me was eating. I had avocado and
grapefruit and cream cheese.

I'm glad we spent last night together —
all night for the first time ever, the whole
delicious night, hours of it, only not not not
not nearly enough. Waking up with you this
morning! I can't wait for more times like
that, only without the parting.

Another letter tomorrow, probably an e-
mail.

Till then — mind the corners.

Acknowledgements

My thanks are due to Diane Samuels, whose play *Kindertransport* has stayed vividly in my mind since I saw it at the Palace Theatre, Watford, seven years ago. To my first readers, for their encouragement: Linda Sargent and Andy Barnett (who also took me to see *Kindertransport*), Adèle Geras, Ann Jungman, Helen Taylor, Naomi Turner and Jean Ure, and particularly to Ann for a riveting account of her trip to Israel. To David Fickling, Bella Pearson and Maggie Noach for being such a supportive editor/agent combination, to Sophie Nelson for her meticulous copy-editing, and especially to Bella for introducing me to the Gershwin Preludes.

THE
SHELL
HOUSE

LINDA NEWBERY

When Greg stumbles across the beautiful ruins of Graveney Hall, an old mansion, he becomes intrigued by its history. He and his new friend, Faith, are drawn into a quest to uncover the fate of Graveney's last heir—Edmund, a young soldier who mysteriously disappeared during the First World War.

But soon Greg finds that his investigations have a disturbing effect. His confused relationships with Faith and Jordan, a schoolmate, and his changing views on love and religion ultimately reveal more about himself than Greg could ever have imagined.

"[A] haunting British exploration of faith and sexuality."
—*Kirkus Reviews*

"A pitch-perfect tale of contemporary teenage life."
—*Publishers Weekly*

"There are some novels written for young people which cause adult readers to wish they had experienced them when younger. This is one of them." —*Financial Times (UK)*